Granger's Crossing

A NOVEL

MARK W. TIEDEMANN

Granger's Crossing

A NOVEL

Blank Slate Press | St. Louis, MO

For information, contact:
Blank Slate Press
4168 Hartford Street
Saint Louis, MO 63116

www.amphoraepublishing.com
Blank Slate Press is an imprint of
Amphorae Publishing Group, LLC
www.amphoraepublishing.com

Manufactured in the United States of America
Cover Design by Kristina Blank Makansi
Cover art: Kristina Blank Makansi

Set in Adobe Caslon Pro, Bickham Script Pro
Library of Congress Control Number: 2022948575
ISBN: 9781943075751

Timons Esaias and Bernadette Harris for comfort,
comment, and companionship along the way

One

ULYSSES GRANGER FIRST SAW the Cortez house from the saddle of an unfamiliar horse. It was pretentious, with aspirations evident in a second story and the makings of a broad front porch. Someday it might be a grand house, but for now it labored beneath a mantle of incompleteness. It stood at the crest of a low rise at the end of a wagon track that came out of the woods a dozen yards to the right of Granger and his three companions.

He did not see his future, only the place where Ham had gone missing.

If anything has happened to Ham, he thought, *I'll have someone's hide.*

He held his irritation in check, but it was a struggle, especially after the river crossing. Granger hated open water. All the way across the Mississippi, in a canoe between two natives of the Fox, he kept trying to remember the Lord's Prayer. "The Lord is my sergeant," he had muttered. The Indians, if they heard, had ignored him. Once more on dry land he recalled the entire prayer effortlessly.

Naturally, when I no longer need it...

A year in the army had knocked much of the boyishness from him, but he still had to work against his youth and the anxiety of not looking foolish in front of more seasoned men. He was twenty, but sometimes felt much younger. He wore his authority awkwardly.

He blamed Ham for going missing and his French and Spanish hosts for losing track of him, but he bit back the impulse to say anything, hearing Ham's admonition, "Don't always lead with your mouth, Oddy."

Oddy. Ham's nickname for him. Granger disliked it intensely—Ham was the only one he allowed to use it—but just now he wanted more than anything to hear his friend say it.

A trio of crows erupted from the trees on the far side of the clearing, circled, then dropped lazily back into hiding. Sweat trickled down Granger's spine beneath his woolen uniform. He shifted in the saddle and looked at their guide.

Lt. Tayon of the St. Louis militia had removed his own scarlet coat a couple of miles back and sat in shirtsleeves and buff vest. Perspiration slicked his young face and darkened the fabric around his armpits. The sun was nearly noon-high and June of 1780 was only a couple of days away. No breeze relieved the heat.

"Well?" Granger said.

Tayon sighed. His left hand rested on the hilt of his sword; a pistol hung holstered below the pommel of his saddle and a musket rested against his back. "It should be deserted. Señor Cortez is on his way south with dispatches for Ste. Genevieve. All his slaves were brought into the village before the battle."

Except, Granger had been told, one of them claimed someone was still out here, which was the reason Ham

Inwood—his friend, his sergeant—had come back out to be sure. Alone.

Granger glanced at the other two men. He had to decide what to do next. He ignored the moil of uncertainty, licked his lips, and straightened.

"Russell, Taylor." He motioned for them to circle around, inside the cover of the trees. Almost silently, they rode off in opposite directions. Seasoned woodsmen and veterans of the last two years of Colonel Clark's campaigns, they made Granger feel awkward and inexperienced, as if he should follow their lead instead of commanding them, a feeling he also kept rigidly in check.

"I am sorry for the inconvenience, Lieutenant," Tayon said. Beneath his accent, his English was excellent.

"You've already apologized, Lieutenant," Granger said, pleased at the steadiness of his voice. "No need to keep doing so."

Granger adjusted his sword belt and checked the powder pan on his rifle, trying not to fidget. Then he heard the bird call signal. He still did not know what bird it was supposed to be, but he had learned the call soon after he and Ham arrived in Cahokia, a month ago.

He resettled his three-cornered cocked hat and urged the mount forward. His nerves danced as he left cover; the buff turnouts on his blue coat made fine targets from a distance. But no shot came. He envied experienced men like Taylor and Russell, who seemed unbothered by danger. He knew it was a mask, but he envied their ability to hide their fear. Perhaps in time, if he lived long enough.

Halfway across the treeless field, he saw a large barn on his right, perhaps thirty yards northeast of the house.

Topping the rise, Granger spotted Russell emerging from the trees far to the left, almost directly across from where he had begun. Close up, the house appeared even more unfinished than from the tree line. Windows flanked wide double doors. One door stood open by several inches. Russell joined them as they made a circuit around the house.

A stable stood just northwest, a split-rail corral enclosing a large area behind it. Taylor was dismounting before the entrance, musket in hand. Directly north was a row of shacks—slave quarters. The only evidence of agriculture was a substantial garden just behind the main house; whatever Cortez was doing here, it wasn't farming. Horses, someone had said.

"Lieutenant," Taylor called. "Something's dead."

Cold fire chased over Granger's scalp and down his neck. He swung his right leg over and jumped to the ground and hurried up to the stable entrance. He caught the odor of rotting flesh and his insides squeezed. Tayon pulled his pistol from the saddle holster, Russell cocked his musket, and they waited on Granger's word.

For a moment, his mind was empty. "Look at the slave quarters," he told Russell and Taylor. He glanced at Tayon, who nodded, and together they entered the stable, into a thick, miasmic stench.

As his eyes adjusted, Granger saw a row of stalls to the left, all empty. Hay piled against the opposite wall, below a half-finished loft. Toward the rear, just before stacks of lumber, lay a disquieting shape on the dirt floor.

A horse, sprawled amid hay, dung, and its own dried blood, a mangled mess. Flies clouded noisily about it. The wounds had been caused by a sword or axe, and it had been castrated. The opened belly showed signs of having been chewed on.

From what Granger could tell, it had been an impressive animal, dark coat almost black, and big.

"That is Cortez's best stud," Tayon said.

"Why…" Granger started to ask. The smell stung his sinuses, watered his eyes. He turned away and saw that not all the stalls were empty. Another horse lay butchered in the nearest. This one was a plainer animal; a blanket stretched beneath it.

"And that," Tayon said, coming alongside him, "was the horse Sergeant Inwood rode out here."

Panic fluttered at the edge of Granger's awareness. He strode to the entrance. "Russell!" When the man came hurrying around the corner of the stable, Granger said, "Search for sign, see if a war party came through here."

Russell touched a finger to his hat and hurried off.

Granger's heart pounded now. After the British-led assault on St. Louis had been broken, the various Indian bands dispersed; word had already reached the village of small raids on outlying farms to the north and west. It was possible some had come this far south. He started to go back into the stable when Taylor came up to him.

"Nobody here, Lieutenant," he said. "There's a hen house, but ain't nothing but feathers and bones. Wolves or foxes."

"Search the barn."

"Aye, sir."

Granger hesitated, unsure what to do next. Tayon joined him. "Why kill the horses?" Granger said. "Doesn't make any sense."

"The stud," Tayon said. "Did you see? It was shot in the forehead." He touched a finger to his own, between the eyes.

"The house," Granger said.

Midway there, he spotted the small cemetery off to the right. The perimeter was marked by rocks laid in a rectangle. There was a single wooden marker, a thick whitewashed plank, expertly carved: Atilio Juan de Cortez 1755 – 1778.

"I thought his name was Diego," Granger said.

Tayon shrugged. "It is. Diego Hernan de Cortez. I do not know who this is."

Stepping onto the porch, into the shade, Lt. Tayon drew his sword. They flanked the door. Pistol cocked, Tayon pushed the open door the rest of the way in with the point of his blade.

The interior was as incomplete as the outside. A hallway stretched back to a rear door. The wall to the right was solid, but on the left only the framework stood. The room contained a heavy table surrounded by six elegant chairs covered with scarlet brocade. An enormous hutch faced them, shelves empty but for a few silver plates and a row of silver goblets, finely made with a pair of engraved rings near the lip. In the center of the table, flies buzzed around an open decanter; dead insects floated in an inch of dark liquid at the bottom. A goblet lay on the floor near the doorway, part of the set in the cabinet. Granger counted eleven of them.

"Lt. Granger."

In the opposite room, a wide stone fireplace dominated the far wall, flanked by two chairs, a table between them. A painting, hung on the wall opposite the windows, showed a man in breastplate, a conquistador's helmet under his left arm, a sword in his right hand, point downward. The man's face was thin, neatly bearded, with large dark eyes, and a crown of reddish hair.

"Family?"

Tayon shrugged. "There is a resemblance..."

To the right of the painting was another door, partly opened. Granger stepped carefully, quietly on the dark wood floor. With the barrel of his rifle, he pushed the door in. He leaned through and found a small room with a narrow bed, a table bearing a wash bowl—the bottom still covered by water—and a candle burned down to less than an inch. A crucifix hung on the wall above the bed.

The house was silent but for the two of them. No one was here. Still, Granger ascended the stairs with the care that came of combat experience, the expectation of surprise.

On the second floor he found two bedrooms with a study in between, all with connecting doorways lacking doors. The heavy iron bed in the first room had been dragged, leaving gouged arcs in the floorboards. The chifforobe had been emptied of clothing that lay scattered across the bed and floor.

Papers and books covered the floor of the study. All the drawers had been pulled from the huge desk. Granger found a few stacks of letters still on the desk and one letter half-written, the quill lying across it, dried out. The handwriting was sharp and angular, compact except for the bold flourishes of some of the consonants. He could not decipher the Spanish. He could read Latin and some Greek, useless languages so far from Suffield, Connecticut.

French would have served him better than the Classical studies his mother had insisted upon.

As he stepped back from the desk he saw an overturned strongbox below the window, its contents scattered on the floor around it, as if someone had been sorting through them, looking for something. A sheaf of letters was tied with a scarlet ribbon. Granger knelt and shifted some of the loose pages. A few lay crumpled behind the desk.

The writing on the envelopes was in a different hand, an elegant cursive. He tugged one out and opened it. Three pages of beautiful handwriting, the last page signed "Eliana."

"Lieutenant."

Granger looked up. Tayon stood in the connecting doorway. Granger refolded the letter and slid it back into the envelope, then tamped it back among the others in the ribbon. He dropped it to the floor, picked up his rifle, and joined the young Frenchman.

This room had been ransacked as well. The smaller bed had been overturned, a chest of drawers toppled, its contents emptied onto the floor. A chair lay broken against one wall, cut lengths of rope tangled with the cracked wood. Blood spattered one wall and the floor around the chair. Granger looked questioningly at Tayon, who pointed at the curtains piled in a corner.

An incongruous shape stuck out from beneath the layers of ivory fabric, a distinct length of polished wood with brass moldings. Granger knelt and pulled up the cloth, revealing the rifle. Ornate brass filigree decorated the patch box, inlaid with silver that swept up the wrist, into the fine work around the trigger guard and hammer plate. Matching inlays dotted the long stock beneath the octagonal barrel.

A high, distant keening started up in Granger's ears.

"It is Sergeant Inwood's," Tayon said.

Granger's mouth was suddenly dry. He coughed and nodded. "You recognize it." His voice was rough, barely above a whisper.

"It is distinctive. Like yours."

Granger looked down at the rifle in his left hand. Both Ham and he had arrived at Cahokia with rifles instead of muskets, which drew attention. Clark had a few riflemen in his ranks, but most of his soldiers, like most militia or Continentals, carried muskets, which were more uniform, quicker to reload, cheaper and easier to obtain. Rifles were special. Granger had heard that General Washington disliked them, but still maintained a company of riflemen to harass the British. They carried an aura, a reputation, and were rare enough that two men carrying rifles coming among a force armed with Long Land Pattern muskets or Charlevilles caused a stir.

Granger swallowed several times before he could speak normally. "We both got our rifles from the same man, Martin Shell. Birthday presents. Ham's birthday is only a couple of weeks after mine and his father had these made for us in Pennsylvania. Heidelberg Township. Mr. Shell had been making rifles for…I don't know." He stood up with both weapons and laid them on the mattress on the floor, cheek piece up. "Look here. An old Spanish *reales* set in the filigree, on both of them. My father gave them to us, for our birthdays, two each, so we had them set into the stocks." He hefted Ham's. "Sixty-one inches. Three hundred yards with accuracy. Ham was the better shot—" He stopped, suddenly conscious of his rambling and the slight quiver in his voice.

"Lieutenant!" Russell called from outside.

Granger went to the open window. Below, Russell waved to him to come down. Granger and Tayon hurried outside. Russell was running west toward where Taylor waited at the edge of the woods. When Granger and Tayon joined them, Taylor pointed at a patch of ground at his feet.

"Tracks."

The body lay in a depression on the west side of a large fallen tree, half a mile from the house. A shallow grave barely covered the human form. Animals had already dug parts of it up, revealing the blue-and-buff uniform, a hand, one shoe, and a hank of blond hair. Granger felt cold and his legs trembled. He reached toward the hair and brushed away dirt until the face stared up, blind eyes open.

"Ham…"

It came out as a breath, as though he had been punched hard in the stomach and could not fill his lungs to speak. He dropped to both knees, staring, hating the sight, unable to look away.

"Mon dieu!"

"His head's been stove in," Russell said.

Granger barely heard him. A rushing sound grew in his ears and his skull felt tight, as though the air had suddenly grown thicker, heavier. Sparks danced at the edge of his vision, which began to dim. He heard a pulse and thought it must be Ham's. He reached toward the body.

The act seemed to break the pressure constraining his senses. Someone grabbed his arm and he looked up at a vaguely familiar face. In the next instant he recognized Tayon, and in the instant after that he felt his sympathy and concern.

"Lieutenant?"

Russell balanced on the trunk, musket in hand, keeping watch even while he attended to what Granger was going through. All of them had lost friends; none had escaped the touch of unfairness in early death. Till now, though, no death had wrenched Granger's insides so deeply. He was not experiencing loss, he was lost.

I am an officer of the Continental Army, he thought, *I must not yield to grief, not now.*

Granger blinked through hideous amazement, swallowed around an impossible pain in his throat, coughed, and looked again at the body. "What?"

"His head," Russell said. "Look."

Granger moved to see what Russell was pointing to. The left side of Ham's head was oddly flattened. He had been struck hard, perhaps by a musket butt, maybe by an Indian war club. Acid filled his throat as he moved hair aside to better expose the wound. He stared at the depression—oblong, from just above the temple down to just behind the ear.

No one's going to mistake us for brothers anymore, he thought. Not that they had ever resembled each other that closely except for the light hair and the hazel eyes. Ham had been shorter, broader, his jaw squarer, his smile brighter…

What do I do now? he wondered, suddenly feeling very young.

Tayon backed away from the body, staggered a few paces and bent over. He gulped air loudly but did not vomit. When he turned around his face was pale. He smiled uncertainly. "Curious," he said. "I have seen death before now. But this…"

"There's all kinds of death," Granger said, his voice ragged and unsure. "It's all different, even if it ends up the same."

He realized then that Ham's was very different. He had seen men killed and as ugly as some of those deaths had been, there was a cleanness to them; the framework of war had mitigated their senselessness, though he sensed that a greater chaos pertained. That was too big, though, too ancient to take personally. This was different. Ham's death did not fit war. Someone, outside the defining madness of military battle, had killed him and then buried him in secret. Granger felt threatened and experienced a monstrous urge to run.

"You said he was your friend," Tayon said.

"I've known Ham for…since we were boys. All my life." He ground his teeth, feeling that he should say little. For a moment he was a boy again and his best friend was gone.

Russell moved, carefully searching the trunk, the ground, the surrounding foliage. "I don't see tracks leading off," he said. "Nothing definite anyway. Two maybe."

"Ham could have—"

He stopped. Could have what? Beaten two or three Indians? Not if they surprised him. And why assume they were Indians?

Granger turned slowly, peering into the woods. He had the feeling of being watched. A sound maybe, something different from the background of birdsong and breeze sifting through branches, triggered a wariness he had learned to trust.

"Lieutenant," Russell said. "Unless I'm missing something, it looks like Ham was brought out here already dead."

"How can you tell?"

"I don't see any of Sergeant Inwood's tracks." He started back the way they had come, stepping carefully, searching. Granger followed him, watching as Russell studied the small signs Granger took on faith were there. Russell knelt and examined a patch of moss for a long time.

"This ain't making much sense," he said finally. "Ground here should be covered with tracks, but someone took the time to smooth 'em out. Not all of them. Got a pair of moccasin tracks…heavy, though, like someone carrying a load."

"Ham."

"Hard to tell how old. Two days, four days. Dry as it's been, sign like this could lie on the ground a week unless something else came along to obscure it. But as much as the body has been gnawed on, I'd say near four, five days."

Gnawed on. Granger swallowed hard and set that aside. *Before the battle, then,* he thought. "Any sign of struggle?"

"No. That's the other reason I think he was carried here." Russell returned to the body. "Had to be Indians, but—"

"Indians do not bury their victims," Granger said, sounding more confident than he felt. "Not in war. Do we follow them?"

"Trail is too old," Russell said.

"Lieutenant Tayon," Granger said, "where was señor Cortez during the last several days?"

"In St. Louis."

"All during the attack?"

"Of course."

"Hey, Lieutenant," Taylor said.

Granger looked up. Taylor stood at the far end of the fallen tree, gazing off into the trees. He started to raise his right arm, to point, when he shuddered. Granger saw it and tightened his grip on his rifle.

The shot was loud. Taylor pivoted off the log, dropping his musket, and fell.

All of them dropped to the ground. Granger crawled toward Taylor, cradling his rifle across bent arms and using his elbows to drag himself forward. He heard someone sprinting behind him and rolled to see Tayon running, hunched low, to the west.

Granger reached Taylor at the same time as Russell. Taylor was waxy white and gulping air. Blood flowed from a puncture in his shirt just below his left collarbone. His eyelids fluttered and his tongue raked over his lips. Russell pulled a large rag from his pocket and pressed it to the wound. Taylor's body strained against the pain and he groaned.

Leaving them, Granger worked his way up the depression to alongside the trunk and risked a look. The woods presented a vast curtain of raggedness between myriad posts. He drew back the hammer on his rifle, searching.

He saw the puff and flash off to his left a moment before the tree alongside his head spat bark and splinters with a loud crack. He raised his rifle, sighted instantly at the point of the shot, and fired. As the smoke cleared before him he saw a branch, twenty-five yards away, swinging from the thin shred still attached.

Tayon rushed through the trees toward the spot, a reckless charge that Granger admired and feared. Then he was up and running, too.

The two men met just past the dangling branch and began searching for signs of their attacker. Granger knelt and reloaded his rifle. Tayon, sword in hand, pivoted slowly, face grim.

"He is gone."

"Just one?"

"It must have been."

Granger stared into the patchwork of sunlight and shadow, heart racing. They were exposed here, he realized. An experienced warrior could easily have shot either one of them by now. A shudder ran through him as he got to his feet.

"We should get back," Tayon said.

Russell had bandaged Taylor with strips of linen holding the rag in place, but it was already soaked with blood.

"Sorry, Lieutenant," Taylor said. He was slick with sweat and could not stop writhing as Russell worked. With the metal tang of blood Granger smelled urine. Russell's hands were red.

"Bullet's still in there," he said. "We need to get him back to the house at least."

For a moment, Granger wondered, *what house?* He stared at Taylor, who was trying not to make any sounds that might locate them for the enemy, and Russell, who grimly ministered to his comrade. A fly whizzed past Granger's left ear, making him wince, but he focused on the situation.

"Lt. Tayon, we need to make a litter."

The two officers cut branches. Using strips torn from Ham's uniform, they tied them together into a travois, all the while nervously watching the woods around them. They worked quickly. Granger took off his coat and folded it into a pillow, grateful at least for the sudden cool as sweat evaporated from his skin. Taylor yelped once, loudly, when they lifted him onto the litter. He passed out then, which Granger counted as a good thing as they began the journey back to the Cortez house.

Tayon pulled the travois while Russell and Granger guarded their flanks.

Two

ALL GRANGER'S ATTENTION reduced to the single goal of getting Taylor back to the house alive. Emerging from the woods, he handed Tayon his rifle and took his place. Russell slung his musket over his back and picked up the tail-end of the travois and between them they half-strode, half-ran across the field to the porch while the young Frenchman trailed after watching the forest

Panting loudly from the exertion, they cleared off the table in the unfinished dining room and laid Taylor on it. He was still unconscious, for which Granger was grateful, but they did not rest. Tayon pulled away Russell's bandage and studied the wound. He was pale and his eyelids fluttered occasionally, but his hands were steady.

The wound still oozed blood. From somewhere Russell found a pot and filled it with water from the well east of the slave quarters. Granger rushed up the stairs to pillage the clothes strewn on the floor. He brought down the cleanest linen he could find and sliced it into strips. They worked in sharp silence punctuated by grunts, bootsteps, the heavy breath of desperate determination. The room seemed to fill with a damp cottony immanence, like prayer, an unspoken, willful insistence that this man not die.

Within an hour the water was boiling and the cloth had been soaked and hung out while Tayon, with a knife that had been seared in flame, worked on Taylor while Granger and Russell held him as he screamed until he passed out again.

Tayon pried the misshapen slug out with the knife-tip. The bullet dropped to the floor. Tayon poured water into the wound. Taylor lay still, pale and all but lifeless. But for the blood flow, Granger would have thought him already dead.

Granger felt useless. He picked up the bullet. It was enormous. He tried to imagine the size of the musket that took it. He wiped it with a rag and dropped it into his pocket.

Tayon backed away from the table. Russell applied pressure until the blood stopped, then bandaged it with clean linen. Tayon blew a long, weary breath and went outside. Granger followed.

The sun had visibly moved into mid-afternoon. From beneath the eaves of the porch, everything appeared peaceful, the expected calm of an ordinary day. Blood pounded sluggishly in Granger's ears.

Tayon leaned against a wooden post. He glanced briefly at Granger. "We should get him back to St. Louis to the doctor, but I am afraid to move him just now."

"So we stay?"

"One night only. If he survives till morning, he should make it to the village."

"You managed that well."

Tayon nodded absently. Sweat ran down his face, into his eye, and he wiped at it. Granger saw his hand trembling now.

"If we're staying," Granger said, "I want to bury Ham. Properly."

Granger expected a protest, but after a few moments the young Frenchman nodded again. "I can stay here while you and Russell retrieve his body."

From his expression, Granger knew Russell thought he was being foolish, but the soldier did not argue. They rested a short while, then gathered up the travois and returned to the fallen tree. Together they removed the leaves and twigs and dirt from Ham's body and dragged it onto the carrier. They worked quickly, a nervous sense that their attacker might take another shot.

"Wait," Granger said. "Give me your knife."

"Lieutenant—!" But Russell handed it over.

Granger, still anxious, dug the second bullet out of the trunk. This one was even more misshapen than the one from Taylor, but just as large.

The trip back was without incident. Granger found a shovel in the stable. In shirtsleeves he started digging alongside the other grave in the small plot while Russell tended the horses. The labor emptied his mind, took the rage he knew he should feel and turned it into shovelfuls of dirt. Twice Russell tried to take over, but Granger waved him off. The third time, Russell simply took the shovel from him. Granger stared at the man, all his muscles burning and sweat stinging his eyes.

He stepped out of the hole and sat down as Russell began flinging earth onto the mound. Granger watched, an ache forming across his forehead and behind his eyes. As long as he worked, he kept the whirl of thoughts and feelings at bay, but as he sat idle everything flooded in, drowning him in shapeless remorse. *I should have come across the river myself...I should have been here...*

No. Someone else had done this. Granger had not sent Ham here to be murdered. Ham had gone because Colonel Montgomery, Clark's second-in-command, had thought a Continental on the Spanish side of the river would be valuable. A few other Americans were present in the village, but no soldiers. Either of them could have done it, or both, there was little else for them to do before the battle. Montgomery had resented their presence since they had arrived attached to John Rogers' dragoons. They should have been part of a cavalry contingent attached to Clark's forces, but the promised horses were nowhere to be found and they all ended up as additional infantry. Rogers' men were welcomed as militia, but Granger and Ham had been regarded as spies for General Greene. Montgomery would have been glad had both of them crossed the river.

But Ham knew Granger's discomfort with rivers, something he expected one day to outgrow, and volunteered to go on his own with a few militia, among them Russell and Taylor. Granger was not responsible for Ham's death, the killer was. Granger backed away from the helpless paralysis of guilt and let anger take its place. *How do you know the difference between grief and rage?* he wondered. Either way, he had to find this killer.

Where to start? He could not ride after Diego de Cortez and ask him what might have fetched Ham back here alone. This side of the Mississippi was another country; he had no authority, no rights. Besides, it made no sense that an ally would do this.

But this is his land…

"Hey, Lieutenant. Look at this."

Russell held up a coin. Granger leaned forward and took it. Gold, glinting in the sunlight. "Spanish," he said. "Are there more?"

Russell scraped the shovel along the walls of the grave. "Here's another one. Two more." He handed them all to Granger.

As he turned them over in his hands, a conviction grew in his mind that nothing here was as it should be. It was much like the sensation of being watched. But now he was the observer and he still could not see what he needed to see.

He looked at the wall of the grave where Russell had scraped to find the other coins. "See if there are more."

Russell started teasing at the wall, spilling dirt. Six or seven inches further and more coins fell to the bottom of the hole.

"Damn," Russell said, bending down to scoop them up.

"Don't," Granger said. His thoughts raced. He looked at the house, wondering how trustworthy Tayon was. In any event, it wasn't their money. "Fetch the Lieutenant."

Russell cocked his head, questioning.

"We aren't thieves," Granger said.

Russell nodded. "No, sir, we aren't. But I wager someone is."

Tayon shook his head, staring down at the gold. "I am at a loss, monsieur. There has been some speculation about where señor Cortez has come by his money, but in truth he

has never spent so much that it seemed unduly suspicious."
He frowned. "I am uncomfortable with this. Perhaps we
should leave well enough alone."

It was not what Granger wanted to hear, nor was it
unexpected. Cortez lived here, after all. These people knew
him. "It just seems curious."

"Maybe that's why he didn't bring his slaves in when he
was supposed to," Russell said.

"Hm? What do you mean?"

"The call went out several days before the attack,"
Tayon said, "to have everyone come into the village. All but
a few people to the south did so, bringing their servants as
well, but Don Diego tried to leave his slaves here. When it
was realized that he had done this, I was sent to bring them
in. Sergeant Inwood came with me."

"Then Ham came back alone."

Tayon nodded. "As I explained to you before, on the way
into St. Louis, one of the slaves told him someone else was
out here, hidden. I told him that was unlikely—I knew how
many slaves Don Diego had and they were all accounted
for—but he chose to return to be certain. That was the day
before the battle." He looked down, his face reddening.
"Events occupied me. It was not until everything was over
that I realized he had not returned."

"Someone hidden."

"Absurd. There was no one else here."

But Cortez left his stud here, Granger thought. "Why
would this slave say there was, then?"

"I do not know."

Granger exhaled loudly, frustrated. "What do you
recommend we do about this?"

"Bury your friend, monsieur. Leave the gold. I think we should say nothing until matters with the British resolve. When señor Cortez returns we can all sort it out. Later." He walked back toward the house.

"Lieutenant?" Russell said.

"Leave it." Granger went to Ham's body a few yards away, knelt down, and laid one coin each on Ham's lightless eyes. Then he pocketed one. He wanted physical proof of what they had found. "Take one," he told Russell. "For our labors."

They finished by early evening. It was not quite six feet deep, but it was enough to keep the wolves from digging Ham up. Granger and Russell lowered the corpse. Lt. Tayon rejoined them and stood alongside Granger at the lip of the hole.

"Neither of us put much value in church," he said, "but Ham believed. He believed all sorts of things I found incredible, even though he was by far the more sensible of the two of us. He thought lightning came from the friction of the earth rubbing against the sky. He had this idea that the world sometimes went faster, which made storms. He theorized once that Noah had to have had more than one ark. After going through my father's edition of Plato, he decided that all the Indians were originally from Atlantis and that they had long ago spoken Greek. Ham understood no Greek, so it made no difference to him that they seemed so different. It was all the same. But this war, though. He thought it was inevitable but he was not convinced it was right."

His throat tightened against a surge of anguish. "We... disagreed over it. But he was my friend, so when I went to fight, he came with me." The stinging in his eyes worsened and he looked up through a haze. The sky seemed too bright, the colors all run together. *I didn't come here for this.* He blinked, hard. "For God knows what reason," he continued, his voice thick now, "he believed in me. And I suppose I believed in him. He was my best friend. I can imagine no better."

He found a piece of wood in the shed beside the barn large enough for an inscription. After they refilled the grave, he used his knife to carve it—Ham Inwood, born 1761 Connecticut, died 1780 Louisiana. The lettering suffered compared to the one for Atilio Cortez. Granger trenched a slot at the head of the grave and pushed the marker in, then tamped earth around it. He promised himself to come back someday and retrieve the body to take home, to Ham's family.

Taylor moaned occasionally, his hands clenching and unclenching as he drifted in and out of awareness. That night, he lapsed into fitful sleep. Russell stayed in the room with him most of the time while Granger and Tayon kept to the parlor.

Tayon found candles and as darkness came the rooms filled with inconstant buttery light.

Granger's mind churned. Nothing seemed to fit anything he imagined as he tried to understand what had happened. Ham's body buried in the woods, the dead horses, the ransacked house still containing its plate, and Ham's rifle left behind. A raiding party would not have killed the horses or left the rifle, nor would they have bothered to hide a body. Ham had been struck from behind instead of shot, but someone was out there ready to shoot them. Added to all that was the testimony of a slave that someone had been hiding here. And then there was the buried gold...

Granger excused himself and took a candle upstairs.

Walking slowly from room to room, he saw little but deep shadows and yellowed shapes in the flickering candlelight, the geography of his friend's death. He sorted through some of the clothes scattered about, but then went to the strongbox. He set the candle on the edge of the desk and sat on the floor.

Granger was convinced now that a search had been conducted. There were bundles that had been left undisturbed, other papers still more or less together in neat stacks, and then the assortment of documents scattered here and there.

Among these he found a few that looked official, one with a dark blue seal affixed. Deeds, he thought, or letters of credit. He turned the strongbox over. The two hasps were broken, the locks ruined. Whoever broke into the box had probably found what he wanted and taken it.

Taken it where?

Too many questions, too many possibilities. Granger was convinced, though, that more than one man had been here when Ham walked in on them. They were looking for something and killed Ham when he found them.

And who had been tied to the chair and where was he now?

Sounds of Russell and Tayon moving around below punctuated the stillness. Granger set the box upright and was about to stand up when he glimpsed a few sheets of paper underneath the desk. He teased them out. Two of them were in Spanish, but the third was written in an angular, legible English. All it said was "Received in gold, 200, January 19th, for purchase. J. Dodge, capt."

John Dodge was the quartermaster billeted at Kaskaskia. According to talk among Clark's men, although he styled himself a captain he was in fact a civilian contractor, charged with supplying them. But beyond a few blankets and some bullet molds he had provided little, and Granger had heard nothing but complaints about the man. He was supposed to have provided the horses for Rogers' cavalry. What had he sold to Diego de Cortez? Horses?

He folded the receipt and tucked it into his pocket.

He took out the coin Russell had found. According to the invoice, he had paid Dodge in gold. The same gold? Had the strongbox contained some? Was this a simple robbery? He looked down at the papers. No, he decided, there was something else, though no doubt they would have taken any gold they found.

But not the plate downstairs?

Gold coins would be easier to explain than plate. Which suggested it was someone who lived here, in or around St. Louis.

He saw the stack of letters then, bound in a scarlet ribbon. He tucked the coin away and picked it up. Whoever had killed Ham, Granger reasoned, had had a grudge against Cortez. They had waited until his property was unguarded before coming out here. It was the only thing that explained the horses, the search, the attempt to hide Ham's body. It was a reasonable conclusion.

At least, it felt reasonable.

So who hated Cortez enough to do this?

He needed to know more about Cortez. These letters, written in an elegant hand, might tell him what he needed to know.

"Lieutenant?" Russell called from the head of the stairs. "We got some food ready."

"Thank you, I'll be right down."

He stood, letters in hand, and picked up the candle. His haversack was in the parlor, with Ham's rifle. Granger kept the letters hidden as he descended, pressed to his arm, away from the others, and tucked them inside the bag. Tayon had built a fire in the hearth. Russell had laid out bedrolls on the floor.

Russell sat by the door, musket across his lap. Granger joined Tayon at the fire where he accepted a biscuit and a cup of watered-down rum.

"I got all the threads out, I believe," Tayon said. "I will feel better when Dr. Gibkin or Reynal looks at him."

"Thank you. Will señor Cortez be back soon?"

"It was my understanding that after Ste. Genevieve he was to head all the way downriver to New Orleans to report to the Governor. He may not be back for months."

"What about this place? Will the slaves come back?"

Tayon shook his head. "They will be loaned to various people until Don Diego returns."

"You've called him that before. Don Diego?"

"He likes to call himself that. Some of the other Spanish habitants think it is pretentious, but they humor him. He fancies himself a *caballero* with a great estate. Perhaps he was, back in Spain." He shrugged. "Some of the other Spaniards are dons. The lieutenant governor, others."

"How long has he been here?"

"Oh, perhaps two years. He has spent nearly all that time out here, building this place. He has ambitions."

"Horses?"

Tayon nodded. "He provided many for us for our cavalry. The death of his stud will be hard."

"If he knew he was going to be gone so long, why did he leave it out here? And his slaves? Unsupervised?"

"That I cannot say. I thought he had brought all his stock into the village. Is it important?"

"It's just—nothing makes sense."

"What do you mean?"

"Just—well, if a raid had been going on here, Ham would never have walked in on it."

Tayon drew a deep breath, shifting uncomfortably. "You are distraught over your friend. I can understand. I knew him a little. He was a good man. But it is war, Lieutenant. Maybe there is a why about the whole thing, but each little piece? There is no why for something like this."

"A false argument depends on the first false statement in it," Granger said.

"Pardon?"

"Aristotle. There is always a 'why,' Lieutenant. Find all the particulars, as you put it, you find the whole. Saying there's no particular reason is just a way to stop looking before you start." When Tayon remained silent, he added, "I *am* distraught. My…friend is dead. But even in the context of war, can you make sense out of what you've seen here?"

Tayon gazed into the fire. After a few moments, he shook his head. "It is, I admit, most puzzling."

"Puzzles can be solved, and I want to solve this one. I want to know what happened."

In the morning, Russell and Granger managed to get Taylor on his horse. He was feverish but not delirious. The ride back took longer than the journey out, but they arrived well before noon. Already the day was hot. Granger had shrugged out of his coat halfway to St. Louis and still sweat ran down his body.

They emerged from the forest at the edge of a vast stretch of cleared land, the common fields in which habitants had already been working again, so soon after the battle. Only five days ago, hundreds of Indians and some number of disaffected trappers had rushed the village—part of Britain's attempt to break the main anchor of the Spanish alliance with the Americans in upper Louisiana. At the same time, an attack fell on Cahokia, across the river. The enemy had been beaten off on both sides. Granger still had not learned how many casualties St. Louis had sustained.

Trenches along the creek ran from a mill pond to the river and marked the southern boundary of the village. More trenches and sharpened stake barricades defended the north and northwest approaches.

Tayon spurred his horse to a run. By the time Granger and his men had reached the thick stone gun tower that stood on the other side of the fields, a small crowd had gathered and two men brought a door. Hands took the wounded American and eased him down. Within seconds, Taylor had disappeared inside the stockade.

As they entered the village precincts, another crowd came from the rear door of the stables owned by Monsieur Gambeau, from whom Tayon had acquired the horses they rode. Gambeau pushed through the crowd, scowling, and shouted orders at his slaves. Granger saw another man leaning against the edge of the stable door, watching, arms folded across his worn hunting shirt.

"Tend the horses," Granger told Russell as he dismounted.

Granger pulled Ham's rifle from the saddle and draped his haversack over his left shoulder. When he looked again, the man at the stable door was gone. Tayon reappeared.

"We must see Lt. Cartabona," the Frenchman said.

"I want to see to Taylor."

"He is being taken to the Lt. Governor's house. That is where we must go as well."

Within the stockade, directly below the tower, three large squares, surrounded north and south by fenced plots with houses, stretched toward the river. The nearest square held the Catholic Church and its courtyard, the Governor's Residence next, and finally the public square, the Place d'Armes. The church precinct contained a number of buildings, all wood, the largest being the chapel itself. The government house was the largest residence in St. Louis, built of stone, and surrounded by a stone fence, as was the Place d'Armes.

Granger followed Lt. Tayon down the dirt path, across the Rue des Granges, and then alongside him to the Lt. Governor's house, which fronted on La Rue Royale. He felt watched, and when he looked around he caught people in small groups, pointing to him, talking. Word had spread, speculation begun. Granger suppressed an urge to shout at them to mind their own business. By day's end, he knew, the story of Ham's death would likely be exaggerated to include a Santee Sioux war party, half a dozen British regulars, and possibly wolves. It might even be preferable to what had happened to Ham—struck from behind and buried in the woods.

He mounted the steps beside Tayon and entered the open door of the big house. He paused to let his eyes adjust. People moved busily on errands. Lt. Cartabona, Lt. Governor Leyba's second-in-command, sat at the big table in the main room, papers spread before him. Tayon spoke quietly to him. Cartabona stood and came over to Granger.

"My sincere condolences, Lieutenant," he said to him quietly in accented English. He was a bit taller than Granger, with an incongruously thin face above a stout neck and broad shoulders. "Dr. Reynal is with your man. He will receive the best care we can provide. Have you eaten yet today?"

"No, sir, but I should see to my man."

"Of course. A moment, please. Lt. Tayon has told me of the events surrounding this and I have instructed him to assemble a party to go out to the Cortez land. They will ascertain whether your attackers are still nearby."

"Would it be possible for me to accompany them?" As soon as he said it, he felt conflicted. He could not see to Taylor if he left.

"It would be best if you stay here. They know the land better. Besides, I would not want another American injured or killed on this side of the river. You understand."

Granger bit back on his disappointment. "Of course, sir. We buried my sergeant. It's not necessary immediately, but I should like to retrieve his body to send back to his family. It can wait till we've made certain there will be no further engagements."

"That might be some time. We are still expecting Langlade and his forces to attack. But I see no objection in the event. May I ask, when will you return to Cahokia?"

"If possible, I'd prefer to stay here until my man is out of danger."

"Your Colonel Montgomery will not mind?"

Montgomery would be delighted to have me away from his men, Granger thought. "I'll send word. I'm sure it will be fine with him. It was his intention that I act as liaison here."

"Very well, then. We will see about finding you lodgings. Your man has been taken this way." He indicated a corridor.

"There's one more thing, if I may," Granger said as he followed. "It's my opinion that señor Cortez's house was being ransacked. Someone killed his stud stallion as well as the horse my sergeant rode out there."

Cartabona's eyes narrowed. "Ransacked...searched?" He looked at Tayon. "Is that also your impression, Lt. Tayon?"

"I confess I can offer no other explanation for what we saw. We found no sign of a war party, though we did not search after Taylor was shot."

Cartabona pursed his lips and rocked on the balls of his feet. "I see. That implies someone from here." He continued to look at Tayon, who shrugged but did not deny the conclusion. "Proceed as instructed. If something should suggest itself..."

"Yes, sir."

"See to your man now, Lieutenant. And please eat." He gave a short bow and returned to the table.

"Come," Tayon said.

He led Granger down a hall, past open doors through which he glimpsed wounded men on cots amid the clutter of rearranged furniture, packs, muskets, and the people tending them. Tayon knocked on the last door and entered.

Taylor lay on a narrow bed, the bandages removed from his wound. It mounded on his flesh, blackened now with red cracks, the skin around it bright red and tight. There was an acid tinge to the air; the room felt very close.

An older man in shirtsleeves bent over Taylor, one hand lightly holding his wrist. His lips moved as he counted. One of the two women in the room was laying out fresh bandages on a small table to the left while the other pressed a damp cloth to Taylor's forehead. She straightened and turned, pausing when she saw Granger.

Her face was round, with large eyes below elegant eyebrows. Her dark, almost black hair was caught up beneath a plain white scarf. Sweat darkened her blue-striped blouse under her arms and around the scoop of her neckline. She smiled briefly through her worry.

Granger could not look away. He had never seen a face like hers, had never been caught so thoroughly. She seemed like a puzzle he felt compelled to solve, at once new and fascinating and at the same time teasingly familiar. Though they had never met, he found himself trying to recognize her.

Granger felt a surge of guilt at the distraction. Dismayed and slightly embarrassed, he brought his attention back to Taylor.

The older man said something to her in French. She nodded and went to the table where the other, older woman worked. This woman, larger, hands wide and sinewy, glanced at Granger and a smile almost broke through the layered weariness and—he recognized it now—loss.

Tayon approached the man. He listened for a few moments, and then looked at Granger with raised eyebrows.

"You are his commanding officer?"

"I am."

The old man extended a hand. "I am Dr. Reynal."

Granger shook hands. "Is he—?"

"It might have been better that I come out to him," Dr. Reynal said, "but we must work with what is, no? We will change his bandages regularly and hope for the best. All we can do now is let him sleep."

"Is he awake now?"

"No, but he was briefly."

Granger went to Taylor. The soldier's face was gray, sweat-slicked. His eyes fluttered open and focused on Granger.

"Lieutenant…sorry about the trouble."

"Don't be. Not your fault."

"Shoulda seen him."

"Don't worry about that," Granger said. He stopped. Taylor's eyes closed and his breathing deepened. *Just worry about staying alive,* he had been about to say. He reached for Taylor's shoulder, pulled back before he touched him. He looked up and found the younger woman watching him.

"We will take care of him, monsieur," she said.

There was a chair behind him. Granger backed up and sat down.

"You should eat," she said, "rest."

"I'll stay," he said. "I won't get in the way, but…I'll stay."

The two women whispered to each other, and then the older one left the room. "I'll bring you something," she said as she went, her accent clearly American. The doctor stepped out of her way and returned to Taylor's side.

"There is not much you can do, Lieutenant," he said.

"Nevertheless."

"As you wish."

Russell came in a few minutes later. He stared at Taylor, his face, Granger thought, eloquently expressionless. Controlled. He went to the man. "Stay here till I return." Russell only nodded.

Granger went back to the main room and inquired after paper and ink. He wrote a brief note, detailing events from finding Ham's body to bringing Taylor back wounded. He almost folded it up, and then added a comment about "Captain" Dodge's possible perfidy in the sale of horses rightfully belonging to Clark's men. Satisfied, he folded it in thirds and returned to Taylor's room.

"See this gets to Colonel Montgomery," he told Russell. "Tell him I'll stay to oversee events."

Again the perfunctory nod. Then Russell seemed to remember himself and touched fingers to his hat. "Aye, sir."

"Have you eaten yet?"

"No, sir."

"Eat first. Then see to this."

He backed out of the room.

Granger sat down again just as the American woman returned with a trencher piled with chicken, greens, and bread. She caught his shoulder as he began to rise reflexively and pushed him back down. She set the plate on his lap, smiled, and went back to Taylor's bedside.

With the first mouthful he realized how hungry he was and ate quickly. When he finished, he looked around for somewhere to put the trencher. The younger woman swept it from his hands and disappeared out the door, leaving him feeling self-conscious. She came back with a tankard for him.

"Thank you," he said quickly, expecting her to rush off again. "Ma'am."

She hesitated, half-turned from him, and stared at him as if trying to make sense of what she saw. Her eyes shifted from his face to his uniform then back up.

"You are different than the other Americans?"

"What?"

"Your uniform, it is not like the others." She shrugged. "For one thing, it is a uniform."

"I'm not—I'm in the Continental Army, with General Nathanael Greene. Do you know who that is?"

"I have heard, *oui*. You are like the other one, the one they say was killed?"

"Sergeant Ham Inwood, yes." He got to his feet. "Lt. Granger." He bowed, feeling awkward.

"You will be going back east after…?" She gestured toward Taylor.

"I don't know. That will depend on Colonel Clark."

"Were you close to this man?"

"Barely know him. But he's under my command."

"So you intend to sit here until he recovers?"

"Well…"

"Sit, please," she said and fetched a chair for herself. "My name is Martine. Martine de Lautin."

"You've been helping Dr. Reynal?"

"Since the battle. Me and Emily," she nodded to indicate the other woman. "Her husband died in the fighting, but she will not go home. I worry for her when we have no more wounded to care for. The first day was bad. I had never seen men shot before. Fortunately there were not many."

"One is too many."

When she said nothing, Granger wondered if he had offended or shocked her. He expected her to excuse herself, then, and leave him alone, which would have been a relief. Instead, she nodded.

"Do you know General Washington?" she asked.

Startled, he laughed, a single percussive bark. "No," he said. "I'm afraid I do not."

"Oh. But your General Greene does, no?"

"Yes, I suppose so."

"My brother is with Marquis de Lafayette, who is with General Washington. Fighting on the side of the rebels."

"I see. That's…we're grateful."

She smiled. "I worry about him." Suddenly she stood. "You will be staying in St. Louis until your man is well?"

"Yes, ma'am, that's my intention." *Among other things,* he thought.

"You cannot just sit here. *Un moment, s'il vous plaît.*"

She left the room. Granger stared after her. He had never been comfortable making conversation with strangers, especially women. Now that she was out of the room, though, her absence bothered him, as if for that brief time she had eased the concern he had been holding onto as if Taylor's life depended on it.

"Best maybe you should get all addled and tongue-tied by females," Ham had chided him once, *"otherwise, the way they could turn your head, you'd never have a dependable thought again."*

Ham had always seemed at ease with women while Granger often lost the power of speech when one smiled at him. Granger was older, but he rarely felt that way around Ham. Even now he felt too young for what was going on around him. The difference in their abilities was so sharp that Ham used it to put him in his place when Granger got too "bookish" and started lecturing Ham on topics for which Ham generally had no interest.

The doctor had left and only the older woman remained. She sat by the window, gazing outside, her long face unreadable.

"Lieutenant."

Granger looked at the door and saw Cartabona, who gestured for him to follow.

In the main room, Cartabona said, "You should not stay in the sickroom all the time, Lieutenant. It would do you no good and could impair your usefulness should you be needed. Madame de Lautin has offered you a billet for the duration of your stay. I insist you accept her hospitality."

Cartabona's tone ended any protest Granger could make. It was framed as an offer but the authority of the voice made it an order. Granger glanced off to the left and saw Martine de Lautin—*Madame* de Lautin—standing by the door, watching.

"Of course, sir," Granger said. "I am only concerned for my soldier."

"Understandable and commendable. But you can do little for him by sitting there watching him. Dr. Reynal will do all he can."

"Yes, sir."

Cartabona nodded then. Matter settled, he returned to the table and his work.

Granger crossed the floor to Madame de Lautin.

"It would seem I am indebted to you for the courtesy of a place to sleep," he said.

"There is no debt, Lieutenant. We will be honored. Let me excuse myself with Dr. Reynal and I will take you to my house."

Three

AS HE WALKED NORTH alongside her, carrying his haversack and two rifles, Granger saw that the village stretched out, like a lazy cat, along the rise above the river. Three main streets ran north and south—the La Rue Royal ran closest to the river, then came La Rue d'Eglise, and finally Rue des Granges, where most of the stables and barns could be found.

He had seen little of the place when he stepped out of the canoe and been swept almost immediately out to Cortez's. He saw now that the men dressed in baggy blouses, kerchiefs, broad-brimmed hats, and dark breeches. Boots were not uncommon, but heavy buckled shoes and moccasins predominated. He also saw buckskins, old military coats patched and recut, and plainer cloth coats. The day was already hot, yet some men still wore heavy clothes. With the women, wide petticoats and bodices, white with blue stripes or piping like Martine's, and aprons. Some hats, but most had scarves covering their hair, which otherwise flowed freely.

All of them, even those who dressed in somewhat finer clothes, showed the sun in their faces, tanned skins from working in the open. Granger imagined few were without calluses on their hands. It was an ample town, not more than a thousand people he guessed, and it would be a hard life this close to wilderness.

The number of Indians mingling with the habitants surprised him. The vast majority of the force that had attacked both here and in Cahokia had been Indian. He knew St. Louis maintained good relations with certain tribes, but it was a shock to see any within the village so soon after an assault from others.

Six cross-streets from the Governor's House, Martine indicated her home.

A sign hung on the left side of the gate—*Fonderie et armurier de Lautin.*

As they reached the gate, it swung inward and a Negro wearing buckskins and carrying a musket stepped out. Granger took a step back and the two men stared at each for an awkward moment.

"Neptune," Martine de Lautin said. "This is Lt. Granger."

The black looked down at Granger's uniform. "American?"

"I am," Granger said.

"He will be staying with us," Martine said.

"Ah," Neptune said, nodding. He spoke to Martine in a stream of French. She laughed, the black man smiled. Martine then spoke and Neptune's smile faded. When she finished, he dipped his head. "My condolences, Lieutenant. I hope your man lives. Perhaps we'll meet again. *Bon jour.*"

He walked off, south. Granger watched him greet others, who responded cordially.

"Is he yours?" Granger asked.

"*Pardon?* Oh, no. Neptune belongs to no one but himself. Please, come in."

Granger hesitated. "You're certain this is no imposition?"

"No, of course not. It is very common to have guests here. There are more people in St. Louis than places. In your case, we will be honored." She stopped just inside the gate and smiled at him. "Come in. Welcome to our home."

Her voice fascinated him, closer to music than ordinary speech.

Just inside the fence a dirt path, outlined by rocks, led directly to the deep porch of the main house. The small yard was largely dirt, with occasional eruptions of unkempt grass and a stunted shrub or two. A vine crawled pathetically up one of the thick wooden beams supporting the overhanging shingled roof. Beneath the shade of the overhang, the whitewashed walls showed the odd construction of the region—vertical posts sandwiching filler of mud, clay, and straw, hard-packed and dried, and coated with a lime wash. Granger had seen few houses in the area built the way he expected, with horizontal logs, but the more prosperous residents liked stone about as much as New Englanders.

Off to the left was another building, open to the yard. Granger felt a wash of heat from it and within its bowels he saw the orange-red glow of a forge. He glimpsed someone moving within and heard the clink of metal.

"My husband is a gunsmith."

"A gunsmith. Would he be willing to advise me?"

"I will introduce you after I show you to your room."

"Thank you, I would be very appreciative."

She led him through the whitewashed main room, past the stone hearth that divided the parlor from the dining room. "Come in, come in," Martine said as she moved toward a door on the parlor side of the fireplace. A hallway stretched perhaps fifteen feet to a rear door. On either side were two more doors. She opened the left hand one and stepped back, waiting for him.

Granger entered a small room containing a narrow bed and a stand with a bowl and pitcher beneath a window. A crucifix hung on the wall above the headboard and a trunk stood on the floor at the foot of the bed.

"It is my brother's room," she said. Her fingers laced together and tightened for a moment, and then she moved past him. "The trunk is mostly empty except for an extra blanket."

She glanced at the bed. "I will leave you alone to arrange yourself. We will have dinner in a few hours, so if there is anything else you need to do there is time." She went to the door. "When you are finished, come to the parlor. I will take you to my husband."

Granger laid the rifles on the bed and opened his haversack. He took out the kit with his razor and brush and laid it on the wash stand, wondering if it would be an imposition to ask about laundering his spare breeches and shirt.

He pulled out the stack of letters. *Does Martine read Spanish?* He returned them to the bottom of his bag. Best, he decided, to get to know the de Lautins before asking them to spy on a neighbor. He dropped the haversack on top of the chest and went out to the parlor, where he found Martine waiting. She led him across the yard to the workshop.

"Étienne!" she called as she led Granger under the roof. The heat pushed at him, like a large invisible hand. Deep inside, barely separate from the iron shadows around the forge, Étienne de Lautin pumped the bellows, left arm driving powerfully. The fire glowed hotter in the flood of air. Granger drew a deep breath, steeled himself, and pushed through into the workshop.

Étienne de Lautin was a broad man, his wrists thick below heavily sinewed forearms. To Granger's surprise, he was also much older than he expected, a dense wave of black-streaked gray hair rolling back from his wide forehead and over his ears. He looked around and grinned at his wife, then noticed Granger. He stopped pumping and walked away from the forge to a bench at the back of the shop. Granger followed, weaving between barrels, a rack containing rough, unfinished stocks, and a lathe mounted on a long table. The workbench contained tools for fine work, scales of different sizes, rags, weapons in various stages of repair.

His wife spoke to him in rapid French and he nodded. He extended a hand toward Granger.

"Lieutenant Granger! *Bon jour*! Welcome to our home. Martine says you wish to ask me something?"

Granger's hand felt overwhelmed by Étienne's larger, more powerful grip. "Thank you for your hospitality, monsieur. Yes, I have a question you may be able to help me with." He took out the misshapen balls from his pocket and offered them to Étienne. "These rounds were taken from a log and from one of my men yesterday. We were fired upon while we were on señor Cortez's land. They seem larger than the average musket ball."

Étienne bounced them a couple of times in his palm, then held them up against the firelight. "Perhaps. I could weigh it, maybe, but that still would not mean much. It does seem large. Over .70 caliber. Not a British musket, certainly not French." He went to his bench and dropped a round on a scale. Then he started adding weight to the other side until it balanced. "Larger than a Charleville. Big even for a British Long Land Service musket. This would be almost .79 caliber." He plucked it off the scale, weighed the second round, and then gave them back.

Granger rolled the mangled round in his fingers. "British muskets are between sixty and seventy..."

"I think there is a Spanish musket—a modification, you understand—that takes one this size, but I have not seen one since leaving New Orleans."

"Would señor Cortez own one?"

"No. He came here with an Austrian *snaphaan* and pistols, none of them nearly this size. If it is the Spanish musket, I would say that whoever shot your soldier must have been very close or very lucky."

"Is there anything special about this particular musket?"

"An *escopeta*. Nothing except the size of the barrel. Spanish muskets tend to be around .69 caliber, some smaller. In Mexico, though, some of the barrels were changed because of the Indians. I have heard it said the Comanche and the Apache are difficult to kill, so *caballeros* would modify their muskets. It is not standard for the Spanish army, though, and before we came here Governor Galvez forbade them. I only saw one, once. But it could be many other weapons. Shotguns, for example, might be so large. It is hardly conclusive." He shrugged. "I hope this helps. Your man, is he...?"

"Still alive. Thank you, monsieur." He pocketed the balls.

"You will be dining with us tonight, then?"

"It would be my honor, sir."

Étienne grinned. "*Tres bien!*"

He returned from seeing Taylor to find the hearth blazing and the aromas of cooking filling the house. Martine was going from lantern to lantern with a taper and the room was beginning to glow from the warmer light. Granger watched from the doorway as she finished, unwilling to interrupt. He could see the table now set with plates and a pair of candles. The rooms did not look so bare in the waning daylight; the shadows seemed to bring the furnishings closer together, fill in the blankness, and created a sense of welcome where before had been reserve.

The front door opened then, and Étienne entered. When he saw Granger, he grinned and waved. "Ah, lieutenant! How is your man?"

"Still holding on. He may pull through."

"Dr. Reynal is very good."

Martine came in from the kitchen. "Dinner will be ready soon," she said. "*Tu t'es lavé?*" she asked her husband. He returned a look of mock dismay, and held his hands out, palms up, as though to show her they were clean. She touched his cheek and walked away. Étienne laughed.

"May I offer you brandy?" he asked.

"Yes, thank you."

Étienne clapped his hands and rubbed them as he went to the credenza. He took two glasses and turned them upright, then poured from one of the decanters about an inch of dark liquid in each. He handed one to Granger and raised the other.

"*Vive la révolution!*"

Granger sipped. The sharpness filled his mouth. He swallowed and felt a flush of warmth spread around his chest.

"That's very good," he said.

"It is not really brandy. It is American. Whiskey. We have a factor who brings it in from Philadelphia." He gestured back toward the hearth. "Please, let us sit."

The heat from the fire washed over Granger as he sat down. Sweat licked his face, but Étienne seemed unaffected.

"You are one of Clark's men, no?"

"Not exactly. I'm with General Greene, of the Continental Army. I came out here with Captain John Rogers and his dragoons."

"You are a Virginian?"

"No. I'm from Connecticut."

Étienne frowned. "Where is that?"

"North. Closer to Boston than Charlottesville."

"Ah. A big country, no? When this is finished, then, you will go back?"

"I haven't thought about it yet. I never expected to be here."

"You thought, perhaps, to be fighting near your home?"

"Closer, at least, yes."

"But war takes us unexpected places. I came here from Quebec by way of New Orleans. I was on the Plains of

Abraham with Montcalm. Terrible day! I lost my home. I thought I would return to France, but I ended up in New Orleans. That is where I met my wife. So it was not such a bad thing, going somewhere unexpected." He leaned forward. "Lt. Cartabona said you lost a man? Not the same one who was wounded with that ball?"

"No, another. A friend of mine was killed here. Out at señor Cortez's place. We found him yesterday."

"Cortez. Hm." Étienne scowled at the fire. "If I may ask, what was your friend doing out there?"

"He was out there to retrieve anyone that hadn't come into St. Louis before the battle. He'd been working with Lt. Tayon. One of Cortez's slaves told him there was someone hiding there, so he went back to be sure. We were attacked when we found my friend's body."

"By whom?"

"I don't know. We never saw him."

"Him? Only one?"

"So it appears."

"Curious," Étienne said, gazing into the fire.

Silence stretched. Granger finished his own whiskey and set the glass down on the small table between them.

"Do you know señor Cortez?"

Étienne shifted in his chair. "I know everyone in St. Louis if they have a musket, rifle, pistol. That is almost everyone. There are two other gunsmiths, of course, but we share the same customers. Sometimes there is too much work for one to do. I did work on Diego's pistols shortly after he came here. He has a fine matched pair. French." He smiled. "But in the matter of Don Diego, I know him slightly better. At least longer. We traveled with him up the river when we came here over two years ago. We shared a boat."

"What kind of man is he?"

"Spanish." Étienne laughed. "*Excusez-moi.* I mean nothing by that." His expression suggested otherwise. He took both glasses and went to refill them. When he returned and handed Granger his glass, he said, "You have been out to his place. You have seen. That should tell you something. Diego is ambitious but not well ordered. He takes on too much and doesn't finish one thing before starting another. I think he is lonely and perhaps obsessed. He speaks occasionally of a woman he left in Spain whom he hopes to bring here after he has established himself. But the way things are going, that could be another ten years! Who would wait so long? He works hard, but... he says he wants to raise horses. He claims he did so in Spain."

A woman, Granger thought, *Eliana...?* He recalled the cleared land, stumps still dotting the pasture. "Do you think that's possible?"

Étienne shrugged. "He supplied Pourré's cavalry with mounts, a dozen of them. But horses need pasture, land to run. We are close to the plains, but Diego's land is heavily wooded, as you saw. He could certainly clear it, but that is much work and he has only his slaves. He hires no one else. I suppose if desire can make a difference—and sometimes it can—then he will do it. Perhaps not the way he wishes, though. We spent many weeks with him, spoke almost daily, and yet I know less about him than some men I've spent less than a day with. He is a close man, solitary."

"Untrusting?"

"Not exactly. More that he simply does not wish to share."

"We found a dead stallion. Lt. Tayon said it was his stud."

"Dead?"

"Shot then butchered."

"*Mon dieu,* that makes no sense. Why…?"

"I wonder that myself."

Étienne stared into the fire, his face expressively disturbed.

"You said he's lonely," Granger said.

"He works and dreams and does business. He has money. Some. I don't know how much." He seemed preoccupied for a moment and Granger expected him to change the subject. But then, frowning, he continued. "He brings lumber to the village. But he has no friends—well, that is not precisely true. There is at least one, Jose Renaldo. But Cortez keeps to himself so much he's almost a hermit. He has only his slaves out there to keep him company, and how much company can they be?"

"Do you like him?"

"What is to not like?" Étienne shrugged. "I suppose. He is a decent man. For a Spaniard." He laughed. "When the call came for volunteers to face the British, Don Diego was one of the first. He came into the village wearing an old but amazingly clean uniform and offered his services to Lt. Governor de Leyba. He had to exchange that beautiful old uniform, though, for the new one the cavalry wore."

"New one?"

"Yes. Like Tayon's. The scarlet one with blue facings? Don Diego had a traditional Spanish one of dark blue with red facings. And the hat! *Mon dieu*, he looked like something! But he did not complain. He helped with the drill, then, and I tell you he is a born horseman."

"Where did he get the horses?"

Étienne shook his head. "East, across the river."

I know where he got them, Granger thought, thinking of the receipt he had found.

"Has he ever told anyone about a brother?"

"No. What do you mean?"

"On his property there is a small cemetery plot. We saw a marker for someone named Atilio de Cortez."

"Indeed?" He ran a finger over his chin, expression thoughtful, as though he were trying to come to a decision. "He never spoke to me of family and I have heard nothing. For that matter, I don't recall a cemetery, but it has been months since I was there. Martine?"

"Come to the table," she called.

Étienne stood. "Do you know if Don Diego ever said anything about having a brother?"

"No."

Étienne raised his hands. "No. Perhaps Tayon?"

"He didn't know either."

"Hm. But I would not be surprised to learn he has a dozen brothers. He only spoke of the woman, his fiancée."

"What did he say about her?"

"A gentleman should be discreet, no? All I will say is that from the way he speaks of her I could not bear to be away from this woman for two days, much less two years." He narrowed his eyes at Granger. "But you are young, perhaps you do not know about such things yet? You have all that to look forward to."

Granger sat back from his empty plate, gorged and satisfied. "I cannot recall the last time I enjoyed a meal so well." The chicken had been spiced, and served with greens, fresh corn, and a chewy bread.

Martine smiled and got up to pour more wine.

Étienne patted his stomach. "Excellent, *mon cher*."

"Thank you very much," Granger said.

"Our Lt. Governor Leyba," Étienne said, "has asked that St. Louis open its heart to our allies. Personally—"

"Étienne," Martine said, warning.

"—I wonder what it is we are allied to." He gave Martine a look. "France, now Spain, elects to support you Americans in your cause, and it is hardly my place to question the counsel of kings, no?"

"I don't see why not," Granger said. "We are."

"*Exactement!* It is unnatural."

"Forgive me, but you toasted the revolution."

"Of course I did. I am a patriot and anything that puts the English in their place is a good thing. For once they are running. But now I speak of your goals. When you have won, what then? You are rebelling against your king. Will you become part of France? Or choose a new king of your own?"

"I'm sure that's being discussed by the men who make such decisions."

"But what kind of men are they? Philosophes? I wonder what kind of country will come from this. Of course, you may yet lose. Unlikely with France on your side, but it could happen."

"It could," Granger admitted, uncomfortable. "My opinions are no longer what they were when I joined the army. I'm not altogether sure what they are anymore."

"War can do that to a man," Étienne said. "But there always remains a center."

"Étienne," Martine said, "has strong opinions."

"Sometimes too strong?" Étienne asked, smiling at her. "As may be. But you, Lieutenant, do you suggest that you fight in a cause in which you no longer believe?"

"Étienne—"

Étienne waved her still. "No no. I am interested. He has come so far from home to fight in this rebellion, and now he has lost a friend. That is no small sacrifice. I wish to know, what is it that makes this worthwhile for him."

"I did not willingly sacrifice my friend," Granger said. "It was never my intention to spend what was most precious to me on philosophy."

"Then—"

"What do I think of what we're doing? When I began I believed it was a just rebellion. 'Justice is often thought to be the greatest of virtues. Neither evening nor morning star is so wonderful. And proverbially, in justice is every virtue comprehended. It is a complete virtue in its fullest sense, because it is the actual exercise of complete virtue, because he who possesses it can exercise his virtue not only in himself but towards his neighbor also.'"

"That is Aristotle," Martine said.

Granger looked at her, surprised. "Yes. My mother insisted we study him, as well as Plato and Homer. I thought I knew when I joined the rebellion what that meant. Complete virtue. I'm not so sure now. I think I'll have to wait till it's over before I can answer you."

"Your friend?"

"Ham never wanted to join this war. I did. We debated it endlessly. My father wanted me to go to college, to be educated. I wanted to fight the British. Finally, when I made it clear that I would thwart his desires, he helped me secure a commission. Ham came with me, though his family did not have any inclination to assist him. He became a sergeant quickly enough and we ended up with Nathanael Greene in the south. That was over a year ago. I've seen a few battles since then. I think it fair to say that enough blood and death will blunt any patriot's fervor."

Étienne nodded, his face grim. Granger thought he saw understanding, even sympathy.

"Excuse me, please." Granger stood and walked away from the table, working to control his reactions to his own bluntness. The image of Ham's body roiled his mind.

He stood before the hearth. He could hear them talking quietly in French.

He felt a hand on his shoulder. He turned to see Étienne standing beside him.

"Forgive me," Granger said. "I did not intend—"

"Think no more of it. I speak too freely, sometimes. Martine warns me to be more circumspect, but I pay no attention." Étienne drained his wine. "It is time for me to retire. I am up early, before dawn. I've had much work since the battle. Many are bringing their muskets to me complaining that they missed because the sights are off or the barrel is not true or the trigger too tight. In truth, most miss because they are loath to shoot a man, but I cannot tell them that. So I work long days. Tomorrow I must spend the day north, in St. Charles. When I return we can speak of pleasanter things, no? I must sleep. I enjoyed our conversation. I bid you good night, Lieutenant."

Granger watched Étienne stretch, say something more to Martine, and walk out of the room. A few moments later a door closed. Granger moved away from the fire, then, grateful to be away from the heat.

"Étienne needs the warmth."

"I beg your pardon?" He turned toward the voice and saw Martine bent before the fire, working with a small shovel to damp it back.

"He has worked so long before a forge that he chills easily," she said. "This is cool for him. It's not so very comfortable for others, though, I'm afraid."

"He must suffer in winter."

"Terribly. But I do what I can to keep him warm."

"I imagine you do."

She laughed quietly and Granger, embarrassed, was glad he stood away from the light so she could not see him blush. He felt simultaneously drawn and repelled, his attraction to this woman strong and unwelcome. *She's married, she's French...*

"You know Aristotle, ma'am?" he asked.

"I, too, had an insistent mother," she said. "It was thought once that I might become a companion to a great lady. Instead I am here."

Granger wanted to ask why, how she had come to be married to Étienne, but he could not just then push the words past his teeth.

"Would it be useful," she said, "if you could speak to the slave who said there was someone else on señor Cortez's land?"

"Yes."

"There is a man—Neptune, you met him when I brought you here—who could arrange that, I think. I will speak to him about it."

"That's…thank you."

"I have a favor to ask in return," she said. "I have been reluctant."

"A favor. If it's something I could do—"

"I said my brother fights for you in the east. We have not heard for some time. I have received no letters. It would be a great favor if you could take a letter to him, to see that he is all right."

"Well," he began, startled. "I'm not even sure where to begin."

"He is with General Lafayette."

"So you said," he said, finding it impossible to explain how large the country was and how many men were scattered across it. "I'll try, in any case."

In the candlelight it was difficult to understand her expressions, but it seemed her smile was sad. "*Merci*, Lieutenant. Try, yes, that is all I ask. In the morning I will find Neptune and we shall see. Now I must go to my husband. *Bonne nuit. Faîtes de beaux reves.*"

She walked past him, to the door, and he waited for her to look at him again. When she did not, he felt both disappointed and relieved. He stood very still until he heard the door open and close again. Then he snuffed all the candles and lanterns. He carried the last lit candle to his room.

He stood in the middle of the room, his mind empty for a moment. There were things he had to do, duties to attend, and yet he was here, in a quiet place. *"It's a hell of a thing, Oddy,"* Ham said. Granger blinked. His vision fragmented through tears. "Not now," he said as he wiped his eyes. He wrenched his thoughts away from what had happened; time later, after all the necessary details had been seen to. *Think of something else,* he commanded himself, *something kind, something…gentler…*

Martine came to mind.

As he undressed for bed, he tried to imagine what had drawn Martine and Étienne together. For Étienne's part, Granger thought he understood. But in her case, he had more difficulty. It was none of his business, though. There were husbands and wives in Connecticut with wide differences in age. The more he thought about it, the more inappropriate his imaginings became.

He wondered what her mouth tasted like.

Four

GRANGER SLEPT LATER than usual and woke reluctantly. He lay half awake, thoughts moving sluggishly until they fixed on Ham. He recalled the speech he had given last night. Pompous, he thought, but accurate. He had joined this fray to find justice. He had seen precious little. Finding the killer at least seemed more purposeful than much of what he had witnessed since joining the rebellion.

In the parlor, coffee, a bowl of porridge, and a plate of bread waited on the table for him, but no sign of Martine or her husband. Granger ate quickly and headed to the Lt. Governor's house.

There he found several sweating, rumpled men gathered in the courtyard, a few wearing the bright scarlet coats of the local cavalry. Others he recognized as men from Clark's militia. Servants brought them tankards. Granger spotted Lt. Tayon on the porch talking to Cartabona and another man.

As Granger approached, the third man asked Cartabona something. Cartabona nodded. The man, tall, black hair beneath a broad-brimmed hat, wearing a scarlet uniform, glared at Granger, his anger almost palpable. He gave Cartabona and Tayon a short bow and stalked off, disappearing into the house.

"Lieutenant," Cartabona said. His expression was grim.

Granger almost asked who the third man was when he glanced past Cartabona and saw Russell just inside the doorway, talking to one of the women who had nursed Taylor, the American. His head lowered and she put a hand on his shoulder.

Granger felt a chill erupt in his chest. "Taylor?"

Cartabona nodded. "Your man died very early this morning. I am sorry."

Granger closed his eyes for a few moments. He had never lost a man under his command. Somehow, his death shook him as though Taylor had been a close friend. When he looked again, Russell was no longer visible through the door. Men moved past him from the house.

"The doctor did his best," Tayon said. "Perhaps I did not do as much as I could."

"No, we—it's not your fault," Granger said. "You did as much as you could. Without you, he would've died out there." He looked at Tayon. "I didn't expect you back yet."

"We returned last night. We found nothing. We have been discussing whether we should go out again."

"Maybe I could go with you this time."

Cartabona shook his head. "Your Colonel Montgomery is here, arrived not an hour ago."

"Colonel...why?"

Cartabona pursed his lips. "You should discover that from him." Cartabona bowed. "If you will excuse me."

Granger watched him walk away, feeling oddly disconnected.

"Why do I feel that everything has changed?" he said.

"I am so sorry," Lt. Tayon said. "You came here to find your sergeant and now—"

"The other man you were talking to. Who was that?"

"Lt. Renaldo."

"Jose Renaldo?"

Tayon looked surprised. Before he could answer, Colonel Montgomery stepped from the house and came toward him. He was a tall man with a thin face and deep-set eyes that almost disappeared in the shadows of his hat. His mouth was set in a perpetual half-smile that had irritated Granger since he first met Clark's second-in-command.

Granger saluted. "Colonel."

Montgomery's hand tapped the brim of his hat half-heartedly. "My condolences on your sergeant's loss."

Tayon cleared his throat. "You will excuse me, gentlemen," he said, saluting.

Montgomery waited until Tayon was well away before continuing. "Bad business. Sergeant Inwood was a good man. So was Taylor."

"Colonel, I—"

Montgomery's left hand cut the air. "It's war, Lieutenant, no need to explain. Are you of a mind for revenge?"

"Sir?"

"We're going after them on the other side. I'm sending a force up the Illinois after the raiding party. I'm here to coordinate with Lt. Governor de Leyba. I want you with our party. This will give you a chance to see us in action the way we prefer, on the offensive."

"Begging your pardon, Colonel, but what about Langlade?"

"If he were coming, he'd have been here, don't you think? Personally, I think they're just using him as an excuse to do nothing. Besides, if he is on his way, all the more reason to catch the first group before they have a chance to join up."

It's been five days, Granger thought. But Montgomery never liked to be questioned. Granger believed he was looking for an excuse to make his own reputation, and now with Clark gone back east he had an opportunity.

"I had hoped to be involved in finding the ones who murdered my sergeant."

Montgomery frowned. "Murdered? Since when do casualties of war constitute murder? No, I don't want you meddling. Let the Spanish deal with it, it's their territory."

Granger considered protesting, but caught himself. Something else was going on here. Montgomery was being arbitrary, he no more needed Granger with this expedition than he cared about being diplomatic with the Spanish. Regardless, his mind was made up and arguing would serve no purpose.

"Very well, sir. When do you wish me to rejoin the company?"

"Do you have any other business to tend to?"

He thought of his desire to talk to Cortez's slave about what he had told Ham, but Montgomery would see that as meddling. "Nothing that won't keep till we return."

"Excellent. Then, as soon as you can, get a canoe back."

"Yes, sir," he said. "I have to retrieve my kit, but I can be back in Cahokia by this evening."

"Make it sooner. I want to move out by first light tomorrow."

"Very well, sir." Granger saluted. Again, Montgomery made his almost-salute, then walked back into the house, leaving Granger feeling frustrated and disappointed. As he thought about it, though, he discovered a part of him that did crave revenge. It surprised him, realizing it; exhilarated him, and then disturbed him.

"Lieutenant?"

Tayon stood beside him again. "Yes?"

"Is everything all right?"

"Colonel Montgomery has requested I return to Cahokia. It would seem...well, I should be leaving soon."

Tayon glanced around. "You should know, perhaps, that this is not all your Colonel's wish. Lt. Renaldo complained about you. He hinted at insult. Lt. Cartabona decided that it would be best if you were removed for a time."

Renaldo. That made more sense, then, as there was certainly no affection on Montgomery's part for the Continentals. Cartabona's request, though, would give him a reasonable excuse to do what would otherwise seem arbitrary.

"I don't even know Lt. Renaldo," Granger said. "How could I insult him?"

"He is a close friend to Don Diego. He was offended that Sergeant Inwood had gone to his property alone. Now he is angry that you were there." He shook his head. "Truly, I am puzzled by his reaction, but when Colonel Montgomery arrived to order you back..."

"I see. Thank you." *I wonder who told him?* He glanced up and saw Russell coming toward them from the house.

"It is unfortunate. I had hoped we could get to know each other."

Granger realized then that he felt the same. Perhaps it was only that they had been through a fight together, but he found he liked the young Frenchman.

"So had I," he said.

Tayon seemed to brighten from within. "You will always be welcome here."

"Lieutenant?" Russell said as Tayon stepped from the porch.

"Yes?"

"I hear you're going back to Cahokia."

"That's correct."

"If it's not too bold to inquire, then, do you intend to replace Sergeant Inwood? As your aide, I mean."

"Are you volunteering?"

Russell's mouth flexed, his only sign of embarrassment. "Yes, sir, I believe I am."

He found Martine working in the garden behind her house, on her hands and knees, pulling weeds. When she saw him, she stood, smiling, and something seemed to tighten Granger's spine and chest.

"Lieutenant..."

"My apologies. It seems I'm to return to Cahokia. Today."

Her smile faltered. "Is something wrong?"

"Not at all. I was quite looking forward to your hospitality. It's been some time since my last home-cooked meal." It occurred to him that, despite his intention to return, events might prevent that. "I'll be accompanying an expedition. It could last several weeks."

"Oh."

"I plan to come back." There was a tone of urgency in his voice that surprised him, which she seemed to hear as well. He turned away. "I need to collect my things."

"Of course." She gestured toward the house, then followed him through the kitchen, the dining room, and stopped at the hallway.

"You said something about a letter to your brother."

She nodded. "But if you are returning—"

"I intend to, but events might take charge."

Granger went to the room, gathered up his belongings, and packed his haversack. He looked around. He had left no impression on it at all. When he left, it would be as he had found it. He shouldered his bag and carried the two rifles out.

Martine waited in the parlor. She had taken the kerchief from her head and was wiping her face.

When she saw him, she stood and held out an envelope. He propped the rifles by the door.

"His name is Jean-Renard Lascal," she said.

"I will try to see that he gets it. Do you have some paper that I may use?"

"Of course." She gestured toward a small desk he had not seen before, to the left of the door.

Granger added the letter to his haversack, and then sat down. He took the pen from its holder and dipped it in the inkpot.

"You said Neptune could help me with señor Cortez's slaves," he said.

"*Oui*, but he is with my husband today, going to St. Charles. I doubt they will return before tomorrow."

"If you would kindly give him my request, then," he said, beginning to write. "If he will speak to them on my behalf, I have some specific questions I would appreciate being answered. If you could read this to him—"

"He can read."

Granger looked up at her. "Indeed? Well..." He wrote.

Who was hiding? How long has he been there? Were all the slaves aware of him? If he did not arrive in the area with Cortez, when did he come to be here? What did Cortez say to explain his presence? Did he specifically order you not to say anything about him? How many horses did Cortez have? Who is the man in the grave in the cemetery plot?

He tried to think of more questions. Martine stood close, watching over his shoulder. Granger caught the scent of her, warm from exertion, sweat mingled with cotton. He set the quill down and closed the inkwell. There was no blotter, so he left the page to dry on its own.

"That should be sufficient."

"Do you really intend to come back?" she said.

"I do. But circumstances may delay that. If they do, I'll be back...eventually." He looked up at her. "Your village seems a good place. There's much to recommend it."

"Thank you for taking my letter," Martine said. "I did not know how else to find out."

"I hope I can do what you ask."

"I'm sure you will. What is it you're doing that you must leave so soon?"

"Punitive expedition. We're going after the enemy force now, before they have a chance to regroup."

"That sounds...they must be well on their way to Prairie du Chien by now. How can you hope to catch them?"

"I'm sorry. I shouldn't have told you."

She laughed. "Why not? Do you think perhaps I am a spy? Who would I tell?"

"Your husband."

"I do not tell Étienne what he does not need to know."

Étienne will not come home today, he thought. Granger made himself look away from her, down at the sheet of paper on the desk. The stillness of the house seemed to press in on him. The fact that she was alone with him, unlikely to be disturbed, dominated his awareness.

You're being absurd, he thought. *She is married, they are happy, content at least, that is obvious. Your inexperience is deceiving you.*

He looked over his list of questions. He folded the paper and handed it to her. "That should be enough. Answers to those questions would be most helpful. I can retrieve them from Neptune when I return—you needn't be involved any further."

"How soon do you have to leave?"

Her tone puzzled him. She took his questions, but she looked at him. Her eyes seemed to shimmer.

"Madame de Lautin—"

"Martine. My name is Martine."

Slowly, as if he might flinch away, or run, she touched his face. Her fingertips brushed his left cheek, traced the line of his jaw down to his neck. Shivers ran across his shoulders. His entire body churned. He wanted to pull away, but she was too close for him to get out of the chair without shoving her away. He drew his head back.

"I'm sorry," he said. He swallowed and closed his eyes. "I don't—"

She bent down and kissed his mouth. Her tongue prodded his lips until he opened them, then slipped past his teeth and flexed against his tongue. He inhaled loudly and pushed his tongue against hers, afraid of the contact, unwilling to break it off. Heat flooded through him. In an instant, he was overwhelmed.

He smelled her. She had been working in the garden, sweating, but beneath that was another odor, richer, new, and he breathed in her salty tang. Her hands held his head in place while she pressed her mouth onto his. Both of them breathed frantically. Hesitantly, his hands went to her waist, followed the lines of her back, came around to her breasts.

Her right hand dropped to his crotch, squeezed, then both hands worked at his buttons. Granger panicked. Instead of pushing her away, though, he tried to unbutton her bodice. Their mouths stayed together, working at each other. Saliva ran down the left side of his chin.

His breeches opened and she tugged at him. She broke the kiss then, groaning deep in her chest. Her hand closed around him. He moaned. Her face was flushed red, eyes wide, feverish. Her chest heaved with each breath.

"Ma'am—"

She put her fingers against his lips. Thoughtlessly, he drew them into his mouth and sucked.

Suddenly she stepped back. Granger thought for an instant that it was done, that she had changed her mind. He hoped so and feared it. Instead, she gathered up her skirt, pulled it high, baring her legs. He glimpsed a dark patch between them just as she came forward again, straddling him.

Deftly, she took him in one hand and guided him inside her.

The hot wetness shocked him. His hips lunged forward, pushing against her. He grasped her thighs, thrust upward briefly, and spasmed. He shut his eyes and grunted with each pulse.

Her arms enfolded his head, pressed his face against her chest. The odor of sweat mixed now with a stronger scent. Her face and neck were slicked with sweat. All they did now was breathe, heavy, exhausted breaths. He thought it was done. But she began to slide on him, up and down, drawing on him. Exhaustion gave way to another wave of frantic want.

He tried to kiss her again, found her chin instead.

"Wait," she hissed. She grabbed his coat, half-stood, slipping free of him and pulled. She fell back toward the floor and he followed. She undid a couple of her buttons and wrenched the fabric aside to reveal a breast. A large, asymmetrical, pink nipple seemed to stare at him. He took it in his mouth while her hands guided him once more into her.

He pumped against her as though in a seizure, and she exhaled explosively with each thrust. The pressure built and built until he came a second time.

Then they stopped. He lay atop her, gulping air. She stroked his back, his hair, touched his face. He could feel himself shrinking until he slipped limply out of her. After a few minutes, she shoved at him, urging him to get off her.

His legs trembled as he stood. Martine lay on the floor, her skirt bunched inelegantly around her waist. He stared at her naked legs, at the mass of hair at her crotch, then, fascinated, at the slow trickle of semen that seeped from her.

Finally, she sat up. She smiled at him, face wet. She laughed. She grasped his thighs, leaned up, and lightly kissed the tip of his penis. Stunned, Granger staggered back against the chair and almost fell across it. He sat down heavily and watched her stand and try to smooth her clothes.

"*Merci*," she said, smiling.

"That," Granger said, his voice ragged, "was my first time."

"Indeed? I am grateful. I feel honored."

Her face was red, but her expression showed more concern than embarrassment. She looked at the place on the floor where they had rutted just now, and then surveyed everything else in the room. She pushed down at her skirt repeatedly. Whenever her gaze swept over him she smiled.

She feels honored, he thought, feeling stupid. He kept shifting from embarrassment to exhilaration, from a desire to leave immediately to a sharp hunger to do it again. Guilt chased surprise. His skin felt suddenly too tight. A drop of sweat ran into his left eye and he winced. He rubbed at the stinging, feet rooted in place, afraid to move, trying to come to terms with what had just happened.

"You should button yourself," she said.

"Pardon me?"

She gestured toward his crotch and he looked down to see his now flaccid penis still dangling in the open. The moment he saw it, the image of her pulling him onto her, skirt shoved up, flashed through his mind, and it began to swell. He looked up and saw her smile. Shame and hope filled him.

"Can we—"

She raised an eyebrow quizzically. "Perhaps. If you return from your punitive expedition." She touched his face. "I think I would like that. But slower, next time, no?"

"Slower..."

"Such pleasure should be enjoyed at length. There is much more."

"What about...I mean..."

"I told you, I only tell Étienne what it is good for him to know."

Granger felt disappointed, and an instant later confused. She was a married woman. He was a guest.

But it wasn't my idea... "Is he away often?"

She grinned. "Often enough. Button up before you go."

He looked down at himself again and laughed. He tucked himself back in and buttoned his breeches.

"I don't know what to say."

"Perhaps 'thank you'?"

"Yes. That. Thank you. I...don't understand."

For the first time, a trace of doubt crossed her face. "You should go now," she said. "I would not want you to get into trouble."

The list of questions lay on the floor. He snatched it up and handed it to her again. His hand quivered. "You'll see that Neptune gets this?"

"You will see my brother gets my letter?"

"Of course. I—" He caught himself before he said "I promise." He knew better. "I will do my best."

Still shaky, he gathered up his things and left the house. He glanced back from the gate and saw Martine standing at the door, watching him. He touched his hat and bowed, then hurried down the avenue.

That night Granger lay in his tent, sorting through the fragments of events that failed to make sense. In the canoe crossing the Mississippi back to the eastern shore, Russell had told him that Colonel Montgomery had decided to remove Granger from St. Louis almost immediately after reading Granger's report. He didn't know what had set the Colonel off, but something Granger had written had made him angry and, Russell thought, worried. That partly explained Montgomery's presence in St. Louis. But then Lt. Renaldo, a man Granger had never met, had brought a complaint about him to Lt. Cartabona. Renaldo was supposed to be Cortez's friend, a man who, from what Étienne de Lautin told him, had few friends.

Thinking of Étienne took him to thoughts about Martine. His first woman and it had happened so quickly. He wanted to go back across the river, find her, have her again. More importantly, he wanted to ask her why. They had known each other less than a full day. She was young and married to a man at least twice her age. Perhaps her motives were that simple, to be with someone her own age.

He had never felt so ignorant, so aware of all the things he did not know.

"Have you ever been in love, Russell?" he had asked earlier.

If the man had been surprised at the question, he did not show it. "A number of times, Lieutenant. Every one as real as the one before."

"I'm sorry, that was not—"

"The lady you were billeting with?" When Granger hadn't answered, Russell nodded. "I can see that."

Granger had left it there, unsure even why he had asked. Russell made no further mention of it.

He wrenched his thoughts back to Ham. Who had been out there that a slave had told him about? What had he found when he walked into that house? He wondered if Lt. Renaldo knew and if his complaint had to do with keeping anyone—but especially Granger—from finding out.

He seethed with frustration. Everything he now wanted was on the other side of the Mississippi River and in the morning he would be moving in the opposite direction. There was nothing for it but to follow orders and see this campaign through. Then he could return.

I will go back. I'll figure this out, Ham. I promise.

Three Years Later

Five

FROM HIS WINDOW on the second floor of the *Indian Queen* Granger watched lamplighters move down the street through knots of revelers. Philadelphia thundered with a cacophony of competing songs, as though each inn and tavern, street corner and boarding house had chosen a different one for its denizens to roar out at full voice, each trying to demonstrate how much more patriotic it was on this July 3rd, 1783. The tavern below his feet resounded with ale-fueled cheer. Part of him wished to be among them, sharing the fervor of triumph. But mostly he wished for quiet and a full night's sleep before tomorrow's departure west.

Letters covered the small desk below the window. The last month, it seemed, his world had become defined by letters. Open before him was the letter from his brother letting him know how much he could get for him in exchange for the land warrants Granger had received in lieu of pay and pension upon mustering out of the Continental Army. The land was considerable—three thousand acres in the Tennessee territory, compensation for a Major's rank— and were he to hang onto it might be worth a good deal more than Gideon could get for him now. But Granger didn't want the land, he wanted coin, and the price Gideon had arranged with a group of speculators was more than Granger had expected.

Then there were letters of credit arranged with Josiah Weatherall and Company, also through Gideon, and cosigned by Weatherall's partners, the McLean brothers, who he would meet later on, in Pittsburgh. They were betting on him establishing himself as a merchant in Illinois Country, where they expected a land boom in the next few years, after the situation with Spain was resolved. They were looking ahead, investing long-term, and had supplied him with the means and merchandise to start a depot on the frontier.

Colonel Morse had written him twice with the suggestion that he might continue in the army in some capacity not specified. Granger recognized them as invitations to be a spy in Colonel Morse's company. Granger had made no secret about his intention to go west. He had replied to the Colonel's offer with vague thanks and a promise to consider it, but for now he had no intention of remaining in the military.

Other letters to family and friends, inquiries, correspondence with families of soldiers he had commanded. All of them seemed to come into his hands since the surrender of the British.

He picked up an envelope addressed to Martine. It contained two pages, one from a Major Stubblin of the 7th Pennsylvania Regiment, informing Martine Orianna de Lautin that her brother Jean Renard Lascal had died. Major Stubblin had told Granger that the boy had never seen combat, a fact not mentioned in the letter. The second page was a letter of condolence from General Marquis de Lafayette. Granger had intended to add a letter of his own. He told himself that this was why he had never mailed it. But he had never been able to finish that letter.

To one side lay a curiosity. The sheet was small, torn along one edge, and had been folded many times. The creases seemed cut into the creamy paper. He had found it shoved deep inside the patch box of Ham's rifle. Granger found it over a year after leaving St. Louis, when he had finally had time alone, away from any curious eyes, to thoroughly clean and inspect the weapon. He'd emptied everything from the compartment—patches, a cleaning worm, a small folding knife, and two surprises: a locket containing a cameo and a clipping of auburn hair and a dried flower—and found the paper tucked far in the forward recesses.

M. de la Vargas, camino del mercaderos. Then, below that, initials. *J.P.R., A.J.C., C.L.V.* Then a rough sketch of a street, squares for houses, and an arrow aimed at one of them near a crossroad. And finally, at the bottom: *Estas nuestros.* The paper was soiled, sweat-stained and worn. It made no sense to Granger that Ham might have put it there. He'd had no Spanish. More likely, it had been hidden there in St. Louis. The question was, who? Étienne or Martine de Lautin seemed the most likely, but that made as little sense.

In the center of his desk, he laid the stack he had just retrieved from the young student he had hired to translate them. *Young,* he thought, *he's not much younger than I am.* Yet Granger had felt a decade older than the quiet, self-conscious man, another connection made through Gideon. Granger had paid him for the work now completed and brought the translations back here, eager to finally read what he had carried with him for three years since leaving St. Louis.

He had not intended to be absent so long. The expedition Colonel Montgomery claimed to be mounting, for which he had pulled Granger out of the village, did not get underway for weeks. When it finally left, he went with them till they burned the first Indian village, which they had found unoccupied. It turned out later that they had been Missouri, who were supposed to be allies. When Granger had protested the action, Montgomery sent him back east, to General Greene.

Granger had actually forgotten about the letters until he was back in North Carolina.

All of them were by the same woman, Eliana. There was no surname attached to any of them, the translator had told him. They covered a span of three years roughly. Some had been reread many times judging by the smudging on the edges.

Granger drew a deep breath and read.

My love,

I live by your words. Our worlds now are so different, the lands we walk through, even the light, though from the same sun, seems changed. I have the city, the valley, the mountains that mark the north, the plain that spreads south to hills and more mountains. We live bordered by limits, the earth's stone foundations upon which the sky rests. The nearest river...

Well, you know how far. You write of rivers. It is these rivers that divide our worlds, not because they flow between us, but because they are what define yours. Always, when you speak of life there, your Mississippi is ever present. Also the Missouri, the Arkansas, the Illinois, the Ohio. All these rivers, like veins, feeding all that land, all green, and no house higher than the trees. You are surrounded by water, but not limited by it. It feeds you, it carries you, it brings you the world.

I am surrounded by stillness and dry streets.

I know, it is a contradiction. How can there be stillness in a city so full? It is a noisy stillness. If you slept beside your river you would hear it, constantly, until you must come to think of it as the natural condition of life, and a stillness defined by ubiquity. So it is with so many people, all moving and talking and singing and crying. It is. And it is like a sirocco, bringing the dry of the desert into the streets, noisy and barren, acting like life, yet when it leaves there is nothing left in its wake. Your rivers draw me. I hunger for them. Odd, it is not a thirst. You would think it would be, all that water, but that is not how I feel. I do not want to drink of them. I want to be on them, by them, in them. I want them the way I want...

Last year we went to Toledo for a wedding, my mother's cousin's oldest daughter. While there, I slipped away for a day and went to the Rio Tajo. I tried to imagine it wider, with denser forests at its edge, and Indians and men with guns. I tried to imagine the light, but it seems such an ordinary stream compared to what I have imagined from all your descriptions. I want to see a river so wide I cannot recognize people on the other side. I want to be on a river that can match what I have seen through your words, through your eyes.

I want to lie with you on the bank of such a thing. The wetness of your new land excites me, and yes, at times I see your river as the passage into the earth, and the earth is a woman, a lover, waiting and ready for the kisses, the hands, the finger, the tongue, the phallus. How can I feel no shame when the land itself is so shameless? And proud of its desires.

You have corrupted me to want, and all that I want has become part of the same corruption. But there is no decay, no rot. So perhaps it is not corruption. Maybe it is the destruction of blindness and ignorance. How many of us will ever have a chance to know all there is? How many of us will ever find the opportunity to be more than what we are given? How many of us will ever touch such rivers as you have touched?

I want to be a river for you.

Make it soon, my Diego. I may in desperation have to find my own way there if you do not send for me. It has been too long and with time expectations may grow unreasonable. But I have no doubt that your rivers will not disappoint me, and because you are now one with them, you cannot disappoint me. But soon, my love, or I will find a way on my own, and you know how that might turn out. Soon. Please
—Eliana.

"My God," Granger breathed. He shuffled through the others. At a glance he saw that they were all love letters. Granger felt a spark of envy, which changed to chagrin when he glanced over at the unfinished letter to Martine, one in a long series he had tried to write her that he had never been able to complete.

Granger pushed back from the desk and rubbed his eyes. He had heard a voice in his head as he read, a voice he knew. Martine.

He skimmed a couple more until he came across a odd paragraph, in a different hand—Cortez's?— scrawled at the end of a letter. *We have it. In hand. It is done and now I am free. I will bring it. I am on my way.*

Bring what? he wondered. Her freedom? Permission? There was no date on this letter, he had no idea when it had been written. And in none of the rest had he found any indication that she had left Spain and was on her way. As far as he knew, she was still there, waiting to be summoned.

He gathered up Eliana's letters and put them in his satchel. He could go over them more closely during the journey down the Ohio for any details that might be useful. This first perusal left him agitated. He had never watched while two others made love, but that was how he felt now. Aroused, guilty, fascinated.

He finished sorting through the rest of the correspondence and stowed it for the morning. That left one letter on the desk, the one that had triggered his final decision to head back.

Lutenint,

> *I have settled here on the east bank of the Missisipi River, across from Saint Louis. I do smithing and*

some trade. I heer things, some might intrest you. Diego Cortez has returned to his place. Word is his fiancé is on her way here. There was a inquest about Sergeant Inwood's death, but nothin come of it. Colnel Montgomery left a year back. There's a question about accounts between him and Dodge. Anyway, this might be of interest. The woman who helped nurse Taylor, the one you told me about, lost her husband a few months back.

I trust this finds you whole.

—T. Russell, sergnt, retired

Granger read it again. Étienne de Lautin was dead. Cortez was returned to St. Louis.

And now Eliana is on her way.

He drank a glass of sherry and went to bed. Sleep came slowly. When it did, he dreamt of Martine, speaking to him, repeating, *I want to be a river for you.*

Dear Gideon

I am on my way back to St. Louis at last. Your connexion in Philadelphia proved the opportunity I needed and I cannot refuse to take it. I have obtained a loan from the company of Weatherall, Mclean, Lee, and Squires, sufficient to see me back to Illinois Country and solvent for at least a year. I've met with the McLean's here (did you know they were twins?) who transferred the gold. Of course, I shall have to repay it. We shall see now whether I have the makings of a good merchant. Together with the funds you secured for me, I have ample to establish myself.

As for the company itself, they hope to establish a new route, bypassing Montreal for trade. I have misgivings. In the short term, the local interests in St. Louis will be set against it. In the long term, however, as Mr. Weatherall explained it to me, it may prove impossible to deny. He suggests that we, now that we are a nation, will move west regardless the obstacles, and I cannot deny the logic. I pity the French and Spanish should they try to keep us out, just as I pity the Indians we continue to displace.

Mark W. Tiedemann

I am writing you from Pittsburgh, where I have been arranging transportation—the cargo will come from Philadelphia soon after—and from there I make my way to Illinois Country. I'll have to travel by the Ohio River. River travel! Odd that a man who has been shot at, chased, starved, and been in the thick of the worst combat should be so afraid of such a thing. It doesn't help that the river route is the most sensible and when we begin moving goods west it will be the only practical route. I will also have to be careful going through Louisville, as I have learned that Colonel John Montgomery is there, sitting on a local commission of some kind. Best to avoid him if I can.

I do look forward, however, to returning to St. Louis. I may be naive on this point, but I feel that as long as I am fair and honest in my dealings, I shall be successful. This gives me the opportunity to fulfill certain promises which I've told you about. There are three requiring attention.

The first and chief matter is the discovery of how and why Ham was killed. I confess I feel this one is unlikely to be resolved. Much time has passed. On the other hand, this may work in my favor. But secondly, I intend to retrieve his body and return it to his family, a promise I made last summer when I visited them. They treated me more gently than I expected under the circumstances. I tried my best to make sense of Ham's death for them, but as it makes no sense to me this proved difficult.

The third responsibility is most private and you will forgive me if I do not discuss it. It involves a letter and another death and certain expectations I acquired on the very day I left St. Louis. Depending on how matters develop, I will tell you sooner or later.

The fact remains, though, that I am returning to so pleasant a village in so beautiful a landscape that I have been unable to forget about it for even a day since. My affection for the place is tenuous, but real, and perhaps so fragile that I will be disappointed upon seeing it once again.

Your last letter informed me of your acceptance into Yale. My sincerest congratulations. You will raise the family stature much more quickly, and perhaps higher, than I. After the last few years I will be content to do well enough not to cause concern on anyone's part. When I have a situation in St. Louis, I will write to you so that you know where to send future correspondence. Good fortune, brother, and God's Speed.

Sincerely yours,

Granger

Six

GRANGER WALKED PAST the gate to Martine's house three times. The sign was gone for Étienne's smithy and gunsmith works. No smoke rose above that part of the compound where the workshop stood and as he loitered outside, Granger heard no pounding of iron on iron. Once he was sure this was the house, he struggled with a different kind of reluctance. After all this time, he realized that he had no idea what to expect. He had imagined several possible outcomes, all of them positive if not wholly wonderful. He had had no reason to doubt any of them. But in truth, he had no reason to hope for any of them, either.

This is childish. Since arriving in Cahokia and finding Russell, he had found excuses not to cross the river. Russell finally questioned him about it, forcing Granger to take the ferry and step onto Spanish soil once more. He pushed open the waist-high gate and walked the short path to her house and knocked on the door.

The latch clattered and the door swung inward. A slender Negro girl looked up at him.

"Monsieur?"

"Um...is Madame de Lautin at home?"

The girl frowned. "*Parlez-vous francais?*"

"Oh, I..." Granger fumbled for what little French he knew. "*Je regrette...non...*um, Madame de Lautin?"

"*Et vous?*"

"Tell her..." He tapped his chest. "Lieutenant Granger."

"*Attendez, s'il vous plaît.*"

She closed the door. Granger raised his hand to knock again, hesitated, considered leaving, waited, and started to knock anyway.

The door opened just as he raised his hand.

The sleeves of her pale blue bodice were rolled up to the elbows and her hair was drawn back beneath a green kerchief, exposing her ears. Sweat darkened the fabric at her armpits, and a small tear above her left breast marred the bodice. There was a streak of dirt on the right side of her forehead, angled from the center part in her hair to her cheekbone. Her skin glowed with perspiration.

Granger noticed all these details in an instant. What took his attention and held it, though, were her eyes, which for a second or two seemed to both soften and deepen in recognition. It might have been his imagination, what he expected or desired occluding reality, because it lasted only a second, fading fast enough to make him doubt its reality. She did not smile and all his optimism shrank.

"Monsieur?"

"Mart—Madame de Lautin...forgive the intrusion, but...do you remember me?"

"Of course. Are you still Lieutenant Granger?"

"No. Still Granger, of course, but I thought it would be easier to reintroduce myself that way. I'm no longer a soldier. It's just Granger now."

She folded her arms, nodding. "I see. So you have returned."

Granger's confusion increased. "Yes. I'm opening a store in Cahokia. I hope to do business here, as well. In fact, I hope one day to live here."

She frowned at that. "Ambitious. Of course, that will depend on many things."

"The Spanish mainly."

"Most certainly the Spanish. But there are other factors."

She waited, then, silently. Granger felt diminished, optimism gone, his anticipation becoming impatience. Awkwardly, he pulled the envelope from his pocket. "You had asked me to do something for you. Do you recall?"

Her eyebrows drew together, creating a single depression between them above her nose. "I gave you a letter for my brother and asked you to find him."

"Exactly."

"My brother is dead, Lieutenant."

Granger's hand stopped midway to handing the envelope to her. His ears warmed. Her expression did not change, and he felt trapped, unable to do anything else. Finally, though, she unfolded her arms and took the letter. Granger's arm dropped as if a string had been cut, letting it fall. He cleared his throat, preparing to leave.

"I'm being rude. It's not your fault he died. Please, would you like tea?" She stepped aside, inviting him in.

No, he thought, *I do not want tea. I want you to be pleased to see me, to welcome me, to smile at the sight of me and then imply that what happened between us was a beginning. I want more, I want an explanation, I want a continuation. Not tea.*

But he said, "Yes. Very much. Thank you."

He crossed the threshold and entered her house now as though he had never been here.

The hearth was cleaned out and the furnishings burdened with parcels. The house looked ready to be vacated. Granger surveyed the room, and then looked at Martine with a new understanding.

"Lucy," she called. "*Une tisane, s'il vous plaît!*" She gestured Granger to one of the chairs before the now fireless hearth.

"You're leaving?" He placed a hand on the back of the chair and watched her, impatience turning to anxiety.

"This house, yes," she said. She gestured toward the chair again. "Please, sit."

"I heard about Étienne." Granger sat, perched on the edge. "My condolences. Are you leaving St. Louis?"

"Not yet. I don't know." She looked at the letter in her hand, and then tucked it into a pocket in her apron and sat down. "Forgive me, Lieutenant, I am distracted. Étienne's sons are coming to claim their inheritance. I must leave."

"His sons...not—"

"His sons are nineteen and seventeen. I have no children by him. By law, they have half Étienne's estate due them. I could pay them if I had money. All there is, however, is this house and his shop."

"That doesn't seem fair."

"It's not all bad. I am inheriting all that he is owed by the people he has done work for since we've been here. If I accept it in barter, I can live quite well. There is some property in New Orleans he signed over to me entirely, but I would have to go there to sell it. I am not without resources. But not the house. Not this place." She looked around wistfully.

Lucy, the Negro girl, came in with a tray bearing a pot and two cups. Martine nodded to her after she set it on the table between them. Lucy left and Martine poured.

"I don't recall you owning a slave," he said.

"I do not. Lucy belongs to Madame Gratiot. She has been helping…" Martine shook her head. "As I say, I am distracted. Forgive me."

"There's nothing to forgive. It's understandable that you might not want company just now." *But I feel responsible…*

She handed him a cup of tea. "Company is welcome. On that account, I am glad you're here. But I have little gladness about anything lately. Things have not turned out as I wished. How long have you been in St. Louis?"

"I arrived yesterday. But I've been in Cahokia a week."

Her eyebrows rose as she poured her own cup. When she sat down, her eyes drifted over the room. "I think I will miss this place."

So will I, he thought, looking around. He had only spent a night and part of a morning here, but he left changed. He had thought she had been equally affected, but that, he saw now, was presumptuous. A life had passed in this house, time and words and, he assumed, mutuality and affection between two people he really did not know. Her expression now showed a kind of longing he knew nothing about, a kind of longing he had in some sense hoped did not exist.

"How did he die?"

"Apoplexy," she said. "As far as anyone can say. He got into an argument with Monsieur Gambeau and went into a seizure."

"Gambeau. The man who owns the stables? What about?"

"I don't know. He wouldn't tell me. My husband took three days dying. He woke only once and called for his dead wife." At that, her eyes seemed to harden. She stared at Granger's knees.

"I'm sorry," he said.

She set her cup aside. "My life is in disarray. It's not your fault."

"If there's anything I can do—"

"Do not make promises you may wish to retract later," she snapped. "Or cannot keep. I am a widow with complications. You should be careful around women like me. I think it is best I sort my difficulties out first, before entangling anyone else in my life."

But I'm already entangled, he wanted to say. *You entangled me three years ago and I've been unable to stop thinking about you.*

He said none of it, finding no gracious way to phrase it. The longer he tried, the more it felt as though his insides were rearranging, heart for kidney, liver for lungs. He wanted. It had never occurred to him before now that maybe he should have learned to stop wanting her. But he had no idea how he might have done that.

He said finally, "That's a most admirable decision." His voice sounded thick in his own ears.

"You sound...surprised? Or disappointed?"

"Humbled, maybe. I'm not sure I could be so responsible under the same circumstances."

She smiled sadly and refilled his cup. "You said you plan to be here some time."

"Yes, I—if I'm successful, I intend to live here."

"You meant that? You mean in St. Louis? I thought... you would have to become a citizen here. Give up your country. You are willing to do that?"

"It's not that uncommon, from what I've heard. But it will depend on the resolution of certain matters."

She narrowed her eyes. He thought he saw recognition in them. "And if you resolve them…why would you stay?"

"There are inducements here," he said.

Martine's expression changed from suspicion to puzzlement to something Granger recognized as fear. Granger felt the fragile arrangement of expectation he had brought here collapsing. Every response from her had been other than what he had wanted, anticipated.

He had played this scene out in imagination innumerable times, a fantasy that had become a touchstone. Relief, joy, embrace, confirmation. Every time it ended with them tangled—on the floor, in a chair, across a bed—finally with the leisure to explore each other as he thought lovers should. This awkwardness never occurred to him, though now that he was here it seemed obvious there would be. Three years and he had never managed to write to her. What else could he expect?

"That would be..." she began. "I wish you good fortune."

For the moment he was grateful for her poise. Something might yet be salvaged. "Me, too. I confess, one of the reasons I wanted to return—"

"Did you? Want to return?"

"Yes, of course."

"It's been nearly three years."

"More than. There was a war."

"Ah. Yes, of course."

Her tone, tinged with criticism, irritated him. He felt played with. He set his cup and saucer aside. "It took some time to track down your brother. I'm sorry it was too late, but I kept my word. You should at least look at the letter I brought you."

Startled, she took it from her apron pocket and opened it. She stared at it for a long time. Eyes wide, she looked at Granger.

"General Lafayette."

"Yes."

"Forgive me, I—"

Granger stood. He wanted to get away from her before his anger overwhelmed him. He had wanted her to be glad to see him, glad enough to embrace him. Her husband was dead. Granger wanted her to welcome him as an immediate replacement—irrational and selfish, he knew, insensitive. Guilt he thought long suppressed stirred inside. He was being unreasonable, but he felt humiliated, even betrayed, and he knew he had no right to be angry.

"Nothing to forgive," he said. "I promised I would bring word back. I've done that. You're obviously busy, so I shall take my leave now. Again, my condolences on your losses."

"Of course...*merci*..." She stood, frowning uncertainly.

Granger went to the door, clutching his hat.

"Lieutenant?"

"Madame?"

"Will I see you again?"

He closed his hand on the handle. "It's probable, madame. It's a small place, after all. St. Louis, that is."

"This is not what you hoped for."

He almost choked, suppressing a laugh. "No."

"It's no one's fault if you came here hoping for something more. But it has been three years. And nothing came of it that was of any use to me."

He opened the door, puzzled and offended. He glanced back and saw her watching him, her face expressionless, her hands folded before her. He bowed and stepped outside. Walking down the Rue d'Eglise, he wondered what she had meant. *Nothing came of it that was any use to me...*

I made all the wrong assumptions, he thought. *Best stay with what I understand from now on.*

Seven

TAYON LOOKED no older than Granger remembered. More comfortable, certainly, in a suit of fine clothes instead of a uniform. His wife, who looked even younger, sat with him at the table and at every pause in the meal held his hand. Cécile's plain face was animated by an enthusiastic good humor. Granger liked her immediately. He even caught Russell, sitting opposite him, smiling.

"We married shortly after you left," Tayon explained. He blushed, laughed at himself, then called, "Missy, *plus di vin, s'il vous plait.*"

A Negro girl came into the room, head bowed, and went to the credenza. She brought a decanter to the table and carefully filled their glasses.

"You were gone when the final campaign started," Tayon said. "February, the next year, the new Lt. Governor, Cruzat, decided to act on the recommendations of Letourneau. He's Potawatomie, an ally. He helped stop Langlade. Anyway, we sent an expedition north all the way to St. Joseph. We had already heard that your own had accomplished much. Beausoleil commanded, I was second, and we marched through the most bitter cold. There and back, five, six hundred miles! We were magnificent!" Tayon laughed. "We planted the Spanish flag in the middle of a British trading post! That is winning, I think. Of course, no doubt the fact that we showed up in the middle of winter surprised them. Only the insane would attempt such a march and attack at that time of year."

Tayon raised his glass in a toast to himself and the victory in which he had participated. Granger laughed and raised his own glass. Tayon drank down the wine and set the glass carefully on the table and pushed it from him with fingertips.

He grew serious. "This idea you have of dealing in goods across the river—"

"I didn't say—"

"You didn't have to." He gave Russell a significant look. "Cahokia may be growing, but if you wish to be a success, you will have to do business here. That might be difficult unless you either become a citizen or..."

"Or?"

"Or take on a partner." Tayon smiled slyly.

"You?"

"Perhaps me. I would be honored, of course. But I was thinking more of the Chouteaus. Their ambitions may be just what you need. I am part owner with them in the grist mill."

"You could, of course, introduce me?"

"Of course, if you like."

"I had given some thought to Gratiot." Charles Gratiot had been a merchant from Kaskaskia who had provided considerable aid to Clark during the war. More than the supposed official quartermaster, Dodge. At least what

Gratiot said he would provide actually arrived. He had moved to St. Louis and Granger had learned that he had prospered and become influential.

"Unfortunately," Tayon continued, "Charles is away, but he would be a good choice as well."

Granger looked at Cécile. "Did you fall in love with his intelligence or because of that uniform he wore?"

She blushed, grinning at Tayon.

"You know," Tayon said, laughing, "I'm not certain she ever saw me in it."

"The scarlet one?" Cécile said. "Of course I did. I didn't think they would ever take them off, they were so proud." She stood. "If you are going to keep talking about war and how brave you all were, I will leave you to it."

"We're talking business now," Tayon protested.

"Almost as bad," she said, smiling. "*Bon nuit.*"

"Madame," Granger said, standing.

Cécile left and Tayon brought the decanter from the sideboard to the table. He refilled Granger's glass, then his own. "Fewer ears are better," he said. "Cécile will guarantee no one will listen who should not. Be aware, however, that I will tell her later what we discuss now."

"You've done well," Granger said.

"Thank you. I have. She is..." He grinned and waved a hand. "There are no words." He sat down and the smile faded. "So, *mon ami*, tell me why you have come back? For a woman or for revenge?"

Granger looked sharply at Russell, who met his gaze. "It's not like it's been much of a secret."

"This is true," Tayon said. "Rumors of you and Madame de Lautin began soon after you left. To be expected, of course, and Étienne paid them no attention. Rumors like that happen all the time. Too many men, too few women. But about Cortez, it was different. So I ask you, why have you come back?"

Granger considered his answer as he took a sip of wine. He had been thinking about this for three years. The reasons were not an issue for him, but who to trust. He trusted Russell. He gambled that he could trust Tayon.

"I want to know what happened. I want to know how Ham died."

"Why is it that you doubt he died as a part of the battle?" Tayon's gaze fixed on his wine glass, which he now turned idly with two fingers on the stem. He looked, Granger thought, like a businessman about to weigh the merits of a proposal.

"Very well," Granger said. "Because nothing made sense out there. Two dead horses to start with, shot and butchered. None of the plate had been stolen, Ham's rifle had been left behind, and the house wasn't burned. It seemed obvious that the place had been searched. We found no evidence of a war party coming through. The fact that Ham was killed in the house and carried away to be buried in the woods fits no explicable combat situation. It's possible a small scouting party might have gone that far west the day before the attack, but they would have no reason to cover their tracks, especially after St. Louis beat back the main assault. I doubt anyone north of Cortez's place would have been left alone, hence my surmise that something happened unrelated to the battle. Ham was murdered and hidden."

Tayon's eyes came up, locked on Granger. "I agree. However, why would anyone do this?"

"I don't know. Perhaps someone knew about the gold buried there. Perhaps someone has some other complaint with Cortez. The killing of his stud seems like an act of petty revenge in that case. But I suspect it also has to do with the stranger Ham was told about, that no one, I assume, has ever found."

"True," Tayon said. "As for people with complaints against Don Diego…there could be dozens. What do you intend to do, accuse them all?"

"No. But if we can find this stranger Ham was told about, it's possible he saw what happened."

"It's possible he would have been killed, too," Russell said. "We just never found his body."

"Somebody shot at us," Granger said. "Shot Taylor."

"Do you believe it was this stranger?" Tayon asked.

"I wouldn't be surprised to find out that it was. But I don't know. I want to find out."

"What will you do if you succeed?"

"Ask why."

Tayon looked surprised. Russell started laughing, a low sound deep in his chest, which triggered a chuckle from Tayon. Within moments the three of them were laughing. Tayon slapped the table.

"Exactement, mon ami! Absolument! Tres bon!"

As the laughter faded, Granger felt a companionable bond with these two men that reminded him of his friendship with Ham. But then he wondered at the way friendships form and if it was not normal to begin with a humble ember and watch it grow to flame. He had been friends with Ham through all the life he could remember, but there must have been a beginning, a time it did not matter, to him or Ham.

Given that, how might he feel about these two men in time? He sobered quickly contemplating the possibilities.

"Cruzat," Tayon said, "decided—officially—that this was all the result of a raiding party. We did not get everyone inside the village, there were people to the north and west, some still working their fields, who were caught or killed after we routed the attack. The British Indians scattered over the countryside and many farms were attacked, so it was not unlikely."

"Officially?"

Tayon shrugged. "I do not think anyone truly accepts that, but…"

"Without a better explanation, that will do?"

"Exactly," Tayon said finally, pouring more wine. "Then you should know some things. Most importantly, the man who came back a little over a year ago is not Don Diego de Cortez."

"What does that mean?"

Tayon leaned forward. "Don Diego returned a little over a year ago. He delivered letters to Cruzat, then went out to his property with his slaves and resumed working as if no time had passed, coming back to the village to do business and, briefly, to answer questions from Cruzat's inquest. He had been gone eighteen months, part of that time to Havana. I have no knowledge what he brought back, that is between him and Cruzat. He was kept here in the village for a few days, at the Governor's House, and then allowed to resume his life."

"Havana," Granger mused. He pulled the folded page from his pocket and passed it to Tayon. "Does this mean anything to you?"

Tayon frowned as he read it. "A name, a street...I don't know. This last, it means 'it is ours.' These other things—initials? People? Where did you get it?"

"It was hidden in Ham's rifle, in the patch box. Before you ask, no, I don't know who put it there." He refolded it and put it away. "Did anyone tell Cortez what happened on his land?"

"I did, certainly. He listened silently, thought about it for a time, and said, 'I see.' That was all."

"He wasn't surprised?"

"Who can say? He may have been shocked to his core. I don't know. You will get an opportunity to meet him, though. You have arrived at the right time. His fiancée is supposed to be arriving in the next week. He is finally bringing her here from Spain."

Granger raised his glass and drank to cover any reaction. So Cortez had finally sent for her. But Eliana arriving that soon? It seemed he had only just beaten her here. He thought he might have time to become acquainted with people, perhaps learn things about Cortez. And his enemies.

On the other hand, he recalled what had been written—*I have it, it is ours*—and wondered if it had anything to do with the note. *It is ours.*

"Who got his horses?" he asked.

"The stable owner, Gambeau," Russell said. "He was one of Cortez's competitors before."

"Wasn't he the one who provided us our mounts that day?"

"He was," Tayon said. "You have a good memory."

"Cortez's horses—did he care for them while Cortez was gone?"

"He did," Tayon said. "Which is apparently how he acquired them. He presented Cortez with a bill."

"You said Cortez is not the same man," Granger said.

"True. I have nothing to base this on but impressions. After he returned, he changed his endeavors. He grows some corn, a few other things. But mainly, he has built a saw mill and sells lumber to St. Louis. Also, within six months of his return he had sold all his original slaves and bought new ones. He owns more than he did before, even some Indians."

"I thought," Russell said, "that was illegal."

"Owning Indian slaves? The governor forbids it, but still it is done."

Granger's optimism shrank. "Sold them. Are they all still in St. Louis?"

"Most, no. They went south. I think a few are still here."

"Why did he do that?"

Tayon shrugged.

"What about the horses? Did he buy new ones?"

"He has a few for his own use. I do not believe he intends trying to raise them anymore."

"How does that make him a different man? I take it you don't mean simply changed."

"No." Tayon scowled. "Small things. Acquaintances he doesn't seem to know, events he cannot recall. He holds himself differently. By all accounts, he was kind to his former slaves, but he has a new foreman who is as harsh as they come."

"But everyone recognizes him as Cortez."

"He looks the same."

"The brother?"

"The thought occurred to me. But how do we prove it?"

Granger remembered the McLean's back in Pittsburgh, but it seemed far-fetched.

"And what," Russell said, "does it have to do with who killed Sergeant Inwood and Taylor."

Granger looked at him. "Do you think it was the same man?"

Russell shrugged. "Maybe there's another corpse out there."

"Cortez," Granger said. "We'd have to dig up that grave and see if anything else is there besides Ham and gold."

"Good luck with that," Russell said. "Far as anyone's concerned here, Cortez is back and has done nothing wrong."

"The grave troubles me," Tayon said. "I do not believe anyone is buried in it. The ground, as far as I now, was never consecrated. Cortez would not overlook such a thing. And let us also be clear. You do not believe Cortez himself is responsible for Sergeant Inwood's death?"

"No, not directly. But someone who obviously hated him is. We may have to learn all we can about Don Diego before we find out who that was."

"But if Tayon's right," Russell said, "and this one ain't the same man—"

"Maybe everyone's waiting to see what happens when his fiancée arrives," Granger said. "If she accepts him, then…"

Tayon nodded. "It would be confirmation of a sort."

"So she's coming. After how long?"

"I think five, almost six years."

"She must be some woman to have that much patience."

"I agree. I am looking forward to meeting her. They will be married here. It's to be quite an event. The Chouteaus, Cerré, Beausoleil, everyone of any means has contributed something."

"Perhaps I should, too."

"It might be a good gesture."

Granger laughed quietly. He felt at ease, more than he had for some time. He looked at Russell and Tayon and realized that he was glad to see them. Had he no reason to return to St. Louis, he might have missed this, and never known it. The last person with whom he had felt so comfortable was Ham.

"You're right, my friend," he said. "It seems I've arrived at just the right time."

Eight

GAMBEAU'S STABLES were near the old stone tower at the western edge of St. Louis. He remembered it from the morning he rode out with Tayon, Russell, and Taylor to find Ham. This was the place from which they had procured their mounts and to which they had returned the next day.

As he entered, the smell of alfalfa and stale enveloped him. His eyes adjusted quickly and he saw rows of stalls for horses, most of them occupied, and a black man pouring grain from a burlap sack into a feed bucket on one of the stall doors. He looked up and Granger thought he was familiar.

"Bon jour, monsieur," another man said, walking toward Granger. He was a stout man, bordering on portly, and wore a wide-brimmed straw hat.

"Good morning," Granger said.

"Ah, American?"

"My name is Granger. I'm looking for Monsieur Gambeau."

"You have found him, monsieur. What may I do for you?"

Granger was briefly surprised; the Gambeau he remembered had been much thinner. "I'm interested in a horse."

Gambeau smiled and took his arm. For the next several minutes he boasted about his stables, the quality of his animals, and the care and feeding they received daily. His stock was, he claimed, the best available in St. Louis. Granger listened, asked a few questions, and encouraged him to expound, and soon he was describing the inferior quality of his competitors and even related an anecdote about how one of them cheated a stranger who had yet to return to the village.

"Ah, but when he does!" Gambeau waved a hand as if to ward off a threat.

"Honest men are rare," Granger said. It was clear Gambeau did not recognize him, but Granger wondered if that was an act. "Your stock looks very fine. Where did you get them?"

"From many sources. I am particular when I buy."

"I've heard of Indian horses, that they're exceptional."

Gambeau made a dismissive face. "I prefer stock that is not so wild. These, for instance, I acquired from a habitant who used to raise them, but since gave up and sold them to me."

"Gave up?"

"In truth, monsieur, he was a man whose ambition exceeded his ability. But he showed fine judgment turning them over to me."

"Was this señor Cortez?"

Gambeau's smile faltered and his eyes narrowed. "Do you know Don Diego?"

"Not at all. I've heard of him, though. I understand he provided horses for the cavalry here during the battle."

"Oui, l'Année du Coup," Gambeau said, nodding. "Or, as the Spanish prefer, the Battle of San Carlos. And that is true, Don Diego provided many horses for Pourré's cavalry that day. Some of these, in fact, were in that battle. Were you here, monsieur?"

"I served under Colonel Clark," Granger said. "We took some of the brunt of the assault across the river."

"Ah. Yes, I heard that was hard fighting. So, which of these fine animals has caught your eye?"

Granger haggled a bit and they finally agreed on a fee. Gambeau also sold him a saddle.

As he was leaving, Gambeau followed him. "Are you intending to stay in St. Louis, monsieur? I mean, obviously you are, but—"

"For how long? I don't know. I'm considering opening a store. I want to get to know the place, though, before I commit."

"A store, interesting. Do you have a place to stay?"

"I have. Monsieur Tayon has generously put me up."

"Tayon, well! You cannot do better. Fine people. Well, then, I shall be seeing you about, then."

"Yes, you will. *Bon jour.*"

As he stepped into the street, Granger looked back into the stable, but could not see the black man. He touched a hand to his tricorne and Gambeau waved in return. Granger started down the street, north, back toward Tayon's house.

"Monsieur Granger?"

Granger turned and saw the black man from Gambeau's stable standing in a narrow gangway.

"Yes?"

"My name is Neptune. Madame de Lautin asked me to do something for you."

Granger recognized him then, the man coming out of the de Lautin residence wearing buckskins and carrying a musket that day Martine had brought him to her home.

The man nodded and gestured for Granger to follow. "We can talk over here."

Neptune led the way back up the gangway, then outside the dilapidated stockade fence that once surrounded the village, built in preparation for the British assault. Granger followed him to the thick prominence of the old tower.

Common fields stretched away, individual plots separated by loose pickets. People worked in some of them, both white and Negro. Far to the north, the earthen mounds rose, sudden hillocks in the landscape, marking the far extent of the township.

Neptune stopped in the shade of the tower. He was not a large man, but Granger sensed his strength, as well as anger held in check by long habit.

"You wanted to learn things about Don Diego de Cortez," Neptune said. "Remember?"

"I was chiefly interested in what anyone might tell me about a guest."

"And there was one. But it's strange, what I heard. I think maybe it be best you hear straight from them. What's left of them, anyway. I can arrange for you to talk to Sasanna. She used to belong to señor Cortez, but she got sold to Monsieur Labadie last year. They all been sold. Sasanna's still here, though, and it's easier now for her to talk to you, if you're still wanting to."

"What did she say?"

"Lot of things didn't make sense. But maybe to you they'd be reasonable. Are you interested?"

"Yes, of course."

"Tomorrow is Friday. Monsieur Labadie goes to Mass in the morning, along with half the French in St. Louis. Come meet me here at sunrise and I'll take you to see Sasanna. Then you can decide what to do after that."

"All right."

Neptune began to move off.

"Wait," Granger called. "It's been three years."

"Yes," Neptune said. "You're wondering why I bothered about this after all that time."

"Yes."

"I said I would."

Neptune walked away.

Martine stood when Granger entered Tayon's parlor, as if startled by his appearance. A smile danced ghostlike across her face. Her eyes shifted toward the door, then fixed on him. Granger's anger at her evaporated, replaced by hope. *Just smile again,* he thought.

"Monsieur Granger," Cécile said, rising. "You have met Madame de Lautin? Let me get you a cup." Before Granger could demur, Cécile left the room. Tayon was absent.

"Madame," he said, feeling awkward.

"I did not—" She smiled hesitantly. "I thought—"

"It's likely both of us made assumptions," Granger said, cringing inside at the flatness of his voice.

She frowned. "I did not expect you to return."

"I said I would."

Her mouth compressed around a smile as she glanced down at the floor. Her hands came together over her stomach for a moment, then separated and disappeared behind her back. When she looked up again, her face was composed in an expression of innocence, perfectly contrived, a well-formed mask of sincerity.

It should, he thought, *look like a lie*. Instead he saw it as an opportunity, an admission that a door could open if he used the right key. All he had were words and he had never been deft in their use.

He cleared his throat. "I'd hoped..."

"Hope is always a good place to begin."

"...that I'd not returned too late."

The innocence turned to interest. "For what?"

I want to be a river for you, he thought, and almost said, but then he wondered where he had heard those words before. A moment later he remembered—Eliana's letters— and remembering, stumbled into guilt. *Not my words, but too perfect to reject. For another time, though. Now they must be my words.*

"To be of use," he said.

She reddened. "That was unkind of me."

Nothing came of it that was any use, she had said. He had no idea what that meant, only how it made him feel. Now, though, even that seemed uncertain, and before anything else he wanted clarity. "The invitation or the rejection?"

She stiffened, mouth compressing to a thin line. Granger's heart raced; it could all end now, the challenge too direct for her.

"I would like to know," she said, "if you would be pleased if I stay."

"Stay? In St. Louis, you mean?"

"Of course."

"I—if that would please you as well."

"That was equivocal."

Granger felt his ears warm. "Yes, it was." *Why is this so damned difficult?* he wondered, frustrated. "When I arrived in Cahokia I very much wanted to see you again. I did not receive the welcome I expected. Perhaps I was wrong in expecting anything. I would nevertheless like very much a chance to realize those expectations." Surprised at himself, Granger clasped his hands behind his back, glanced away for a moment, and cleared his throat. "Is that less equivocal, madame?"

When he looked up again, Martine was smiling. "*Oui,* Monsieur Lieutenant. That is excellently clear. An offer has been made which may allow me to stay without depending on the charity of friends. Although several would gladly take me in, I do not wish to be a burden."

"An offer?"

"Señor Cortez has asked if I would be willing to be a companion for his new wife. She is, apparently, a lady used to a certain luxury."

"Cortez…"

"I would have a room in their house and certain duties, but it would allow me to remain." She raised an eyebrow. "If that would agreeable."

A series of reactions passed through Granger, none of them comforting. The two that emerged most clearly seemed incompatible on some moral level, but he could not deny them. Firstly, that Martine would stay. Secondly, that she would be in a position to learn things he wanted to know. The first excited him, the second shamed him, but there was no choosing between them. He wanted both.

"If you leave…" He cleared his throat again. "I'd be glad if you stayed."

She nodded. "Then I should accept his offer."

"When did this happen, if I may ask?"

"Yesterday, a few hours after you left. Jose Renaldo came with the proposal. Will you be attending señor Cortez's wedding celebration?"

"I—when will it be? I only recently heard about it and I've been told conflicting times."

"When the bride arrives. Here we must be flexible. Schedules can only be so fixed and times often conflict. It depends as much on the river as on desire."

I want to be a river for you…

"Um…yes, I…as long as I'm invited."

"Oh, you will be. Tayon will see to it."

"Then I look forward to it."

"Good. Then I would look forward to having a dance with you."

"I would—I would like that."

"Then I appreciate your forgiveness of my rude behavior."

"Nothing to forgive. Although I do not dance well."

"But I imagine you dance sincerely." She smiled, bowed, and headed for the door. She passed by him and he caught her wrist.

The touch seemed to lock them both in place. She did not move, did not seem even to breathe. Granger left his fingers lightly curled around the inside, the tips against the soft area alongside the tendons, where he felt her pulse tap. He wanted to tighten his grasp. She did not pull away.

Then she curled her hand up and lightly stroked the edge of his hand.

"There is much to like here," he said.

She smiled at that. "There is. *Adieu*, monsieur." She slipped free and left.

Granger stared at the door in her wake, wondering what had just transpired.

"You should be careful."

He started, and looked around. Cécile stood in the doorway to the kitchen.

"Excuse me?"

"Be careful. With her. She came here to see you. The first thing she asked when we sat down. 'Is Lt. Granger here?' I know Martine a little. She has had a difficult year, monsieur, and this is the first time in months that I have seen her look..."

"Look?"

"Hopeful."

He found Neptune waiting as promised, with two saddled horses, one of them the animal Granger had purchased the day before, on the west side of the tower. Neptune wore his buckskins today and a musket hung in a saddle holster. Neither man spoke as they rode away from the village, around the north tip of the big pond bordered by a few more buildings than he remembered, though still dominated by the mill on the far side. The common fields had been pushed farther out.

They entered the veil of trees and undergrowth and, instantly, the two were alone. Granger watched Neptune for a time. Neptune sat his horse with practiced ease. He reminded Granger of the few free blacks he had seen in the army, though none had shown Neptune's unconscious confidence. All of them had seemed to expect calamity at any moment, as though they sensed their freedom to be conditional and temporary. Neptune showed no sign of that constant, oppressive anticipation.

He also managed to keep far enough ahead to make conversation impractical.

After an hour's ride, they emerged from the forest onto a broad expanse of cleared land that extended west and north of the house and outbuildings a hundred yards from the tree line. The house, in French style, had a wide shingled roof that reminded Granger of a hat, sloping into the overhang of the broad porch that wrapped around the entire structure. The other buildings looked far more prosaic, especially the slave quarters, which were little more than wooden boxes with thatch to keep out the rain. Neptune dismounted at the nearest box. Down the row of them Granger saw dark faces peering from the doorways, watching.

Neptune leaned into the darkness of the shack and spoke quick, clipped French. A small woman emerged, her hair showing white in jagged lines pulled back in a fuzzy ponytail, dressed in a plain blue shift belted by a length of twine. She stood barefoot at the threshold of her door and snapped back at Neptune. He laughed.

"This is the man who asked about the stranger at Cortez's place," Neptune said.

The woman looked up at Granger with an expression at once terrified and resentful. She turned sideways to him, as if wanting to retreat and ignore him. But she stayed, staring at him as if trying to see his intent in his face. She frowned, finally, shook her head, and said to Neptune, "No." She went back inside the darkness.

Neptune followed her.

Granger looked at the main house, then at the tree line to the south, then at the other slaves, who alternately looked at one another, the dirt, and him, all the while pretending to ignore the shouting coming from Neptune and the woman.

"Monsieur."

Neptune stood in the doorway. He motioned for Granger to enter.

Granger dismounted.

"She will speak this once," Neptune said. "Get what you want now. There won't be another chance."

The heat in the room nearly drove him back outside. The only door was open but somehow did not vent the cloistered air within. It pushed at him until he was entirely inside the windowless space, and then it enveloped him, making it hard to breathe.

As his eyes adjusted, he found the woman sitting on a rickety cot, legs drawn up against her chest, arms around them. She rocked slightly, a shape in the lightless volume, visible more by her clothes than her skin.

"You're Sasanna?" Granger asked.

"That's what I called," she said, voice almost inaudible.

"You speak English."

"I come from Savannah."

"Did Neptune tell you what I want to know?"

She nodded.

"Then tell me."

"Why you want to know?"

"A good friend died there. I want to know what happened."

She snorted. "Maybe safer not knowing."

"For whom?"

She stopped rocking then and Granger felt her gaze fix on him.

"All right, then," she said. "I tell."

She uncurled and sat on the edge of the cot, hands on her thighs. Her voice carried a sing-song quality he had heard in some slaves in the Carolinas, inflected with a French accent.

"Don Diego buy me in N'Orleans five year ago. He treat me better, not like those before. We come up the river to here where he plan big plans. Gonna be horses, he say. Gonna be range. Gonna be fine days. Gonna be so good that when he done he gonna free us. So we come here. But there too much work. Gotta clear the land, build, find the time to start the plan. Don Diego, he not good at planning. All everything happen same time, he never stay workin' on one thing long enough to finish. But he a decent man. Just too much to do, not enough time ever. He never get mean." She aimed a finger at Granger. "That's important. We all believe what he say, that we be free. That's important."

She shook her head, frowning, as if trying to decide what to say next.

"He got horses," she said. "Buy 'em from an American. Some folk in the village weren't too happy 'bout that. Some come out, have words with him. Couple times. Last time, there's shoutin' and Don Diego run 'em off."

"How many? Did you know who they were?"

"'Bout four most times. Couple of 'em important men. I don' like to say they names."

"Gambeau maybe?"

Reluctantly, she nodded. "He one."

"Go on."

"'Bout three month 'fore the war time, a man show up. On foot. Dirty, unshaved, look like he been living in the open for months. Said he was by hisself, but I never think that true. He kept looking west, south, like he expectin' someone. Maybe he hope he alone, maybe he escape something. But he said he alone and Don Diego believe him. He took him in."

"Who was he?"

"Never told. Skinny, old clothes, coat looked like a soldier's, but so dirty it hard to say. Torn. He look torn. Heavy black beard, long, dirty hair. He nearly dark enough to be mulatto—from the sun, though, not his mother. Not right." Sasanna touched her forehead, a gesture Granger barely saw. "See it in his eyes, his mind slipped loose. Don Diego put him up in upstairs room and we don't see him too much after that. Sometime, we hear shoutin' in the night. We figure then that Don Diego knew him from before. Sometime it so angry to make a chill in the bone.

"We start missin' things after that. Chickens, mostly. Don Diego thought we took 'em. He act sad about that, gave us leave to eat more, thinking maybe we just hungry, but it don't stop. I think he start to believe us, but by then he spendin' time in the village helping get ready for war. Gone a lot. When one of his pigs went, he got angry. Got his gun and his horse, went out, all day and the next. Never found nothin'. At night the shoutin' was worse."

"Do you think this stranger took them?"

"Took 'em where? In his room, kill 'em and cook 'em? Don Diego wouldn't go riding out looking for someone else if that true. No, it weren't him. He stay in his room. We bring food into the house, set it on the table, and leave. We come back, it all eaten. The someone he kept expecting took things. We never see who. We hear him, sometime, out in the wood, but we never see him.

"Don Diego thought on it long time, what to do, but then it come time to fight the redcoat, he say. He had a uniform from when he in the army, before we know him, but he didn't use that one. He had a new one, say it the uniform of the St. Louis militia cavalry. It so red, he stand in the sun and it hurt to look at him! He look amazing! We all proud. He saddle his horse and ride into St. Louis to drill with the militia. At first, he come back.

"After the uniform, the fightin' got worse upstairs. We see the stranger then, couple times, come down to watch Don Diego ride off. He come out the house and watch him go and just kept staring after, like he was fixed and couldn't move. He look angry as any man ever been. We all afraid to go near him. Nobody look at him and we try to decide what to do 'bout him. Don Diego trust us to keep his place, but this was a white man. What happen if he tells us to do somethin' and we don't? We say Don Diego told us what he expects, we do that. But it's not so simple sometime.

"What he do, then, was come to the shed one day and look through all the wood till he find a piece. Asa kept askin' what he need, but he never answer, just kept lookin' till he find what he want, then he took that piece in the house.

"Day come Don Diego say he be in town all the time, then, 'cause the attack was close, but we be fine. He want us to make sure nobody come burn the place down or steal his horses. Some of them he took with him for the fight, but he left his studs and brood mares behind. We didn't have to worry none, he say, 'cause they coming to make war on St. Louis, not the farms. He'd be back when it was over. He ride off then. The stranger heard that. Must have. He come down and went out into the woods. He didn't come back for a day. When he did, he went back upstairs. Last time I seen him, that day. Next day, some soldiers come from town and tell us we got to get inside the walls. Didn't matter, they said, what Don Diego told us, we goin'."

"Why didn't you tell him right then about the stranger?"

She was quiet for a time. "We talk about that before. We decide that if Don Diego wrong and the redcoats come, we go hide in the woods and leave him behind. Let *them* do somethin' about it. We stand by that then, decide to leave him all alone there. They tellin' us to get to town, must be danger. He get killed being alone here, well, that ain't our fault. But that way we don' go against Don Diego."

"So why did you change your mind when you got to St. Louis?"

"Lucien did that. Said it wasn't right, that we be murderin' that man no matter how it look. Asa beat him later, but it was too late then. I see what Lucien mean, but sometime you gotta set one right thing aside to do another, bigger right. Lucien, he got religion back then, said Jesus wouldn't approve. Turn out bad, though, and he hate hisself after."

"That's all? What happened after?"

"Nothing. The attack come, it ended, and we stay in St. Louis almost a month 'fore they send us back to Don Diego's land. Vasquez, he a trader, he oversee us after that. He been there some time, we find out. What we saw broke our heart, those horses dead. Don Diego was so proud of that stallion, it come all the way from N'Orleans special. We clean up, we work the place till Don Diego come back."

"He'd been to New Orleans and Havana."

"We heard that. Wherever he been, it worked on him."

"What do you mean?"

Granger repeated the question when she did not answer. She said, "Well, it was like him, but not. He wasn't the same when he come back. Not different so you wouldn't know him, but not the same. Look the same, sound the same, mostly act the same. But he changed."

"Time can do that."

"Wasn't time."

"How do you mean?"

"Don't know how to tell you. But Don Diego, he never would've sold me before. Never would've sold any of us. He promised we be free. But we all gone now. Most of us gone from St. Louis even."

Granger looked at Neptune, standing in the doorway. "Her and Asa," he said, "are the only two left around here. The rest were sold back down the river."

"Couldn't get no price for me," Sasanna said. "Too old. Asa, though, he the best carpenter around. Monsieur Chouteau bought him just to keep him close. Monsieur Labadie bought me to help Don Diego out."

"He needed money?"

She shrugged. "Never seemed to want for it before. Then he got new slaves out there. Some Indians. Got a foreman now, too, runs 'em. I hear there are whippin's like in Georgia." She looked at him then. He could see her clearly now and the resentment in her eyes cut at him. "We were gonna be free. Now I gonna die like this. Monsieur Labadie, he not a bad man, he don't mistreat nobody, but it ain't free. That stranger poison everything."

"What became of him?"

"He gone when we come back. Run off. Maybe the redcoats caught him. I hope so."

"You said Cortez bought the horses from an American?"

"Most of 'em. Bought from a man downriver, maybe thirty head from him."

Dodge, Granger thought. "Did you ever see him again? Afterward?"

"No. Jus' that one time to buy and a few days later to bring the horses. After that, he never come back."

Granger wanted to do something for her. The bitterness in her voice, the smallness of what might once have been a proud, maybe beautiful woman, offended him on her behalf. Till now, he had never understood the outrage of the abolitionists. Slavery was an odious fact of life, intellectually contradictory to what he thought the world ought to be, but no more than an uncomfortable fact. If asked, he disapproved, but he had never been moved by it.

"Who are his friends?"

"Never had any, really. Señor Renaldo come out most, I s'pose he a friend. Nobody else."

He put a hand on her head, lightly. "I'm sorry."

She scooted back from him, drew up her legs again, and began rocking once more.

At the door, he asked, "When you returned after the battle, you cleaned up the house, correct?"

"Yessir."

"Did you find anything missing?"

At first he thought she would not answer. But then she said, "His old uniform was gone."

"His old one?"

"The one he come here with, from before. That gone. He kep' it in a trunk. Ever'thing else that was in there was still there."

"Did he take it with him when he left to fight?"

"No."

"And he never came back for it?"

"After that last time he left, we never see him. Not till he come back from Havana."

Granger was uncertain what that might mean. He left an old uniform behind to go fight for St. Louis wearing a new one. Sasanna and the others would have noticed it missing when they cleaned up. Whether it made any difference now, he could not say. "Thank you," he said.

Stepping from the room came as a relief. The outside air felt cool and light. He squinted into the morning sky. He climbed back onto the horse.

"Dodge was the quartermaster for Clark's army," he said as Neptune mounted his own horse. "Cortez bought horses from him."

"Monsieur Dodge did plenty of dealing here."

"And Colonel Montgomery knew about it."

"Without doubt."

"But Monsieur Gambeau ended up with them."

Neptune grinned. "Gambeau bought horses from Dodge before Don Diego did. Dodge used Gambeau as his agent for all kinds of things for a while."

"I thought you worked for Gambeau."

"I work for many people. This morning, I'm working for you." He turned his horse and started off.

Granger glanced back at the slave huts and for a moment saw Sasanna watching him, just before she retreated into the darkness.

As they rode back, Granger kept looking off into the woods. Forest gave way to plains here in patches. Lush outcroppings of black walnut, cherry, and oak, as dense as anything in Connecticut or Massachusetts, suddenly yielded to cottonwood and maple and sycamore, with underbrush thickly difficult to pass through, loose congeries of vine and ivy, mosses and fern. Then came the cleared sections, with tall grasses or stretches of clover. Farms abutted frontier, tentative fingers thrust into the tangles of new land.

Neptune now rode alongside Granger.

"She said the stranger walked out of the woods," Granger mused aloud. "From where?"

"Might be anywhere. Some *coureur de bois* travel all the way to the western mountains, more than a thousand miles.

Go far enough west and south, there's Spanish Mexico. This around here is one kind of frontier, but Europeans been all over west of the Mississippi. British got traders coming down from the Hudson Bay talking and trading with the Mandan—"

"The who?"

Neptune grinned. "Mandan. Far enough away that you never heard of them. Man could get lost and wander a long time before staggering into a place like this."

"Europeans?"

"Spanish, French, English, Scots, Irish, Portuguese, Dutch, Italians, Swiss. Monsieur Gratiot is Swiss. What would you call them?"

"You *do* read, don't you?"

Neptune frowned.

"Don't be insulted, Neptune. I know many whites who can't read and some who can but don't, and wouldn't know all the nations you just mentioned."

"Don't understand that."

"What?"

"In your country there are laws against slaves reading. Many do anyway. Why someone who has every freedom to do so would refuse is beyond me."

"They have no interest. Books are dead things to them."

"Not to you?"

"I've always found books to be good companions. They tell the truth more often than most people."

Neptune laughed. "So you're impressed that I talk about Europeans instead of just saying white people."

"So far, Neptune, I'm simply impressed with you. But indulge me. Someone—a European—walks out of the woods, from the west. You heard Sasanna's description? That doesn't sound like a seasoned trapper, does it?"

"No. Sounds like someone who got lost."

"Lost from where?"

Neptune was silent for a time. "Seems there were more questions you should've asked her."

"True. I should've asked her if their arguments were in French or Spanish."

"Spanish."

Granger glanced at him. "How do you know?"

"I asked after I got your message from Madame de Lautin. The stranger spoke Don Diego's native tongue."

"You already knew all this?"

Neptune nodded. "I thought you should hear from one of them for yourself first. Maybe you had more questions I didn't think of."

"Did I?"

"The question about the uniform."

"I didn't know about the uniform. I just wondered if anything was missing. Stolen."

"I saw Don Diego the day he rode south. He was wearing an old blue Spanish uniform."

"So either Sasanna lied or he came back when no one else was there."

"Or someone in the village loaned him the blue uniform. Lots of possibilities. Things were in turmoil that day, anybody could've left the village, come back, done anything, and no one would've noticed."

Neptune stopped his horse. Granger rode on a few yards, and then turned. Neptune seemed to be studying him, eyes narrowed.

"What is it you plan doing, Lieutenant?"

"Depends on what I learn."

"It won't be much if no one helps you."

"You're helping me."

"So far. I've done what I said I would do. Now I have to decide if I'll do anything more."

"And you can't do that unless you know what I intend to do with what I learn."

Neptune smiled grimly. "As you say."

Granger knew he could not do this on his own. Even with Russell and Tayon helping him, he was an outsider here. Habitants had no reason to talk to him, much less trust him. Trust, he knew, never existed one-sided.

"It's my aim," he said, "to find out who killed my friend and why."

Neptune drew a deep breath and looked away. "I've seen a lot of vengeance. It's all a waste. Nothing's ever made right."

"What about justice?"

"Is that what you want? When you find out what you want to know, will you be content with justice? Because you won't be able to do that on your own, either."

Granger felt a flare of anger, but he understood what Neptune meant.

"I don't know," he said finally. "Ham was nearer a brother than a friend. I had no choice but to come back here to learn the truth."

Neptune looked at him and nodded. "I'll help you. But you know that once you start looking, people will get angry over it. You stir this up it might go bad for you."

"Could be worse for you."

"Could."

"So why help me?"

"Sasanna, Asa, the others. It wasn't right, what Don Diego did. Maybe I'll find out why myself."

"All right. Then tell me, who else can I trust?"

"When the time comes, Cruzat will do what's honorable. He's a fair man. But you need to know before you go to him. You're staying with Tayon. He says you're a friend. Tayon is quick to be friendly, slow to give friendship, but his judgment is sound. You can't do better. For the rest, let me think on it."

"What about Jose Renaldo?"

"What about him?"

"He made a complaint about me last time I was here, on Cortez's behalf,"

"Did he now?" Neptune urged his horse forward again. "If Don Diego has a close friend, it would be Renaldo, at least from what I seen."

"Have they always been?"

"Renaldo had been here a year or more before Don Diego arrived, but I suppose it might be possible they knew each other before. You could ask Father Bernard. He pays attention."

They rode in silence for a time. Then Granger said, "The stranger. Cortez knew him. He came looking for Cortez."

"How do you know that?"

"Because it makes more sense than an accident. Cortez would have no reason to take him in if he really were a stranger and even less reason to keep him a secret unless there was something between them." Granger studied the shadows around them. "And he didn't come alone."

"How do you know?"

"Someone else was stealing the chickens."

Neptune laughed. "Sounds to me like you have an idea who the stranger was."

"I do. But we need proof, and I can't see any way of getting it unless…"

"Unless?"

"Unless we find out who stole the chickens."

Nine

THEY WERE TALLYING the last of the stock that had arrived by flatboat a few days earlier. Dry goods mostly, but also tools, coffee, and kegs of rye, now all stored in Russell's barn behind his foundry on the north end of Cahokia.

Russell had left one crate aside and pried it open. "What is this?" he asked, stepping back.

Granger came over from where he had been making entries into a ledger and looked at the bulky iron contraption. "A circulating stove. Latest thing. People in Philadelphia have been calling them Franklin Stoves. For the parlor."

Russell examined it. "Well, ain't that an amazing thing. That ought to do well here." He straightened up and started re-crating it. "You ought to give one to Madame de Lautin."

"What?"

"Might make up for things."

"What 'things' do you think I need to make up to her?"

Russell shrugged. "I don't know. I heard it didn't go well, that's all."

"Heard from who? Never mind. If I gave her one, where would she put it? She's going to be staying out at the Cortez place."

"I heard that, too. Did you ask her why?"

"To be a companion for Cortez's new bride, when she comes."

"Whose idea was that?"

"She said Jose Renaldo presented the proposal."

"Renaldo. You know, he's been paying attention to her since her husband died."

Granger's chest tightened. "So?"

"Enough so I'd be concerned if I had an interest in her myself." He hammered the last nail in and straightened up. "Unless you don't have any interest. I don't mean to presume."

Granger didn't know what to say. He went back to his ledger. "Did we get anything from John Dodge?"

"Not yet. Why do you want to talk to Dodge?"

"He sold those horses to Cortez. Someone didn't like that. He could tell us who else he dealt with."

"Gambeau, you said."

"You know Gambeau. Do you think him capable of killing Ham?"

"No, not likely. He wouldn't even have the brass to try. But there are a few men he works with who would. If he had enough coin."

They continued working in silence. As far as Granger could tell, the only things he was short was one keg of rye whiskey and a bolt of linen. Under the circumstances, he felt vindicated. He had come to Cahokia by land, with only a pack horse, and sent most of his stock by flatboat up the river to avoid trying to haul it through territory controlled by John Dodge's band. He had been aware of being watched as he made his way north, but no one had bothered him.

"Dodge never goes anywhere without three or four ruffians," Russell said suddenly. "And I wouldn't recommend going to him. If you meet with him, don't tell him you were in the army. There's no love lost between him and the army."

Granger set the ledger aside. "Why wasn't he arrested? He's a thief."

Russell grunted. "Who was going to do that? The Spanish are insisting everything east of here up to Kentucky belongs to them even though we fought for it. Congress don't want to stir 'em up anymore than they have to right now until it all gets settled. Last thing they'll do is send a detachment of regulars to Kaskaskia to try to arrest a man who supplied a lot of goods to the habitants. So what if it wasn't his to trade? Colonel Montgomery is in Louisville telling everybody what a patriot Dodge is. Dodge's got Cruzat convinced he's enforcing Spanish law over there and intends to be a good citizen when the treaties get signed. Besides, he's got about twenty or so men. Not the most disciplined bunch, but hard men with no conscience to speak of."

"What about the folks living in Kaskaskia?"

"Oh, they'd like nothing better than to see Dodge gone."

"He might not talk to me," Granger said, "and if he does, he might not have anything to say worth hearing. But I'm convinced he's the reason Montgomery pulled me out of St. Louis and had me go up the Illinois on that raid."

Russell looked at him. "How do you figure?"

"Something you told me back then. You said he read my report and got angry. Next day, we're heading east. Neptune told me Montgomery knew all about Dodge's activities."

Russell nodded. "They were together in it, then."

"That's my thinking."

"It's still likely he won't even agree to meet."

"It's still worth the attempt." Granger finished his entries and closed the book. "Does she reciprocate?"

"Hmm?"

"Martine de Lautin. Does she return Renaldo's interest?"

"Oh. Hard to say. She's still grieving, but that don't mean a lot here. These folks like to act as if they live in a city, but life here's hard and sometimes short. They tend not to let tradition get too much in the way of getting on with things. Personally, I think Renaldo's being inconsiderate. But as far as anyone knows, he hasn't said anything she might take offense at." He came over by Granger. "Meaning no disrespect, but what part of my letter brought you back? Her or Sergeant Inwood?"

"Neither. I'd been making plans to return before I received it. Your letter hastened them, that's all."

"Uh huh. Tell that to someone who don't know better. You wouldn't have planned to come back without a good reason and these are the only two that matter. My opinion."

Granger laughed. "Fair to say. Very well. Both. I don't know which is the more important. But I also don't think I can choose which to give up on."

"Might be you should think on that further," Russell said. He started to turn away. "Like I say, folks here, some of them don't live long. Everybody knows they could die tomorrow. Sickness, Indians, a drunken argument, even drowning. Consequently they don't wait on what they want."

"Meaning?"

"Meaning if you got intentions, you better act on 'em sooner. Might not be a later. Meaning no disrespect."

"None taken." He looked toward he river. "I'm considering giving a couple of kegs of whiskey for the wedding celebration."

"I'll be sure to attend, then."

Sleep eluded him that night. His thoughts refused to settle. He lit the lantern beside him and, anxious, pulled out the letters. He sorted through them, and started reading one.

Diego,

There are times I would give anything to be a man! You have such freedom. There are so many things in the world, so many experiences to have, and so much denied us by circumstance. Better perhaps not to want what cannot be freely enjoyed.

Still…I do not believe that. Ignorance is no remedy for injustice, and knowing where and how injustice confines us can only hasten the day when the prison is torn down. Because if one of us can know, can see, then all of us can, and on that day no one can keep us bound when we do not wish to be.

The Americans seem to know this now. Are they not tearing down their prison? But you will say that is political, and doesn't apply to individuals. You will say that, but I know you will not believe it. You only pretend to accept what is so that you also will be free to want, and, being a man, take what you want.

But not everything you want can be taken. You cannot take me. You did not. I gave myself. That was an act of rebellion, you know. It may be true that you believed yourself to be acting as a man and asserting a prerogative, taking possession of something promised, something you feel you deserved because you had asked for it and it was granted. You asked my parents, and they gave you their blessing, but it was not real until I consented. Even though I had no right to refuse according to the laws and traditions of the prison in which we live, had you come to me to make a claim someone else—even my parents—had granted you, it would have been pillage, robbery, rape. I am the only one who could make it otherwise, and I did, and you received what you thought was already yours only because I agreed to give it freely.

Agreed. A weak word. I wanted. In the center of my soul, Diego, I wanted. I cannot say even now if it was you I wanted, only that I wanted. Is that wrong of me? Is that sin?

You are the one who called into question the very idea of sin, who told me that there is right and wrong but sin is something invented to keep us from knowing either. I did not know what you meant for a very long time. I am not certain now that what you meant and what I now understand are the same, but I am eager to find out.

But it began with the wanting, with the hand in the pit of my stomach, drawing at the outside world, wanting it to come inside. Hunger does not describe it, nor an emptiness that needs filling. It is both and neither. A paradox? What would Zeno do with it? For a woman, it is always halving, coming closer, so near the warmth of it caresses her face, but the touch never quite happens. Is it because she is incapable of such sensation or of such reach or is it the inability to defy paradox? Or is it only because we are only ever allowed to reach, never grasp?

I am fortunate that nothing of consequence followed that night, Diego. I would have done what I did with you in any event, because I wanted you. I may even love you. But it would have been a shame on my family for there to have been consequences. For me, perhaps freedom. Having consented to our marriage, they would have packed me off after you as quickly as propriety would permit, and I might even now be by your side, before you, around you, in every way with you. As it is, I must wait, and content myself with your letters, which grow ever more necessary to my sanity.

Your letters prove that I have wanted wisely, that you are not ashamed in the peculiar way of those who talk of the new and of revolution and of the drawbacks of society and then condemn those who actually try to live according to those ideas. Hypocrisy does not begin to describe such perversity! But you are not like that. You believe what you told me, you want what you said you did, and when I tell you my feelings, what my body desires, what my mind craves, you do not ignore it, *nor chastise me for shamelessness. You give me more. You describe what would be if you were here now. You suggest.*

Oh, yes, you suggest. That alone is worth the wait. I find what books you mention, I try what may be tried, and I am building an imagination. It is my hope that I continue to give you new things to imagine as well.

Granger folded the letter and returned it, with the others, to his haversack. His thoughts were focused now. He tried to imagine this woman, but all he could see was Martine.

Weary, he snuffed the light, and told himself that at his first opportunity he would return the originals to her—to Eliana. It would be a way, he believed, of settling one thing, at least, so he could clear his mind and do what he needed.

Ten

GRANGER FELT STRANGE entering the grounds of the church. His family had been Congregationalist, but only on Sundays. The mistrust of Rome had nevertheless been part of his upbringing. Stepping through the wide gate along the Rue d'Eglise, just west of the abandoned government house, felt more like entering another country than crossing the Mississippi had. A dozen feet inside, a large wooden building supported a square tower that rose out of a peaked roof, and on the roof of the tower, a cross. The main door was about six feet wide and ten high. Just inside, to the right, a podium supported a large silver bowl with water, surrounded by candles all burning at different heights.

Tayon and Cécile took seats in the third pew from the front, a conspicuous position that drew curious looks from others as Granger sat with them. Unfortunately, it only gave him a limited view of the rest of the gathered parishioners. He glimpsed Martine, though, in company with another couple, on the opposite side of the center aisle.

The people immediately around him comprised the obvious wealth of the town. As well as more opulent clothing than he expected on a frontier, he saw a few ornate wigs and one or two male faces wearing powder. Mixed in with the fine satins and linens and silks was plainer attire such as he would see in any town in the east worn by established merchants.

The service lasted almost two hours, by which time the air had become thick from humidity and smoke from candles and the priest's censer. The last blessing administered and the command to go in peace was followed by obvious relief and a barely restrained exodus into the courtyard. He had never attended a Catholic mass before. It was alien and disturbing, but also fascinating. The Latin resonated from all the lessons his mother had insisted on, though the ritual chanting still slipped by his comprehension. If he intended to live here, he needed to understand even this.

Emerging into the courtyard after the service, Granger stopped, catching sight of Martine near the gate, speaking with two men. The couple she had come with stood to one side.

Both the men talking with Martine looked familiar. The taller of the two had a thick mein of dark red hair. He was thin, with wide shoulders, and the straight bearing of a career soldier of rank. The other man was stout, black-haired, with deep-set eyes in a wide face.

"Tayon, who are those two?"

"That," Tayon said, "is Don Diego de Cortez. The other man is Jose Renaldo."

Granger understood the familiarity then. Don Diego bore a strong resemblance to the painting he had seen in his house that day of the conquistador. He had last seen Renaldo the day Montgomery pulled him out of St. Louis.

"Excuse me," Granger said to Tayon and Cécile. He crossed the courtyard to the small gathering.

"Lt. Renaldo," Granger said, smiling. "*¿Como estas?*"

Renaldo frowned at him. "Do I know you, señor?"

"We've never met," Granger said, "but I've heard of you. And you must be Don Diego de Cortez."

Cortez gave a short, polite bow. "Señor."

"This is Lt. Granger," Martine said.

"An American," Cortez said.

Renaldo's mild confusion changed to recognition. "You were here before, señor. For *l'Anneé du Coup.*"

"The Battle of San Carlos," Granger said. "I was, yes. Served with Clark."

Renaldo leaned closer to Cortez and spoke rapidly in Spanish. Cortez's expression changed, his eyebrows rising briefly.

"So, we fought as allies," Cortez said. "Though on opposite shores."

"We did. I understand you were in the cavalry here?"

"I had that honor."

"I heard that you, in fact, provided many of the horses."

Cortez frowned and looked at Renaldo, who gave a small nod. "That is true, señor. I do not care to boast."

"That's admirable. I'm sure everyone here appreciated your generosity and sacrifice. I know we appreciated your participation."

Cortez smiled at that. "How long do you intend to stay this time?" Cortez asked.

"I'm considering making St. Louis my home, sir."

"But—forgive me, señor—did you not just fight a war to make a home?"

"More to decide where that home would be."

Cortez's lips pursed briefly, a smile in his eyes. He gestured toward Martine. "Do you know Madame de Lautin from before?"

"I do. We met. Briefly." He saw amusement in Martine's eyes.

"She has had some misfortune," Cortez continued. "You may be aware that I am to be married soon and I have offered to assist her in a small way."

"You've asked her to be a companion to your new wife, yes, I'd heard. That's also very generous of you."

Cortez tilted his head in modest acknowledgement. "It is not entirely selfless. My good friend, Jose, has expressed interest in Madame de Lautin's well-being."

A chill chased across Granger's scalp as he looked at Renaldo. "Indeed."

"She has agreed to come live in my house after the wedding," Cortez said. "As for Jose, that is entirely a matter between them. Of course, he enjoys a challenge, so it is our duty to ensure it is not too easy for him."

Cortez grinned, but Renaldo did not seem to share the jest and managed only a grim smile.

"Would you please excuse me, Don Diego," Martine said. "I promised Madame Gratiot I would help her today. We must go."

"Of course," Cortez said, bowing to her.

Martine curtseyed quickly, smiled at Granger, and said, "Señor" to Renaldo. She joined the couple waiting at the gate and the three of them left. Renaldo scowled at Cortez.

"I thought Monsieur Gratiot was away," Granger said.

"He is," Renaldo said. "East. Meeting with your government. There has been some disagreement over debts owed."

"I'm sure," Granger said. "It wouldn't be the only one."

"That was Monsieur Cerré accompanying them," Cortez said. "As for that, I must be off myself. My Eliana is due soon and I have much work to do, so if you will forgive me, señor Granger...?"

"Of course. A pleasure to meet you, señor."

"Have you been invited to the celebration?"

"Not formally."

"Consider it done. You will be most welcome."

With that, he tapped the brim of his hat and walked out of the yard.

Leaving Granger facing Renaldo, who frowned at him.

"Is there something the matter, señor?"

"Why have you come back?"

"You mean after you did what you could to send me away three years ago?"

The shock in Renaldo's face was gratifying. Renaldo stepped closer.

"You should leave," he said. "You will only stir things up that do not concern you."

"Aren't you forgetting that a friend of mine died in your friend's house?"

"A friend? I thought—"

"Sergeant Ham Inwood was my friend. We'd known each other since we were children."

Renaldo's scowl changed then, a softening that was no less wary for the flicker of understanding in his eyes. "This is very personal for you," he said.

"Very."

"I see." He stepped back. "Then I will say to you, señor, that Don Diego is *my* good friend and if I can, I will see that no harm comes to him or his. *Buenos dios,*" He bowed, pivoted, and walked away.

Tayon came up beside Granger. "Is there going to be a problem?"

"I don't know," Granger said. "But I hope so."

"Come," Tayon said. "Father Bernard has agreed to speak with you."

A thin man in a brown robe stood in the door of the church, watching them. He smiled distractedly, but his eyes squinted between deep fans of creases, the skin of his face dark from years in the sun.

"Father Bernard," Tayon said. "This is my friend, Granger."

Granger, unsure how to greet the priest, bowed awkwardly, then extended his hand. "I'm honored to meet you, father."

"Are you indeed?" the older man said, his smile growing. His accent was neither Spanish or French. Granger thought he heard traces of German. He looked at Granger's hand for a few moments, and then took it, clasping it tightly.

"Father Bernard," Tayon said, "has been here many years and knows everyone. You may ask him your questions knowing he will tell no one else." With that, Tayon bowed to the priest, and left the church.

"Um..." Granger began, "I don't—I'm honored to meet you, father, but..."

"May I introduce myself fully? I am Father Bernard de Limpach, Order of the Capuchins."

"Granger."

"Just that?"

"It's my preference, Father."

"As you choose. Did I understand correctly that you were here during *l'Année du Coup?*"

"Yes. With Colonel Clark."

"We are, of course, grateful." He slipped an arm in Granger's and led him toward the sanctuary. "Are you by chance Catholic?"

"No. My family is Congregationalist."

"Your family. What about you?"

"I haven't thought about it for some time."

They stopped at the edge of the first row of pews. Granger looked up at the hand-carved cross on the wall behind the altar. "Someday we may have a proper apse," the priest said. "The habitants built this just before the attack. They did the best they could and I admit they did well. Still, a good solid building of brick or stone, with more windows...the first church was log, not even planed wood. This is a Catholic community, Monsieur Granger."

"That doesn't bother me, in case you're wondering."

"The question crossed my mind. You're from a country with a long antagonism toward Rome."

"I'm not my country."

"I see. Will you continue attending services?"

"Does everyone attend now?"

Father Bernard laughed. "Regrettably, no. Though they all come to me with their troubles. Eventually. Even those like you, who are not Catholic."

He sat down on the first pew and gestured for Granger to sit. "You wish to know about Don Diego de Cortez."

"Yes, but—"

"I will tell you this about him. You heard our bell this morning? It is a fine bell. Diego de Cortez was one of the soldiers who helped transport it upriver, part of a cadre from Havana. Jose Renaldo was with them, too. It arrived here in 1774. Diego was very taken with St. Louis and thought he might return. He came back four years later to try to start a life. Do you know that his betrothed is coming? Within a week or two, I believe."

"So I've been told."

"It was a difficult journey, bringing that bell. St. Louis is very proud of it."

"And grateful to Don Diego?"

"I doubt most people here remember him from that. Benito Vasquez bought the bell. Don Diego has never reminded them of his part. He is a very private man, monsieur. So before I say more, I ask you, why do you wish to know about him? Why should I tell you more than I have?"

"Fair questions. Did Tayon tell you about my friend?"

"He did. I am sorry for that. But as I understand it, Don Diego was here, fighting with the cavalry, when your friend died, and he was on his way south when you and Tayon were attacked."

"Because I believe his enemies killed my friend."

Father Bernard's face showed no change, but Granger sensed the mind working through the ramifications. He waited, anxious, unmoving. He had heard that Catholics regarded confession as a sacred obligation, that which passed between supplicant and priest inviolate. It was an idea he could respect, but he wondered what constituted confession and what mere knowledge.

"You speak with the clarity of a Jesuit. What, though, will you do when you find answers?" Father Bernard regarded him thoughtfully. "Since Diego returned from New Orleans, he has attended often, much more often than he ever did before, though he no longer goes to confession."

"What changed?"

"That is a good question. As a priest, I should not complain—there is something sad about suspecting someone's piety. A war was being fought. Much more killing happened in the Gulf of Mexico than here. The British attacked Havana, did you know that? St. Augustine too. Perhaps Diego saw too much. Perhaps he killed when he did not want to." Father Bernard shrugged. "I am curious. Not, I am sure, for the same reasons as you."

"Is he a bad man?"

"No, not all. Not before or after. Just remiss. He was not the most organized man. That has changed somewhat."

"I'm told he sold all his original slaves when he returned. Did he ever say why he did that?"

"My son, I am ever concerned over why men should own other men in the first place. No, he never said why. Some of his friends bought them. Most have gone down river."

"Do you like Don Diego, Father?"

"I love all my parishioners."

"Of course you do. I didn't ask that."

Father Bernard smiled. "I see. Are you certain you never took any schooling from a Jesuit?"

"My mother gave me a grounding in the classics."

He nodded. "I like most of my parishioners well enough. I try to like others. Diego is...difficult to like."

"Any particular reason?"

"He lets no one in. There is a wall around him. He is certainly likable, but there is a sadness in him, difficult to see unless you know what to look for. But he has a quick smile, always a pleasant greeting. But no intimacy. Which also makes it difficult to tell who may be an enemy, at least someone who would descend to theft and murder. I myself would like to know the answer to that."

"No one has confessed to it?"

Father Bernard shook his head. "No."

"Has he ever spoken to you of his brother?"

"Only that he had one."

"'Had?'"

"I am under the impression that he died. Also that it was not a pleasant relationship."

"He never said so directly?"

"No. But the pain is evident. If you know what to look for."

"Like the sadness?"

Father Bernard shrugged. "The only man I ever saw Diego truly angry with was Charles Gambeau. But it passed quickly and nothing came of it."

"What was it about?"

"Business. Horses."

Granger stood. "Thank you for your time, father. You have a fine church."

"Perhaps I will see you in it more?"

"Stranger things have happened."

Eleven

Diego,

There are moments, my love, I feel time passing without me. I am in a cave, watching the world change, cities rise and crumble, lives collide, and I am waiting. I see the caballeros and I imagine their attention, the desire in their eyes, and what may follow from the smallest encouragement. And I wait. I will not lie to you, my Diego, the waiting is punishment to my spirit.

Do not let me become dry, do not allow me to desiccate, turn to dust, all the while watching the river flow by. I am practiced now in waiting, in finding anticipation sufficient to stay my feet, hold back the desires that are best in your embrace.

A young officer called yesterday on my father. He came inquiring after my sister, Marietta, but I was introduced to him while papa and he were in the parlor, discussing matters. I confess I no longer miss those talks. I see them as little more than barter, two men haggling over merchandise in the market, but I must occasionally endure them as arrangements are sought for my sisters.

The officer was not handsome, but there was a vitality in his eyes and in the set of his shoulders. For a few moments I wanted to touch his face, feel the skin under my fingers, draw on the warmth that is so different from mere heat. I fear I licked my lips, for his eyes danced with surprise and not a little speculation. I excused myself as quickly as seemed suitable and retreated to my room where I spent time imagining you, your face, your hands, all that you are, and your especial heat, which always seemed like melted butter with chilis.

I withhold myself, Diego. I want. I want you, but I also simply want, and I feel stretched by wanting. Do not delay longer than necessary.
Your own,
Eliana

"Benito Vasquez paid for the bell," Tayon said over dinner. "It was a special day when it arrived, and I do remember some Spanish soldiers accompanying it. I never realized that one of them had been Don Diego."

"Or Renaldo?"

"Him, yes, because he stayed, part of a transfer from the garrison in Ste. Genevieve. A few of them stayed, but not all."

"Are any of the others still here?" Granger asked.

"Some, I'm sure. I would have to think…"

"Are any of the others friends of Don Diego?"

"No. I'm certain the only one he resumed friendship with was Renaldo."

Granger pushed his plate away and picked up his glass. "What do you think of Jose Renaldo?"

Tayon shrugged. "Good officer, fine horseman. Honest, as far as I know. We haven't had many dealings." He narrowed his eyes. "Ah, you wonder about his intentions toward Martine, no?" He smiled. "Or perhaps hers toward him? *Mon ami,* you are too reticent. We are on the narrow edge of the wilderness here. There is no time for caution. If you want something, you should say so, otherwise someone else will claim it. Not, perhaps, very civilized, but…" He shrugged.

"You sound like Russell."

"Indeed? Well, good advice is good advice."

Granger considered denying that he had any intentions toward Martine, but that was absurd, and he had done a pathetic job hiding them. The problem was, he didn't know where the limits were, what he could expect, or even how much he wanted…Her. *Say it,* he thought, *be plain, truthful. Say how much you want her.*

Confusing matters more was this arrangement she had made with Cortez, to be companion to his new wife. Granger worried over that, part of him not wanting her to go, suspecting there was a danger in it. But on the other hand, having her there, perhaps to tell him about Cortez, about Eliana, might be useful.

So am I using her? She used me, it would only be fair.

"Did Étienne know Cortez?" Granger asked. "I mean, why is he offering this position to Martine? Why him and why her?"

"Hm. You know, the de Lautins arrived here the same time as Cortez, in '78. I don't know how well they knew each other, but you are right, it is a curious display of generosity. Or maybe not. It may be exactly what it appears, an opportunity for Cortez to have someone for his wife to depend on for the first months of her new home."

"Perhaps." He drank his wine and circled his thoughts like an enemy, unhappy with himself.

"You should simply go to her and ask," Tayon said. "Openly, without dissimulation. Then you will know. And she will know."

"We'll both know," Granger snapped. "Then what?"

"Then you decide."

Twelve

GRANGER MADE THE CROSSING back twice a week to help Russell set up the store in Cahokia. Russell's ferry was impressively stable—a broad platform stretched between two long canoes—but on each crossing, Granger clenched his teeth and tried to achieve a calm that stayed just out of reach, relief flooding him every time he set foot on the opposite shore.

Taking across the two stoves was the worst, especially when a sudden eddy near the shore rocked the ferry and Granger expected the heavy crates to topple. They had been purchased already, but a crowd gathered at the house of Pierre Chouteau, who had bought one of them, and Granger took orders for three more, one from the American widow, Emily Chandler. He began to believe he might make a success out of the commercial part of his return.

One morning he arrived at Russell's smithy to find Jose Renaldo waiting for him.

Heat rolled out from within the smithy, keeping Renaldo near the outer edge of the sprawling pergola. Granger saw Russell, shirtless and sweating, hammer in one hand, the other working the bellows even as he kept an eye on the Spaniard.

"Lt. Granger," Renaldo said, bowing.

"I'm no longer in the army, señor. Call me Granger. What can I do for you? Have you come to order a circulating stove?"

Renaldo smiled. "No. I wish to discuss with you a matter of some delicacy."

"Which would be?"

Renaldo cleared his throat. "You may or may not be aware that I have a certain regard for Madame de Lautin. Especially since the unfortunate passing of her husband."

"Very considerate of you."

"*Gracias,*" he said, bowing his head. "As a consequence, I have been in her company a great deal. We have become close."

"Señor, are you suggesting that I stay away from her?"

Renaldo smiled. "I am gratified that you grasp of my meaning. However, I doubt your intentions would be sufficient. St. Louis is a small place, it would be impossible for you to avoid all contact."

"It would, if I had any intention of doing so."

Renaldo's smile faded. "Meaning what?"

"Meaning I have no intention of leaving her alone. I have every intention, in fact, of seeking her company as often as possible. That is, assuming my attentions are welcome."

"They are not."

"Did Martine tell you that?"

"They are not welcome by me."

"But that's irrelevant," Granger said. "It's her choice. Isn't it?"

Renaldo shook his head. "I came to you in a spirit of openness, one *caballero* to another—gentlemen—to inform you of how matters are. I thought you would be reasonable and take the honorable course."

"Let me ask you plainly, señor—did Martine make you any promises?"

"Implicitly—"

"No, sir. Implications will not do. Did she tell you that your expectations are valid?"

Renaldo's expression closed in a stony mask. The fingers of his left hand tapped at the skirt of his coat. "Very well," he said. "Then I will be plain. Leave."

Granger laughed, startled. "I beg your pardon?"

"You should leave. It will not be safe for you to remain."

"Do you intend to challenge me? A duel?"

"That, of course, would be illegal."

"However, if circumstances and honor force you to it, legality is irrelevant."

"Something like that."

"I admit, I admire your brass."

"Good. Then we are agreed?"

"You're blunt, sir. I'll be blunt in return. No."

Renaldo looked more puzzled than angry, but the anger was there. His lips pulled back and he sucked air through his teeth.

"What do you want?"

Not the question Granger expected. If Renaldo were sincere, bargaining would never occur to him, at least Granger assumed. "Truth for truth?" Granger asked. He stepped under the eaves, into the muffling heat.

Renaldo nodded.

"I like it here. I think it would be a good place to live. Naturally, that involves Martine de Lautin."

"You should reconsider," Renaldo said. "I will block you."

"You will try. But I have questions on a different matter."

"Yes?"

"Why did you have me sent away? Martine was not at issue three years ago."

"I did not. I expressed my displeasure at foreigners invading the home of my friend. It was your own colonel who sent you away. I had nothing to do with that."

"How'd you even know I'd been to Don Diego's place?"

"You said truth for truth. It is your turn."

"So it is. I also want to know why my friend died."

Again, Renaldo looked puzzled. "The man who was shot the day you went to Don Diego's hacienda?"

"No, but I'd like to know who did that too. My life-long friend, Sergeant Inwood, who was murdered in your friend's house before the battle began. He was the reason we were out there. He'd gone missing and we were looking for him." Granger took a step toward Renaldo. "You didn't know? St. Louis is a small place. You knew we'd gone out there and come back with a wounded man the very next day, soon enough to complain, but you didn't know about Sergeant Inwood?"

"It was war—"

"No, señor, that will not do. My friend was murdered inside Don Diego's house, then carried into the woods and buried."

Renaldo showed no surprise, no sign of the disbelief a fantastic claim might elicit. Instead he looked, if anything, worried. "You don't believe Don Diego had anything to do with it, do you?"

"No, but I believe his enemies did. You're his friend. Are you going to tell me you have no idea who they might have been?"

Renaldo's face hardened. He reached inside his coat and Granger's body tightened, ready to grapple with the Spaniard. Renaldo brought out a leather bag, though, and dropped it on the railing. It clinked.

"For you, señor," he said. "For your trouble. Take it and go back to your new country. This is not a place for you. If you stay, people will be hurt."

He walked out of the smithy, and then stopped. "If you disturb the peace of my *amigo* you will answer for it."

Granger snatched the purse. "I don't want your money."

"Keep it. I will not take it back. Use it to go home."

Renaldo strode away.

"He showed up about two hours ago," Russell said, coming to join Granger. "Asked if you were going to be here today. It sounded like he already knew this was one of your regular days here."

Granger hefted the purse. "Things just keep getting more interesting," he mused and opened the bag. He whistled as he spilled gold coins into his palm.

Russell picked one up. "Looks like the ones we found in that grave. How much is there?"

"Enough, I'd say, to get me home."

"He came ready to see you leave." Russell gave him a curious look. "You ain't leaving."

"Of course not." He returned the coins to the bag. "Everything I want is here."

"Curious. Did you notice that when you changed subjects on him he didn't hesitate? Didn't even have to think about what you were talking about."

"I did. He didn't come here to talk about Martine, only to get me to leave."

"You don't think he's interested in her?"

"He may well be, but I'd be surprised if it's from real affection."

"How can you tell?"

Good question, Granger thought. It was just an impression—the absence of certain reactions, of any warmth or sentiment when Renaldo talked about her, as if she was no more than an object he wanted to own. Not all that unusual, Granger knew, he had known many men who beneath their civility had no regard for the women they pursued, but the show Renaldo had made, the pretense, made a poor mask. He hefted the bag of coins. "Just a feeling," he said.

"Do you think he knows who killed Ham and Taylor?"

"If not with certainty, he at least has suspicions." Granger dropped the bag into his coat pocket.

"What about Martine?"

"What about her?"

"Think she feels anything toward him?"

"No, I do not. But that doesn't explain why she's accepted Cortez's assistance."

"By the way," Russell said, "Dodge sent word. He'll meet us at the Great Nobb in two days."

"Great Nobb?"

Russell gestured east. "About five, six miles. You remember. Canteen Mound?"

Clark had met with a number of Indian tribes there early in his campaign, Granger recalled. He had never been there, but he knew about it.

He sent word back to Tayon that he would be gone a few days and the next morning they were up at dawn, horses packed. Russell had hired two local men he claimed to trust—"just in case"—and they rode out beneath a low overcast sky. They could have walked the distance in a couple of hours, but Russell wanted time to prepare.

By mid-morning Granger became aware of an immense wall to the north, indistinct through the confusion of forest, but rising up from the land like a great sleeping behemoth. As Russell led them nearer, Granger thought of the outcrops of earthworks north of St. Louis and the stories that they had been built by long-absent Indians. He wanted to ask if this enormous mass came from the same source, but it was so close it seemed to demand silence. None of them spoke, the only sounds the clop of their horses and the occasional trills and whistles of birds.

Abruptly, Russell turned north and within minutes was leading them up a ramp of earth that hugged the side of the mound and brought them onto a terrace. Another rise hulked at least forty feet higher up. After a short ride, they came on the remains of campfires and Russell dismounted.

From this elevation Granger overlooked a vast area and saw a number of smaller hillocks surrounding this one. He thought of the earthworks around Yorktown and imagined a great battle conducted here, with siege works and palisades and trenches.

Ridiculous, he thought. But the idea that something great had once happened here persisted until he heard Russell order his two men to canvas the area.

Silently, Russell and Granger tethered the horses, then cleaned the site and built a fire. By the time it was crackling, Russell's men returned to report they had found nothing. "Looks to be we're the first ones here," one of them said, opening his canteen. "You want to set up a crossfire?"

"Yeah," Russell said, "but I want you in the open. I don't want him thinking ambush. I want him mindful, no more."

They nodded and searched for likely perches.

"I'd heard he was dangerous," Granger asked, "but a crossfire? Here?"

"Take no chances and chance won't take you," Russell said. "He's still pretending to some legal authority, but people are getting tired of him. He insists he's still an officer and has charge of the militia, but I don't think he was ever such."

"He's a thief," one of the other men said.

"But he does have a body of men," Russell continued, nodding. "Claims he's head of the regular militia. I expect soon enough he'll abandon the pretense and be the brigand he's becoming. But for now he still wants to appear on the side of the law."

"He was working with Montgomery," Granger said. "Montgomery's in Louisville trying to recover his reputation and answer charges that he defrauded Virginia."

"A lot of us suspected some such," Russell said.

"Why'd Dodge suggest meeting here?"

"Oh, that was my idea," Russell said. "I didn't think it wise to travel fifty miles away to where we might have a little trouble getting out. Besides, Dodge being willing to come here says something."

"Such as?"

"That he's more curious about you than you are about him."

Granger laughed. "I never knew you were devious."

They spent the day in occasional hushed conversation and quiet, waiting. It reminded Granger of days and nights during the war passed just this way, a small group of men huddled together, still and alert, as often hoping nothing would happen as longing for a break in the monotony. The reserve acquired in such times lent an appearance of wisdom and maturity to men both younger and not much older than Granger and he had wondered many times if they all harbored the same fear and inadequacies. By the end, he had grown adept at keeping his credulity at a distance, stashed safely out of reach most of the time, while acting the experienced leader, veteran and witness to the shocks of responsible horror, the flensing of innocence, and loss of youthful certainty. Such companionable silences masked many failings, doubts, and unwanted secrets.

Russell asked him about what had happened after he had left Clark's militia to return east. Russell had stayed on in Illinois Country after the expedition in pursuit of the scattering bands of Indians the British had united for the attack on Cahokia and St. Louis. Granger told him about rejoining Greene in the Carolinas and then the final campaigns that trapped Cornwallis and ended the war. He had been seconded then to Washington's staff and ended up in Newburgh during the demobilization. He had been in the room when General Washington confronted the officers plotting mutiny. The threat of civil war permeated the camps, though no one said the words.

"You carried both rifles all through it?" Russell asked.

"I did. I told Ham's folks that his had been lost. I couldn't give it back, not then. Not yet."

Russell nodded as though he understood, and, Granger decided, maybe he did. War bred superstitions among soldiers, attachments to keepsakes and tokens, investments in objects that otherwise were only things but took on the substance of meaning out of circumstance.

Late afternoon, one of Russell's men whistled. A few moments later they all heard the horses making their way up the slope. Russell signaled and the other two sprinted to their positions, muskets in hand.

Five of them rode up onto the terrace. As soon as he saw him, Granger realized he had seen Dodge before, in Clark's camp. He looked taller than he was because of his almost gaunt physique. His face was darkened by several days' beard, but his cheeks were deeply etched above a square jaw. As he came close, he fixed his gaze on Granger and did not look away when he dismounted.

His men remained on their horses, eyeing Russell's sentries unhappily.

"Major Granger," he said, stopping before Granger. "I'm glad to make your acquaintance."

"I'm at a loss, sir," Granger said. "I'm no longer in the army."

Dodge smiled. "As you prefer. I retain certain connections in Virginia. I have heard you intend establishing a store in Cahokia." He looked at Russell briefly. "Perhaps I can be of service at some point."

"Perhaps." Granger gestured at the campfire. "We have coffee."

"Thank you."

Russell poured a cup and Dodge squatted by the fire.

"I have questions," Granger said, "about someone you've done business with in the past. Don Diego de Cortez."

"I remember the gentleman, though it has been years since the last time we had any communication."

"He bought a number of horses from you."

Dodge's face clouded. "I should caution you that any allegations of improper conduct on my part—"

Granger held up a hand. "I'm not concerned with your end of any transactions. I want to know about señor Cortez."

Dodge's eyebrows raised. He sipped at the coffee for a time, then shrugged. "He paid in coin, for which he received twenty horses. All broken and saddle-ready. As far as I am aware, we were both satisfied."

"Why did he buy them from you? I understand there were others in St. Louis who could provide him with horses."

Dodge snorted. "Half-broken wild animals. Good stock, though, but Cortez wanted animals he could rent immediately. Besides, he was barred from buying them in the village."

"Barred?"

"There were others dealing in horses, among other things. Some of whom I did business with. A small group of them cooperated to maintain an exclusive trade. Cortez, as I recall, was determined to break it and offered me better than any of the others were willing to pay."

"Any names in particular from that group?"

"Oh, a few rather prominent gentlemen, some of whom are still important. They're a practical lot. Their politics change easily when it's to their advantage. I would rather not tell you anything that might make it difficult for me to do business with them in the future."

"Charles Gambeau is hardly a prominent man."

Dodge nodded. "You are quite right. He was one, but it was my observation that he was no more than a factor for someone else. As the others always represented themselves, it wasn't one of them. Not as far as I could learn. I never did discover who was backing Gambeau's purchases. Even so, when Cortez offered me a higher price, I gave Gambeau a chance to do better, but all he did was curse me. *Nous avions un marché, lui et moi!*" Dodge smiled. "We had a deal. Indeed we did, but it changed, and Gambeau seemed singularly unable to grasp that."

"Why didn't he just go back to his benefactor for more?"

"It's a question, I grant you. Knowing him, I'd hazard a guess that Gambeau was cheating his benefactor and couldn't ask for more."

"Gambeau owns all those animals now."

"Does he? Interesting. May I ask, Major, what your interest is in this matter? I'm agreeable so far because I believe there's a possibility that we might profit by each other at some point, but I would prefer to know what I'm staking here."

"Fair enough. Do you intend to do any business in the future with Cortez?"

"I'm told he's building a sawmill and is already providing lumber to St. Louis and even St. Charles. If he makes a success of it, he'll need partners to expand."

And you would love to be the only one on this side of the river he deals with, Granger thought. "Then you should be concerned about his well-being."

"As you are?"

"He has enemies, which is nothing unusual. My concern at present is to discover who they are. They've done me injury and I need to know where to send the bill."

Dodge nodded slowly. "Sounds reasonable. Go on, then."

Granger glanced up at Dodge's four men who watched and listened in silence.

"Was that your only dealing with him?" Granger asked.

"Just the one purchase. I thought there would be more, but…"

"Were you there, on his place?"

"I delivered the horses myself." He shrugged, frowning. "He told me he intended breeding horses and he already had a couple of fine animals he'd brought with him from New Orleans."

"Was there anyone in residence with him?"

"No, he lived alone, just him and his slaves."

"Did you hear anything from Gambeau after your dealings with Cortez?"

"He sent me a very offensive letter, but that's the last time I communicated with him."

"Who are you dealing with now?"

"At present, no one. I was trading with Monsieur Gratiot, but he hasn't contacted me in several months."

"One of the horses Cortez brought from New Orleans was for stud. It was killed."

"In battle?"

"No. It was shot in its stable and butchered."

Dodge frowned. "That makes no sense. Why would anyone kill a horse?"

"That's a question, isn't it?"

"Not the act of a sane man."

"I wouldn't think so, no."

"I'm afraid I can offer no insight in the matter, other than to say that Gambeau has been known to trade with some lawless sorts. Trappers and men who spend too much time among the savages."

"Anyone in particular?"

"You might take notice of a man named Chavreaux. I did some business with him myself. I found him difficult. There were a few others, but Chavreaux was a regular with Gambeau. Furs."

"You've been helpful. My thanks. May I ask, though, why you agreed so promptly to meet with me? This has been a long journey for you."

"I wished to meet you and take your measure. I also have a boon to request."

Granger felt a stir of unease. "A boon."

Dodge reached inside his coat and pulled out a letter. "I would appreciate it if you would use your good offices to see that this gets to the appropriate person or persons in Congress. It is a list of replies to a series of complaints—untruths and calumnies—leveled against me by the former military authority in this area, namely Colonel Montgomery. He has been actively disparaging my reputation since his return to Tennessee and I have been unable to leave my responsibilities long enough to properly answer them. I took it upon myself to come here so that you might judge my sincerity and integrity."

Stunned, Granger accepted the letter. He glanced at Russell, who was staring blankly at Dodge.

"I'm not sure why you believe I have any entrée with the Congress," Granger said. "I'm a private citizen—"

"Please, Major. I understand you must present yourself as such for the benefit of the Spanish, but accept that my sources are sufficient to my needs. You possess a good reputation, and I'm certain you know who should see this."

"You'll forgive me if I promise nothing. I'll do what I can, but the results are out of my hands."

Dodge made a magnanimous gesture. "That is as may be and I accept your provisos. But I would take it as a great favor if you would forward this to whomever you believe most effective."

"Well..."

"You may of course read it beforehand. I have no need of secrecy, especially not in the service of my good name."

"Then given the provisos I've offered, of course."

"Then I am satisfied."

Dodge got to his feet. As he walked toward his horse, Granger took a gamble. "You're leaving? You don't wish to share the camp for the night?"

Dodge turned sharply, surprise in his face. Granger waited, hoping he would refuse. Gradually, Dodge smiled again. "Thank you, no. I have matters to tend to in Kaskaskia. We can make a good five, maybe seven miles before dark."

He gave a slight bow. "A pleasure to make your acquaintance, Major."

He swung up to the saddle, wheeled his mount around, and the five of them rode back down the slope.

Russell let out a deep, loud breath. "That was…"

"I know. But the last thing I want is for that man to think I'm afraid of him."

"Gambeau is a parasite," Tayon said, helping Granger and Russell unload the kegs of whiskey they had ferried over for the forthcoming wedding celebration. Granger was contributing two kegs, but Tayon had bought three more and had brought Neptune along to help load them into the charette waiting several yards up the bank. "But a murderer? No, *mon ami*, he has not the *acier* to kill."

"What about this man Chavreaux?" Granger asked.

"Ah, well, that is different. He is a *coureur du bois*, a fur trapper, trader. He has been so all his life and no man survives so long without the necessary hardness. In his case, it is a hardness he seems to enjoy. He is a cruel man. He may even be a murderer, but I have never heard anything more than rumor."

"Only thing," Neptune said, "he's done work for Gambeau, but he doesn't like him. Why he'd do something like that for him…"

"What about for himself?" Russell asked.

"Can't see it. Unless there was something in it for him. As far as I know he never had dealings with Cortez and Cortez never had anything Chavreaux would want."

"Gold?" Russell suggested.

Neptune shrugged. "Gambeau might go looking for someone's gold, but how would he know it was there?"

"But Gambeau was angry at Cortez," Granger said. "Here's how I see it." They loaded the last keg on the back of the two-wheeled cart and Granger wiped his hands on his pants. "Cortez bought those horses from Dodge, horses Gambeau expected to get. He would've made a profit on them just the way he is now, renting them out. Cortez paid more and paid in gold. That hurt Gambeau's trade. It also put Gambeau in a very difficult position if Dodge's surmise is correct and someone else was backing him and he'd been cheating. But then Cortez gives those horses to Pourré's cavalry, which probably cut Gambeau out of even more money. He already heard Cortez paid in gold coin. So when everyone else is in town, he goes out there to look for the gold and maybe do some damage to Cortez's property."

"Killing his stallion," Russell said.

"Ham finds him, walks in on him. There's a fight and Gambeau kills Ham."

None of the others appeared convinced.

"Yes, there are problems with it," Granger admitted. "Gambeau would never have been able to do that on his own, Ham was a good soldier."

"Not only that, "Russell said, "but if the issue was money, why would he leave all the plate?"

"You're thinking Gambeau didn't go there alone," Neptune said. "Chavreaux?"

"What about the stranger who was supposed to be hiding out there?" Russell asked. "Where was he all that time?"

"Still hiding," Granger said.

"I have a larger problem in all this," Tayon said. "If, as we suspect, it is Cortez's brother living there now, what happened to Don Diego?"

"And who was stealing the chickens," Granger said.

Neptune laughed. "You also have to take into account," he said, "that John Dodge is a brigand and might be lying through his teeth."

"Perhaps," Granger said. "But I don't think so. Is there any chance of learning if Monsieur Gambeau was in the village that day?"

"It's almost three and a half years ago, *mon ami,*" Tayon said.

"Where did you take Cortez's slaves when you brought them back?"

"To Gambeau's stable first."

"Was he there? Do you remember?"

"Yes, of course. Arrangements had to be made for Don Diego's slaves."

"So he knew where you were going and what you were doing. And afterward? When you and Ham came back?"

Tayon shook his head. "I don't recall. When we returned with the slaves, I had to attend to other matters. I honestly don't even remember when Sergeant Inwood left, only that he asked me about what the one slave had said. I don't remember seeing Gambeau then."

"I can understand Gambeau looking for revenge," Neptune said, climbing into the charette. "He's a petty man, easily crossed. But killing your friend makes no sense."

"I agree," Tayon said. "There is no reason for it. As for Don Diego, we may know for certain in a few days, when his bride-to-be arrives. If anyone will know he is not the same man, she will, no?"

Tayon mounted the charette with Neptune. "I will see that these are stored and on hand for the celebration."

Neptune took the reins and flicked them. The lone mule stirred and the cart rolled away, toward the north gate of the village.

"There do seem to be problems with your idea," Russell said.

"Yes," Granger agreed. "But until I hear a better idea, I'm sticking with it. Charles Gambeau had something to do with Ham's death."

Thirteen

THE DAY ELIANA ARRIVED, was a clear sky with a sharp chill. Granger awoke to find Tayon already gone and breakfast waiting. After he ate, he pulled on his new fur-lined deerskin coat and headed up the street to Charles Gratiot's house.

The former government house, though still the largest in the village, was too deteriorated, parts of the roof collapsed, so Victoire Gratiot, Charles's wife, opened her home for the wedding celebration. Granger made sure the two casks of Monongahela Rye had arrived at the house. Three barrels still waited in Tayon's house.

Three days earlier a rider had left Cape Girardeau and arrived early last night to bring the news that the bateau carrying Don Diego's bride was on its way, and St. Louis had been seized in a spasm of activity. It seemed that half the kitchen slaves in the village had been loaned to the Gratiot house to work on the celebration and tend to the contributions brought from the other habitants on trays and in baskets. Long tables had been set up in the main room. Wine, cider, beer, even coffee and tea would be available throughout the event.

Granger drifted outside. Across La Rue Royale, the Place d'Armes writhed with activity. Merchants laid out their best, more tables had been set up for the celebration, and a platform had been erected at the far end, just above the riverbank, for speakers. A group of women were busy draping bunting around it. Fires smoked; pigs and deer were already on spits.

At the river end of the open market, a lone man stood at the head of a long plank leading down the sloped bank to the water's edge, where flatboats and bateaux crowded against the bank. He seemed oblivious to the noise and activity, either in the Place d'Armes at his back or the gathering knots of river men, *coureurs dus bois*, local merchants, and Indians on the beach below—his gaze fixed to the south, on the Mississippi.

Granger made his way north, then down onto the slope and south to get a better look at him. Wooden planks covered the sandy soil. A couple of Spanish soldiers were shouting at some of the river men and gesturing for them to move their boats.

On the island forty or fifty yards from the landing even more people gathered. Men were fitting barrels, driftwood, and other objects beneath the long gangplank extending down from the Place d'Armes to support it. Granger drifted back up toward the edge of the market, found a spot from which to observe the man.

Cortez was finely-dressed in a dark green coat, a gold vest, and ruffled blouse, buff pants and high, polished black boots. His hands clasped behind his back, he possessed a military bearing. After watching him for a time, Granger went to Riviere's tavern.

Already the place was crowded, mostly with men who worked on outlying farms or at trades in the employ of local elite. They were dressed as well as they could afford and were spending a good portion of what they had on ale or rum. Surveying the room, he saw Jose Renaldo at a small table by a window, alone, a mug cradled between his hands.

Granger bought a tankard of cider and slid into the opposite chair. "Lt. Renaldo. I'm surprised to see you here instead of on the landing with your friend."

"Señor American," Renaldo said. "You are still here." He glanced around the room as if looking for an excuse to leave.

"I said I intended to stay. Would you like me to return your money?"

"Yes, you did. And no, I would not. Keep it."

"It's not an inconsiderable sum. I wonder why a man would part with so much for so little return?"

"When you come to misfortune here, my conscience will be clean." He frowned across the table, his expression thoughtful rather than resentful. "You will be attending the festivities today?"

"I'm looking very much forward to them. But I take it you're not?"

Renaldo shrugged. "As of today, everything will change. Nothing I do will matter."

"Is that a bad thing? I understand Don Diego has been separated from his lady for several years."

"You know a good deal more than you should. But St. Louis is not a place where secrets can easily be kept, so I should not be surprised."

"You've been his friend a long time."

"What is it you want, señor?"

"At this moment? I'm just being friendly."

"Hm. Yes, I have been Diego's friend for many years, and so I respect, even admire, the friendship you must have had with your man, but there comes a time when you risk losing yourself over what can never be recovered."

"I didn't say anything about that."

Renaldo shook his head and looked away. "You did not have to."

Granger saw something then unexpected briefly cross Renaldo's face: sadness. It lasted a moment, and dissolved into a kind of weary resentment, but it was enough to cause Granger to wonder what had happened. What had he lost that he had decided was unrecoverable?

"Señor—"

Renaldo pushed back from the table and stood. "I have matters to attend to. For my *compadre*. You will excuse me."

"The money—"

"You will please not speak of it. Keep it. I will sleep better knowing I have done all I could for you."

Granger watched Renaldo make his way through the crowd toward the door and as he disappeared from view, Granger glimpsed Monsieur Gambeau, sitting at a table on the far side of the room, watching him. People moved between them, blocking the view.

Russell emerged from the throng, drink in hand, and sat down where Reynaldo had been.

"Morning," Russell said.

"Good morning."

"What was that all about?"

"You saw?"

"Saw. Didn't hear."

Granger leaned to one side to get another glimpse of Gambeau, but too many people now blocked his view.

"Looking for someone?" Russell asked, turning.

"I thought Gambeau was here."

"He was. I saw him leave with two others, looked like *coureurs du bois*."

"You didn't know them?"

"I've seen one of them around, but no, I didn't." Russell took a long drink, sighed loudly, and looked around the room. "By the way, the de Lautin brothers are in town. Come to collect their inheritance."

Granger studied Russell, his pulse raised. "So?"

Russell took another drink. "Rumor is the brothers don't want the property. They may want to sell it. They certainly don't intend to live here."

"Sell. Then why not—?"

"Madame de Lautin could probably borrow the money to buy it from them. But they've made it clear they don't intend to let her have it. Seems there's some dispute. They aren't her children and they apparently don't consider her their mother."

"Well. That presents some possibilities."

They had been making connections with some of the local merchants, but it was slow going because of the antipathy of Spain toward American claims on the east side of the Mississippi. No one knew how it was going to come out, so Granger found reluctance to do more than token business. Owning property in the village, opening a store in their midst, would change things.

Even so, the idea excited him.

"Where are they?" Granger asked.

"I don't know. But they'll be at the festivities tonight."

"Find Tayon and see if you can find them and let them know we're interested in discussing it with them."

Russell nodded, finished his drink, and stood. "Oh, Neptune was looking for you."

"Did he say why?"

"No, but he wanted to meet up at the tower."

Russell worked his way through the crowd.

Granger sat, watching the traffic in the street, listening to the babble around him as he finished his cider. Because he understood so little, between the French, Spanish, and Creole, Granger heard it as a kind of music.

He was nearly finished when señor Vasquez appeared in the doorway.

"Caballeros! Ella es viniendo! Los barca es viniendo!"

The room erupted with shouting and cheers and most of the men rushed the doorway.

"What is it?" he asked a man pushing toward the exit.

"They sighted the boat," he said, grinning. *"¿Vienes?"* When Granger gave him a quizzical look, he said, "It means 'are you coming?'"

In the short time Granger had spent in Riviere's, the riverfront had filled with people. It seemed almost everyone had come to the bank to watch the approach of the boat being pulled now by a team of oxen along the shoreline. Granger managed to squeeze through close to the gangplank.

The morning chill burned off, and Granger, in his heavy coat, sweated in the press of so many people. It was just past noon when the river end of the plank was raised to the bateau as it butted against the shore. Men tied it off to thick wooden stanchions driven into the sand-covered clay.

The plank was about five feet short of the gunwale. Water lapped between boat and beach. More men took up the ropes and strained to pull the bateau closer; the hull tilted, but the distance remained. People shouted instructions, encouragement, suggestions, voices blending into incoherence. The crew of the boat joined in, two of them finally extending their own gangplank, which almost reached the shore side plank. An argument began between one of the boatmen and two men on the bank.

Suddenly a woman appeared at the edge of the bateau gangplank and the shouting died away. Granger stared. She wore a loose bodice, sleeves reaching to the middle of her forearms, and full skirts, all in bright green with white lace at the neckline. She wore a dark green scarf, but, grinning, yanked it from her head as if in defiance. Her thick dark hair, struck with reddish highlights, was caught by a nearly invisible gold ribbon. She smiled, making her face wide, almost moon-like. Then, suddenly, she grabbed her skirts, strode boldy down the plank from the bateau, and jumped across the gap to the gangplank on shore. The boards groaned and flexed, almost knocking her down, but she caught her balance and began bounding up toward Cortez.

Now we'll see, he thought, *now we'll know if that's the man he's supposed to be...*

The crowd burst into shouting and applause. Gun shots cracked the air. All around were smiling faces, laughter, a kind of manic exultation as though a long-sought ambition had finally been achieved. At the top of the plank, Diego de Cortez stood with his arms spread. The woman stepped into them and they kissed.

Granger felt a wrench of surprise, and then a startled recognition of jealousy.

I read her letters, he thought. *I know her.*

Her letters were part of his memory now, and the picture he had made of her came as much from what he had never seen as from her own words. Her thoughts, given to a lover with whom she had experienced far more than was proper between unmarried people. Just as he had with Martine de Lautin.

Two expectations tangled in his mind. In a sense, he had already made love to Eliana. He could not help but feel attached to her. Nor could he alter the impression that Martine had written those words to him.

He wanted to know Eliana now, as a person, the way he knew Martine, with a voice, and a smile, rather than words on a paper attached to another woman in memory. He envied Cortez, who would wed her today, and take her home, and know her as thoroughly as flesh can know flesh.

He was amazed at himself. Joy, suspicion, guilt, envy, now lust. He took a tentative step to the right, then left. He laughed. Trapped. Looking up, he saw Martine, a few yards away, watching him. Her face seemed empty—she did not smile or frown, she showed nothing. But her eyes did not waver. Granger raised his hand. At that, she looked toward

Eliana and Cortez, and Granger felt a need to know her the way he knew Eliana.

He started working his way through toward Martine. By the time he reached where she had been, she was gone.

He turned in place, searching, and then looked back up at the platform. Eliana and Cortez stood side by side now, waving at the crowd, producing more cheers. Eliana seemed flushed, her smile wide and giddy. Cortez—Granger wondered if he imagined it—seemed relieved.

They began to move toward the village. Granger looked around for Martine again and pushed away from the river. The crowd forced him south until he finally found himself well away from the center of town. He had lost all trace of Martine. Knowing he would have a chance to see her later, during the celebrations, did little to dampen his disappointment.

"I thought you might be down here."

Granger turned to find Neptune a few paces away. "Oh. Yes, you sent word. My apologies."

Neptune shrugged. "No need. Did you see what you expected?"

"No." He looked back the way he had come. *What did I expect? That she'd realized he wasn't who she expected and reject him? It's been years.* "What was it you wanted to tell me?" he asked, turning back toward Neptune.

Neptune casually looked around him, nodded for Granger to walk with him.

"Yesterday I talked to a man named Joseph, used to work for Gambeau. He was there that day your friend and Monsieur Tayon returned with Cortez's slaves."

"Yes?"

"Gambeau left with two other men a couple of hours before they came in."

"Does this Joseph know who the other two men are?"

"He only knew they were fur traders. Chavreaux was in the village that day, so I imagine he was one of them."

"Did he tell anyone about this?"

Neptune grunted. "Who would he tell?"

"Lt. Cartabona."

"Why would he listen to a slave?"

Granger winced inside. Testimony of slaves was forbidden under Spanish law, as it was under French law and American, unless it corroborated an owner's statement. *But did you really expect to settle this through legal means?*

"It would be helpful to know with certainty who those two men were and if we can find them."

"Find them. Do you think they'd talk to you?"

"I suppose that depends on how the question is put."

They walked in silence for a time before Neptune said, "I have to be cautious, monsieur. I work for Gambeau from time to time."

"I understand. If it becomes possible, I can do something about that. You've been doing work for me anyway."

"I do work for many people in St. Louis. But Gambeau provides me a place to sleep. It would be good to have somewhere else to go if I'm to foul my own nest."

"If you want to stop, I understand. I have no wish to put anyone else in harm's way."

Neptune scowled at him. He shook his head. "The thing is, monsieur, I don't really like Gambeau. If I quit on you, I'll let you know beforehand." They wandered back toward the thicker crowds. Near the Place d'Armes, Neptune said,

"I do for you because it is my choice, because I am a free man. I do many things for many people, because I am a free man. In return, people do things for me, because they, too, are free, and it is their choice. So it will be with you. And till then, I am pleased to know you and help if I can."

With that, Neptune gave him a sharp bow from the waist and headed west. Granger thought it best not to follow.

Just then, voices drew his attention eastward. Coming up the middle of the Place d'Armes, flanked by a huge throng, Cortez and Eliana walked arm in arm, both smiling as if this were the first day of their lives.

Granger managed to get a place in the second to last row of pews on the left. Father Bernard took control of the service, the Mass proceeded, and suddenly, it was over. Don Diego and Eliana stood, embraced, and Diego kissed his bride.

Their mouths touched—and she pulled back. It was a small motion and Granger believed if he had not been watching intently, and without the knowledge of what these two people already shared in another time and place, both distant, he might have thought nothing of it. When they separated, though, she looked puzzled for another moment. It was what Granger had hoped to see in their first encounter, on the landing. But that, he realized, had been a hurried act, a show as much as anything, both of them more caught up in themselves and the theater of the moment than in who they were to each other. This, their second kiss, was the serious one, the reacquaintance. It meant more. Then she pressed her mouth to Diego's again, her arms around him, pulling him close. The kiss continued until a few people began making polite noises of mirth or embarrassment. Father Bernard's eyebrows rose and he started to lean toward them. They parted and Eliana gazed up at Diego, her face expressionless for a few moments. Then she smiled. The newly-made husband and wife turned to the gallery and a cheer erupted. They strode, her hand in the crook of his arm, down the aisle.

As they passed by him, though she was smiling brightly, her heavy eyebrows were drawn together, a sharp crease in the space between them. It was a brief look, more impression than clear detail, and then they were past, through the throng in the foyer, and out the doors.

Everyone began moving into the center aisle, following. Granger let himself be carried along until he was through the gate and into the street. He managed to leave the flow and make his way another street over, then down to the Rue d'Eglise, and back to the Gratiot house. People entered and exited the Gratiot property in constant streams, singly and in groups. A few more shots sounded, loud singing, cheering, laughter. Distantly, he heard a fiddle playing.

The furniture in the main hall had been moved to make room for dancing. A group of musicians gathered in the southwest corner—two fiddles, a flute, a guitar, and a clavichord. Tables with food and drink were interspersed with chairs along all the walls. Granger found a barrel of his whiskey on the largest table among three other kegs. Mugs, cups, and glasses filled the spaces between them and people lined up.

"Ecoutez! Attention, s'il vous plait!"

Cadet Chouteau stood in the center of the room, a glass in hand, turning slowly. Though the younger of the Chouteau brothers, his face was rougher than Auguste's, a square jaw and intense, deep-set eyes already framed by sharp crow's-feet. The room fell silent. Cadet proposed a toast—Granger heard Diego and Eliana named—and everyone raised a glass roughly toward the south end of the room.

Don Diego and his bride emerged from a hallway, hand in hand. Diego bowed to Cadet, and then did the same to the room at large. He brought Eliana out to the middle of the floor, took a position with his right hand on hip, left arm extended, palm upward supporting Eliana's hand. They gazed at each other, smiling. Cadet gestured to the musicians, who, heads bobbing as one to a count of four, struck the first chord simultaneously.

Granger did not recognize the tune. Don Diego and Eliana faced each other, bowed, and then came together. He held her properly and she seemed to smile in amusement. Then they danced.

Granger worked his way to the front line of spectators. Not fifteen feet away, Eliana Cruzita de Salvador, now de Cortez, danced with her new husband while everyone watched. Granger wondered if she matched anyone's expectations, if any of them had imagined her as she turned out to be. She was not what he had expected, but he had been picturing her as Martine.

Both women had rounded faces, but Martine was not plump. Nor did she have a mole on her left cheek. Nor were her eyebrows as thick or as arched. Nor were her eyes green, nor her chin dimpled, nor her hair dark red. The list of details ran on. Eliana looked nothing like Martine de Lautin and Granger struggled to see her for herself.

The hair startled him the most. Dark enough to appear brown in poor light, more than one shade of red rippled as it moved in time to her whirls and pirouettes. She leaned back, her steps sure and elegant. Watching her, even the music seemed better. Her body was suffused with a compelling energy, most evident when she laughed, which she did easily. She danced with evident ability, as though she had learned at the same time she learned to walk.

By contrast, Don Diego danced as though he had learned it as a drill. He grinned, but his body simply did not respond as fluidly, and Granger imagined him having difficulty keeping pace with his new wife before the evening ended, and perhaps even after. More than that, though, it seemed obvious they did not know each other. They came together, whirled through a number of steps, and then parted to circle each other. From time to time, Eliana's smile faltered. Granger saw uncertainty in her face. But then she would move more deliberately, step more decisively, and laugh, as though by force of will she could bridge whatever now lay between them.

The more Granger watched her, the more the reality took its place in his mind.

The dance ended. Applause filled the room. Diego looked flushed, his smile tentative. Then, blinking, he noticed the guests, and turned with Eliana to bow.

"*Gracias,*" he said.

The musicians took up another tune and more couples stepped onto the floor.

"Granger!" Tayon clapped him on the back, grinning. "I almost missed the ceremony," he said. "Have you seen Cécile? She should be here."

"No, sorry. I also don't see Jose Renaldo."

Tayon swept the room, frowning. "Curious."

"Did Russell talk to you this morning?"

"He did." He craned his neck.

The musicians worked through something like a minuet. Don Diego still danced carefully and stiffly, while Eliana seemed part of the music. But something had changed. Both now smiled at each other with unreserved affection. The period of reacquainting had moved to a new level.

The music changed again, picking up tempo while the dancers rearranged themselves into two rows, men on one side, women on the other. Granger thought it was some sort of reel, but he did not recognize the steps at all. The men bowed, the women curtseyed, and almost formal pirouettes brought them round each other and back to their places.

"I need to talk to you," Granger said to Tayon.

"Of course. But you should dance. This is an opportunity for you to meet someone in more favorable circumstances. Ah! There she is."

Granger laughed as Tayon hurried off. Shaking his head, he turned away—

—and saw Martine, sitting in a corner with Tayon's wife and another woman. Granger stopped, unable to look away. Martine laughed at something the other woman said, covering her mouth, then, with the same hand, gestured as she replied. In that small sequence, Granger thought he had never seen anyone more appealing.

She looked around then and saw him.

And changed.

Her smile softened, her eyes fixed on him, and she became beautiful. He found her more difficult to look at, even as he wanted to keeping staring at her.

Eliana is married, he thought, *and I am not.* It jarred him. Dismayed, he gave Martine a quick smile and looked away. The dance ended, and people milled around waiting for another tune. He searched the room until he found Don Diego and Eliana, in the opposite corner, chatting with Cadet and Lt. Governor Cruzat. As he watched, two more men joined them, one of them Jose Renaldo. By their postures and expressions, the conversation was light.

But then three men, including Gambeau, approached. At first everything continued cordially, but then Gambeau said something and Cortez frowned. Renaldo stepped so as to be between one of Gambeau's companions and Cortez. Granger watched the faces as they changed, some becoming embarrassed, others cautious. Cortez stared at Gambeau in silence until the smaller man flushed deeply, bowed clumsily, and strode away. Cortez then spoke to the two men who had been with Gambeau. They, in turn, scowled, gave crisp bows, and left.

Someone clasped Granger's left arm. Russell, who leaned close to his ear.

"If you're interested in that property I told you about...?"

"Yes?"

"The owners are of a mind to sell. Tayon's with them. Would you be willing to meet with them now?"

"Right now?"

"They're in a festive mood."

Granger looked past Russell, searching the room for Gambeau, then saw Martine still talking with her friends. Suddenly buying her house seemed like the best idea he had ever heard.

"Certainly," Granger said. "Where?

Fourteen

WITHIN TEN MINUTES they gathered in the main office of the lt. governor's stone house. Auguste Chouteau came with two other gentlemen—Gabriel Cerré and Lt. Governor Cruzat—and the de Lautin brothers arrived a few minutes later.

The brothers both appeared well along toward drunk. They dressed expensively in silk; one of them had spilled wine on his wrinkled coat. The older of the two had removed his wig and balanced it on his knee. Introductions were made, Tayon doing most of the talking and translating. When Granger's proposition was explained to the brothers, both raised eyebrows and shook Granger's hand vigorously.

"They want to sell," Tayon said finally. "They are not so taken with our village," he added wryly, "and would like to return to New Orleans. As we already have two other gunsmiths, they see little point in trying to restart their late father's business. They wonder if you are interested in that part of the estate? As far as that goes, I have my doubts that either of them ever lifted a hammer to strike an anvil. They wouldn't know how to do the work if they wanted to."

"The business or just the shop?"

Tayon spoke to them. Auguste Chouteau made a few comments. The brothers studied Granger, nodding in a show of sagacity, but they continued drinking during the negotiations.

"They see your point," Tayon said. "There is a forge, a lathe, some grinders, and a great deal of raw stock. Half a dozen rifles and muskets in various states of completion, tools. They have at least taken an inventory. The tools they may wish to take with them, but I do not think it would be terribly expensive to convince them to sell you the entire lot for, say, one hundred dollars. That would raise the price of the entire property to five hundred."

Granger calculated silently. "Three hundred dollars," he said, "and they can take the unfinished rifles. Someone in New Orleans, I'm sure, can complete them and they should get at least ten or twelve dollars apiece for them."

More discussion ensued. Neither Cruzat nor Cerré said much, Tayon and Chouteau dominating. The younger de Lautin grew visibly unhappy, but his brother cut him off and he walked away to sulk. Tayon smiled. Cruzat gave Granger an appraising look.

"Three hundred and fifty," Russell translated for the older brother.

"Then he leaves the unfinished rifles."

Tayon almost laughed. He reported the counter-offer. The older de Lautin scowled.

It took another fifteen minutes, but finally the sale was agreed. Gabriel Cerré sat down at the desk and drew up a bill of sale, two copies. Everyone present signed both. The sulking brother refused at first, but after his older brother grabbed his jacket and spoke sharply, he relented.

Cerré folded one copy and handed it to Cruzat, who tucked it into his jacket. "He will hold that until payment is made," Tayon explained. "Please do not pay them without witnesses present. I half expect one or both to regret this in the morning."

"Then let's finish it now. Wait here and I'll return with the money."

Russell went with him to Tayon's house. In the room they had given him, Granger pulled out the bag from Renaldo and the purse he had brought with him from Philadelphia. Between the two he had nearly four hundred and twenty dollars. He hefted Renaldo's bribe, his inducement to make Granger leave. Granger had offered to return it and been refused. *He said I should use it to go home,* he thought. *Well, if this is home...*

Everyone had remained in the small room. The money was counted out twice for the de Lautins. After the second count, the older brother grinned and shook Granger's hand. Cruzat poured small glasses of port wine as a toast and handed Granger the bill of sale.

"A proper deed will be forthcoming from New Orleans," Tayon said, "but this has the force of law. You understand, of course, that to actually live here you will have to become a Spanish citizen."

"But—"

"Oh, don't look so dismayed, *mon ami*! It would not be so bad. It can be done now. Lt. Governor Cruzat can receive your oath." He leaned close. "Americans do this all the time. Commerce."

Tayon made it sound trivial, little more than a formality to conclude a transaction, rather than the profound change it was. *Perhaps it's not so great a decision*, Granger thought. It had always been a possibility, one of the consequences of his return. Now that the choice was at hand, though, it frightened him a little.

"Do I have to sign something?"

"It is an oral oath," Tayon said. "You are on your honor here." Tayon grinned. "Americans have honor, no?"

Granger laughed, feeling anxious.

How much do you want what you think you want? he wondered. He found Russell watching him, unsmiling. Something about it pushed him.

"Very well," he said. "Let's get that done, then."

Within seconds, people shifted position, and Cruzat opened a drawer in his desk and pulled out a sheet of parchment. He held it in his left hand and stood before Granger, who straightened out of reflex.

"Usted ahora llevará el juramento de la lealted a España y su rey," Cruzat said.

"You will now take the oath to Spain and the King," Tayon translated.

Granger nodded. Uncertain what else to do, he placed his right hand over his chest. Cruzat smiled and began talking. When he stopped, Granger looked at Tayon.

"Just say yes."

"Yes. *Sí.*"

"En su honor usted ahora es un tema de su majestad santa, rey Carlos el terero."

"You are now a citizen of Spain, *mon ami.*"

Cruzat extended his hand and Granger clasped it. He turned and saw Russell, still watching him, slowly smile and nod.

He drank the port and shook hands. Cerré babbled something in French that Tayon began to translate, but was interrupted. Tayon slapped Granger on the back, laughing. The brothers stood by the door, murmuring between themselves, the older hefting the purse. The clink of the coins added a delicate sound to the laughter and indecipherable conversation.

"Tayon," he said, "would you ask señor Cruzat a question for me?"

"Of course."

"Ask him if, as a new citizen, I might call on him in a few days to discuss a matter of concern."

Tayon frowned. "Remember, *mon ami*, he presided over the inquest about your friend. He is aware of the facts around the event."

"Does he know who I am?"

"Of course he does."

"Then—"

"I suggest you have a little more patience before you make this an official matter."

"Please. Ask him."

Tayon spoke to Cruzat for a time. Cruzat glanced at Granger and nodded.

"He understands what you wish to discuss," Tayon said, "and he is willing to speak with you, but it will be at his convenience."

"I see." Granger nodded at Cruzat. *"Gracias, señor."*

Cruzat smiled and extended his glass for Granger to touch with his own. More port was poured. After a few more minutes of awkwardly translated conversation, the de Lautins begged to be excused and bade everyone enjoy the rest of the evening. They left, in company with Tayon.

"You should," Gabriel Cerré said suddenly, in heavily accented English, "be aware that most people here also speak Spanish, monsieur."

"I speak neither French or Spanish, monsieur. Not well, at any rate."

"But you have good fortune in your friendships."

"It seems so," Granger said. "I would still do well to learn both languages quickly."

"Even if you do, monsieur," Cerré said, "you may still need a habitant to translate meaning."

Diego and Eliana were absent when Granger returned to Gratiot's house. A group of people gathered around the musicians, singing something very slow and melancholy, which changed almost instantly into a tarantella, everyone shouting and stamping their feet to keep a ragged time. The dancing seemed less organized now, more spontaneous. Outside in the chill evening air, fires snapped, sending sparks skyward. Granger crossed to the Place d'Armes.

A lone dulcimer trilled a series of chords over and over while a circle of men danced. People sat against the fence in small groups, drinking and talking. At the far end a pair of fiddlers ripped through a vaguely familiar tune while three Indians intoned a sonorous choral accompaniment and pounded the ground with their feet. Granger drifted, a low panic driving him, from group to group, searching faces now demonic in the firelight around which they congregated, looking for Tayon or Russell or even Neptune. He came to the river side of the market and stepped through the wide gate. The ramp down to the bank was still in place, and he saw small fires on several of the boats tied to the shore and more on the almost invisible island in the river.

"*Bon soir*, Lieutenant."

He started at the voice and looked to the right. A shadow stood a few yards away, just outside the fence. Martine.

"Madame," he said, his voice thick.

"You are looking for something?"

"I…"

"Do you think you will find it here?"

"I do."

Martine came closer. When she stepped into the light of the fires behind them, her face looked red and damp. Tears, he thought, and raised a hand to wipe at them. She stopped just out of reach.

"It seems," she said, "you own my house."

Granger's fingers curled. "How—"

"Étienne's sons. They could not wait to tell me. If I had known they would sell it so soon, I might have been able to buy it myself, perhaps through an intermediary. They do not care for me very much. I have never understood why, they were little enough involved in Étienne's life when we met. Perhaps they thought I was a threat to their inheritance. Which has turned out to be less than they hoped, I'm sure. So they did not tell me about wishing to sell my house until they had already done it. I think they enjoy my difficulties." She half laughed, half grunted. "A jest. A final humiliation. My house is now owned by a stranger. Not even French, but an American. I must buy it from you now if I want it. I cannot live there now in any case. What would people say?"

What would I say? he wondered.

"When you said you intended to stay," she said, "you meant it."

"I came back with that in mind."

She cocked her head to one side. "Why?"

"I had hoped you wanted me to," he said.

"You...I thought—"

"Does there only have to be one reason for it to matter? Would you believe me if I said I came back only for you?"

She looked away and silence stretched. The sky reflected on the river now, darkening quickly, above and below the same color, the same deepness.

"No," she said finally. "I would not believe that."

"But if I said you were one of the chief reasons?"

She smiled and turned her face away from the fire, into shadow. "Perhaps. Yes, I could believe that."

"Would that be sufficient for you?"

"I don't know. But it is not unwelcome."

Granger seemed to see her more clearly, isolated for a few moments from everything around them, and his pulse rushed.

"The other reasons," she said. "Could they interfere?"

"I hope not. I intend not."

She nodded. "I suppose I'm glad that the house did not go to a complete stranger. In any event I am happy Étienne's sons no longer own it. Thank you for that, Lieutenant."

"My last rank was major." He licked his lips. "But I told you, I'm no longer in the army. My name is Granger. I would be honored if you would use it."

"Granger, then. Except when I forget. Which means that I am Martine, not madame."

"Martine, then. There's no reason you can't live in your own house."

"Pardon?"

"I would welcome it. Under any circumstances."

"Lieutenant—Granger—perhaps you should say nothing more—"

"Or say much more. If it would make it less inconvenient, we could marry."

She gasped. "You jest."

Granger felt a surge of desperation, a need to convince, as completely as she had bound his feelings in a desire he still could not be certain she shared. He took her arm and led her away from the bonfires and the small knots of people. When he felt far enough away and deep enough in darkness, he pulled her to him and kissed her.

Briefly, she tensed, but then opened her mouth, welcoming him. Tongues dancing, acceptance became willingness and then hunger. She worked a hand inside his coat and pressed a palm against his chest. He followed the line of her jaw with his lips to her neck, letting her now ragged breath fill his ear. Granger felt encased in a private space into which no one could see, alone with her. An illusion, he knew, but strong and growing stronger. He drew back. A moment to draw air, check himself before he lost all control.

A temporary suspension.

Martine let her head fall against him. She withdrew her hand and stepped back. He sensed her gaze as she raised her head, her eyes hidden in the lightless envelope.

"I'm completely sincere," he said.

"I believe you. *Merci.*" Her voice was thick, uncertain. "Somehow I don't think it would be fair to impose my conditions alone. Let me consider it." She stepped away from him then, breaking all contact. She glanced around.

As she began to walk away, Granger said, "Are we—" She stopped and looked back. Granger swallowed. "We aren't really strangers, Martine. Are we?"

It was difficult to tell in the darkness, but he thought she smiled. She turned her back to the river and walked away, through the celebration, into the noise, and out of reach. Soon after he lost sight of her, Granger wondered if they had spoken at all or if he had imagined it.

Fifteen

HE DRIFTED SOUTH and west, seeking solitude. As he left the festivities behind, the events of the evening seemed to take on weight. *I bought a house, changed my country, proposed marriage, all in less than an hour.*

It seems I've decided.

He might feel better about it had Martine accepted. But she hadn't said no.

For now, he needed to let his decisions soak through him, settle, and become in some way normal.

Ham would think I'm a fool. But he'd understand, or at least accept it.

Granger came to the slope at the western edge. The stockade fence, unmaintained these past three years, had gaps, and he edged through one into the near absolute darkness outside the village. Clouds blocked patches of stars in ragged streaks. The thick tower was a blunt obstruction to the south, visible only by the faint trace of light from the village on its crown. He walked a few yards out from the fence and stopped. Within moments he felt isolated, separate from his surroundings. He let the feeling continue and it carried him further from connections even of memory. He was entirely himself, unaffected and for the first time since before the war saturated with anticipation that did not frighten.

Gradually he became aware of voices. Coming out of his reverie, he located them in the direction of the tower. Granger moved carefully, stepping quietly, probing with the toes of his boots as he approached the stone structure. Finally, he laid a hand against it and started working his way around to the other side.

Laughter stopped him. A woman. A few quick words from a man, another laugh, and then quiet rustling.

Granger backed away.

He saw the dim outline of a wide gap in the fence and stepped through.

He smelled the stables before he recognized where he was, just a bit north of Gambeau's.

The rear doors glowed faintly, limned by lantern light from within.

Granger sidled up to the edge of the doors, back against the wall, and listened. His perceptions now seemed soft and swaddled from drinking. He wasn't drunk, but he was affected. He moved slowly.

The sounds came, low and isolated. A shuffle, the snort of a horse, a brief ticking. Silence, then the ripple of liquid poured into a metal cup.

"*Bien,*" someone said. Someone else grunted.

Granger leaned to the edge and peered around. Three men—Gambeau and the two who had been with him earlier—sat around an upturned barrel. A lantern hung from the post between two stalls cast light on their cards. One of them started to look up and Granger jerked back.

He made his way back to the corner of the building. He paused, getting his bearings, and then walked to the front. As he stepped into the street, movement to his right caught his eye. He stopped. A shadow floated against the dark wall. He began to say something.

The motion triggered his reaction before he recognized it: an arm swinging toward him. He ducked, felt a fist brush his hat from his head, and then stepped back, quickly.

Granger raised his arms as the shadow advanced on him. "Whoa!"

"Qui êtes vous?"

"Emile!" someone shouted.

The shadow stopped as light rimmed its bulk. Gambeau stepped from behind it with a lantern raised in his left hand.

"Monsieur Granger?"

"My apologies," Granger said, stooping to retrieve his hat from the ground. "I didn't intend to disturb you."

"No, not at all," Gambeau said. "Forgive my friend, he thought…I don't know what he thought. Are you all right?"

"Well enough. I didn't expect to be assaulted."

"Of course not. Please, come inside. May I offer you something? I have some rum."

"Thank you, but I think I've drunk enough. I was clearing my head, away from the festivities."

"Please, I feel badly. You are a customer."

Granger looked at the two men. The one who had attacked him watched, no trace of chagrin in his wide face. He was a head taller than Gambeau and beneath his hunting shirt Granger saw powerful shoulders and arms. Granger could not help thinking he had seen him before today.

"I suppose for a short time," Granger said.

"Excellent!"

Gambeau took his arm and led him into the stable. The other man was standing a few yards inside the door; Granger saw the butt of a pistol tucked into his belt. Gambeau chattered in quick French and he smiled and went back to the barrel.

He poured from a fat jug into a tin cup and offered it to Granger.

The other man came up behind him, still unsmiling, until Gambeau said something and he sat down on one of the stools around the barrel.

"We were having a game of Ombre," Gambeau said. "Would you care to join us? We can change it up to Quadrille."

Silver coins gathered in the center of the barrel head, surrounded by three hands of well-used playing cards. Both Gambeau and the other man drank from tin cups. The big man who had attacked him drank from a tarnished goblet. Granger watched it as he lifted it from the barrel to his mouth and set it back down. Granger made himself look away. He remembered seeing similar goblets at Cortez's house.

"I'm afraid I've spent all my money tonight," Granger said. He sipped the rum. The sugary burn seemed to linger from his throat to his belly. "This is good. Thank you."

"Spent all your money?" Gambeau said, resuming a seat.

"I bought the de Lautin house."

Gambeau stared at him. "That's...congratulations, monsieur. I did not know you intended to live here. You realize you will have to—"

"Become a citizen of Spain? I already have. Lt. Governor Cruzat took my oath earlier tonight."

"Well. I suppose that makes us neighbors. What do you intend to do?"

"I'll open my store."

"Partnering with Monsieur Russell across the river? Clever."

Watching him, Granger sensed that Gambeau was not pleased. He wondered if Gambeau had planned to buy the place from Étienne's sons. Gambeau studied his cards intently. The other two men studied him, as though waiting for a decision.

"Excuse me," Granger said suddenly, "but we haven't been introduced yet. I'm Granger."

The big man's eyes shifted to him, but he said nothing.

"Forgive me," Gambeau said absently. "These are my associates. Emile and Davidet."

"Emile Chavreaux? I've heard of you."

The big man straightened, frowning. "And I have heard of you."

Davidet's attention was fixed now on Chavreaux. Granger recalled where he had seen Chavreaux before. Standing at the door of the stable when Granger, Russell, and Tayon had returned with Taylor, three and a half years before.

Granger finished his cup and handed it back across the barrel to Davidet. "My thanks. I should get back, though. My friends will wonder if I've gone off and gotten lost."

Gambeau seemed to come out of his funk and stood. "We can perhaps do business, then. You should come by when you are settled and we can talk."

"Perhaps. Good evening."

Granger turned his back to them and walked out of the stables, his body electric with anticipation. A blow, a shot, a knife. He had provoked them, though he did not know how, but Gambeau was displeased that he had bought that property.

He walked out into the night and nothing happened. He wound his way to Riviere's, which was still open, and went inside looking for someone he knew. The rum was further impeding his thoughts. He sat down at a table and rubbed his eyes.

He sat there for a time until he felt more in control.

So that was Emile Chavreaux, he thought, and shuddered. He had encountered men in the war who had lost the connection to humanity that bound most people to shared limits, men who could kill without thought and no remorse. Chavreaux gave that impression. A dangerous man if provoked. Was he one of the men Gambeau had left with that day?

Is he the one who actually did the killing?

He doubted Gambeau would have done it. He would have paid someone else. It seemed to Granger that Gambeau was a man whose ambitions were greater than his nerve, and that tended to make him irascible and petty. He wanted more than he had and seemed unable to achieve his goals. What was there about Martine's house that bothered him that someone else now owned it? The forge? The other equipment? Or just the fact that it wasn't going to be his?

Details combined to give him an idea what had happened that day. Tayon and Ham had gone out to bring in Cortez's slaves. Cortez had left them there even though the order had gone out to everyone to bring them in. Obviously he wanted his property defended, but not necessarily from the British and Indians. Gambeau timed it so that he and his companions would be there after the property was vacated. He probably did not know about the stranger hiding there. They intended to search the place for something. The gold? How would Gambeau have known about that?

When Ham returned unexpectedly, they were found. The question was, what were they doing that they had to kill Ham? They might have made any number of excuses or even hidden from him. Ham had caught them doing something they could not allow anyone else to know about.

Granger was certain it had to do with the stranger. Cortez's brother. Had they found him?

Too many details remained hidden. But Granger thought he knew the general outlines of what had happened. Proving it would be difficult, maybe impossible.

Renaldo knew part of it. But convincing him to talk would be a challenge.

I'll worry about that later. I have time now, I live here.

Granger left Riviere's and returned to the Place d'Armes. The revelry was still in loud, boisterous progress. Granger drank more, chasing a warm muzziness in his head. He sang with a group of trappers and they all laughed together, half at his inarticulate mimicking of the lyrics, half at their own inebriation. He sat by the dulcimer player for a long time, watching his fingers, until his cup was empty. He returned to the main house and drew a draft of his own whiskey. At no time did it appear that the party was about to end. More food came, replacing the ruins of what had already been consumed.

Drunk, knowing it, and feeling both foolish and pleased, he decided it was time to retire. He walked unsteadily back to Tayon's house.

He went the wrong way, though, and got turned around. He wandered down the streets, away from the party. Fewer people were about, and it was night. He found Riviere's again, but it was deserted. But now, at least, he knew where he was, and carefully chose his direction.

And stopped halfway down the Rue d'Eglise.

He looked back.

I'm being followed...

He searched the shadows, but there was nothing to see. Fences, a few dim glows behind them picking out their edges. He tried to silence his own thoughts, his own body, the way Russell had tried to teach him long ago, in the woods on the hunt for redcoats and Indians, and listen to the air. But the distant babble of the celebration invaded his consciousness, and his own inebriation made it impossible to concentrate. His hand came up to his waist, but he was unarmed.

He continued north.

It was less a sound than a feeling. He whirled around and strode back.

"What?" he demanded. "Who's there?"

Someone stepped from a shadow, into a pool of moonlight. A shape, no more, faceless.

Granger lurched to the left and collided with a fence. As he rebounded, a hand closed around his throat. Panicked, he tried to jerk free. He sensed more than saw the shape of his assailant. He shoved his hands forward, groping for a face. Before Granger could find a grip, the man shoved him from side to side. Spittle ran down Granger's chin.

"*Qui vive?*"

The hand left him and he heard running. To his right, a gate opened.

"Monsieur?"

Granger coughed, rubbed his throat, and looked at the man leaning out from his gate.

"It's...thank you...I'm all right."

The man muttered "*Le sot!*" and retreated, slamming his gate shut.

Granger listened again. Nothing. Shaken, he continued north, back to Tayon's house.

Sixteen

"THERE ARE BRUISES." Tayon sat back, frowning at Granger as if he had gotten himself assaulted on purpose. Granger felt like apologizing. "You didn't recognize him?"

"I didn't even see who tried to choke me." Granger felt embarrassed. He had been too drunk to defend himself and knew he was lucky to have survived. He took a mouthful of coffee. "But I suspect it was Chavreaux."

"Why?"

"I recognized him. He'd been with Gambeau that day."

"He has been in business with Gambeau for years."

"He had one of Cortez's goblets."

"What goblet?"

"There was a set of silver goblets in Cortez's house. I didn't pay much attention to them, but last night I saw one very much like them, in Chavreaux's possession."

"It's been over three years. Is your memory that good that you can recall a goblet?"

Granger hesitated. Tayon's point was valid, he couldn't be sure. But the impression had been strong. *Is an impression enough?* Tayon waited and Granger looked away. "I'm fairly certain."

"Hm. It could be coincidence."

"Could be. How likely is that, though?" He winced as he stood, his neck stiff. "You may be right. I need to have another look at those goblets to be sure, though. Do you think he'll be out at Cortez's place today?"

"Chavreaux? Hardly."

"And Gambeau?"

"I doubt it. They have made no secret of their animosity. Do you still wish to go?"

"Of course. I wanted a reaction. I didn't expect this, though." He gestured at his neck.

"This man who attacked you—you think it is the same man who killed Sergeant Inwood? That Emile Chavreaux killed Ham?"

"If he was there, he struck the blow. But if he was there, it was because of Gambeau. The question is why."

"And Cortez?"

"I thought—I expected some kind of confirmation yesterday that the man claiming to be Don Diego is in fact his brother."

"You expected Eliana to reject him? In front of everyone?"

"I don't know. Yes. Maybe."

"It has been years since they have been together. And what would she then do? Turn around and return to Spain?"

"So she'll try to make things as she wants them to be?"

"Or as she needs them to be. It's possible we were wrong about Cortez, too."

"No. None of you think it's the same man as before. In spite of Eliana's reactions, I'm still convinced that man is not Diego but Atilio."

"*Mon dieu!* Very well, then. The party leaves in an hour. We will see what we may."

"Tayon—thank you. You've been generous with me."

Tayon smiled awkwardly. "Think nothing of it. Tell me, though, what do you think of the bride?"

"She's lovely."

Tayon gave him a skeptical look. "You, I suspect, will never be guilty of exaggeration. By the way, have you told Martine that you bought her house?"

"She already knew. Her stepsons told her."

"Oh?"

"I told her she didn't have to leave it."

"What did she say to that?"

"She didn't."

Tayon sat down again. "Let me ask you, *mon ami*, what is it you want from her?"

"Nothing. I— "

"No no no! A man does not offer such a thing to a woman from whom he wants nothing."

Chagrined, Granger kept silent. He was torn between what he thought he wanted and what he thought might be possible.

"I advise you to decide," Tayon said. "Indecision is the worst thing with a woman. Decide. But perhaps you should finish this thing with Cortez first. It would be unfair to entangle her in something that may damage you." He patted Granger's shoulder. "I must see to our horses. One hour."

❧

Three charettes waited behind a larger, four-wheeled wagon in the street by the Place d'Armes. Around them, the crowd seemed as dense as it had the day before, at the peak of the celebration. Trunks unloaded from the boat piled onto the little two-wheeled carts while the oxen waited, snorting white clouds of steam in the brisk October air.

Granger tied Ham's rifle, in its case, to the saddle of the big chestnut mare. Tayon had gone to Gambeau's stable earlier that morning and brought the horses back. Gambeau, he reported, had not been there. Neptune had saddled the horses for them.

Granger had decided at the last instant to bring the rifle. He looked around to see if others were going armed, and found a few muskets in saddle holsters, some swords, and the occasional glimpse of a pistol under a coat.

While many of the men had donned their best coats, most of the women dressed in their work-a-day cotton and wool, wrapped in shawls or wearing long overcoats obviously taken from the men. Cécile rode with several others in a single wagon, one of four carrying people out to the Cortez farm.

Around mid-morning, Cortez and Eliana emerged from the Gratiot house. The crowd cheered. Don Diego held Eliana's hand firmly in the crook of his left elbow. He was grinning like a boy, eyes darting from face to face.

Eliana seemed pale and uncertain. Smiling, but reserved, not the same woman who had leapt from the boat and bounded up the ramp to meet her fiancée boldly and eagerly. That eagerness was diminished, replaced now with caution, a controlled politeness, and the look of someone reserving judgment. She allowed her husband to help her up into the wagon, where she drew a cloak around her and cast only fleeting looks at the well-wishers.

Don Diego pulled himself into the seat and grabbed the reins.

Must've been a long night, Granger thought. His own head still ached dully, as well as his throat.

The entourage was trapped for the time being by the crowd, but finally several men began shouting at people and opening a passage. Granger searched for Martine but did not see her in the crowded street. Cortez's wagon, drawn by two mules, lurched forward. Granger patted the horse's neck and she twisted her head around to nuzzle him, knocking his hat off. Laughing, he mounted.

It still took nearly half an hour to get out of the village and onto the road leading west. At one stretch the track narrowed and even those on horseback had to go single file. They reached the property just past noon.

As he emerged from the woods, Granger was startled by the differences. The house still had two floors, but the attempt at a Spanish style, with its mud-coated walls, had been abandoned, and Don Diego had completed it more in the local style, with a broad roof sitting over it all like a big, lazy hat. It seemed to squat on its land like an indolent cow. Smoke flowed from a pair of chimneys, one on the west end of the house, the other in the center. A new fence surrounded the cemetery plot.

The stable had been rebuilt, larger than Granger remembered, and there were now two barns. He did not see the slave quarters. The grounds had the look of care and attention, dirt pathways leading to the various outbuildings, and a road heading southwest, toward the tree line. The overwhelming impression was of order, strikingly different from his first visit here. Granger dismounted and led his horse toward the new stable with the other riders. A long post ran the length of the building, water troughs on one side in easy reach for the horses. After tying his mount and taking the rifle from the saddle, Granger went to the stable door, Tayon following.

Within, the stalls were filled with both horses and a few cows. A trio of slaves looked up from their work, one hoeing back hay, another doing a repair on one of the stalls, the third holding a shovel, all frozen for the instant, staring at him as though waiting for a command. The stable itself appeared well-organized, clean.

"It has been over a year since I have been here," Tayon said. "He has done a great deal of work."

"Impressive," Granger said.

As they turned to leave, they found a man standing in the entrance, watching them. He was shorter than Granger, but wider across the shoulders, and his square face showed deep lines in the dark skin. His hair was black, tied back, and he wore a plain linen blouse, coveralls, and moccasins. Granger's eyes settled on his hands, which were large and veined and powerful.

Before he could say anything, the man pivoted smoothly and walked away. Startled for a moment, Granger glanced at Tayon before stepping outside the stable.

Granger searched the immediate grounds, but whoever the man was, he had disappeared. In the distance he saw the shapes of workers in a field, bent to their labor. To the north he glimpsed, obscured behind a stand of trees, a row of crude structures—the slave quarters, moved now a good three hundred yards from the main house.

"Who was that?"

"Salvatore," Tayon said. "Diego's foreman. A silent, unpleasant man."

"Indian?"

"Yes, but no one knows from where or which tribe. Ah. There he is."

Don Diego led a group of men toward the southwestern edge of the homestead, pointing and talking, occasionally pivoting to face them as he made a sweeping gesture. Granger and Tayon caught up to them by the time they reached the trees. The group spread out, sifting through the dense growth, suddenly silent for the next forty or fifty yards.

They emerged at the edge of a great swath of cleared land, still peppered with stumps. To one side a pile of logs remained. A hundred yards across the clearing, a bulky structure rose against the new tree line—a mill.

Granger moved alongside Tayon. "He cleared all this in the last year and a half?"

"Impressive, no?" Tayon said. "He owns twenty-two slaves now, half of them Indians. From the look of it, he works them very hard."

Granger thought he heard disapproval in Tayon's voice.

A few hundred yards north, he saw the beginning of a plowed field.

"He has bought five more slaves," Tayon said. "We have been getting a lot of lumber from him the last several months. He's still far short of what Kaskaskia produces for us, but if he keeps this up he could pass them in the next two years."

"What about your mill?"

Tayon shrugged and scowled. "Someday we may catch up to both."

"How is he paying for all these slaves?"

"A good question, *mon ami*. He always had a little money, but for the most part he did business here as everyone does, on credit. A few months after his return, though, he paid his debts and began all this. Maybe he dug up that buried gold, no?"

Don Diego's arms flailed as he spoke. He walked quickly, every part of him animated and excited. Cortez talked quickly, his accent thick enough that Granger could not tell if he spoke French or Spanish.

"What's he running it with?" Granger asked.

"Hmm?"

"I don't remember a stream or a creek around here."

"He is using slaves."

Granger was startled. "They're turning it by hand?"

Tayon grunted. "He is ambitious."

"Of course, but..."

"He has plans—no, that is not fair—he *is* digging a channel to divert a stream past it, to turn a water wheel. That could well take another year or two, though, and I'm not certain the stream will be powerful enough."

Granger tried to imagine the amount of labor involved. A hand mill took a great deal of effort. He had seen them in use back in New England, for the construction of a new house or barn, but not for production of commodity lumber.

"Who does he work on the mill? The Indians or the Negroes?"

"I don't know, *mon ami*," Tayon said with a sigh. "Does it matter?"

Granger tried to make what he saw conform to what the two former Cortez slaves had told him, of an almost compassionate man they seemed to serve willingly. What he saw here signified a powerful will, an obsessive drive. All this in eighteen months. Granger wanted to ask if any of Cortez's slaves had died under such conditions.

"I suppose not," he said finally.

Don Diego had stopped in the center space, between one boundary and the other, talking to the group about the mill, then about the cultivation, then about—he stopped when he saw Granger and Tayon. His eyes shifted between them a few times, then settled on Granger. He approached the two men.

"Señor Granger, I am pleased you have come."

"Don Diego," Tayon said, "I did not tell you last night, that he provided the excellent whiskey."

"Ah!" Diego smiled broadly and stepped toward Granger. He patted Granger's shoulder and shook his hand. "*Gracias! Muchos gracias! Excellent!*" He licked his lips and seemed to concentrate. "Your gift was most welcome."

"My pleasure, Don Diego. My friend Tayon must take credit as well. May I say, you speak English very well."

"It deserts me sometimes," Diego said, grinning. "*Gracias.* I learn in Havana. Many sailors. How do you like my home?"

"It's very impressive. How long have you been working on it?"

"Many years. Many, many years. *Cela semble éternel.*"

The group laughed.

Tayon translated. "Seems forever."

"Ah," Diego said, "you do not speak French?"

"Poorly. I'm learning, but it helps to speak slowly."

"Forgive me. You should learn more quickly, though. You will be *en desventaja.*"

"Disadvantaged," Tayon said. "You will be at a disadvantage."

"*Sí, sí.*"

"Yes, yes," Tayon said.

Diego made an exaggerated growl and slapped Tayon's shoulder. Tayon laughed.

Diego's gaze settled suddenly on the rifle resting in the crook of Granger's left arm. Granger's scalp tingled, seeing the reaction. Don Diego started to reach for it, but stopped inches from touching the stock.

"That is...what? An American long rifle?"

"Yes, it is."

Casually, Granger undid the ties and slid the rifle out. He draped the sheath over his right shoulder and held the piece in both hands, out toward Cortez, who ran his gaze slowly along its length, pausing at the butt where the Spanish coins glowed brightly.

"It is beautiful," he said. "What is the range?"

"I can shoot accurately up to three hundred yards, depending on the wind."

"May I?"

Granger let him take the rifle. Cortez laughed. "Heavy. What size?"

"Forty-eight caliber."

"So small?"

"Rifled. You don't need the size as much."

"Ah, *sí...*" He stared again at the inlaid coin, and then turned it over to find the other one. Granger thought for a moment he saw displeasure, perhaps even recognition. But that would be impossible, since by all accounts Don Diego had never seen this rifle before.

He handed it back. "If there is time, perhaps you will demonstrate?"

Granger looked across the field. "Pick a target."

Murmurs rippled through the gathering and Cortez grinned. He turned slowly, surveying the area until he stopped and pointed. Granger followed his aim down the shallow slope toward a line of thick trees that formed a wall. One tree shot up from the others, leaning to the right in the beginnings of an arc.

"You see the dogwood?" Cortez said. "There is a branch midway up?"

Granger saw it, a lone offshoot, bare except for a clump of browned and crumpled leaves waiting for the next heavy rain to knock them off. He estimated it at about two-hundred-thirty yards, an almost horizontal target that might be a meager four inches thick.

"What part do you want me to hit?"

Laughter broke out around him. Cortez looked startled, and then clapped his hands and joined the others, laughing loudly. When he recovered, he said, "At the base?"

Granger nodded and primed the pan. He raised the rifle, pausing to watch the smaller branches around the target. No breeze, and then a flutter. He sighted down the length of the rifle and waited till the air stilled.

The flint snapped, sparking the powder, and the rifle barked and shoved against his shoulder. Thick smoke occluded his vision for a moment. When it cleared, the branch aimed visibly lower, a chunk of it now missing where it met the trunk. Applause rippled but he immediately reloaded. He did it quickly, the way he had learned to during the war, and before the last man stopped clapping, he stood once more, aimed, and fired. The branch now rested completely against the trunk, pointing downward.

Cortez hooted.

Granger reloaded again. "Would you like it pruned completely?"

"*Sí, sí!*"

Granger aimed once more and touched off the weapon, heart pounding now, pleased to be using Ham's rifle, proud of the accuracy.

The smoke cleared and the branch was gone, fallen into the underbrush.

The applause was louder now and people clapped Granger on the back. Cortez almost danced with excitement. Granger took his time reloading now, but he left the pan empty, and slipped the rifle back into its sheath.

"I have never seen shooting as fine!" Cortez said. "I am amazed, señor."

"It's been a while since I had a chance to shoot."

Conversation swirled for a time and Granger answered questions and accepted praise until Cortez clapped his hands to get their attention.

"Your pardon, señors, but soon there will be food and drink. We should continue if you still wish to see my mill." He walked away and most of the group followed.

"His French is as bad as his English," Tayon said. "Worse, I think. Do you wish to see the mill?"

"No."

Tayon patted his shoulder. "Then come, let us pay our respects to his new bride."

Seventeen

GRANGER HESITATED at the threshold. For a few moments, blood rushed audibly in his ears, muffling sound. He saw Tayon, a few steps into the hall, beginning to turn toward him. Beyond, midway down the hallway that stretched to the back of the house, a man stood, staring at him. For an instant's impossible recognition Granger thought it was Ham. He seemed to raise a hand to point at the ceiling above his head. Granger blinked, the illusion transformed into someone else, someone living, a yellow nimbus of hair glowing around a stranger's face, smiling, hand up, waving, bidding them enter.

Granger stepped through the door. *Obligation accepted*, he thought. The pulse faded, sensation resumed. The man he had mistaken for Ham went through a door to his right.

The house reverberated with voices. People gathered at the far end of the hall, through the back door. The walls were finished, papered in a dark green. The plank floor caught light and shimmered. A rack to the left, just inside the door, held muskets and swords. Granger set the rifle in among them, and then walked down the hallway. He looked through the first doorway to his left and found a parlor filled with visitors, the hearth ablaze, light shafting in from the two windows looking out on the front porch.

Three and a half years and the memory of disorder remained strong, so that Granger was uncertain he was even in the same house. The walls all appeared finished, the enormous hutch filled with plate. He made his way to the hutch. Five goblets stood on one shelf. Brightly polished, each bore a twin band etched near the rim, a pair of delicate braids.

"Granger," Tayon called from the other side of the hallway.

He crossed the hall. This room, too, looked as it should, completely different from his last visit. Shelves covered three walls, containing a modest collection of books. Granger counted five chairs and a settee, as well as two small tables and a sideboard, more furniture in one room than he had ever seen in a local house.

Everyone stood or sat in a semi-circle around the woman occupying the high-backed chair facing the windows, mostly women, including Cécile and Martine. The light fell on Eliana like soft snow, brilliant, clean, and edgeless. She looked up at Granger and he stopped, transfixed by her eyes. Martine leaned close to her left ear and spoke.

"Señor Granger," Eliana said, smiling. "I am glad you came. I have been told excellent things about you."

She extended her left hand. Granger stared at it for an awkward moment. He took it, bent, and touched his lips to her knuckles, quickly, dryly.

"Señora," he said.

"May I know your given name?"

Her voice was not as he had imagined it from her letters. She sounded rough, as though she needed to clear her throat. Perhaps after the last couple of days she had talked too much, made it raw.

"Given name," he said. *At least she didn't ask for my Christian name.* "Ulysses."

"Ulysses..." She smiled. "How brave."

"Most people just call me Granger."

"Is that what you prefer?"

"It is."

"Then it is Granger. You do not like your name?"

"It's...cumbersome."

She laughed. "To be a pagan among so many must be difficult."

"Pagan? I confess I never thought of it that way. To be honest, I never cared much for Homer."

"But you have read him?"

"Yes."

"And Virgil?"

"That, too."

She clapped her hands, looking for a moment like a delighted child. "We must have you to visit! I had hoped for someone with an education, and here it turns out to be an American!"

Granger glimpsed Tayon's smirk.

"There are others quite well read here," Granger said. "The Chouteaus, I understand, have a large library."

"Merchants," she said dismissively. "I would rather know the poets."

"I'm a merchant myself, señora."

"Yes, but you are an American. Somehow I do not think business is the only reason you are here."

"No, it's not." He looked at Martine, but she avoided his gaze. A moment later she excused herself and left the room.

Eliana smiled, triumphant in her observation, and Granger thought he had never seen a woman so perfectly formed. She was enchanting and he was enchanted, though he knew it would not be for long.

"Just now," she said, "Americans are more interesting than anyone else because they have done this remarkable thing. You cannot be merely merchants."

"Or poets?"

"Perhaps not, but just what you are is poetic."

"And just what are we, señora?"

She tilted her head, examining him, eyes narrowed. Not an innocent gaze, but guiltless, and Granger imagined he saw invitation, promise, the potential for knowing...

"Aspiration," she said.

"I'm sorry? I—"

"You personify it. Not for the world, though certainly there are among you those who do, but you aspire to be... more."

It would be easy, he realized, to tell her that he knew her. She elicited trust and he felt like a thief withholding from her. *I know you*, he thought, *I've read your soul...in translation, certainly, but it came through...I can help.*

He stepped back politely and made himself smile. "There are others waiting to meet you, señora," he said. "I hope to talk to you later."

"Of course! I am glad to have met you, señor Odysseus."

He bowed politely and backed away. Tayon followed.

"Ulysses?"

"Granger."

Tayon laughed and glanced back toward the parlor. "She's beautiful, no?"

"Beautiful, yes."

"I hope Don Diego doesn't sequester her out here all the time. It would be a benefit to see her in town, in the market."

"You sound infatuated."

Tayon grinned. "I'm young, and it's natural to be taken with a beautiful woman."

"Like your wife? I suppose it's well that she's here."

Tayon slapped Granger's back, laughing. "I'm hungry."

They found the dining room behind the parlor, with a door to the kitchen area. Granger went through to the rear door. A few yards from the northeast corner of the house was a cooking shed from which smoke billowed out of a pair of chimneys. Like the day before at the Chouteau house, the food was laid out in a buffet. Chickens, venison, and pork, as well as maize, wheat cakes, bread, and puddings.

"I need to look upstairs," Granger whispered to Tayon, who nodded and took his plate off toward the salon. No one paid him any attention as he went to the rear staircase.

Heart racing, he ascended the stairs, wincing at each creak of a tread, and emerged into the gallery that still ran the length of the house. He crouched reflexively and pressed back against the wall.

At the first door, he hesitated. If he went back down the stairs now, he could be out the back door and away before anyone knew he had come up here. But he could just as easily encounter someone—perhaps Don Diego himself—on the way down the steps. It would then be a waste of recklessness.

He gripped the handle, pushed it down, and eased the door open.

Until he entered, he had no idea what he expected to find. The memory of the ransacked space conflicted with order. The study contained a desk, a trunk, a chair, and a book case. Granger closed the door softly behind him and went to the desk. A single sheet of paper lay on the leather pad, blank. A stack of blank paper stood to the left, an ornate pewter inkwell to the right. The wood glowed darkly, clean and smooth. Granger opened the trunk, grateful to find it unlocked. Tucked among neatly folded clothes he found three large leather-bound folios containing letters, all in Spanish. Leafing through, he saw that many of the pages were yellowing with age.

He took one to the desk where he searched for something with new writing, but there was nothing. He returned the folios and burrowed through the clothes. At the bottom lay a uniform, fading blue with red trim. Gold epaulets lay on top.

Granger closed the trunk. He left the study and crept down the hall to the next door. Entering, he found a bare room with a blanket on the floor beneath the window. He was about to leave when another object caught his eye. Metallic, half-hidden by the blanket, the length suggestive. Granger carefully pulled away the cloth. The musket seemed shorter than standard and the lock exaggerated and bulky. The stock had been decorated with nailheads in the shape of a crucifix. A powder horn and shot bag lay near the end of the barrel. He did not want to move it. He leaned over to peer at the bore, which seemed larger than it should. He replaced the blanket and left the room.

At the opposite end, past the stairs, he came to the final door. He opened it and stepped through into the bedroom.

Martine spun around, startled, mouth wide, standing before the open armoire.

"Lieutenant—"

"What are you doing?"

He closed the door quickly.

"I am—" Her face reddened as she glanced around the room, as though seeking a way out. "I will be living here," she started again. "And—I thought—" Then she looked up at him, scowling. "What are *you* doing here?"

Granger ignored the question and turned his attention to the room. Again, the order surprised him. Everything about the Cortez property collided with his memory. The bed was no longer askew, the floor was clean, the other furniture...

He went to the armoire. Martine stepped back. He found it half filled with fine suits and another uniform. Blue, much cleaner, newer. He shuffled through the clothes again.

No scarlet uniform.

At the foot of the bed stood two large trunks. Both were locked. Eliana's.

Footsteps sounded in the hall outside. Granger looked at Martine, who reflected the panic he suddenly felt. His pulse beat loud in his ears now. The latch moved.

Martine grabbed his coat and pulled him against her. Before he could say anything, she kissed him. He stiffened for a moment, then relaxed, and her arms went around his neck. Her lips opened—

"Oh! I beg your pardons!"

Granger stepped back and looked toward the door. Eliana stood there, hand raised toward her mouth, which was forming an embarrassed smile. Her eyes danced.

"Señora," he said. "I—please forgive us, we meant no disrespect."

"Of course not." She closed the door behind her. "Have you been to this house before, señor?"

"Yes," he said. "Years ago."

"Is it as you remember?"

"To be perfectly truthful, it could not be more different than it was then."

She nodded slowly, mouth puckered. She walked toward the window and gazed out. "It is a beautiful place, don't you think?"

"More so because you're here," he said.

The words shocked him as much as her. She gaped at him, face transformed. Granger did not look away, stunned that the thought had become spoken words with no hesitation. He glanced at Martine, whose eyebrows were raised. He thought—he expected—she would rebuke him. Instead, her smile eased back.

"Forgive me, señora, I speak out of place."

"You *are* American."

She said it as if it explained everything. "I am. But I've become a Spanish citizen."

"Then you intend to stay in St. Louis."

"I hope to open a dry goods store." Again, he glimpsed at Martine, whose expression now was carefully neutral.

Eliana's smile was briefly filled with amusement, but then it faded. "I know we have never met before yesterday, but..." She searched his face, worried and fascinated. Then shook her head. "Forgive me. It is all so new. So different. But your words please. I am not offended. I look forward to our next conversation, señor Odysseus."

"You speak English very well."

She bowed her head. "Thank you. I was told I should learn it as well as French if I intended to live here."

"Better than Don Diego."

She frowned. "Yes...curious, is it not?"

"He said he learned it in Havana."

When she did not reply, Granger stepped away from the door, toward the stairs, drawing Martine with him.

"Señor?"

"Yes?"

"I am not sure everything is as it should be. If I have questions, will you give me answers?"

Then why did you marry him? he wanted to ask. "If I can."

"True answers."

"Of course."

"*Gracias.*" Eliana smiled slowly and nodded. "I am glad you are here, señora de Lautin. I would speak to you privately. That is, if you are unoccupied at the moment."

Granger felt Martine's hand squeeze his just before she released him and turned back. "Of course," she said. "Until later, Lieutenant?"

"Of course."

Granger went downstairs, his legs trembling, dread graying his thoughts.

Granger stood at the short fence surrounding the cemetery and stared at the lone marker. The wood had grayed, but it was otherwise unchanged. Grass grew thickly around it. He could find no trace of the other grave, no swelling of the ground, no difference in the grass. He resisted an urge to enter the enclosure, kneel where Ham was buried, touch the earth.

He turned away and found Don Diego, watching him. Several paces away Salvatore stood.

"Forgive me," Granger said. "I meant no offense."

Don Diego cocked his head to one side as he came closer. He gazed down at the marker and Granger thought he had forgotten about him.

"Your brother?" Granger asked.

The question seemed to startle Don Diego. He looked owlishly at Granger, and then nodded. "He is not there, of course."

"Then how do you know?"

"That he is dead? A brother knows. My brother...do you have a brother, señor?"

"Yes."

"Then you know what it is like, to love someone and also wish they did not exist? My family, we are old and proud. We have traditions, a name that demands much from us. Atilio tried, but he had his own way, and it did not always meet with approval. Sometimes...well, he went to Havana to find his fortune with the army. We thought, good, serving the king, the country, even in such a remote place, that will be honorable. But then we heard reports that he did not serve well. Atilio was always strong-willed and did not yield to authority easily. An admirable thing in a man who also has the ability to stand by his willfulness."

His English had become much better, more fluid, as he spoke.

"What happened to him?" Granger asked.

"He was sent finally to Mexico, to the frontier, and we never heard of him again. Reported lost. We only hope he died honorably. But lost...it is so ambiguous, no? Who can say where he went? How he died? If..." He pressed his lips together tightly, glaring at the marker. Then he sighed loudly. "You lost a friend. Did he die bravely?"

"Everything Ham did, he did bravely."

"You were *amigos*?"

"My best friend. Almost a brother." He watched Don Diego take that in. Then added, "He never disappointed me."

Don Diego nodded slowly and turned away. "You are very fortunate to have had someone like that in your life, señor. I wish you had not lost him." Before Granger could say anything else, he walked away, toward his house.

Salvatore remained where he was, staring at Granger. Granger waited until he turned away.

As the day continued, Granger noticed Eliana moving from room to room, engaging people in conversation, her laughter becoming sharper and more anxious as evening approached. The brightness of her changed from attractive to raw, almost repulsive. Then he understood. She did not want anyone to leave. Granger watched, feeling helpless, until eventually there were only a handful, and Don Diego was making farewell noises to them.

Martine avoided him. He did not make it difficult for her—there would be time later to find out what she was looking for—and as the afternoon grew late he made the rounds to say goodnight.

He went with Tayon to the stable. The slaves had their horses saddled and ready. Carriages and charettes made their way out, among single riders. Granger and Tayon spurred their horses and headed for the road back to St. Louis.

Away from the farm, in the thickness of uncleared woodland, the darkness became oppressive. It was nearing six o'clock, Granger guessed, and the sky was ice gray.

"What did you think?" Tayon asked.

"About what?"

"All of it. The señora especially."

"I don't know. She seemed anxious."

"Anxious, yes. That's one way to see it, I suppose."

"Why?"

Tayon shrugged. "She seemed afraid to me." Granger waited. Finally, Tayon said,

"It seemed to me that she did not want to be alone with her husband."

So you saw it, too, Granger thought. But in all her letters he never once detected fear. Unless it was fear of being left in Spain. *Would she cooperate with such a deception in order to have the life she imagined?*

"*If I have questions…*"

They rode the rest of the way back in silence.

At the stockade, two Spanish soldiers met them.

Eighteen

LT. GOVERNOR FRANCISCO Cruzat poured wine for Granger and Tayon.

"You are a citizen of Spain now, señor," he said without preamble, fixing Granger with an appraising look. His English, heavily accented, was clear and fluid. "Until now, if anything you did caused unrest or broke laws, short of a serious offense, I would have been satisfied sending you back across the river and barring you from return. It is different now."

He raised his glass in a silent toast and sipped along with Granger and Tayon. Then he nodded to the lone Spanish soldier still in the office. The man saluted and left, closing the door behind him.

Cruzat sat down behind his desk. "Last night there was too much. Too much revelry, too much drink, too much food. Too much. Now we may talk with clearer heads and no distractions."

Granger glanced at Tayon, who watched Cruzat, his expression guileless. Granger's heart seemed to beat a little harder. "Of course," Granger said.

"My position here," Cruzat said, tapping his desk

with an index finger, "is both simple and complex. I am to maintain good order and the loyalty of the habitants to Spain. That means being on dependable terms with most of the people. I say 'dependable' because that is preferable to merely 'good' terms. It may seem a minor distinction, but I assure you it means everything in a time of crisis. I have less than twenty soldiers. For anything more, I must rely on militia. I would rather not. As a veteran of your recent struggles, I'm sure you understand. You were here, I am told, with Colonel Clark. You know, then, the problems with militia, especially as you were not."

"No, sir, I was a Continental, detached at that time from General Nathanael Greene."

"Then we need not quibble over terms."

"No, sir."

"I have merchants jealous of their privileges, more than a score of Indian tribes that make regular visits here expecting protection or presents or justice they cannot achieve on their own. I have fur traders and foreign traders coming and going. I have a population disproportionately male and laws regarding mixed relations that are continually ignored that nevertheless cause problems. I have had killings and thefts and more domestic squabbles than I care to remember. And above all this, I am to encourage new residents, who bring their own problems with them. I tell you all this to make my position clear. I am not, I believe, a frivolous, vain, or arbitrary administrator, but personalities will always play a part. You were an officer?"

"I was. I retired a major."

"Then you understand my meaning."

"Perfectly."

Cruzat nodded in satisfaction. "Your return caused concern. Everyone knows why you are here, even though most will say nothing about it. I am aware of the rumors, I know about the incidents of your previous visit. I conducted my own investigation. I wish to ask you, one gentleman to another—or, perhaps, more importantly, one officer to another—why *are* you here?"

Granger studied Cruzat. *He knows the rumors, he knows the past…he wants confirmation or contradiction, something he can rely on.* He glanced again at Tayon, who was studiously not looking at him.

"There are several reasons—" Granger began.

"You know the one I am interested in."

"As I was about to say, the one you're asking about concerns the death of my sergeant and one of my privates during the *l'Année du Coup*." Cruzat nodded and Granger continued. "I'm here to see if I can learn how and why my men were killed, especially my sergeant. We were friends. Since childhood."

"Do you have some idea about that?"

"Hypotheses. Guesses, really. More than I did before."

"Do you suspect Don Deigo de Cortez?"

"No. Though he's very much at the heart of this."

Cruzat drank more wine. "My position—my task—as I said is one of maintenance. I cannot afford to create discord that might damage Spain's position here. So I am often forced to do nothing, to overlook events when paying them too much attention would result in such discord. It is often preferable to allow those concerned in disputes to settle them without my intervention. In this instance, though, I would like to prevent any mistakes."

"On my part?"

"On anyone's part. However, I am not entirely a bureaucrat. I am, I believe, a conscientious man. I would prefer to see justice done. But in this instance, I want to know in what direction that might lie. So tell me, señor Granger, who do you suspect and for what reasons?"

"Charles Gambeau and Emile Chavreaux."

Cruzat did not seem surprised. "Go on."

"I don't know the reasons. I have suspicions. Gambeau and Don Diego were rivals over the supply of horses. I believe during the preparations for the battle he and some confederates, one of which was Chavreaux, went to Cortez's home, searched it, killed Cortez's stallion. And my friend, who I believe found them when he went back out there in search of someone reputed to be hiding on the property."

"What were they searching for?"

"I don't know. I think they went through all of Cortez's papers."

Cruzat leaned back and gazed into a middle distance, his expression intensely thoughtful.

"What happened when you and Monsieur Tayon went out there?" he asked.

Granger described the day. Tayon confirmed and added a few details. Cruzat asked a few questions for clarity, and then refilled his glass as he pondered.

"So who shot at your man?"

"We never saw him," Tayon said.

"But the ball was enormous," Granger said. "I was told it came from a Spanish modification, an *escopeta*." Granger hesitated before adding, "I found such a weapon today in a room in Don Diego's house."

Cruzat's eyes came up at that. "Interesting," he said finally. "I will tell you some things now. Monsieur Tayon was insistent that there be an investigation. Searches were made and when Don Diego returned from his mission there was an inquest. In between Tayon's insistence and the inquest, I made inquiries. We have not been idle on this matter. I considered the possibility of a band of disaffected *coureur du bois* who could prey on people far outside the precincts of the village. Indians perhaps. There were, you may have heard, a number of unfortunate incidents of that sort, people we were unable to bring into the village, caught on their farms by roving groups of angry Indians in the aftermath of their defeat. But we found nothing like that. Like you, señor, I recognized that Don Diego was at the heart of this matter. It was the only thing that made sense, though I confess what sense it made was tenuous at best. Nothing was stolen from his house and only his horse was killed—and the one your sergeant rode out there. Why? There seemed no logic to it.

"But I learned some things about Don Diego in the course of my inquiries. Nothing I could use in any meaningful way, but knowledge should never be discarded lightly.

"Don Diego came here in 1778 from Havana via New Orleans. Before that he was in Spain. But I discovered another de Cortez who had been in Cuba for several years before that."

"Atilio," Granger said.

"Exactly. His brother." Cruzat sorted through some papers on his desk until he found what he wanted. He cleared his throat and translated. "Atilio Juan de Cortez of

Madrid joined His Most Catholic Majesty's army in 1771. His family had purchased him a commission as an ensign. Within six months, he had risen to the rank of lieutenant, whereupon he was sent to the New World. He arrived in Cuba in early 1772 and spent the next two years in the garrison of Havana. Except for a single expedition to New Orleans and up the Mississippi in 1774, he did nothing worth mentioning. He became captain, then seemed to stagnate. Abruptly, in 1777, he was sent to Mexico. There was a question of impropriety. He served in Mexico City until 1778, when he was sent, along with units of several regiments, north to deal with a matter of Indians attacking Spanish settlers north of the Rio Grande. The campaign lasted several months and was unsuccessful and costly in manpower. Slightly over half the force returned. Atilio Juan de Cortez was formally listed as deceased after this, lost somewhere in the upper reaches of Tejas."

He set the paper aside. "Upon further inquiry, the 'impropriety' mentioned turned out to be the theft of a very large amount of money that had been sent as a dowry for the marriage of one of the officers. An officer who was dead, of fever. The chest went missing, three men were suspected, but nothing was proved. Two of the officers were reassigned—one of them was Atilio de Cortez—"

"And the other was Jose Renaldo," Granger said.

Cruzat's eyes narrowed. "How did you conclude that?"

"He came here with Atilio in 1774, part of the escort for the bell Benito Vasquez donated to the church.."

"You have learned more than I thought. Yes, it was Renaldo. He was here when Diego Cortez arrived in 1778. He had stayed as part of the garrison in Ste. Genevieve.

Some time after Don Diego arrived here, Renaldo resigned and moved to St. Louis."

"A different Cortez. Did they all know each other in Spain?"

"It's possible."

"So if they stole the dowry," Tayon said, "then did Renaldo bring it here?"

Cruzat picked something up from his desk and flipped it toward Granger. Gold shimmered in an arc and he caught the Spanish coin.

"You paid for your new house with these," Cruzat said. "Where did you get them?"

"Renaldo."

"A loan?"

"A bribe. He wants me to leave St. Louis."

"You kept it?"

"He refused to take it back. He told me specifically to use it to go home. Well, I intended to make St. Louis my home, so…"

Cruzat smiled briefly. "The dowry that was stolen was all in gold coins. Obviously there is no way to tell if these are part of it, but it is suggestive, don't you think? We have silver here, but not very much gold."

"Very." Granger tossed the coin back to Cruzat, who caught it deftly. "Have you asked Renaldo about it?"

"Again, we come to the difficulty of my position. I experienced some problems two years ago, requiring a sum of money. Renaldo was most helpful. It would be ungenerous of me to question him after his own generosity, but it did not stop me from asking a discrete question or two."

"Tell me, does *camino del mercaderos* mean anything to you?"

Cruzat's eyebrows rose. "It is a street in Havana. Why?"

"I came across it on a document."

"It is one of the principal commercial avenues from the harbor."

"And the name M. de la Vargas?"

Cruzat shook his head. "I am not familiar with that name. Do you have this document?"

"Not here."

"Do you have any thoughts to its meaning?"

"I was hoping you might suggest something. This Havana connection between Renaldo and Cortez."

"Suggestive." Cruzat shrugged. "What else?"

"If Gambeau knows about this money, that could explain what it was he was searching for."

"But how would he? I have found no previous connection between Don Diego and Monsieur Gambeau."

"Other than the horses you mean?" Granger said.

"Horses?"

"Lt. Governor Leyba was here at the time. Don Diego bought a large number of horses from John Dodge, who was supposed to be Clark's quartermaster, horses he then lent to St. Louis for Monsieur Pourré's cavalry. Prior to that, Dodge had been dealing with Gambeau. That sale caused a rift between Gambeau and Cortez. They were competitors."

"That I did not know. How did you learn about this?"

"I found a receipt in Cortez's house and recently I asked Dodge about it."

Cruzat frowned. "It seems you have been poking into places you perhaps should not."

"He found it when we went there searching for his sergeant," Tayon said quickly.

Cruzat still looked dubious. "What became of these horses?"

"Gambeau owns them now," Tayon said. "He stabled them after the battle. From what I heard, when Don Diego returned, he presented him with a bill, and Don Diego signed the horses over to him."

Cruzat smiled. "Then, yes…other than the horses."

"You said there were three men involved in stealing this dowry," Granger said. "Do you know who the third one was and what became of him?"

"That name I was unable to obtain," Cruzat said. "I was given to understand that he is an aristocrat and under the protection of the governor. This is always a difficult situation."

"Vargas?" Granger suggested.

"As I said, not a name I know, even among the elite in Havana."

"No way to find out if he has had contact with any of the people here then?"

"I have found no way."

"Isn't Don Diego aristocracy?"

"Yes, but his family is not so powerful and the connection to the main branch not so close." Cruzat leaned forward. "So. What do you think?"

"A number of things," Granger said. "Firstly, the man you all call Don Diego is actually his brother. Everyone has remarked on how different he was when he returned. I think he was the one hiding out there, who Ham went back to find and found Gambeau instead. I think it's possible Gambeau was looking for that money. But…"

"But it still makes little sense," Tayon said. "Why kill an American soldier? What were they doing that Ham caught them at?"

"Exactly my problem," Cruzat said. "Like you, I suspect. I have pieces of a puzzle that make most of a picture, but not all, and I cannot afford to act on what I have. I need to know the rest. We can talk and imagine and concoct stories that make it all plausible, but we have no proof. Yesterday made proof even less likely."

Granger looked at him, nodding. "Because she accepted him."

"Yes. I thought, briefly—but no, she married him. Why would she do so if he were not Don Diego?"

"It has been years since they spoke face to face," Tayon said. "How could she be certain?"

"If she was not certain, why not wait a few days?" Cruzat shrugged. "You said a number of things?"

"Yes," Granger said. "Gambeau and the horses. He has no money. From what I understand, he never did, but Dodge allowed that he had been buying from him in coin. Where did he get it? Obviously, he had a sponsor. If true, then when Cortez outbid him, why didn't he simply go back to the sponsor for more money?"

"The benefactor did not have it?"

"Or Gambeau had been cheating him and couldn't ask for more without revealing that."

"I see. It would be evident in any case and Gambeau would be obligated. So you suspect someone else?"

"I'm fairly certain Gambeau went to Cortez's place, but not on his own initiative. He was acting on behalf of someone else."

"Jose Renaldo?"

"It bears consideration."

Cruzat sighed. "All speculation without proof. I have none. You have no answers." He stood. "I am grateful for you speaking candidly with me, señor. Do me the courtesy, should you find your answers, tell me, especially before doing anything about them. I am sympathetic. But I will not tolerate precipitate actions that will disrupt the harmony of my village."

"I'll try, sir. Thank you for your candor."

"That was remarkable," Tayon said as they walked toward his house. Night was coming quickly, stars already scattered overhead.

"He wants me to solve his puzzle for him," Granger said.

"Why?"

"Because it might cause him problems later if it's not solved."

"But why you?"

"Because I'm an outsider. If anything goes wrong, it won't be laid at his feet."

"Clever. I always suspected Cruzat of possessing a streak of deviousness."

"He was lieutenant governor before Leyba, wasn't he?"

"He was. There were disputes. There always are, but he was recalled. Leyba unfortunately was even more disliked, but then he died in office. Lt. Cartabona filled the role until a new man was sent from New Orleans. Cruzat."

"He said something about difficulties that Renaldo helped him with?"

"His family was taken hostage by river pirates on their way here to join him. Not for very long, the ransom was paid and they were released."

"Renaldo gave him the money?"

"Some certainly. I always suspected, but he never said. So. What will you do now?"

"Talk to Renaldo."

Jose Renaldo opened his door. He frowned at Granger and Tayon, but silently stood aside and waved them in.

"Señors," he said as he closed the door. "I would ask to what I owed this honor, but I think I know. May I offer you wine?"

"We just came from Don Diego's," Tayon said. "You were missed."

"Of course I was." He crossed the candlelit room to a small table that held a silver tray with a decanter and glasses. "You have also just come from Cruzat." He poured them glasses and handed them over. "So what questions have you come to ask that I will not answer?"

Granger felt his anger stir and decided not to fence. "The third man. Who was it?"

Renaldo hesitated as he started to refill his own glass. "I have no idea to what man you refer."

"The dowry, the third man. Atilio. Havana."

Renaldo smiled. "Obviously you know everything. You need nothing from me."

"Who is de la Vargas?"

Renaldo frowned, surprise in his eyes. "Who?"

"You don't know?"

Renaldo sighed. "This grows tiresome. You're groping in the dark for something you can't understand. Leave."

Granger took a step toward him. Tayon's hand on his arm stopped him.

"I need to know why my friend died," Granger said.

"Is that all?" Renaldo said. "You haven't understood it yet? He was where he should not have been. What more is there to understand?"

"Why did Gambeau kill him?"

Renaldo's eyes widened. "Ah. But how do you know it was Gambeau? As far as I can tell, it was a raid by Indians. But I cannot answer you because I don't know. I have no idea if or how Gambeau might be involved. I can surmise, but then so can you. And a surmise is only that—without weight."

"What was Gambeau looking for?"

Renaldo shrugged.

"How," Granger tried once more, "did Gambeau know about the dowry?"

"How could I possibly know that?"

"That's what Gambeau was searching for."

"Was it?"

"It's possible Gambeau killed your friend, too."

Now Renaldo's mask of polite attention slipped. "I have no idea what you mean."

"We both know that man out there, married to Diego's fiancée, is not Diego. He's Atilio. Everybody in St. Louis knows he's not the man they once knew, that he's someone else. He's Diego's twin. Which means Diego is probably lying somewhere dead and Gambeau killed him."

"Do you have any proof of this?"

"No. But you do. You know."

Renaldo sighed. "I continue to have no idea what you mean. There is certainly no proof. So I think you should leave now."

He turned his back to Granger. Granger felt his restraint give way and he advanced on Renaldo.

Renaldo spun around, extending his arm. Tayon hissed and Granger stopped at the glimmer of steel. A knife-point hovered inches from his throat.

"If you persist," Renaldo said, "then you will invite death. You are ignorant and that ignorance will get you killed."

"Then enlighten me."

"No. That could get someone else killed."

"Eliana?" When Renaldo did not react, Granger stepped back. "Martine?"

Granger saw the change in Renaldo's expression, almost imperceptible. The knife wavered.

"What does Martine have to do with this?" Granger asked.

"Nothing," Renaldo said. "And it should stay that way. Keep away from her, señor. You cannot protect her."

"And you can?"

"Better than you." He looked to the right. "Tayon, take your friend home. Then try to convince him to leave St. Louis."

Tayon took Granger's arm and tugged him toward the door.

Outside, walking back toward Tayon's house, Granger tried to understand the connections. He was embarrassed, like a boy who had given too much away. Just as they reached the gate of Tayon's house he remembered, years back, Étienne telling him that they had come up the Mississippi in Cortez's company, on the same boat.

"They were connected," he said aloud. "Back then, they were associated. But that was only coincidence. Wasn't it?"

"Leave it for tonight, *mon ami*," Tayon said. "Perhaps he is right. Perhaps digging too deeply will only shed more blood. And not the blood you expect."

But Granger's imagination would not stop. He sat before Tayon's fire, glass in hand, sifting everything he knew, everything he guessed. He kept returning to earlier, finding Martine upstairs in Cortez's house, searching.

Searching for what?

Perhaps Étienne knew. Perhaps something passed between Cortez and him and now Renaldo believed Martine knew what it was. Or where it was.

Nineteen

THE GATE OF HIS new house stood ajar, and the front door was wide open. He stepped into the main room, pausing while his eyes adjusted. The hearth was a gray-black hole in the wall. A single rush-seated chair stood to one side of it. The only light came from the open door, all the windows shuttered. Granger unlatched the shutters and opened them, letting mid-morning sunshine flood in.

He drifted through the house. The furniture in the room he had used the first time he had been here was all that remained. Martine had left the bed, the bureau, the stand with the water bowl and pitcher.

She had also left the enormous iron stove in the kitchen. He put a hand on its now-cold surface. He wondered if she wanted it, having left it only because it would be difficult to move. The cupboards contained nothing. A butter churn stood outside the rear door, some curds clinging to the sides and bottom.

The shed in back contained a few more chairs and a small table. A stack of firewood stood alongside the shed. There was a large section of a tree stump where the faggots had been split, but no axe.

Mark W. Tiedemann

In the shop the fire pit was cold. Tools hung from rafters, lay on workbenches, along with several stocks in various stages of completion. There were brass fittings, iron pieces, a stack of barrels, and other things Granger could not identify. He needed to take an inventory and decide what to keep. He could doubtless sell a lot of this to one of the gunsmiths.

A strongbox sat on one of the workbenches with a note. *These are all the papers pertaining to the property. Martine.* His breath shuddered; he had never owned anything like this. Elation churned with trepidation.

Granger raised the lock and opened the box. Stacks of documents filled a bit more than half of it. He leafed through them—receipts, notes of credit, IOUs, a title— until he found one that seemed out-of-place. He tugged it free. The paper was thick, larger than most of the others, and was fixed by a large official seal at the bottom. It was in Spanish, which he still could not read, but the title, in a florid script, read *Declaración jurada.* His scalp tingled as he skimmed the text and found two names—Atilio Juan de Cortez and Jose Pasqual Renaldo.

He closed the strongbox and carried it into the room where he had spent one night years ago. He set the box on the bed and folded the document in his hand. Not sure where to keep it, he tucked it into the inside of his coat. He took deep breaths, convinced he had found something that would answer most of his questions. *I should give this to Cruzat,* he thought. *Or wait to see what else transpires…*

He wandered the house. He noticed patches on the walls where pictures or samplers had hung. In the main bedroom, a crucifix still marked the wall against which the bed had stood. He wondered why she had not taken it—it was, he thought, her brother's. He took it down and carried it out to the shed, and returned with the table, which he placed in the parlor, before the hearth. He then searched for a broom to start cleaning out the fireplace. He found one in the shop, though he had to beat it against a post to shake out the charcoal and grit.

When he returned to the parlor, he heard someone calling. "Mister Granger?"

Standing in his door was a woman, a sack in one hand and a broom resting over her left shoulder like a musket in the other. Behind her were two Negroes and a pair of white girls who by appearance were her daughters. She looked familiar. Her accent was distinctly American.

Then he remembered—Emily, the other woman working for the doctor with Martine, back when they had brought Taylor in. Granger invited them in and immediately followed a few more women, including Cécile Tayon, who carried a large wicker basket filled with small bags, vegetables, and other items.

"*Bon jour*," she greeted him. "We have come to help."

Within half an hour, the house was filled with neighbors, cleaning, preparing food, supplying a few pieces of furniture, most of it obviously well-used and sometimes repaired, and toward noon Granger found himself hosting another party.

Russell showed up mid-afternoon with Neptune and a charette filled with Granger's personal belongings brought from across the river. "Looks like you're welcome here," he said.

"I didn't expect this," Granger said.

"Seems you've been accepted by the right people. Does it bother you changing countries?"

"Not as much as I thought it might. What about you?"

"I'm still an American."

"I mean—"

Russell waved a hand. "Lots of Americans have been doing this for years, everybody knows it don't mean much. Besides, you have something you need to do. You do what you have to. When it's done, well." Russell shook his head. "I'm not troubled. You're still the same man." Russell watched the women, girls, and the slaves moving through the house, cleaning, arranging furniture.

"By the way," Granger said, indicating the American woman.

"Oh, yeah," Russell said. "That's Emily Chandler. She's American, her husband died during *l'Année du Coup*, and she owns a good spread of land south of here along the Meramec River. She has five daughters and at least three of them are near marrying age. She ordered one of those stoves last month. I sent off to Philadelphia for it. Should have it by spring."

"I suppose someone's going to have to put it in for her."

Russell shrugged, a slight smile tugging the corners of his mouth, and to Granger's dismay red crept up his neck into his face.

"Seems like a lot of trouble to go to for a stove," Granger said.

"Maybe."

"Oh, I have a favor to ask." He led Russell into the shop. He handed him the document he had found. "Take this back across the river with you and put it somewhere safe."

Russell unfolded it and frowned. "Spanish. Looks legal."

Granger indicated the names. "I don't know what it is yet, but I want to keep it secret for now. It was in with the papers for Étienne's business."

Russell nodded as he refolded it and slipped it inside his vest. "I'll see to it."

For a few moments Granger stared at Russell, struck by his generosity. Since he had arrived, Russell had helped without question. Tayon as well.

Emily and Cécile directed the work until things were nearly done, at which point ale appeared and discipline, little as there appeared to be, broke down. Granger found himself in awkward conversations with non-English-speaking people, translations going through either Russell, Cécile, or Emily, whichever of them was nearest when need arose, though he understood more and more.

Toward evening, people left until only Emily and Cécile remained, along with Emily's two daughters and slaves. The house seemed to glow now from a score of candles, the fireplace, and one lantern hung on a peg by the door. Granger now possessed a good-sized table, numerous chairs of various shapes, a trunk, two small cabinets, pillows, sheets, and a partially-stocked larder, as well as an assortment of china and cutlery. He sat with the women before the hearth, a glass of sherry in hand. He could not remember who had brought that, but he silently toasted them for their generosity.

Emily Chandler wandered the house and grounds, finding little things to do, and Granger wondered about that until he realized she was waiting for Russell to come back. But the sky was already darkening and Granger knew Russell would not be back tonight. Cécile watched her for a time with an amused moue, but finally suggested that it was time to leave Granger to himself. It had been a long day and there would be time later for more celebrations. Granger mouthed a silent "Thank you" to her and watched Emily gather up her daughters and slaves and follow Cécile back to the Tayon house.

Over the next few days, he worked with Russell and Neptune to haul across the river a large amount of merchandise for his intended store. He was glad now he had stocked himself as well as he had with Monongahela Rye because every day he played host to an impromptu party as various men came to see him.

He knew most of them already, had laid the groundwork for a relationship with them, but now it was more formal. Real in a way that it had not been. A string of afternoons and evenings spent shoring up future relations with St. Louis's merchants accompanied the initial outfitting of his establishment. By the end of the week, he had orders, made a few sales, and Neptune had moved his possibles into the shed in back.

All in all, Granger felt it had been a good week.

Twenty

HE PLACED HAM'S rifle on the mounts above the hearth and propped his own against the wall by the bedstead. From a pack he took a pair of pistols and placed one by the pillow. The last of the guests had left a couple hours earlier. Neptune had gone back across the river with Russell to help with what inventory remained, so Granger was alone in his new house.

Back in the parlor, he lit two candles and opened his portable desk. He took out the letters and the translations and spread them out. He needed to talk to Martine. He knew it had been unlikely that she would show up today, but he was still disappointed.

After making sure the pitcher by the bowl on the stand contained water, he undressed, cleaned his teeth, and snuffed the candle.

A dreamless time passed in the close darkness. The imminence of deep sleep pressed against him, banished abruptly by a sound. His pulse quickened instantly as his hand closed on the butt of the pistol.

He glanced at the window, a deep blue floating against black, and listened. Slowly, he sat up, waiting. He decided

Mark W. Tiedemann

finally that he had heard nothing and began to lay back
down when he heard another sound, this time clearly
within the house.

He slid out of bed and crept to the bedroom door.

"Lieutenant."

His heart rammed against his ribs. "Martine...?"

He set the pistol on the bureau and stepped into the
hallway. He made out the shape of the doorway by the dull
glow from the embers in the hearth, and against that frame
a woman's outline

"Martine...let me light a candle—"

"No! Please."

The shape came toward him. He felt something light
scrape across his face, then a hand on his chest. He took it
and squeezed, pulled her against him. His lips brushed her
forehead, nose, finally found her mouth. She pressed him
back and strained against him, as if trying to mold herself
to him. His back against the door jamb, he held her, hands
running across her back, down her sides, her own hands on
his chest, fingernails scraping. He was afraid to stop kissing
her, that she would back away, even though she opened her
mouth and thrust her own tongue against his. When they
broke the kiss, both of them exhaled loudly, the sounds low
and thick. He found the buttons on her bodice and began
undoing them.

She pushed away then, and stepped out of reach, until
the wall behind her stopped her. They breathed heavily,
filling the space with a dense urgency. She panted as if she
had been running. He did not move. The air seemed filled
with pulse. With effort, he waited.

"Lieutenant..." she said finally, a whisper.

"Granger. Please. Martine."

She laughed. "I am shameless. I am staying with the Gratiots until Diego and Eliana are ready for me. I crept from their house and came here...no one knows, I think."

"Why?"

"I need...we must talk."

He saw her retreat back to the parlor, a shadow against shadow. After a few moments, he recovered some control and followed.

The hearth glowed a low, dull orange, enough light to see that she sat in one of the chairs by it. But it gave little warmth now, and Granger shivered—he wore only leggings. He considered fetching blankets, but he did not want to leave her presence. He took the chair opposite.

"I can offer you some sherry or whiskey—"

"Nothing, thank you."

They sat in silence for a time. She sat stiffly, gazing into the embers, hands folded in her lap. He leaned forward as she turned toward him.

"What were you looking for?" they asked simultaneously.

Startled, they gaped at one another, and then laughed.

"At Don Diego's—" he said.

"Upstairs...I almost screamed when you came in—"

"—thought no one would be there—"

They stopped and sat back, watching each other.

"Why did you do this?" she asked suddenly, waving a hand at their surroundings.

He almost gave a glib answer—it became available, an opportunity he could not pass up—but caught himself. "I wanted a reason to stay," he said. "I wanted—"

"You wanted?"

"I told you what I wanted. I don't speak French well enough. Maybe if I did, you'd understand me. I want you."

"I see."

He waited. When she said nothing more, anger rushed through him.

"You see what? I thought—I hoped—to have a very different reception from you, but you've been acting as if nothing happened."

"Nothing did."

"Are you so accustomed to fucking strangers that you consider that nothing?"

She frowned. "We all fuck strangers, Lieutenant, no matter how well we think we know them. But no, to be as honest as I can, I am not accustomed to doing what I did. You were the only other man besides Étienne I had done that with up till then. I had reasons for doing it. You did not know them. I used you. For that, I beg your forgiveness. But forgive me also if I doubt your sincerity. Have there been no other women in your life since? Three years is a long time."

He laughed. Her language startled him almost as much as her candor. "Is this deliberate? Are you really so ignorant of your own consequence? You changed everything!"

"I don't understand."

"Maybe because you were the first. I don't know. But I left here altered."

"Because of me."

"Yes."

"Not because your friend died here?"

"Had he died anywhere, it would have hurt the same. Even the manner of his death. It enraged me, yes, but I would have gone on, crippled perhaps, affected, but the same man. Ham's death only made life harder, it didn't change me. But you...yes, you made me different."

"I'm sorry."

"Why?"

"You might be somewhere else now, living the life you wanted."

"No, I wouldn't."

She was silent for a time. "I'm fond of this house. It was a good home. I was sorry to lose it. If I had born Étienne a son, I would not have. But it proved not to be possible."

"You mean you and he didn't—"

"Oh, no." She laughed. "Étienne and I, we were insatiable together. But I never conceived. What I did with you was in desperation. He was so much older than me, I thought perhaps... When I say nothing happened, I mean that I did not get a child."

Everything shifted. Granger felt foolish and angry, but very quickly sympathy took their place. All his assumptions broke down. *I truly did not understand.*

"So...it was not me..."

"You are a handsome man, Lieutenant, but not that handsome. In time, perhaps, I might find more about you. But you know nothing about me."

"I know enough."

She shook her head. "Despite what you say, you came back because of your friend. Everyone knows. They wait to see what you will do."

"I won't deny it. But that was not the whole of it. How do I make you believe me?"

"You are making a home here. Anything you do out of revenge..."

Granger had indulged that conversation with himself often and had no desire to have it with Martine. He waited.

"Now I must be truthful with you," she said. "The day you came here, the day you returned, I was living in a kind of dream. Étienne was gone. I was very lonely and very angry. Why had he died? Why had I been left this way? And Jose had been around often enough that even in my grief I knew what he wanted. I was very frightened. I could have easily taken your arrival as salvation, but I am not a weak woman. I have never accepted that I have no strength, that I have no right to be my own person. I resented you tempting me to betray the independence I had been struggling to build inside. No matter who would take Étienne's place, it had to be my choice, not something done out of anguish or desperation. *My choice*. To do that, I had to be my own, entirely. I was prepared to never see you again to achieve that."

"I—"

She held up a hand. "Then you did something I did not expect. You did not insist. Given what I did before, you may have imagined you had some right to me, that I had made you a promise. Other men would assume so. But you didn't. You accepted that things were as they were and you did not press. I could feel your disappointment, but you walked away. You accepted. You may never know how much that meant. Men assume their right to decide. Women have to fight for it and usually we lose.

"I thought you were acting in order to convince me to yield. But the more I considered it, the more I realized that you gave no hint of artifice. It came from yourself, from who you are. And I thought perhaps I should not discard you so lightly. I thought you could be worth the risk.

"So I ask you what you wish to do now? You have my house. You said I could live here."

"Yes."

"What would you have done if I had already been gone?"

"To be honest, the thought never occurred to me."

Martine laughed sharply and covered her mouth.

"You must finish this business over your friend. Whatever you do, it may be that you cannot live here after."

"That's possible."

"I treated you coldly when you first returned. I'm sorry."

"There's no reason to be. Now that I know."

"Knowing why can make such a difference?"

"Sometimes knowing why is the only thing that matters."

"You must explain that to me. Étienne's death...even if I knew why..."

Granger leaned forward. "We had a neighbor who wrote a lot of letters to the newspapers. Not just our local publication, but to Philadelphia, Boston, Richmond. He'd done this sort of thing most of his life, I think. He loved being a firebrand, stirring the pot, as he called it. He had a deft mind and I enjoyed his writings, even when I disagreed with him. He could argue both positions in some issues, equally well. He had a talent for infuriating people. After '76 things changed. He had always counseled caution in his letters, always, most of which were published anonymously— he signed them 'Aeneas Virgillus'—and even my father respected him, though as the conflict spread it became more difficult to abide some of his ideas. He wouldn't be swayed by popular opinions. He had his convictions and he stood by them. He thought independence was a bad idea, that we would be opening ourselves to invasion by other countries—like France. He didn't think we could defend ourselves long enough to really become a country all of our own, not without Britain to protect us. And he thought that Parliament had a point, even if they were handling things badly. They had fought a very expensive war, a good deal of it here, and the treasury was empty. His quibble with Parliament was over how they decided to tax us, not whether they should or could. In that he was in sympathy with many revolutionary firebrands. He drew the line at open rebellion. Many folks felt that way before Concord. After Concord, people began dividing into camps. One wanted to break with Parliament no matter what, the other wanted to make them pay attention to the original issue and reconcile. Our neighbor was of the latter opinion.

"One night, a mob dragged him out of his bed. Him and his wife. They coated him with hot tar and added goose feathers. His wife was made to watch. They threatened to cut off his member and made her beg for his life. They might have done worse, but his two sons came from their own homes and found them before much more happened. They were armed and had brought a couple of others. They found the abductors all in black face, some wearing petticoats, none of them willing to be recognized. Shots were fired, no one was killed, and our neighbor was rescued. Though removing tar and feathers is a painful thing and tends to strip away skin. A few nights later, our neighbor's house was burned down, as was one of his son's. Our neighbor's wife died in the fire.

"He left with the rest of his family soon after. My father told me later that one of the men in the mob—we all knew who they were for the most part, even though no one suggested bringing any of them before a justice; what good would it do?—bought the land for half its value. As far as I am concerned, we lost a good neighbor. He was a generous man with broad interests and a good collection of books, of which I often made use. His sons were fine company on hunts and were generally well-liked. He had a daughter I fancied, even though I never had the courage to tell her so. She's gone as well. Of course. His only crime was to see things a bit differently. He mistrusted popular opinion, which I've come to think is a good habit to cultivate.

"At the time, however, I had more sympathy with his persecutors. My blood was up, I was outraged by the British. I couldn't understand how someone could be tolerant of the oppression, could argue against the self-evident right of taking up arms. Like others, I thought he was someone to be scorned. I blamed the British for forcing us into mutually exclusive camps. It was a kind of madness. I wondered why he could not at the least keep his ideas to himself while brave men were fighting and dying for the cause. I did value the fact that he, too, was brave. He also had the courage of his convictions and expressed his own opinion. It would not have occurred to me to do what was done to him and his family. At least, at the time I didn't believe I would do something like that. But the men who had done it spoke in the same terms that I did, supporting the revolution. Only some of them did so for reasons other than justice."

"Still you fought for your revolution."

"I did. I thought, if we can make a place where something like that can never happen again, then it would all be worth it. By the end, though, I knew that wasn't possible. The best thing—the only thing—is to do what we can when opportunity arises to make justice possible. Build it daily. To do that, you have to know why. You have to understand. There are reasons and they must be revealed. If possible. Hidden truths can be as harmful as lies."

"So what is hidden here?"

He hesitated. "Do you really want to talk about that now?"

"We may not have another chance. Why not?"

"All right. What does Cortez have that Gambeau was looking for? That you were looking for?"

"Oh." She seemed surprised. "You know?"

"That there is something? Obviously. But what? Gambeau was in Cortez's house when Ham found him. There were others, Gambeau couldn't have overpowered Ham on his own. Whether he struck the blow himself or not, Gambeau is responsible."

"Then…?"

"I want to know why. Before I move against Gambeau I want to know what he was looking for. What's this all about?" When she remained still for long enough, Granger said, "Some kind of document, I imagine. That's what was searched."

"It—this is complicated. Yes, a document. A testament of some kind. Étienne knew, but I did not, only that it came from Havana."

"You never saw it?"

"No."

"Did you tell Cruzat?"

"No. Étienne said that it could not be used until another document came from Madrid."

"What could—? A pardon?"

"Étienne never told me. How could you know?"

"A reasoned conclusion. Don Diego's brother, Atilio." He wondered if he should tell her what Cruzat had told him. "Atilio was involved in some scandal in Havana. He was assumed dead in Mexico."

"But you think he is alive. That he is now married to Diego's bride?"

Granger sat back, gazing into the hearth. Elements came together in his mind smoothly—perhaps too smoothly. "A pardon might free him to act on the other matter. Diego may have requested it, of course, to clear his family name. And Eliana was bringing it with her. It may be that her family refused to permit her to marry Diego until the scandal was resolved. That's why it has taken so long for her to come."

"How could you know all this?"

"I'd rather not say now. Later, when it's finished."

Martine let out a long breath.

"So," Granger continued, "what does all this have to do with you and Étienne?"

"We met Diego on the journey up the Mississippi, coming here. He became friends with Étienne—that was never a hard thing to do—and Diego entrusted the document to him. He thought it would be safer if he not have it. He said he was concerned about misunderstandings."

"The argument Étienne had with Gambeau, then?"

"Was likely about that. I have no idea how Gambeau learned about it. He was already here when we arrived."

"So what were you looking for?"

"The document. It went missing some time after Étienne died. I thought perhaps Étienne had given it back just before, but Don Diego claims no. I'm not even certain he knows what I'm talking about."

"But you don't even know what it is." He felt a twinge of guilt keeping from her the fact of its discovery, that it was in his possession.

"I thought I would recognize it if I saw it. It must be something…official?" She made an exasperated noise. "I thought—if he does not have it, Gambeau may. But I don't know what to do in that instance."

"What good would it do Gambeau anyway?"

"I don't know."

"It wouldn't. But it might benefit someone else." Granger gazed into the hearth, turning his thoughts over.

"Do you believe some one else—"

"Renaldo."

"Oh."

It surprised him when she stood. "I should go," she said.

"Should you?"

"Do you wish me to stay?"

"Very much."

"Do you love me?" she asked.

"I want you. It's difficult to tell the difference sometimes."

She sighed and seemed to relax. She sat down again. "When I saw you at my door, my heart nearly broke again. After Étienne died, it took a long time to realize that I would survive. I couldn't imagine feeling the same way about anyone else, though I knew it was possible. I didn't love Étienne when I married him. Fond of him, yes. Marriage is not based on love. There's too much else to consider. But I was his second wife and he had learned from his first how to be kind and considerate and how to make me feel welcome. I think that is when I began to love him, when I understood that I was welcome in his life. I wanted to give that back to him. It became love. Wanting is not sufficient, but you are right, it is difficult to see that. The other takes time. Do you have the patience for that?"

"I'd like a chance to find out."

"And what about your friend? Can you set it aside and go on no matter what you discover?"

"I can't answer that."

"It is not a fair question. I will stay in St. Louis until you can say, one way or the other."

"I—the question is, will you stay here, tonight."

"And the answer is, no. I cannot."

Granger's disappointment was like a folding up inside. "I see. I understand."

"But I can stay for a little while."

He looked at her sharply. She came up to him and held out a hand.

"I think, though," she said, "we can use something other than a chair."

They engaged in a wordless dialogue, sentences made by touch, feverish exchanges of unpunctuated intent. He felt it like fear, a deep-body knowledge, dangerous and inescapable. He marveled at the explosive exhalations that took her, the panic that enveloped them rushing toward climax. He drank her in and she feasted on him. They laughed and moaned and made sounds that were both and neither. He disappeared within her and was happy to be so lost; she found him again and delighted in her discovery.

In between, he asked "Why tonight?"

She traced his ear with her tongue and said, "Two kisses...I couldn't bear not having the rest."

Sweat pooled between her breasts and around her navel. He drank it and she trembled and they took each other again.

Somehow, she stirred before dawn. He awoke slowly as she gathered her clothes.

"Stay," he said.

She shook her head. "Not yet."

He considered arguing, but knew it would not change her mind. "Come back, then."

"When I can." She buttoned her bodice. She leaned over him and kissed him. He started to pull her back into bed, but she broke loose, laughing. "Go back to sleep. You have much to dream about now."

"Hardly a substitute for reality."

"Anticipate, then. I must go."

"Martine." She paused. He said, "Thank you."

She drew on her cloak, touched his lips with her fingertips, and left.

Dear Gideon,

I hope this finds you well. Please pass my good wishes on to the family when you see them. I trust your path is clear and your way unencumbered. It is frustrating in the extreme to know something and to be unable to act upon it. The enigma of Ham's death is now clear to me and yet there is nothing I can do. I have taken my knowledge to the Spanish lieutenant governor, we have gone over the matter at some length, and he then thanked me and bade me keep it to myself. I wonder, is it that I'm an American and he has no interest in upsetting residents of longer standing? Or is he playing at something else? In the meantime, I see Gambeau three, sometimes four times weekly and can say nothing without creating a situation that may prove hostile to my own purpose. Likewise with Renaldo, who I am convinced is behind it all, but I cannot say how as he continues to appear as Cortez's friend.

As I now conceive it, what must have happened is this: before the battle, Gambeau, being in charge of the largest stable in the village and in a position to watch the comings and goings of people into and out of St. Louis, took his opportunity to invade Don Diego's home after seeing Ham and Tayon return with all of Cortez's slaves. He would have had several hours, in his es-

timation, to search the place for any document in question. Or the gold. He went there with a confederate or two and began the search. Ham, in the meantime, had been informed that someone was still hiding on Cortez's property and took it upon himself to go back to find him. He came upon Gambeau and his partner (I suspect Chavreaux) in the midst of their ransack and was somehow overpowered and killed. Panicked, Gambeau abandoned his search and returned to St. Louis. A few days after the battle, I, Tayon, and two of Clark's men went there to find Ham.

The rivalry between Gambeau and Cortez is plain. Cortez undercut him in the local horse trade through an advantageous purchase from Dodge. Added to this is the matter of Eliana's arrival with what I believe now to be a pardon for Don Diego's brother, Atilio. All of this springs from events in Havana many years ago. I suspect Don Diego has been waiting for that matter to be cleared up before exercising his claims, so there can be no possible barrier to dealing with whatever may be clouding his future. But if she did bring such a pardon, why has Cortez not acted? Perhaps he doesn't know where the original document is, either. Diego knew, but if this is Atilio...

This is incomplete, obviously. The matter of who shot Taylor is unresolved as is the question of who carried Ham's body into the woods to bury. Not Gambeau, certainly! But these things float, loosely connected to the events, and I am unable as yet to resolve them into a coherent picture.

Winter approaches. We have already had snow. Martine has returned to Don Diego's house as companion to Eliana. Russell and I begin to grow the store. It would be easy to slip into the routines of life here and let all this pass.

Most sincerely and with affection,
Granger

Twenty-one

SNOW LAY SIX INCHES deep in the streets when Russell brought the last charette filled with Granger's merchandise up to his new shop. Flakes drifted, windblown, and the air just above the rooftops roiled with chimney smoke.

Granger had received a note from Martine.

Lieutenant.

> *You may find this of interest. Don Diego travels south once a month, usually with Salvatore. They left again this morning. They are gone between three and four days, long enough for a journey to Ste Genevieve. Perhaps this is important?*

Yours, Martine

Granger felt a skip in his thoughts at that word, "yours." He had seen her rarely since that night she had come to him, always in company with Eliana de Cortez, sometimes also accompanied by Jose Renaldo, who spent at least a day a week out there. Granger did not believe himself a jealous man, but he experienced a raw resentment at the thought of Renaldo paying court to Martine.

The next morning Neptune took him to meet an Osage named Kashesegra. Three days' journey southwest brought them to an encampment where, in halting French, Granger had learned that, yes, a white man had passed through Osage lands almost four years ago, followed a few days later by an Indian of an unknown tribe who had managed to elude capture. The white man had been ragged, face thick with beard, thin, and with the unpredictable appearance of the touched, so the Osage left him alone. He had been heading for St. Louis anyway. The Indian following him was a different matter and it bothered Kashesegra still that he had evaded them. Granger had learned little new. The meeting only confirmed what he had already suspected. But Neptune thought it had been a good encounter, that in future Granger might trade with Kashesegra and that friends among the Osage were never a bad thing to have.

Leaving, they headed southeast, arriving after a couple more days at the village of Ste. Genevieve. Granger found a scattered collection of dwellings less organized than St. Louis, older, and if possible more homey. There was no stockade around the village and the streets were wider and there seemed to be fewer people out. Granger saw a similar expanse of cultivated land sprawling west from the town, common fields.

Granger spent a few days talking to the habitants, introducing himself as a new merchant with good con-nections for American goods, while Neptune went off on separate inquiries among other parts of the community. When they left, heading north along the *corde du roi* road to St. Louis, Granger had acquired a few more customers.

"Some know Don Diego," Neptune said as they rode. "He does come down here regularly. Stops in with the garrison commander, visits a couple of others. But always stays about two miles just southwest of town at a small holding owned by a man named Serrifet."

They rode in silence for a time. "Do you think it might be worth a look?" Granger said finally.

They turned off the road, dismounted, and led their horses through the thick woodland, circling back to the outskirts of Ste. Genevieve. It took several hours and it was nearly dark by the time they reached the edge of Monsieur Serrifet's property.

They crouched within the tree line, watching the sprawling house, candle light flickering now in the windows. In the encumbering dusk, it looked more like something grown than built. There was a pen off to the right containing a few hogs, an outbuilding, a lean-to, and a ragged fence around acreage now fallow for the winter.

A door opened and a man emerged with a pan, which he emptied into a garden patch on the left side of the house. He paused at the door and for a moment Granger wondered if he could see them. But then he went inside, banging the door shut.

"I don't see any dogs," Neptune said.

"Hmm."

"What do you think is here?"

"Not what. Who?"

Neptune lapsed into silence at that. Granger waited another hour before slipping from cover and making his way, hunched low, across the open ground to the house. At each step he expected to hear the dog or dogs he had been unable to locate, but nothing happened. He reached the porch without alarm.

Holding his rifle in one hand, he reached up to a post and stepped onto the porch. He put his weight down carefully. The boards did not creak. He mounted the porch and crossed to the wall, then made his way from window to window.

Most were covered in hide that had been scraped thin and oiled to a translucency that, in places, allowed a view in. Others had glass panes, which gave him a clear though slightly distorted view.

He came finally to a small room with a lantern on a table, a cot, a chair, and a crucifix on the wall. A figure occupied the chair. It was difficult to tell through the oiled skin, but a blanket covered the man's legs and he sat crookedly, head propped by a pillow. He did not move.

Granger ducked away from the window and squatted, back to the wall. *Could it be this simple?* he wondered. He searched the darkness surrounding the house and tried to assess the chances that no one else would have guessed in a year-and-a-half. But he had seen unlikelier things during the war, opportunities unrecognized, gambles unmade, what should have been obvious overlooked. As he considered it, he realized that he hadn't imagined this possibility.

The sound of a hammer drawn back sent a shock through him as he looked up at a man standing at the corner of the house now aiming a musket at him.

Granger braced for the shot. But another figure appeared behind the man, grabbed the musket barrel, pulled it away from Granger, and pressed a pistol barrel to the man's head.

"We ought to talk inside," Neptune said.

Monsieur Serrifet appeared to be ancient, his lean face a mask of fine lines, darkened by a life of hard work. A scattering of white hair clung to his skull. His mouth showed the indrawn look of lost teeth. But there the ravages of age ended. He was shorter than Granger, but he stood military-straight and his shoulders were still impressively broad. His hands were large and veined and powerful.

Just now, he also seemed very angry.

But his anger receded under Neptune's explanations, becoming finally embarrassment and suspicion. Granger followed the rapid French as best he could, but in essence Neptune explained to Monsieur Serrifet who Granger was and what they were trying to do. The old man asked a few questions, his eyes fixed on Granger, wary. Granger could not blame him. The circumstances did little to encourage trust.

"He's been caring for him for over three years," Neptune said. "When Don Diego returned, he asked that the care continue and that his presence remain a secret until he could come home on his own. He's been paid."

"What happened to him?" Granger asked, feeling he already knew.

"Beaten and left for dead."

"May we see him?"

Neptune relayed the request and Monsieur Serrifet answered quickly. "It would do no good," Neptune translated, "he recognizes no one, just sits. The only time he shows any presence is when he's read to."

"Is that a no?"

Neptune grinned. "No."

The old man led them to the small room. Granger stepped around Monsieur Serrifet to get a clear look at the broken man in the chair.

It was hard to tell. The right side of his face was a tangle of scars and distortion, the eye rolled up and showing on white, the corner of the mouth drooping under the trimmed mustache and beard. He could see now that the legs lay at an angle, even in the chair, and one hand was an immobile claw. The only obvious sign of identity was the dense dark red hair.

"Both legs had been broken," Neptune said as Monsieur Serrifet spoke, "the right arm above the elbow and the hand crushed. He had been savagely beaten, to the face as you see, and there are scars from a knife over his chest and stomach. Finally, there's a bullet wound above the heart. They missed evidently, intending to kill him." Neptune sucked air between his teeth. "How he managed to stay alive is…"

Granger stepped in front of the man. "Which one?"

Neptune shook his head.

Granger squatted. "Don Diego?" Nothing. "Atilio?" He reached toward the man.

"Non!"

Granger glanced back at Monsieur Serrifet, who glared at him. Granger withdrew his hand.

"I know who did this. I intend to find some justice, if possible. But it would be a great boon to me if you could tell me what happened."

Again, nothing. Granger, disappointed, straightened. He started to turn away.

The man in the chair grunted. Granger looked down and saw his unbroken hand slowly reaching toward Granger.

His single good eye was fixed on the rifle. Granger held it out for him and his fingers slid across the stock, lingered on the coin, then fell to his lap. The eye came up to Granger's face, moist now, and a tear broke loose to trail down his cheek.

"Mon dieu!"

Serrifet was leaning over the man then, patting his shoulder. But he continued to stare at Granger. More tears flowed, but Granger thought he now saw the beginnings of old rage emerging.

"Don Diego—Atilio?—and Salvatore brought him," Neptune continued to translate. "Right after the battle. Set him up. Salvatore stayed around, guarding. Monsieur Serrifet knew Diego Cortez from New Orleans, before the two of them came upriver. Soon after the brother returned, Salvatore disappeared, but the regular visits began. There's been money, supplies. This, however, is the first good sign he's seen."

"Has there been any trouble? Any sign that someone else has been coming around, looking for him?"

"Not that he knows. Monsieur Serrifet is a canny old warrior. He's from Quebec. He's been managing well. Till now. He's put out that we got around him."

"He nearly did for me."

Neptune passed that on and the old man nodded, chattering in French.

"He knows," Neptune said. "Says a year ago you'd be dead, but he's been feeling slow lately."

"I'm grateful," Granger said. "Did either Salvatore or Cortez leave anything else with him? Some papers?"

"You found some of his secrets, that doesn't make you welcome to the rest."

Granger laughed.

"What do you want to do?"

"I think it's time finally to have a long talk with the current Don Diego."

Twenty-two

WITH WINTER COMING, Granger came to an arrangement with Neptune. There was room for him to stay. In exchange, Neptune began building a wall to enclose the old smithy, which Granger intended to use as a store. Granger offered to pay as well, but Neptune put him off. "We can discuss that later," he said. "We'll see how this works out first." The wall was going up quickly.

"Should probably fetch another load of lumber," Russell said, studying the progress of converting the workshop into a store. "River will be icing up soon."

"Does it freeze over?"

"Often. There's this in between time, though, it's just full of floes and I can't cross with the ferry."

They carried the last crate of iron pots through the gate, into the still-drafty shop. Granger had built a modest fire in the pit, which cut the chill and gave a dull reddish-orange light.

"You figured a way to keep supplied yet?" Russell asked.

The question irritated Granger. A few weeks earlier word finally arrived from New Orleans about the conditions of the Treaty of Paris and the Spanish reaction had been predictably unpleasant. Spain insisted that England had no right to cede everything on the east side of the Mississippi to the United States, that the Spanish claim extended well into Illinois Country and down to the Ohio. Orders had come with the news to enforce an embargo on the river to prevent American commerce. Granger wondered what his chances of becoming a citizen here might have been had the official news arrived before he had purchased Martine's house.

Russell still came and went as he pleased, as did several other Cahokia locals, but newcomers, few as they were for the time being, were met with tense questions and a cold hesitance.

"I still haven't figured out how I'm going to get these people to actually pay for anything," Granger said.

"You mean with actual money? Well."

Both men laughed.

"*¿Hola? ¿Está usted abierto para el negocio?*"

Diego Cortez stood framed in the doorway to the shop, bulky in a heavy, fur-collared coat, grinning at them. Outside, past Cortez, two women waited with another man.

"Pardon?" Granger said.

"Wants to know if you're open for business," Neptune said from where he watched outside the unfinished wall.

Cortez looked at Neptune and nodded. "*Sí!* We have come to see what you offer."

"I'm not ready for customers yet," Granger said, "but since you've come all the way from your place, I'll be glad to show you what I have."

Cortez nodded again, mumbling "*Gracias, gracias,*" and stepped into the shop.

The two women followed him in. One was Eliana, the other Martine. Granger politely bowed to both of them. The second man was Renaldo.

Cortez turned, surveying the space. "This was a blacksmith's shop?"

"Yes. And a gunsmith."

"Ah, *sí*. Do you intend to continue that trade?"

"I'm not much with making things," Granger admitted. "There are already a couple of other gunsmiths in St. Louis. I'm considering paying them to finish what was left behind and selling it here."

"Monsieur Granger," Martine said. "Would you mind if I took señora Cortez inside? I would like her to see—"

Granger had not seen her in weeks and found himself reluctant to let her leave his presence so soon. "Of course. Be my guest. The door is open."

Cortez and Renaldo watched the two women walk toward the porch of the house. "I am understanding that you bought this place from Madame de Lautin."

"From her late husband's sons. Yes."

Renaldo frowned at him, but Cortez continued.

"She is a fine lady, Madame de Lautin. She and my Eliana have become friends. She is introducing Eliana to St. Louis, a task for which I am unsuited. We have taken her into our home until she decides whether to stay or return to New Orleans."

"That's very kind of you, señor."

"Ah." Cortez raised his hand dismissively.

"But you already knew that," Renaldo said.

Cortez walked along the stacked crates and boxes, one hand on his hip, gazing at them. "Pots...blankets...axes...

why have you come to St. Louis, señor Granger? Surely you could make your fortune more easily in your own country."

"It's a bit crowded back there, to be honest."

"But heading this way, no? So you think to be here when the rest arrive?"

"Seems like a worthy strategy to me."

Cortez laughed. "Spoken like a military man."

Cortez suddenly looked around, noticing Russell as if for the first time.

"I need to see to the cart," Russell said, touched the brim of his hat, and headed out.

A few moments later, Neptune resumed hammering planks into place.

"Are you considering expanding your trade to Ste. Genevieve?" Cortez asked.

Granger glanced at Renaldo. *Does he know?* "It's a possibility, certainly."

"There is not much there of interest," Cortez said. "But you asked to speak with me after returning. You wish my advice, no?"

"I'd be foolish not to listen to people who have lived here many years."

Cortez smiled grimly. "I'm not sure I can be counted as such."

"But you do know people there."

"A few. Old friends."

Renaldo looked from one to the other now, suspicion in his eyes. He sensed that something else was going on. Granger did not know how much to risk.

Suddenly, Cortez turned to Renaldo and spoke in rapid Spanish. Renaldo, smiling, replied, but Cortez became insistent. Clearly unwilling, Renaldo bowed to them both and walked out the gate.

"He had an errand," Cortez said, "which he interrupted when he saw us. I had not invited him along, but he insisted on accompanying us. So. What were you doing in Ste. Genevieve?"

Granger called up to Neptune, on the roof of the shop. "Can you see him?"

"He's heading down the street," Neptune said.

Granger turned to Cortez. "Don Diego, don't you think it's time to bring your brother home?"

Cortez's eyes flashed briefly before he turned away.

"You are meddling in things—"

"In things that what? Don't concern me? I assure you, these things do concern me. I lost a friend—a brother—because of these things. I want to know why and how Ham Inwood died."

"And you suspect me?"

"No, I do not. I suspect your enemies."

"We all have enemies."

"Not all of them are murderers."

Cortez drew a breath. "Death simplifies nothing. There are matters that must be resolved in good order or there is danger of losing everything. I have already lost so much. I implore you, señor, leave it alone until I am able to bring it all to a conclusion."

"Just what is it you're waiting for? Surely you have what you need. Unless I'm mistaken, your wife brought the final document."

"How do you know about that?"

"I didn't with certainty. Till now."

Cortez seemed to vacillate between anger and surrender. He sighed. "It is for nothing without my brother. It must all be done legally or it can be undone. I have to have my brother back. You have seen him, señor. He has been so since the injuries. I have been waiting for some sign that he is returning."

"And then what?"

"Then I can deal with my enemies."

"It started in Havana, didn't it?"

"I do not intend to talk about that. Not with you, not yet."

"Who is M. de la Vargas?"

Cortez's eyes flashed. "How—"

"Assume I know, never mind how. Who is he? The third man in the theft of the dowry?"

"This is impossible. No one—how can I trust you?"

"Because I don't give a damn about it, not in itself. I don't care what was done, only that it somehow led to my friend's death. Your enemies killed him and I want to know who they are."

Cortez looked away, pale and angry.

"Gambeau was never in Havana," Granger said. "How is he involved?"

Cortez snorted. "Did you know that before the battle he organized the others to withhold their horses from Leyba, attempting to thwart his intention to confront the British? I broke their hold. After that Gambeau was discredited and Leyba was vindicated."

"That must have caused some resentment."

"You saw the results."

"Why didn't you—"

"Seek revenge?" Cortez said, smiling sadly. "For what? Nothing had happened. That was all I could do, ignore Gambeau's treachery and bide our time. Until Eliana came and I could act openly. Legally. Taking revenge too soon would have undone everything else." Cortez looked at him. "Your demonstration with that remarkable rifle impressed me greatly."

"Thank you."

"It's a beautiful piece. I was much taken with it. I would like to buy it from you."

Granger stared at Cortez, stunned. "Buy it."

"*Sí*, buy it. How much do you ask? Such a fine rifle, I would pay—"

"It's not for sale, señor. I'm sorry."

Cortez laughed. "But you are a merchant. You sell things. I wish to buy."

"I sell things that are available to be sold. Not that."

"But—"

"I told you, it belonged to my best friend. The best friend I ever had."

"Your pardon, *amigo*. I meant no disrespect. But please. I heard of the effect it had upon my brother. He saw it and there was…recognition."

"I—" Granger felt a pang of shame. He remembered the look on the broken man's face, the tears. What would he give up to have Ham back? "My sympathies, sir. Let me consider it. Perhaps an exchange?"

Cortez nodded, disappointed. "Certainly."

"I want to know what happened. All of it."

Cortez was silent for a time. Finally, he shook his head. "It seems we both want more than we can give."

"Think on it," Granger said. "Will you be attending Pourré's party in a few days?"

"*Si*, my Eliana wishes it."

"Let me know then."

"And you will do the same?"

"I will do the same."

Cortez raised his right hand in a brief salute, pivoted, and left the shop. He called for his wife.

They gathered on the porch and talked, Eliana seeming to plead, eyes on Cortez, expectant and, Granger thought, a little fearful. Martine said something, and finally Cortez, grinning, nodded and made an exaggerated bow to both women. He saw Granger, then, and raised a hand, greeting and farewell, and walked out of the yard, into the street.

Martine approached Granger.

"You will be at Pourré's?" she asked.

"I will. I'll see you there?"

"Yes. Most certainly." Her eyes seemed to grow larger.

He started to reach out to her face. "I miss you."

She smiled. "My message was useful, it seems."

"Things are moving along. How are you getting on out there?"

"It's better than I'd hoped. I think I would rather be somewhere else, though."

Granger felt a surge of pleasure. "I will see you in a few days, then."

Eliana waited at the gate, watching them with something Granger thought very like envy.

Twenty-three

POURRÉ'S HOUSE was adjacent to the church, on the north side, and against the western edge of the village. The sound of dozens of voices enveloped Granger as Tayon, Cécile, and he entered. They shrugged out of their heavy coats and handed them to a servant girl. Tayon clapped his hands together and rubbed them as he surveyed the crowded main room. The air was warm from the fire in a huge hearth.

"Ah," Tayon said, tapping Granger's shoulder. "Come."

Granger followed his friend through the maze of people to a short, muscular man speaking to three others.

"*Mon ami*," Tayon interrupted. "I wish you to meet Beausoleil. This is my friend, Granger. He was here in *l'Année du Grand Coup*."

The stocky man bowed at the waist. "A pleasure, monsieur. Tayon has expressed his opinion of you. You are welcome in my home."

Granger bowed and then extended a hand. "Likewise, monsieur."

"Beausoleil. Everyone knows me as Beausoleil. We must sit together some time and talk about the battle."

"I would be very interested in that...Beausoleil. And you can tell me about your campaign to St. Joseph."

Beausoleil bobbed on his feet, grinning. "Excellent. Please, let me get you a glass of wine. Do you know Monsieur Labadie? Tayon, you must introduce him around."

As Beausoleil went to a table to get Granger a glass, Granger saw Martine entering, in company with Don Diego and Eliana. She saw him and for an instant she smiled. Then Eliana said something to her, she nodded, and took Eliana's cloak.

Don Diego removed his coat and surveyed the room, his left hand propped against the wide belt he wore as if holding the hilt of a sword. When his gaze came to Granger, he paused, bowed slightly, and continued on into the next room.

Eliana watched him, her face expressionless. Then another woman came up to her and she smiled.

"Marie Josephe," Tayon said. "Beausoleil's wife. Come. There are others I wish you to meet."

Tayon moved him around the party, and he found himself engaging in conversations with people, practicing his meager command of French, sometimes amusing those with whom he spoke. He heard a violin playing in another room.

He ended up in conversation with Gabriel Cerré, a man named Reveau, and Beausoleil about the battle. Beausoleil was interested in how the action had unfolded around Cahokia. His English was fair, but when it faltered, as Granger's French did, Cerré translated.

"I understand," Granger said finally, "you led the cavalry."

"Such as it was," Beausoleil laughed. "Thirty riders of various ability. Not a coward among them, you understand, but clumsiness is as fatal as anything. Only ten of them were professionals. If not for Diego de Cortez, it would have been worse. He is an exceptional horseman and worked with the militia for weeks prior."

"Don Diego trained the cavalry?"

"Superb rider. He was not, however, the only one to train. I did. Tayon is a fine horseman. I think, though, we would not have been so prepared without Don Diego."

"How much action did your cavalry see?"

Beausoleil rolled his eyes. "It was chaos. In truth, we lost sight of each other very quickly. We did not regroup till after. Some did not return till the next day."

Granger wanted to ask if that included Don Diego, but did not.

The talk drifted from the battle into horses, then finally into small gossip, and soon Granger wandered off. For another couple of hours Granger roamed through the party. Two men took up violins eventually and began playing in the parlor. They needed new strings by the sound of it and Granger made a mental note to see if he could order them from Philadelphia. He noticed then that the women present all wore dresses that were several years old, a few showing signs of fatal wear.

"Señor Granger?"

Don Diego stood nearby, hands clasped behind his back.

"Yes?" Granger said.

"I have been considering your proposal. I think, perhaps, an accommodation could be reached."

Mark W. Tiedemann

"The rifle is still not for sale."

"Of course not, and I understand that. However, you would have no objection to making it available?"

"No, not at all."

"Arrangements are being made. I will inform you of the time and then I would like you to do me the honor of a visit to my home."

"With the rifle."

"Exactly."

"Of course." He glanced around the room. "I don't see your friend Renaldo."

"He will be here later. He had some personal matters to which to attend." Cortez leaned in closer. "I must thank you, señor. I cannot tell you how much this means."

"I believe I can imagine."

Cortez gave a short bow and walked off.

"Good news?" Tayon asked, coming up beside him.

"Very," Granger said. He had told Tayon about the last week, including Cortez's visit to his shop. He wanted Tayon informed, but for some time he had kept a distance between them, thinking too close an affiliation at this point might work against them. "I think he's bringing his brother home."

Tayon's eyes widened. "Then we will finally find out what happened?"

"Let's hope."

Granger went to find another drink, and walked into the next room, where Eliana was talking with two men and a woman. Granger backed out of the room, reluctant now to say anything to Eliana.

"May I speak with you?" Martine walked along at his side.

"Of course."

"Not here. I've arranged to spend the night in the village, with Cécile Tayon. I will come to your house later."

She broke away then and Granger watched her disappear among the other guests.

The rest of the evening went by slowly, Granger wishing time to move faster so he could take his leave and go home. Conversations spilled around him, leaving little behind. The Widow Chandler asked about her stove, when she might expect it, Gratiot inquired about a shipment of grain, which was a euphemism for whiskey, and others asked about his future plans.

Finally, Tayon let him know that Cécile, Martine, and he were going home. Granger stayed another quarter hour before heading to his own place.

The gate was open when he arrived. A light flickered through the front door. Granger rushed inside. Tayon, Cécile, and Martine were leaning over someone sprawled on the floor amid overturned furniture. Tayon, holding a lantern, looked up.

"*Mon ami,* Neptune is injured."

Granger reached them and looked down at Neptune, blood covering his mouth and one eye beginning to swell. His chest heaved, but he was unconscious.

"What happened?"

Martine stood. "Tayon and Cécile escorted me here. We found the door open and Neptune like this."

Cécile wrung out a cloth in a pan of water and applied it to Neptune's eye.

Russell had gone back to Cahokia earlier in the day and had not returned. Granger looked around the rest of the room. A chair lay in splinters, the table below the window was on its side. In the uneven lamplight it looked chaotic. Granger went to the hearth and took another lantern from the hook above the mantle and saw the empty space above the hearth. After lighting the lantern, he stirred the embers in the fireplace and added a few pieces of wood. Once they caught and burned steadily, he threw on a heavier log.

Neptune moaned and tried to roll over. Granger carried the lantern down the hall to the bedroom where he located his pistol and a pillow and brought them back. He eased the pillow beneath Neptune's head.

Martine was in the kitchen, igniting the stove. She ladled more water into another pan and set it atop the platen.

"No one was here but Neptune when you arrived?"

"No. We almost went back to Beausoleil's house to get you, but Tayon thought it best to wait for you and not let anyone else know what had happened."

Neptune groaned loudly and Granger went to him. He was trying to sit up now, but one hand went to his left side and his face contorted in pain. Granger reached for him to help and Neptune's free hand closed on his upper arm with startling force. Tayon stepped to his other side and between them they moved Neptune back to the wall. Cécile put the pillow behind his head.

"Damn," Neptune hissed. He looked around owlishly. "Where is he?"

"Who?"

"Didn't see him. It was dark. Big." He started to lean forward and his face contorted. "Ribs." He rested for a few moments. "Came in, someone was here. He hit me with... something..."

Granger went out to the store and brought back a jug of rye, noting as he did that nothing there seemed disturbed. He held it for Neptune, who took a liberal swallow. Cécile lit more lanterns and the room began to glow brightly. Granger closed the door and began a search.

It did not take long to find the one thing that was missing. He returned to the parlor, where Tayon and Martine had Neptune sitting in a chair.

"Ham's rifle," he said. "He took Ham's rifle."

Twenty-four

LT. GOVERNOR CRUZAT was still awake and admitted them. He listened to Tayon describe what had happened, glancing repeatedly at Neptune, who leaned against the wall by the door, holding a rag up to his head.

"And the only thing missing is a rifle?" Cruzat asked Granger.

"As far as I can tell, señor. The parlor was in disarray, but I think that was from the fight with Neptune."

"So he knew what he wanted," Cruzat said. "And you suspect who?"

"Chavreaux," Granger said. "I would say Gambeau, but I doubt he could have overpowered Neptune."

"That's the truth," Neptune said.

"But likely he would have done it at Gambeau's command."

Cruzat nodded. "Then let us go see."

Within minutes, he had rousted his sergeant, a solid man named Blanco, and a pair of soldiers and the lot of them marched down the street to Gambeau's stable, Cruzat carrying a lantern before him. He banged on the doors until a light shown under the edge of it. Gambeau, face slack from sleep, looked out at them. Cruzat snapped at him and shoved past the baffled stable keeper. Then the two of them stood in the middle of the building arguing in rapid French and occasional Spanish while the soldiers searched.

"He is not here!" Gambeau bellowed finally, in English for Granger's benefit. He glared at Granger. "I don't know who you are looking for!" He looked away as he realized what he had just said.

"When was he last here?" Cruzat demanded.

"He left three days ago. I don't know for where. He is not beholden to me."

Cruzat continued on in French. Granger heard his name a couple of times, causing Gambeau to frown at him.

"How do you know it was Chavreaux?" Gambeau said. "You trust the word of this—"

Neptune stiffened.

"I'd be careful if I were you, monsieur," Granger said. "Neptune also is beholden to no one and has suffered injury."

"But not at my hand! Why do you assume it has to do with me?" He glared at Neptune. "And you, you have betrayed me! Didn't I give you a place to sleep, food from my table? Now you work for this foreigner!"

"You didn't give me a thing," Neptune said. "I worked for it."

"Bah! My question remains, why do you assume this has to do with me?"

"Because it does," Granger said. "I know what you did. I will prove it."

For an instant, Gambeau's outrage changed to fear. Then he shook his head. "You don't know, monsieur. You think you do, but you don't. That can be dangerous. Stay away from me."

The soldiers finished their search. Chavreaux was nowhere in the stables.

"Where does he sleep when he stays here?" Granger asked.

"We have already searched," Cruzat said. "He is not here."

"I know," Granger said. "I want to see his doss."

Cruzat spoke to one of the soldiers, who led Granger to a stall near the rear of the stable. He held a lantern up for Granger as he stepped into the space. An old blanket lay atop hay. To the left was a low shelf with a variety of possibles—beads, a leather pouch containing dried beef and corn, and, to Granger's surprise, an old French gorget—and below this a pack. Granger knelt and opened the flap, gesturing for the soldier to bring the light. From within he took the tarnished goblet with a double-band of braids etched near the rim, and brought it out to Cruzat.

"This came from Don Diego's house."

He caught the sudden fear in Gambeau's face, quickly masked, as Cruzat took the goblet from Granger.

"You are certain?"

"There's a set of them in his house. They were there three years ago."

Cruzat held it up to Gambeau. "What do you know about this?"

"It is Chavreaux's," Gambeau snapped. "He has had it for years. I don't know where he got it. The man is away from St. Louis six months of the year. Who knows who sold it to him?"

"You said he's been gone three days," Granger said. "Doesn't mean he'll be gone long. Otherwise why are all his belongings still here? If he intended to be gone for longer, he'd at least take his haversack. In fact, he's not gone at all, is he?"

Cruzat stepped closer to Gambeau. "Until something more compelling tells me otherwise, I will believe señor Granger. I will have order! I want Chavreaux. If you attempt to protect him, I will have you as well. Do you understand me?"

"I don't know where he is," Gambeau said sullenly.

"Do you understand me?"

Gambeau lowered his eyes and nodded.

"Very well. I expect you to inform me if you learn of his whereabouts."

He spun around and strode to the door, signaling for his men to follow.

Gambeau's eyes came up and fixed on Granger. "You have no business causing all this trouble."

"You were there. You saw what happened. Before I'm done, you'll tell me what happened. And why."

Gambeau spat on the ground.

As they headed north, back to their homes, Tayon said, "Don Francisco has been wanting a reason to banish Chavreaux for a long time. I think he would like to do the same to Gambeau—the man has been selling rum and brandy to Indians for years. This is as good a reason as any he has ever had."

Cruzat stopped adjacent to his residence and came up to Granger. "Señor, I regret the inconvenience you have suffered. I understand your interest, of course, but I must ask you now to withdraw from any action you may contemplate. This is now an official inquiry. This is in my hands, señor. I apologize on behalf of St. Louis and Spain for the injury done you and to your associates. But please, stay away from Gambeau and do nothing about Chavreaux. Let me deal with this. I do not need complications."

"Of course," Granger said.

Cruzat continued to hold his attention, eyes narrowed as if searching for any disingenuity or duplicity. Finally, he gave a sharp bow and went to his house.

"Mon ami," Tayon said.

"There's a problem," Granger said. "Cruzat may catch Chavreaux, might even find the rifle, but I might not learn anything more about what happened."

"You would do well to listen to Don Francisco. He's a decent man and more honest than most."

"Oh, I don't doubt that. But we have different aims."

At the gate of his house, he bade Tayon a good night.

He watched his friend head down the street toward his own home. For a moment he worried about Tayon. He had aligned himself with Granger and was in danger. It had never been his intention to put anyone else at risk, but he could see no way around it. What troubled him was that he had paid too little attention to what others might have at stake on his behalf. It crossed his mind to withdraw before anyone else was harmed, but it was probably too late. He owed these people a great deal. It humbled him to realize how much they cared for him to do these things. *I have to see it through. All of it.*

"What are you going to do?" Neptune asked.

Granger held up a hand until Tayon rounded a corner. Then: "Come."

Granger descended one street and headed back to Gambeau's stable. A light still shone around the edges of the doors.

"Go around back," Granger said. "Watch for anyone leaving."

Neptune vanished silently.

Granger waited only a short while and one of the doors opened. Gambeau slipped out and hurried down l'Rue de Granges, north. Granger let him gain some distance before following, keeping to the fences, the shadows.

Gambeau led him straight to Renaldo's house. Gambeau banged on the gate until, at last, it opened and he entered.

Satisfied that he finally had proof of the direct connection, he went back to get Neptune and the two returned to Granger's house. Neptune went inside the shop, and Granger entered the house.

Sitting before the fireplace, Martine looked up at him. In her lap was a sheaf of papers. The sight of them jarred Granger. She held them up.

"Where did you get these?"

Granger had not noticed that his portable desk had been thrown to the floor and the contents spilled.

"Cécile went home." Martine looked down at the letters, frowning. "We cleaned...these were in your..."

"Yes."

"They are Eliana's."

Granger said nothing.

"Explain," she said.

"I took them from Cortez's house the day we found Ham."

"Did you know what they were when you took them?"

"No. Only...later I told myself I wanted to know something about the man who lived there, but at the time..."

"They've been translated."

"I don't read Spanish."

Both of them spoke softly, as if afraid to disturb someone's sleep.

"What did you learn?" she asked.

"I learned that the man she wrote to is honorable, educated, adventurous...in fact, could not possibly be a murderer."

"But you learned much more about her than about him."

"I did, yes."

"Do you approve of what you learned?"

"I don't understand."

"Is she attractive to you? Do you want her?"

Granger's pulse quickened. "I want you."

"But you know more about her than me. Are you certain you know who you want?"

Granger's anger flared, but he bit back a sharp response. It was, after all, a fair question in the circumstances, and he knew he had confused the two of them in his imagination. He believed now, though, that he had them separated. He knew who and what he wanted. After a few moments, he said, "Yes."

Martine's expression softened. "I've been reading some of these. I can see this woman in Eliana, but not clearly. The one living here now is...subdued. Wounded, perhaps." She looked up. "Did you find the rifle?"

"No, it's…Chavreaux likely has it. Cruzat is looking for him."

She held up another piece of paper, the note with the Havana address and the initials. "And this?"

"I found that in Ham's patch box. I thought you might have put it there, but I think Étienne did."

She shook her head. "Étienne had a different document. I have no idea what became of it. I think he gave it back to Don Diego."

"That's what you were searching for?"

She nodded. "It was a full sheet, with a seal. It looked official. I did not read Spanish then, but I recall this address. I remembered it when you returned. I thought it might be important."

"It may be. Whoever was in that house and killed Ham was searching Don Diego's papers."

She looked suddenly sad. "You keep losing things here. Are you certain you want to stay? You may yet lose yourself."

"Or find myself."

She smiled faintly. She put the note back on the pile of letters. "I will not share you with a ghost. I will not share you with this, either. How many times have you read them? How many times have you imagined my face with her words? Which of us did you return for?"

She dropped the stack on the floor and stood.

"I will tell you this," she said, "neither of those people are the ones in those letters."

"What do you mean?"

"There is no confidence in either of them. They are strangers to each other. If those are from Eliana, then she is a stranger to herself." She picked the letters up again and shuffled through them. "Have you ever wondered what this passage means?" She bent closer to the candle and read.

> "*I dreamt of the chameleon last night, which surprised me. I had long ago stopped imagining him. All that remained were our games and the wicked memories of a chimeric youth. I wonder if you give any thought to what we did, the tricks played, the not knowing from one time to another. Remember when you dined with us and reported to your commandant for discipline over some minor infraction you did not commit? Not even I knew. Not knowing, that had appeal, there was risk, and it thrilled. I will miss us. You became one and I longed for the gamble.*'"

Granger remembered the passage. "It made no sense to me."

"Nor would it to me, but I have heard them talk of the chameleon. I'm still not certain, but it seems to me they mean someone real."

Granger's mind seemed to rush suddenly, associations caroming off each other, half-formed ideas finding the rest of themselves. "Atilio," he said. "She knew Atilio. And Diego."

Martine nodded.

"But there aren't any other mentions in any of them," he said, waving at the letters.

"You don't have them all, obviously. In all that time do you think this is all two lovers would write to each other?"

Granger's heart started pounding. *Yes,* he thought, *obviously these couldn't be the only ones, but they were all I had, the only ties to Cortez and the events leading to Ham's death and even with that I missed something...*

"She knows she married the wrong man," he said. "She knew and did it anyway."

Martine's eyebrows arched. "The wrong man? I'm not so sure. But what else could she do? Go back to Spain?" She dropped the letters onto Granger's desk. "We must be careful. It would be easy to cause damage that can never be put right."

"'We'?"

Martine did not look at him for several moments. When she did, her eyes glistened in the candlelight. "Reading these, I thought of you. I do not say I feel as she does, but there was nothing foreign in her sentiments."

"I want to be a river for you," he said.

"Yes."

Granger wanted to say something, encourage her, but nothing seemed adequate. He waited, wanting to hear a specific declaration from her, afraid she meant something else.

"I do not want to be hurt anymore," she said finally. "Is that possible and still let myself love? Permit trust?"

"I don't know," Granger said, wincing at his own candor. "But I don't think we have much choice about it."

She nodded. "I think Étienne knew," she said. "I think Diego told him." She stood.

She started for the door. Granger caught her halfway there.

"What you said, about losing everything. You've lost things here as well. But you stayed."

"I lost them here," she said. "If I'm going to find them, it won't be anywhere else." She leaned toward him and kissed his cheek. At the door, she said, "Finish this."

The door closed and Granger stood still, listening to the blood in his ears, and beyond that the answerless fear of having nearly lost everything.

Dear Gideon,

I have never been so inclined to surrender. The store is now open, I have customers and people treat me more and more as one of them, and yet I wake mornings wanting nothing so much as to return east and give all this up.

Chavreaux has disappeared. No one has seen him since the night of the robbery and there has been no further intrusion.

I feel closer than ever to understanding what happened to Ham and yet, upon examining my evidence, I'm just as far from knowing. It would be both liberating and frustrating if it should turn out that a band of marauders fell on Cortez's house when Ham was there. They would have long since vanished and I will never know.

But I do not—I cannot—believe that is the truth. The dead horses reek of revenge, petty revenge at that. I have no doubt that was Gambeau's doing. My observations of him tell me he is a vindictive, cunning coward. He probably killed those horses—the one Ham had ridden out there on, which was from Gambeau's own stable, to allay suspicions—because he wanted to hurt Cortez, the man who had taken valuable trade from him because he could pay in gold. And now there is this matter of a missing document.

Mark W. Tiedemann

But he did not kill Ham. That was Chavreaux, who was there as well. The goblet is proof, at least in my mind, and Chavreaux is of that segment of humankind capable of murder without conscience.

What is the document they sought? The revenge, the vandalism, I can see all that, but so much of it seems too complex for either of them. My only conclusion is that someone told them what to look for, sent them. I am equally certain that Jose Renaldo is behind it. But why? He was likely a partner with Atilio in the theft in Havana, yet nothing seems to connect him to it. Why was he not punished the way Atilio was and sent to Mexico or jailed? The third man Cruzat could not name, an aristocrat. A protector?

Which complicates this to another level. Hence my despair.

But they are guilty. I must, however, wait and allow Cruzat to conduct affairs in a lawful, authorized manner. He will have his men search for Chavreaux, but it is a vast area and he has few resources. I doubt he will find him.

In the meantime, I have other concerns. Martine will not come to me until I have finished with this. I do not blame her, but it galls me. Wanting to know what happened to Ham has driven me all this time and I thought nothing could be stronger, more imperative. I was wrong. But the difficulty is, if I never resolve the former, how will I be able to tell if I have finished it for myself?

There's no leaving, though. I have obligations. Despite the Spanish embargo, I'm taking orders for goods from Philadelphia. I have no idea how much of this will arrive or how long it will take. The habitants care little for the impasse between the United States and Spain and conduct their affairs as if none of that is an impediment.

Come spring I will decide. If I find no way to move forward on any of my hopes, I will give it up and come home. I would regret that, but I see no way to avoid it. I know what I believe but until someone comes forward to confirm or effectively refute my conclusions I cannot act on them nor can I be rid of them. Such would be an unendurable circumstance and I see no benefit to anyone in such a state.

Take care. I will write when I have something new to tell you.

Your brother,
Granger

Twenty-five

THE MISSISSIPPI FROZE over by the last week of January. Russell began making forays across the ice and by February he could bring shipments over on a sledge. In the second week of that month the stove Emily Chandler ordered arrived, which surprised Granger. He had expected it to be another month at least, maybe even after the first thaws. But the Ohio was not frozen and the stove had been hauled by wagon north from the confluence.

Along with it came another shipment of whiskey, fabrics, an assortment of iron and copper pots, and a selection of books, many in French. Post came as well, not only for Granger. Russell often brought the mail, and he also brought an assortment of newspapers from both Philadelphia and Boston.

It was 1784 now and Granger learned that British troops had finally left New York in November and that Annapolis had been named the new capital by Congress. General Washington resigned as commander of the Army in December. A small notice in a Boston paper revealed that Maryland had barred the further importation of Negro slaves. Loyalist estates were being broken up and sold to patriots. In France, two brothers had lofted something called a balloon into the air. There was a drawing of it, a huge bulbous contraption floating over the ground in Paris.

Russell hired a charette to deliver the stove and Neptune helped load it. Neptune had lost a couple of teeth in the assault the night of the burglary, but had otherwise recovered. Between the three of them they got the crate into the back of the two-wheeled cart, which groaned under the weight.

"That's a lot of iron," Russell commented, his breath coming out in great puffs of steam. "Any notion who's going to put this in for her?"

"I suppose," Grtanger said, "since I'm selling it to her, I should. But I thought you might like a chance to spend some time with her."

"Why would you think that?" As Granger continued staring at him a grin stretched his face. "Something to consider."

Granger looked from Russell to Neptune and back. Neptune was smiling and not looking at Russell. The swelling around his eye was almost gone now, but he still squinted it.

"Tell me," Granger said, "how well do you know the Widow Chandler?"

"I know her a little," Russell said. "Not well." He struggled not to smile. "Not well at all."

"I've done some work around her place," Neptune admitted. "But I know her hardly at all."

"So," Granger said, "is it one of her daughters has your attentions or the widow herself?" He glanced at Neptune who gave him a startled look. They both knew the object of Russell's interest.

Russell cleared his throat. "Her daughters are fine ladies, but are maybe a bit young."

"We'll remember you said that," Granger said.

"Good morning, señors."

Granger looked around to see Renaldo standing a few yards away. *"Buenos dias,"* he said, knowing as he did that he once more got the pronunciation wrong.

Renaldo came up and examined the stove. "I should perhaps consider one of these. Monsieur Cerré is most pleased with his. You are delivering this to someone?"

"The Widow Chandler," Russell said.

Renaldo grinned. "I had heard she purchased one."

"As did Lt. Governor Cruzat," Granger said. "I'm hoping their good opinion of it will cause others."

"Don Francisco's is already installed, is it not?"

"He's been using it for weeks now," Granger said.

"I am on my way to see him. I will ask him and if he is as pleased as Monsieur Cerré, I will come back."

"Gracias, señor." Granger thought he had done better that time. "I should be back in a few days."

Renaldo touched the brim of his hat and walked on.

"We might make a go of this after all," Russell said.

Granger fetched his haversack and his rifle in its leather sleeve. Russell inspected the harness on the pair of oxen, and then climbed up to the makeshift bench he had fitted to the front of the cart. Neptune went back inside the shop.

"A few days you say," Granger said as they left the southern gate.

"Unless she already has a hearth ready to receive it," Russell said, "a few days at least." He was quiet till they crossed over the stream. "I understand she sets a good table."

"Well. Perhaps she'll put us both up while we work on this and we'll be finished before any inconvenience occurs."

Russell's eyes slid toward him but he said nothing.

They left the main road just south of Louisburg and struck southwest. The snow threatened to trap them a couple of times, but the oxen managed to pull them free. The charette rattled as though it might collapse.

The road took a rightward turn around an enormous oak and dipped into a depression. Granger snapped his whip wishing for the oxen to hurry, to use the momentum to carry the charette up the other side, but one wheel thudded down, tilting it to the left, almost spilling Granger over the edge.

"Damn," Russell hissed as he jumped down. The snow came up to his knees. "We're only a mile or so from her house."

Granger looked around at the colorless woodland, white with black etched lines of trees and limbs. Everything felt closed in, the sound muffled.

"It doesn't look so bad," Russell called. "Some shoveling and a push on the back, the oxen should pull us free."

Granger stood up and turned to reach down for the shovels. A flash of light caught his attention and he looked up.

Something hard slapped his left shoulder. His vision tilted. He heard shouting. Russell must have been in trouble. Granger tried to see where he was, but as he turned again he lost his balance and fell.

Then the pain began, all across his left shoulder and upper arm. His skin there felt hot.

He heard another crack and he remembered then what it was. A shot. He had forgotten how strange they sounded in winter, with snow so deep and the air so cold, distant and near at the same time, more like something breaking than an explosion. He tried to stand, but the pain lanced through him and he fell off the bench, onto the floorboard. All he could see was a canopy of ice and snow -laden branches.

He only remembered pieces and parts, fragments of what followed. Russell talking, making no sense. The sudden pain of moving, being dragged off the charette. Cold as he lay in the snow. Russell coaxing him to stand, stumbling. The woods around him bobbing sickeningly. More voices sometime later, then darkness. Hands removing his coat, his blouse, warmth. Faces in candlelight. More pain.

When he finally opened his eyes and knew that he was awake, and remembered his name, he found himself in a large bed in an unfamiliar room. His entire left shoulder, from his neck down to his shoulder blade, the arm, and his side ached. He knew before he tried that he could not move it. Then he felt the pressure of bandages. A smell of rum and burning oil overlaid the stink of his own sweat.

"Mr. Granger?"

A woman sat beside him. It took a few moments to recognize her.

"Mrs. Chandler?"

"Emily please. No need for formalities here." She leaned toward him, smiling. "Lie still. Are you thirsty?"

"I think...yes..."

She sat on the bedside then and brought a thin reed to his mouth. "Draw on this," she said. "My own notion, so you don't have to try to sit up."

He took the wooden tube in his mouth and sucked. Water flowed. He swallowed, nearly choked, drew again. It felt wonderful going down his throat.

"What—"

"You've been shot," she said. "Fortunately, it happened in winter. Russell packed it in snow and the cold has worked to prevent infection. That and a liberal dose of rum in the wound. Not a bad wound for all that I'm sure it hurts terribly. You had two blouses and two coats on. The ball was practically on the surface, easily removed. We cleaned it, cauterized it, and you've been unconscious two days since." She smiled. "You won't be losing any limbs, I'm glad to say."

"I'm delighted to hear it."

"But you won't be going anywhere for a while, either. I hope you don't mind staying under my roof for a time."

"The ball. You said it was removed?"

"Yes—"

"How large was it?"

"Seemed smallish to me."

Smallish? Before he could ask further, she reached to the table and picked something up. She held it out, between thumb and middle finger, a misshapen lump that still retained enough roundness for him to recognize. His ears warmed as he estimated it to be slightly less than .50 caliber.

"Thank you."

She put it aside.

Granger closed his eyes. "Your stove—"

"Russell took a couple of my slaves out to fetch it."

"How did I—"

"Drink some more water and go to sleep. We can talk later."

"But—"

She pushed the reed into his mouth and obediently he drank. She pulled the blanket back to look at his bandage, stroked his head, and left him. Despite himself, he fell quickly into a deep sleep.

Granger opened his eyes. His shoulder seemed less painful now. He tried to sit up and the pain erupted anew. He leaned onto his right side and pushed, carefully.

"Here, now," Russell said. He slid an arm under Granger's back and eased him up.

"Thank you..."

"Stupid," Russell said. "You'll open up again."

Granger's breath came hard as he settled against pillows, waiting for the pain to subside. Black-brown spots danced around his vision. He sat still until it passed, then looked around the room. Daylight came through the single window.

"How long have I been here?"

"Five days now," Russell said. There was a tightness in his voice Granger had not heard since their time with Colonel Clark.

"What happened?"

"You were shot."

Granger grunted. "Is that what this hole in my shoulder is?"

Russell grinned. "The wagon got stuck. I was behind it, trying to see how deep we were. I told you we could shovel enough out to allow the oxen to pull us loose. You probably stood up to get the shovels when I heard the shot. You fell. I pulled you off the bench, onto the floorboard, and grabbed my musket. You kept trying to get up and I told you to stay down. I didn't see any blood, so I didn't know how bad you were. I guessed which direction the shot came from and went around the front of the oxen. When I looked out, another shot damn near took my head off. I heard the ball whistle by. But I saw the smoke, about eighty, ninety yards away. I aimed at it and fired, then took a chance to run up and grab your rifle. I ran into the woods and tried to find him.

"By the time I reached the spot, though, he was gone. I tracked the steps about another thirty yards, but I couldn't see anybody through the trees. I figured I could keep tracking him or help you. I didn't know how bad hurt you were. I unhitched the oxen, got you on one, and took the other and led you here. I've been back out there trying to pick up a trail. I found it, but it leads straight to a creek."

"Have you been here all this time otherwise?"

"No, I went back to St. Louis to let Neptune know what happened. I told him and Tayon. They'll watch the store and the house. Tayon discreetly informed Cruzat. Maybe a couple of others know. But then I came straight back here."

"So Cruzat knows. What will he do?"

"I don't know."

"Thank you. I owe—"

"No, you don't. We got each other through a war for a time. It's what we do."

"Emily showed me the ball."

"Did she?"

"Ham's rifle."

Russell nodded. "That's my opinion, too. Chavreaux?"

Granger closed his eyes. "Most probably."

"We don't know—"

"Of course we do. The question is, did he happen on us by luck? How did he know?"

"I'm sure you got some notions about that."

"I do, but they don't quite make sense. The risk—"

Russell grunted. "You and your sense. Not everything makes sense."

"Yes, everything does. We just don't always get a chance to see how." He coughed and his shoulder twinged. "I need to think, Russell."

Russell nodded and stood. "I'll be around another day or two if you need me. Mrs. Chandler—"

"Emily?"

Russell smiled. "Emily. She'll take good care of you till you're back up and around."

"Russell. Thank you."

Russell touched his hat in acknowledgement, then left the room. Granger sat there, alone, enjoying wakeful quiet for a time. His thoughts, though, kept moving into the bleakness of what had happened. He gazed at the window and ran over in his mind everything he knew. He was missing something, though, a detail he felt certain would make it all plain.

"Hungry?" Emily Chandler stood in the doorway, holding a tray, steam rising from the food on it. She set the tray on the table beside the bed. "You risked opening your wound sitting up, but since you did you should eat."

Suddenly, he was ravenous. The food—a bowl of stew and warm bread—smelled better than any food he had ever smelled before. She perched on the bed, brought the bowl over, and began spooning meat, potatoes, and vegetables into his mouth.

He ate half the bowl before he leaned back.

"Wait, rest. That's very good. Thank you."

She set the bowl down and handed him a mug filled with weak ale.

"You're being very kind to me. Thank you."

"You brought me my new circulating stove. Which Russell has managed to install for me. I'm sure he never intended to do that, but..."

He laughed. "He did, actually. Russell is a surprising man." After a pause, he said, "In fact he's a good man. I've been fortunate here in my friendships."

They sat in silence for a time until Emily Chandler sighed.

"I've always found that talking something through with a good listener is one of the best ways to solve a problem. My late husband taught me that, but I think I already knew it. He was a good listener. I'd be happy to provide an ear if you need it."

"Part of the difficulty is that, although I've been here almost five months, I still don't know the people well enough."

She smiled. "Well, I can certainly tell you anything you need to know, though it may be biased."

"Forgive me, but you don't seem to come up to the village very often."

"Oh, you might be surprised how much you can learn in a day or two talking to the right people. For instance, you might be interested to know that Jose Renaldo has been paying a good deal of attention to Martine de Lautin since her husband passed away."

"I know. I notice though that no one has said anything to me."

"No, they wouldn't. They'd figure it was up to you to notice and do something about it if you had a mind to. Custom keeps the men from bringing it up since it's personal, the women would assume it would be entirely between you and Renaldo and Martine."

"But you're telling me."

"I'm not French. Besides, I'm well-acquainted with just how unobservant men can be."

"Martine told me about it. She's not happy with the attention."

"Are you going to do anything about it?"

"I intend to."

"I wouldn't wait too long. A woman can maintain a lot of patience if she knows something is in the offing, but it's never unlimited. I like Martine, she's a decent woman. It'd be good to see her happy again."

Granger swallowed more ale. "Would you send Russell in here? I have an errand for him. And then I may ask a great favor of you."

"I'd be happy to oblige."

Twenty-six

IT WAS THREE DAYS later when Martine came into the room. Granger felt feverish, but he straightened himself against the pillows. She stood in the doorway, staring at him for a long time, pale and frowning. He was relieved to see her. Then a deep, slow pleasure left no room for anything else, not even the fever, which it seemed intent on making its own.

"*Mon dieu,*" she said. "Is it—"

"The bullet is out, it didn't even go all the way through," Granger said. "I'll be fine in time. Thank you for coming."

"Emily was not very informative, only that she needed help with something." Martine shrugged off her cloak and removed her scarf as she came toward him. "When?"

"Oh, I guess it's been six, seven days now. I've actually gotten up a time or two."

Matter-of-factly, Martine leaned over him to look at his bandage. Without a word, she removed it. She winced when she saw the wound. "Do you know who?"

"I have a good idea. But I need proof. Have you been to the village in the last few days?"

"Four days ago." She looked around the room, found the pan of water and extra bandages made from scraps of old linen. She went to the door and leaned out. Granger heard her speaking, but his ears rang slightly and he could not make out the words. She came back and picked up the pan. "I will be back."

A quarter of an hour later, she returned with fresh, hot water. She washed the wound, gently, but each touch made him tense.

"There is a little infection," she said. "Not much. But we must keep it clean. I'm going to put on some rum now, it will hurt."

It did. Granger bit down, closed his eyes, and waited. Martine finished and applied a new bandage.

"There is some speculation that you are dead," she said, "or that you are here entertaining the Widow Chandler. Or her daughters. It is not an unexpected rumor. I wondered myself, until I spoke to Neptune."

"Would it bother you if I were?"

Martine's eyebrows arched. "You have made no promises to me."

"I did offer to marry you."

"An offer is not a promise. And I've made no promises to you, other than to stay in St. Louis longer than I intended." She smiled wanly. "And to help you find your answers. I think I'm glad I did."

"If something happens to me, what about Jose Renaldo?"

Her smile vanished and her shoulders tightened. "He holds no attraction for me. His attentions have been kind, even generous, but obvious." She looked at him as if to say *"Does that answer your questions?"*

Granger extended his hand. After a moment, she took it and he squeezed. Her smile returned. "We must put matters to rest." She touched his face briefly, and then drew a deep breath. "I told you there is something not right in that house. So it remains."

"Not right how?"

"She does not sleep with him now, not since the new lodger. Several days ago, Don Diego and Salvatore went south again. They returned with a wagon this time. Don Diego asked me to go into St. Louis for some things. I offered to help him unload the wagon, but he said no, he and Salvatore would tend to it. He wanted me to leave then. There was nothing I could do. When I returned, one of the upstairs rooms was occupied, though I am barred from entering it. Eliana carries food there three times daily and often stays there for hours. There are new tensions as a result."

They brought him home, Granger thought. "Has Renaldo been out since then?"

"Once, but he didn't stay long. He seemed worried when he left, but I do not think he knows about the lodger."

"Have you seen him at all?"

"No. Eliana will permit only Don Diego upstairs."

"Diego visits the new lodger?"

"Not every day, but sometimes."

"Interesting. Do you have any idea who he is?"

Martine shook her head, though her expression suggested she had suspicions.

"It's the brother," Granger said. "The question is, which one? Atilio or Diego."

"How do you know?"

"I've seen him. Cortez has been keeping him down in Ste. Genevieve, hidden. He's badly hurt, a cripple. Couldn't even talk."

"Why would he keep him hidden?"

"He had to until Eliana arrived. His life is still in danger. What else has Cortez been doing since then?"

"He has taken to riding out two or three times a week. He is gone perhaps three, sometimes four hours, and when he returns he seems worse than when he left."

"Worse how?"

"He will not talk about what troubles him, but despair is consuming him, as if something terrible happened and he feels responsible. When he is not drinking or out riding, he is at the mill. It is so cold but he has the mill working anyway, and Salvatore drives the teams of slaves to cut trees even in this. Others he has working on the new stream bed. A few have lost toes to frostbite, but one has died. Eliana stays in her room when she is not with the lodger, reading or writing letters."

"Letters to whom?"

She frowned, but said, "I don't know. She never finishes one to send."

Granger thought for a time. "Does he let her leave the house?"

"Occasionally. With me sometimes. Never to go into St. Louis, but only to call on a neighbor."

"Can you bring her here?"

"Why?"

"I need to speak with her. There are questions maybe she can answer. I couldn't think of a way before that wouldn't raise suspicion."

"This might anyway."

"Maybe. I need to know that Salvatore or Renaldo don't follow her."

"Salvatore..."

She looked away. He found her hand. "What is it?"

"He frightens me. Something about him...he is Indian, but I have no idea what kind. He is not from here."

"Has he left Cortez's place in the last ten days?"

"Not that I know."

"When did he arrive out there originally?"

"Shortly after Diego returned, a boat came with slaves, and Salvatore was with them, overseeing them. No one knew where Diego had found him, but he stayed after that. He has been foreman for Diego since."

"There's something else?"

She nodded. "Étienne's sons...a *coureur du bois* found them, three weeks ago."

"Found them. Dead?"

"Yes. They had been...someone had butchered them and left them in a shallow grave."

Why would they be killed? he wondered. "Oh. They weren't supposed to sell your house to me. Someone else wanted it, but they...if you can get Eliana here, you should see if you can arrange a place to stay for her. Or don't go back at all." He sighed. "Martine, I'm going to stay here as long as Emily allows. It might be useful if the rumor started that I'm hurt very badly and might not live. But I don't want any visitors except you, Russell, and Neptune if he needs to see me."

"And señora de Cortez?"

"And Eliana, yes."

She looked uncomfortable at that, but nodded. "What about Tayon? He will be most concerned."

"Tell Tayon to find and keep watch on Gambeau."

"Gambeau? What—"

"Please. Ask Neptune if he can do the same with Renaldo."

"And for you? What can I do for you?"

"You've already done more than enough. But your company would be welcome after...after this is done."

"Whatever it is."

"Yes. Whatever it is." He swallowed. "I—"

"I know," she said, cutting him off. "That would be a fine thing. But tell me later." She stood. "I must get back. It will be night by the time I return." She gave him a look he could not read, but he thought he saw kindness and welcome in it. "I am glad you took the house. And...I am glad you're here."

She leaned over quickly and kissed his mouth. Then she was gone.

Granger closed his eyes. *It's too much*, he thought, *I'm trying for too much...*

But quickly, with Martine's taste on his tongue, he fell asleep.

Twenty-seven

A WEEK PASSED before Russell brought him a message from Martine and the fevers stopped completely. The message read simply: *She will not come. I am sorry. M.*

He gave Russell a letter he'd prepared for Cruzat, and the next day Jose Renaldo rode up to Emily Chandler's house.

Granger leaned against the post on the porch above the steps, a blanket draped over his shoulders, and watched him dismount. Renaldo wore a heavy coat, wool with a fur lining, the skirt below his knees. He trudged through the snow toward Granger, his breath fogging the air.

"Señor Granger," he said. "I'm glad to see you are alive. When I heard that you were shot, I thought…well, I *did* advise you to leave, but I never expected anything like this to happen."

"I'm certain no one did," Granger said.

Renaldo stopped at the bottom step. "I came to see how you are doing. I feel a small measure of responsibility."

"Why would you?"

"I knew you would come to some grief—not this, of course—and I tried to persuade you to go. Perhaps if I had been more persuasive…"

"You would never have persuaded me. Don't trouble yourself."

"I see. It is cold, señor, may we talk inside?"

"It's not my house." Granger pushed back from the post and knocked on the door. Emily Chandler opened it. "Would you object if señor Renaldo came in to talk to me?"

She looked past Granger at the Spaniard and shook her head. "Not at all. Please."

Beneath his wool coat, Renaldo wore a dark green brocaded coat and dark gray trousers tucked into his boots. He sat near the stove and Granger took the chair opposite.

"All of St. Louis is concerned for you," Renaldo said. "Should you return, I am sure you will have more trade."

"Is there any reason I should not return?"

Renaldo gestured at him, palm up. "This is not a good omen, certainly. To be shot. And by your own rifle. That is not to be ignored. I will be honest with you, likely there will be no further attempts on you, but it is not a certainty. Events may follow their own lead. It is a chance I recommend against."

"So you still want me to leave St. Louis. I'm touched by your concern, but I doubt it is altogether disinterested."

Renaldo smiled as if embarrassed. "This is true. I have certain…ambitions…of a personal nature which you could complicate."

"Martine is not interested in you."

"Did I say it concerned her?"

"You did before."

"Yes, well. I have some regard for you. Respect. I do not wish us to be competitors."

"Is that what you think we are? I was unaware."

Renaldo's frown deepened. "I find that difficult to believe, señor."

Granger felt the stirrings of anger. *That won't do you any service,* he thought, *put it aside. He's goading you.* "There's no reason for you to be telling me this unless you thought you had something to lose."

"I do not lose."

"We all lose something, sometimes. In this instance I believe you've misjudged matters."

Renaldo lost all expression. After several moments, he sighed heavily. "I'm here to do you a kindness. I suggested before that you leave St. Louis. There is nothing for you here but grief. I even provided the means. You chose to ignore that advice. Now I must be more insistent. If you choose to remain here, you and I may come into conflict, and that would be unfortunate since it concerns matters in which you have no interest."

"That's presumptuous. It assumes my interest is irrelevant."

"I assure you, it is. You're intruding."

"Now that we understand each other, was there anything else you wished to discuss?"

"Would it serve any purpose?"

"Probably not."

"In that case, I will bid you *Buenos dias.*" Renaldo stood. "You should not presume upon Madame de Lautin's affections. They are not yours."

"Isn't that for her to say?"

Renaldo, puzzled, waited for further explanation. Still wearing the same baffled, slightly worried expression, he put on his coat, bade Emily good day, and left. Granger watched from the doorway as the Spaniard mounted his horse, touched the brim of his hat, and rode away.

"I was listening," Emily said. "Sounded like a threat to me."

"It was. It was also a mistake. I know what's going on now." He stepped back inside and closed the door. "When Russell comes again, I need to arrange transportation back to St. Louis."

Emily frowned. "I'm not so sure you should yet. You seem to be healing well, but you're not so whole that you couldn't reopen that wound."

"I appreciate that. But events won't wait."

Three days later Russell came. To Granger's surprise, Martine was in the cart with him. She did not smile when she saw him. Russell offered to help her down, but she braced one hand on the side of the charette and jumped to the snow. She strode up to Granger where he waited on the porch.

"What did you say to Jose Renaldo?" she said.

"I—"

"He came to the house and insisted I choose. I asked between what and he said between you and him. I objected at having such a demand made and he became furious. Diego intervened and insisted he behave in a more civil manner in his house and then they began arguing. Eliana took me aside then and told me to go into St. Louis. She helped me pack a few things and then had Salvatore take me to the village. Diego and Renaldo were still shouting at each other. I don't think they knew I was gone until I was halfway to St. Louis. What did you say to him?"

Granger worked to suppress a smile. "Only that neither of us had claim on you and it was your choice. He seemed to think he had priority over your affections."

"You—" She hesitated. Her expression changed as she seemed to think through what Granger had said. Finally she nodded. "I see." She smiled. "It's cold."

Russell was the last to come inside. When he closed the door, Granger said, "Renaldo made a mistake. I believe I now know the cause of Ham's death."

"You know who did it?"

"Chavreaux."

Russell nodded. "What about Taylor?"

"That I don't know. Yet. But regardless, Chavreaux didn't act on his own. He was employed."

"Renaldo."

"Absolutely. Through Gambeau and his associates, but it was Renaldo's coin."

"How can you be certain?" Martine asked.

"As I said, he made a mistake. He told me."

"That was bold of him," Russell said. "Or stupid."

"I don't think he knows he told me, but he did. He gave me what I need to discover the rest. Did Cruzat say anything about my letter?"

"He wasn't entirely convinced, but he agreed to what you asked for. Getting shot worked in your favor."

"I'll bear that in mind."

"Why would Renaldo do this?" Martine asked.

"Possibly revenge," Granger said. "But more likely desperation. He's been trying to find something—that document you mentioned. That's why he had Gambeau and Chavreaux search the house, that's why he's been courting you, and that's probably why Étienne's sons are dead. He thinks you have it. He was convinced Diego gave it to Étienne. Either by marrying you or buying your house, he believed he would have it whether he found it or not."

"But what is it?" Russell asked.

"I believe it ties him to a theft in Havana years ago. Something he did with Atilio and one other."

"Why wouldn't Don Diego reveal it before now?"

"Because his brother was still disgraced and there is a third party that the Spanish government is protecting. Maybe this de la Vargas. Eliana brought a royal pardon for Atilio. Now they're just waiting for the right moment."

"Why would Gambeau do all this for him?" Martine asked.

"Renaldo perhaps knows something about Gambeau to threaten him. Or just for money."

"But they're friends," Martine said. "Renaldo and Don Diego."

"I don't think so. I think Atilio knew Renaldo in Havana. Diego? It's possible they all knew each other in Spain, but if so they don't anymore. Given the last few times he's paid a call, do you honestly believe they're friends?"

Martine thought for a moment and shook her head. "No. I have seen friends fight before. This is different."

"The trick will be to get Renaldo to admit all this in front of other witnesses," Russell said.

"Yes," Granger said. "Well, I have an idea about that. Martine, is the guest still residing at Cortez's house?"

"Yes."

"Good. First, though, I need to go back to St. Louis. Then we take the next step."

"First thing in the morning," Russell said, "right after dawn."

"Good." Before Russell left, Granger said, "Russell. Whatever happens, I want you know I—"

"Save it," Russell said. "You can say what you need to after."

Russell went back out to tend to the cart and make other preparations. Granger got to his feet and headed back to his room. Martine followed him and closed the door behind her.

"He is a good friend," Martine said.

"He is. If this goes wrong, would you—?"

"Of course," she said. "You are provoking Renaldo."

"Of course. It's the only way to change the situation enough to force his hand."

"To make him confess? Do you truly believe he will?"

I have no idea, Granger thought. He said, "I don't know what else to do."

"Someone else could die."

"It's possible. I almost did."

She came toward him. "And that would make me very angry." Suddenly she raised her right hand, balled into a fist. Granger stepped back, waiting for the blow. But she held back. Her face twisted briefly, her hand dropped, and she pressed against him. He winced as her head dropped onto his wound, but he put his arms around her and held her.

She sniffed loudly and squeezed him, then stepped away. Her eyes glistened.

"This has been very hard," she said. "I wanted to be here, be with you. I feel unnatural, denying myself, keeping you at a distance. When you were hurt, I thought, another one, again. And I didn't allow—I didn't—"

Granger reached for her again, but she backed out of reach.

"Life here is hard," she said. "I cannot count the times I wished to be back in New Orleans or even all the way back in Provence. Somewhere life could not be taken so easily, by so many things. An illusion, I know, there is no such place, but here there is so very little to mask the harshness. We try, we have parties, we are all friends, we do what we can to make a little theater of life to cover up the dangers, but we all feel how close an end could be."

"Then why do you stay?"

"Because I know I have nothing anywhere else. Here is the only place I have found where I could have something of value that is mine. And it hurts to think of losing it, again and again. There is only one thing worse, though."

"Never having it at all."

She nodded. "Do not lie to me, Lieutenant. Do you want me?"

"Yes."

Her eyes narrowed and her breathing deepened. Granger felt his pulse quicken, a self-conscious tingle, knowing he was being judged. Finally, she turned to the door and threw the latch, locking it.

"I will hold you to that," she said, coming back to him. "I will not leave you again."

Twenty-eight

GRANGER WOKE in the darkness, fully alert. He rolled slowly over. The only light came from the window, filled with deep, metal blue from the rising half-moon. He sat up, his shoulder complaining a little, and looked toward the window. Silver light traced the contours of Martine's face where she lay beside him. Fragments of the last few hours danced through his mind—eagerness and caution mingled, becoming a slow intensity. Just then Granger could not imagine living without her.

His senses teased the way he remembered from the war, waking for no apparent reason, alert to insubstantial disturbances. Usually it was a sentry or another man going off from the camp to relieve himself or even an animal that had come closer than it should. But once in a while the threat was real, and he had learned never to ignore the warning.

Emily did not keep a dog. Granger thought now that she should.

He got to his feet and silently found his breeches and boots. His rifle stood next to the door. By touch in the insufficient moonglow, he picked it up, undid the ties on the sheath, and let the leather fall away from the trigger and lock. He bent to drop the sheath silently on the floor. Cradling the weapon in his left arm, he pushed the striker forward and poured powder in the pan. He hefted the rifle in his left hand—causing his shoulder to twinge deeply—then reached for the door latch.

He stepped back and pulled the door open. The shape of someone framed in the darkness startled him. His right hand closed on the grip of the rifle and he began to swing the barrel around. But the shape rushed at him, black on gray-black, a motion without detail, and slammed into him.

He fell back, the rifle barrel jammed horizontally against his wounded shoulder. He bellowed as he hit the edge of the bed. Half on the mattress, his attacker dropped onto him. Fearing he might pass out from the pain, Granger heaved against the weight, the rifle wedged between them. His assailant pushed himself up, and suddenly a steel shape caught the moonlight from the window, an arm raised above him. Granger pulled the trigger.

The explosion deafened. The flash illuminated, briefly, the stolid broad face of Chavreaux, hovering in the dark, arm raised, knife ready. His eyes caught the orange-white burst from the pan, and he hesitated, rearing back a little. Granger's ears rang, but he felt the weight shift off the rifle, and he pushed.

Chavreaux lost his balance and staggered back. Granger let the rifle go and rolled to the left. A hand groped at his leg and he kicked back, into the dark. Free for a moment, Granger crawled across the floor. Behind him, he heard Chavreaux stumble to his feet and collide with furniture.

Granger reached the wall and stood. A faint strip of moonlight across the floor showed him his rifle. Empty now, but it would make a good club. He started to lunge for it, but Chavreaux stepped into the pale light, straddling the weapon just as another body leapt onto Chavreaux's back and they spun around.

Suddenly lantern-glow filled the room. Emily held a musket and one of her daughters held a lantern. Against the wall, near the corner, Chavreaux seemed frozen for a moment, eyes wide, arms reaching back to try to wrest Martine from her hold. Naked, she clung to his shoulders, arms around his neck. She seemed to be nuzzling him until Granger realized that she had sunk her teeth into his ear. His mouth gaped in a rictus of pain and rage.

He whirled around and slammed Martine against the wall. She grunted, her grip loosened, and Chavreaux pulled an arm away, spun, and threw her toward the bed.

Russell pushed past Emily then. Chavreaux charged at him and snapped a punch at Russell's face, knocking him back against Emily and her daughter.

Granger snatched up his rifle, stood, and rammed the butt at Chavreaux. Granger's shoulder balked and the blow landed on Chavreaux's chest instead of his jaw. Chavreaux grabbed the stock and pulled Granger to the right. Granger glimpsed the knife again, coming up.

Emily fired. Chavreaux crouched. For a moment none of them moved. Then Chavreaux rushed through the door.

"Damn!" Granger reached for his powder and shot.

Emily grabbed it first, handed Martine her musket, and picked up Granger's rifle. Her daughter came back into the room with the lantern. Granger watched as Emily expertly reloaded the weapon. She handed it to him and took her musket back.

Russell was beginning to get to his feet, shaking his head as Granger ran through the house. The main door stood open and he rushed into the night, after Chavreaux. The cold stung bitterly. The moon cast glassy light across the farm, setting the snow and ice aglow like blue fire. Granger moved away from the house, to a place where he could turn to see most of the compound.

"There!"

Martine's voice, loud in the cold air, to the left. Granger ran. Blood pounded in his ears and he felt unnaturally warm.

On the far side of the barn, he glimpsed a shape. It crouched, manlike, and then a brilliant flare hid it as it fired a weapon. The sound thundered around them. Granger heard the warble of the ball past his right ear. He raised his own rifle just as he saw the man turn to run. Too dark to be sure, he aimed at the blackest part of the shape, and squeezed the trigger. When his sight cleared from the brightness, Chavreaux was gone.

Emily appeared beside him, then, took the rifle from his hands, and replaced it with a musket. Unthinking, he cocked the hammer. Martine stood at the edge of the porch, still naked, trembling from the cold. Emily took her by the shoulders and drew her back inside.

Cautiously, Granger searched the outbuildings, and as much of the surrounding ground as he could before the cold and the new pains drove him back inside.

Russell was sitting on the edge of the bed. In the lampglow Granger could see his left eye beginning to swell shut. Martine had pulled on a robe and sat shaking on a chair nearby. She looked up at Granger and gave a weak smile. Granger hugged her and kissed her forehead.

"Thank you," he said.

"Sorry," Russell said. "Been a while since anyone beat me."

"Let me see," Emily said then, bringing a lantern close to Granger. She studied the bandage for signs that the wound had opened. Finding nothing, she then held the light close to Russell's face.

"I'm all right," Russell protested. "You should change his bandage, be sure."

"I'll do it," Martine said. She winced when she stood.

"Here now," Emily said and pulled the robe open to look at her side and back. "You're going to be bruised." She prodded gently. "Nothing broken I can tell."

Martine closed the robe and reached for Granger's hand. "He could have killed us all," she said.

"He panicked," Russell said. "He intended to kill Granger, not all of us."

"Maybe," Granger said. "Will you be able to travel tomorrow?"

Russell nodded. "It's only an eye."

"Come on," Emily said, taking Russell's hand. "We'll get a compress on that."

Alone, Martine led him to the bed and began changing his bandage.

"I—" he began.

She put her hand to his mouth and shook her head. In silence, she worked, and he watched. When she was finished, she lay next to him, holding each other till morning.

Twenty-nine

PEOPLE STARED as the charette rolled into the village. Doubtless after weeks of hearing how close to death he had come, seeing Granger driving the charette must have been a shock. Russell rode alongside. Martine, Emily and her daughters rode in the back of the cart, all bundled against the cold. It was late afternoon. The journey had been tedious and Granger's shoulder ached. He was exhausted, but he stopped before the governor's house.

Russell went to the door and knocked. Cruzat stepped out, accompanied by a sergeant, and came up to the charette.

"Señor, I am gratified to see you well."

"At least not dead," Granger said. "It will be a while before I'm well."

Cruzat bowed in assent. "I have taken your recommendations. We're prepared. When do you wish to begin?"

"First light tomorrow. I think I need to rest tonight."

"I agree. Tomorrow we shall resolve matters, one way or the other."

"One way or the other. Thank you."

Cruzat gave him a quick salute as he stepped back. Granger urged the horse onward, toward his own house.

Tayon, Cécile, and Neptune met them at the gate. Granger managed to climb down on his own. He embraced Tayon and clapped a hand on Neptune's shoulder. He gave no resistance to being supported as he went inside.

"Mon ami," Tayon said, "I am very glad to see you."

Granger hugged him again, and then went to one of the chairs by the hearth. Neptune added a couple more logs to the blaze.

"I spoke to Cruzat," Granger said. "He's ready. Tomorrow."

"Tomorrow," Tayon said. "Do you need anything beforehand?"

"I don't expect anything to go awry, but if it does, will you see to Martine? Protect her?"

"Of course."

Martine frowned at him. "Protect me from what?"

"Renaldo."

"Why would he—"

"I don't know. But it shouldn't come to that."

She raised an eyebrow. "It had better not."

Tayon grinned at her. "I think she's serious, *mon ami*. You had better not disappoint her."

"If that seems likely, I'll depend on you to save me from it."

"Oh no! In matters of men and women, we are all on our own."

Granger grunted, a smile pulling at his mouth. "Then at least a word of warning?"

"I'll do what I can."

Martine was smiling now. She shook her head and walked away to help Emily and her girls settle in.

"I want you to ride out with me tomorrow," Granger said to Tayon. "Russell and Neptune. I want you both already out at Cortez's, on the perimeter."

"You expect Chavreaux to show up?"

"I expect he's already somewhere near there."

Russell nodded. His eye was not completely closed, but the swelling and discoloration were alarming. Granger reflected that Neptune had been beaten, Russell injured, and he himself had been shot. He could not imagine the frustration and anger that would result if he failed tomorrow. He closed his eyes and let his head fall back, feeling the weariness.

"You are all staying to eat," Cécile said from the kitchen doorway. "Bread is almost ready and there is a gumbo."

Tired as he was, Granger suddenly felt ravenous. He breathed deeply and caught the aroma of baking.

"It's good to be home," he said.

A hand touched his face and he looked up at Martine standing beside him. He caught her hand and kissed the palm. He saw Tayon watching them, looking pleased.

"Something amusing?" Granger said.

"Infinitely." He walked away, grinning.

Martine squeezed his hand. "I will help Cécile."

He watched her go and thought, *I want to stay, I want to make this home.* And then: *I hope I can.*

He slept poorly, waking up often. Finally, before dawn, he stayed awake. He washed his face, pulled on a heavy coat, and went out to the yard.

Russell and Neptune were finishing preparing horses. A pair of Cruzat's soldiers stood by the gate.

"How long have they been here?" Granger asked.

"Since last night," Russell said. "They took watches, one slept in the store, the other walked the property. They'll accompany you out later." He reached inside his coat. "Here. Thought you might need this now." He handed Granger the document he had kept for him.

"Excellent," Granger said. "Thank you." *I am very fortunate in my friends,* he thought. *Very.*

Russell and Neptune, muskets in their saddle sheaths, mounted.

"Good luck," Granger said.

Russell touched the brim of his hat and Neptune nodded. The two rode out. Granger's pulse increased. *It begins.*

Granger went back inside and began preparing his own kit. Then he set to cleaning his rifle. As he worked, the others emerged, and soon the house bustled with activity. By the time the sun glazed the windows, breakfast was ready, and Granger was finished.

Martine emerged from the back of the house in her heavy cloak.

"I'm going with you."

"If I say no, I imagine you'll just wait till I leave and follow on your own?"

She smiled ruefully.

Granger laughed. "I'll be glad of your company."

Cécilé took Emily and her daughters to her house. Granger brought a pair of pistols and his rifle, helped Martine into the wagon, and climbed in after her. Drawn by a pair of mules Cruzat had provided, and, accompanied by the Spanish soldiers on horseback, they headed west to Cortez's.

The passage was easier than Granger expected through the snow; the wagon only got stuck once, briefly. He chafed at being unable to help push it out of its rut. The day was warming up and Granger saw signs of melting all around, but it was still cold and he doubted the snow would disappear anytime soon.

They reached the Cortez house just before noon. A row of horses stood tied to the rail facing the broad porch. A wagon stood off to the west, two mules still in harness. Four more soldiers stood flanking the front door and Granger felt a wave of relief—Cruzat was taking this seriously. He looked toward the forest surrounding the compound but all he saw was a tangle of white over black tracings.

He retrieved his rifle, and, Martine beside him, entered the house.

He found them all gathered in the parlor, the painting of the conquistador a silent, magisterial observer. Cortez, Renaldo, Gambeau, Cruzat, Tayon, and one of Cruzat's corporals and another soldier. Eliana was absent but Granger knew where she was.

Granger set the sheathed rifle against the wall and shrugged out of his coat.

"I wish to protest," Gambeau said, snapping to his feet. "I have a business to run, chores, and you already stole my best worker."

"Interesting that you believe I could steal something you never owned in the first place," Granger said. "Sit down, monsieur."

Gambeau, scowling, resumed his seat.

Cruzat watched Granger, eyes half-lidded, speculative. "I have explained that we are all here to resolve certain questions regarding unaccounted deaths. I will leave it to you, señor, to elaborate."

"Thank you."

Renaldo was staring at him, impassive, waiting. Granger addressed him first.

"Where is Chavreaux?"

Renaldo started, frowned, and then laughed. "How would I know?"

"Because he works for you."

Cortez fixed his attention on Renaldo then.

Renaldo smiled at him. "I assure you, señor, this is an absurd accusation."

"But it is not an accusation," Granger said, and before Renaldo could respond, he went on. "I know he works for you. Or rather, he works for Gambeau, who works for you. You've been careful to put some distance between yourself and your agents, but you made a mistake and showed your hand. For the moment I'll let you worry over that. Allow me to sit down. I'm still recovering from my bullet wound."

There were no other chairs in the parlor, but Martine brought one from the dining room. "Thank you," he said as he sat.

"A few years ago—almost four now—my closest friend was murdered here, in this house. It would have been simpler to believe he had been the victim of a raiding party, a casualty of war, but there were things about it that made no sense in that context. It troubled me and I couldn't dismiss it. What Tayon and I found when we came here looking for him was confusing and strange and no matter how I arranged the facts in my mind, I kept returning to the conviction that Ham Inwood had been murdered. One of the reasons I came back was to see if I could learn why and how. I believe I know."

"How can you know?" Cortez asked. "So long ago. No witnesses."

"I admit, it's been a difficult task. All I really had was my conviction and the promise of logic. I had to gather enough detail with which to construct a plausible picture of what happened and then see if I could validate it. I couldn't just make accusations, as señor Renaldo pointed out, I had to back them up with sound conclusions and evidence. That, indeed, seemed unlikely. Until I was shot." He looked up at Martine. "Could you bring me something to drink? I believe you'll find goblets in the cabinet in the opposite room."

"I confess to being fascinated," Renaldo said. "Please, continue. I have always enjoyed a good fable."

Martine returned with one of the silver goblets, half-filled with wine. Granger smiled at her and took a sip. He cradled the goblet with both hands in his lap.

"The first question," he said, "was why Ham had come here alone. That was easily answered. Tayon will corroborate. Ham was told by one of Cortez's slaves that there was still someone here. This was just before the battle, *l'Année du Coup*, and people in the outlying farms had been ordered to come into the village. Don Diego was already in St. Louis as part of the cavalry under Monsieur Pourré, but he had left his slaves here. Ham and Tayon had come out to bring them in, but there was someone else here, hiding. Ham rode back to find him and bring him in. This was a day or so before the battle. Events took charge and his absence was unnoticed till after the fighting. I was then requested to come across the river to look for him, as he was my sergeant. I took two men, Tayon accompanied us, and we came out here.

"I will never forget that day. We found two dead horses in the stable. Both had been shot, one had been butchered, an animal that must have been magnificent, a stallion that I later learned señor Cortez had brought with him when he came here to settle. The other was the horse Ham had ridden out. This was a petty bit of viciousness. The house had been ransacked and searched. The plate was still here, as was the food in the larder. Don Diego's papers had been gone through, though, which was peculiar if a raiding party had come upon the place. And then we found Ham's rifle, still here, on the floor. It was a fine weapon and unlikely to have been left behind by raiders. But it had been abandoned.

"One of my men found tracks leading into the woods. At the end of them we found Ham's body. It had been carried far from the house and partly buried. That was the most unlikely and puzzling part of all of it. Those four things taken together fit no pattern of warfare. I could only conclude that something else had occurred. That Ham had been murdered."

The tension in the room nearly hummed, and everyone's attention centered on him.

"Now, Ham was a seasoned soldier, he was not likely to just walk into a deadly situation. So it vexed me to understand what had happened. He had been struck from behind, that was obvious from his injuries. Given where we found his rifle, it seemed just as obvious that he'd been killed inside this house. Upstairs."

Cortez seemed to shudder, but he said nothing. Gambeau looked ill.

"I don't believe whoever killed him thought that through very well, since what they did instead—carried his body into the woods to bury—raised even more questions once it was discovered. Of course, they no doubt thought it would never be discovered. But then there was the dead horse in the stable that belonged to Monsieur Gambeau." Granger shook his head. "A murderer may have his reasons for killing a man, but why kill the horses?

"I expected to remain in St. Louis several weeks at least, as liaison between Colonel Clark and the village, but apparently my presence created a problem for certain people and I was summarily recalled. I was unable to return until last year."

"And by now whatever you hoped to learn," Renaldo said, "is long turned to dust. You have nothing."

"On the contrary, señor, I have a great deal. I know who the stranger was, hiding here. I know who was here searching through Don Diego's papers. I know what it was they were looking for. I know who killed Ham and who tried to kill me. And finally, I know who directed all these actions."

"So much certainty from so little reality," Renaldo said.

"Again, quite the opposite. Firstly, you objected to my presence here. I couldn't understand that until I learned of the connection to a man named Dodge, who was supposed to be our quartermaster. He was instead selling our supplies for his own profit and Don Diego had purchased a number of horses from him—our horses. That mattered to Gambeau, as I discovered that prior to Don Diego, Dodge had been selling horses and other supplies to him."

Gambeau came to his feet again. "That is a lie!"

"I have it from Dodge himself," Granger said. "Would you be willing to call him a liar to his face? I could arrange it." He waited for Gambeau to say more. Instead, the man sat down, scowling.

"I thought not," Granger continued. "Don Diego cut you out of what had been a profitable deal, and you had every reason to resent him. But it went further, didn't it? You were acting as a factor for Lt. Renaldo here, who was providing you funds for buying the contraband. What did he say when he found out you'd been outbid? I imagine he wanted to know why you didn't tell him before it was a done deal, so he could give you more money. How did he feel when it turned out you'd been keeping a portion of his money for yourself? You couldn't tell him without letting him know how much Cortez had paid Dodge and no doubt he could calculate the difference and understand, finally, how you had been cheating him."

For the first time Renaldo looked away from Granger, narrowing his eyes contemptuously at Gambeau.

Granger allowed time for Gambeau to grow fearful under that gaze. "It must have been easy for Renaldo to convince you to come out here and find something for him, something that would hurt Don Diego. After all, you were seriously in his debt. But you mishandled it, and Renaldo realized the potential danger and protested to Lt. Cartabona that my presence was objectionable. I wonder if Cartabona would have agreed, though, without Montgomery's decision to send me north. In any event, I was removed. When I left, two questions preyed on my mind—who was the stranger and who had been in this house when Ham came in?"

"Do you have answers now, señor?" Cortez asked. One of his hands was balled into a fist on his thigh, the knuckles white.

"I do. Gambeau and Chavreaux were here, searching the house. I know Chavreaux was here because he took a trophy." Granger raised the goblet. "He had one of these, from the set I saw in this house almost four years ago. Chavreaux often works for you, Monsieur Gambeau. I doubt he reads Spanish, if he reads at all, which meant he didn't come here alone. You came out here with him. I know this because one of your stablehands saw the two of you leave on horseback that day. There might have been a third man, but I'm convinced Chavreaux did the killing. Just as he did the beating."

Cortez's hand trembled.

"What beating, señor?" Cruzat asked.

Granger kept his gaze on Cortez. "The vicious beating of Don Diego's brother. Atilio."

Movement caught his eye and he turned toward Renaldo, who had straightened in his chair and was staring at Cortez.

Renaldo waved his hand dismissively. "That is a fantastic assertion."

"Perhaps," Granger admitted. "But true nevertheless."

"Can you prove this?"

"Of course. He's upstairs. We can see for ourselves."

Cortez's eyes closed and he seemed to struggle for composure.

Gambeau laughed nervously. "Monsieur, this is absurd! Why would anyone, even Chavreaux, beat someone so savagely?"

"Because you were looking for something and it wasn't here," Granger said. "Renaldo insisted you find it. He described it to you, told you exactly what to look for, but it was gone. Chavreaux was trying to torture it out of Cortez."

Gambeau laughed once more before subsiding into a sullen stillness, eyes on the floor.

Renaldo folded his arms, his face a mask of disgust. "None of this explains how I am behind any of it. If Gambeau had a dispute with Don Diego, what does that have to do with me?"

Tayon spoke up. "Because Gambeau would never have done anything so bold on his own."

"Besides," Granger added, "how could he know there was anything here that might be useful to him? He couldn't. Even if he had an idea, he couldn't use it. And he was right, there wasn't, not directly. There was only something here useful to you."

"You sound as though you know what this mysterious document is," Renaldo said, his voice flat and hard.

"Did I say it was a document?" Renaldo's face went rigid, and Granger went on. "But I do know what it is. It took me a while to find it. Don Diego had given it to Étienne de Lautin for safe-keeping. Étienne in turn had hidden it." He pulled the paper from his pocket, unfolded it, and handed it to Cruzat.

Cruzat opened the paper and read silently, frowning. "This," he said finally, "is a *Declaración jurada* from the imperial court in Havana."

Granger was watching Renaldo, who paled at these words.

"According to this," Cruzat continued, "a previous action of condemnation has been made void and a new judgment rendered. The formerly-accused Atilio Juan de Cortez has been found innocent and Jose Renaldo has been found guilty of the crimes of theft, bribery, and libel." He looked up at Diego. "Did you know about this, señor?"

Cortez opened his mouth, but said nothing. He nodded.

"This," Cruzat said, "along with the pardon you brought exonerates your brother and names a new culprit." He looked at Granger. "The paper you showed me?"

"A claim, pointing to a solution," Granger said. The initials should have been obvious from the start. A.J.C. Atilio Juan de Cortez. J.P.R. Jose P. Renaldo. I don't know who the third set is, but I'm sure Don Francisco does. As to your involvement," he said to Renaldo, "it became gradually clear. First you wanted me thrown out of St. Louis. Then, when I returned, you tried to bribe me to leave. You paid me a substantial amount of money to do so, money you refused to take back when I said I had no intention of leaving. How could you afford a payment like that? I wondered. Then Lt. Governor Cruzat told me something that made it sensible, about the theft of a large sum of money in Havana several years ago. A theft involving Atilio de Cortez and you."

"Me?" Renaldo said. "I was never charged."

Cortez glared at Renaldo. "You bribed the judge and placed all the blame on my brother, when all he did was give you a place to stay."

"That is hardly all," Renaldo said. "No matter. There is no proof. I will challenge this!"

"Well there is that document," Granger said. "And there is the money. It must have been a great deal of money." Granger shrugged. "And there is the rest. When bribing me failed, you spread rumors about me in order to damage my business. That failed because I already had the good word of my friend, Tayon. Things were becoming awkward because I wouldn't go away. Of course, if you had done nothing at all, I might never have found anything. When I went down to Ste. Genevieve, though, the silence of the one man who could harm you was challenged. Did Don Diego tell you? As long as he remained silent and unresponsive, you were safe, but now there was the chance that he might talk. You arranged to steal the rifle. And then you told Chavreaux to kill me, which he nearly did."

"This is impossible," Renaldo said. "How can you know this?"

"I said you made a mistake. When you came to visit me. You gave me sympathy. You said how tragic it was, that I had been shot by my own rifle."

"So?"

"How could you possibly know it was my rifle?"

Now Renaldo's face lost all expression, as though he was pulling back, burying himself under layers of blank, unyielding walls. A scurrying tingle ran down Granger's scalp and he sensed the danger coiling in the man.

"Renaldo does not know where the money is," Granger said. "He was sent here when Atilio was sent to Mexico. Someone must have suspected something. Perhaps Vargas arranged it? In any event, Renaldo didn't know then and he doesn't know now. They all had a little of it, but Atilio left the bulk of it for his brother Diego, along with an account of what happened. Diego is of a very different nature. It must have been Diego who saw to this judgment. When Don Diego arrived here, Renaldo must have thought the time had come to retrieve the gold and divide it up. But that's not what happened, because Diego is not Atilio."

"Why would Don Diego not reveal all this himself?" Cruzat asked.

"Because Atilio and Diego are twins. Renaldo or anyone else could challenge any accusations he might make by claiming Diego was, in fact, Atilio. How could it be proven otherwise, especially with one dead? Ordinarily I doubt anything would come of it, but there was danger here. A major complication at the very least. Don Diego did not trust Renaldo. I wouldn't be surprised if Renaldo knew the brothers back in Spain. They used to play games wherein they pretended to be each other. An innocent enough game then, but it complicated matters now. What Diego needed was a royal pardon. When Atilio went missing in Tejas, killed apparently in the service of the king, there were grounds for a pardon. It's even possible he sent a copy of this *Declaración jurada* to support the request. Eliana was to have it with her when she arrived. Renaldo couldn't be sure, so stealing the letter was a risk worth taking."

The corporal had moved closer to Renaldo and now stood just behind him to his left.

"And then Atilio, a man Renaldo believed to be dead, showed up here, very much alive, coming from the southwest. This complicated matters because he knew what you had done in Havana and could accuse you from firsthand knowledge. Diego may only have known some of it from his own time in Havana, no doubt answering questions about his identity. It must have galled you to learn that Chavreaux hadn't, in fact, killed him after Diego returned, because you still needed to keep Diego close. After all, you still needed to retrieve the document acknowledging your guilt in the theft and exonerating Atilio. And, of course, you wanted the gold."

"There is no way you can prove all of this," Renaldo said.

"I don't have to," Granger said. "All I had to do was convince señor Cruzat that you engineered the attempt on my life. I think I've done that. There is absolutely no way you could have know I was shot with my own—with Ham's—rifle."

"I am satisfied in that regard," Cruzat said. "You are under arrest, señor Renaldo. You will be transported to New Orleans. The rest can be proven there, but you will answer for the attempt on señor Granger's life."

Cruzat nodded to the corporal, who touched Renaldo's shoulder. Renaldo jerked at the touch and stood.

"What about me?" Gambeau said.

"You will also answer to the charges," Cruzat said. "Take them back to St. Louis and lock them up."

The soldiers moved the two men out of the room, down the hall, and outside.

"My compliments, señor Granger. I am satisfied with how you managed this affair." Cruzat tucked the paper away in his coat. "Will you accompany us back to St. Louis?"

"I will, but first I have some matters to clear up here."

Thirty

GRANGER KNOCKED on the door at the top of the stairs. After a few moments, it opened a little and Eliana peered out. Her eyes dropped to the rifle cradled in his hands and she looked fearful. She looked past Granger to Cortez, standing just behind him.

"Please, señora," Granger said and gently pushed the door open. She backed away and let them all enter— Granger, Cortez, Cruzat, Tayon, and Martine.

He found the brother in the bedroom where he had found Ham's rifle. He still sat in a chair, legs askew, a distracted, unfocused look in his eyes. Granger came up to him and squatted. He held out the rifle where the broken man could see it.

The reaction came. The eyes focused, the head raised. Behind him, Granger heard someone gasp. Then the man extended a hand toward the rifle.

"Do you remember?" Granger asked. "He came to help you."

The eyes came up further and found Granger's. He gave a slight nod, the returned his attention to the rifle.

Granger looked around. "Bring me that chair," he said,

pointing. Cortez fetched it and Granger placed it before the brother and laid the rifle across it. Granger stood and stepped back.

Then the man looked up again, searching the faces before him until he found one. His mouth opened slightly and it seemed to Granger a sound emerged, but it might have been nothing but a heavy breath.

Eliana pushed past Granger and knelt by him, clutching his hand.

"How did you know?" Cortez said.

"He reacted to it in Ste. Genevieve. I thought if he had more time with it, he might come further out. He eats, he cooperates in being dressed, he's not completely gone. It was a guess."

"No," Cortez said, "how did you know all this involved my brother?"

"Oh, that. It was the only thing that made sense."

"You will be so good as to explain it to us, Don Diego," Cruzat said.

The other Cortez was now looking at Eliana and it seemed to Granger he wore a smile.

"Atilio was sent to Mexico," Cortez said after they reassembled in the parlor. "Punishment for what he had done for Renaldo, which, as you surmised, was simply give him a place to hide what he had stolen. It was known what Renaldo had done, but there was never enough proof, and Renaldo was able to shift suspicion to Atilio. They never found the money. No witnesses came forward. So there was an official reprimand, a court-martial. Renaldo was discharged after a brief time in prison. Then they transferred Atilio to Mexico. He was in General Muñoz's command. Do you know the Comanche?"

"No, I'm afraid I don't," Granger said.

"You will one day. Fierce warriors. We always thought the Apache were fearsome, but the Apache made peace with us so we could help them against the Comanche. General Muñoz sent many expeditions against them in the old mission districts east of San Antonio. Never enough soldiers, though, and we never got the Apaches to fight as we do." He shrugged. "My brother died during one of these expeditions."

"But he didn't die."

"No, not entirely. Muñoz sent him with an expedition to help the beleaguered Apache to fight the Comanche. The Comanche took him prisoner. He had not even killed any of them. There was another prisoner among the Comanches. An Apache. He had been educated, in fact, in a mission. He spoke good Spanish and even some French. He had been a slave for the Comanches for a year by then. They beat him regularly, but he told them he liked it. It made them furious when he smiled at them with each blow. Atilio liked him. They were very similar. Broken inside, but held together on the outside by a stupidity that didn't recognize death when it came. Broken, yes, but able, finally, to escape. They got away together after a month among the Comanches. They beat Atilio, too, but the Apache cared for him and kept him alive and they got away. They disappeared into the desert. They wandered. No one knew where they were."

"Until they came here."

Cortez nodded. "That Indian was devoted to my brother. I think he was the only reason Atilio survived."

"He's the one who was stealing the chickens."

Cortez smiled at him. "You know about that?"

"One of your slaves told me."

The smile vanished.

"It's Salvatore," Granger said. "Isn't it? He's your Apache."

Cortez hesitated, then nodded.

"What happened to the money?" Cruzat asked.

Cortez's demeanor changed. He seemed suddenly resolute as he looked at Cruzat. "I don't know. I thought Renaldo had it. He claimed he only kept a portion of it for himself and that the rest was hidden." He shrugged. "When I arrived in Havana and tried to locate it, I could not find it. I assume the man you described as their benefactor acquired it and buried the entire matter."

"And Vargas?"

"An old man who knew them both. Someone Renaldo took advantage of. I thought perhaps that was where the money was, but…"

Granger kept silent. Cortez, if nothing else, seemed to be a very good liar.

"Salvatore shot my man," Granger said. "In the woods."

"I assume so. If he did, it was to defend my brother."

"Why didn't you just turn Renaldo over to the governor?"

"Based on what? My word against his? It was a sword I could not draw. Not until Atilio was pardoned."

"Am I correct?" Granger asked. "That is what Eliana brought? The pardon?"

"She and my family petitioned the king for years to get it," Cortez said. "It was finally granted and she brought it. But I did not know how to go about using it."

"You can give it to me," Cruzat said. "I will see to it that the appropriate steps are taken." He sighed loudly. "No matter now. This is over as far as I am concerned. I am sending Renaldo to New Orleans for trial. Are there any other matters here that need to be addressed?"

No one said anything. Cruzat stood and gathered his cloak and sword.

"Señor Granger. You have handled this affair very well and honorably. Should you choose to remain in St. Louis, I will be most pleased. As long as we may expect a more peaceful tenure?"

"I'd like nothing better."

Cruzat bowed and excused himself.

"Are you going to tell Russell?" Tayon asked.

"What? That Salvatore shot Taylor?" Granger thought for a moment. "It wouldn't be right to keep it from him."

"He thinks Chavreaux did it. Might it not be better to let him believe it is finished?"

Granger felt uncomfortable with the idea, but he saw its merit. "I'll think about it."

"I must thank you most sincerely, señor," Cortez said. "You have removed a darkness from my house. You are always welcome here. If there is anything I can do for you..."

"Perhaps another time." He got to his feet. He clasped Cortez's hand and held it a few moments longer than necessary. Cortez frowned just as Granger released him. "

It's getting late. I'd like to sleep in my own house tonight." He looked at Martine. She nodded.

As they stepped out of the house, Tayon said, "What about the money, though?"

Granger shrugged. "Who knows?"

As they headed for the front door, Tayon said, "Where is Salvatore, by the way?"

Thirty-one

OUTSIDE, RENALDO AND Gambeau waited in the wagon bed, hands bound. Cruzat made a sign and the corporal climbed onto the bench and took the reins. The other soldiers mounted their horses. Granger turned back to Tayon.

"Stay here, would you? Cortez and his wife may need you and I'd rather Martine wait till I come back to get her."

Tayon nodded. "Of course. Cruzat is leaving a pair of soldiers here as well. They will be protected." He gripped Granger's arm for a moment, then went back inside.

Granger climbed onto the wagon seat next to the corporal. The entourage wheeled about to head back to St. Louis.

Cruzat took the lead, with two soldiers behind him, the wagon, then the other pair of troops. Granger surveyed the edge of the trees, wondering where Neptune and Russell were.

Gambeau sat with head lowered, sullen and defeated. Renaldo looked up at Granger, resentful and angry, all pretense gone. Granger recognized hatred, a killing animosity.

"You are very clever," Renaldo said. "From nothing you unraveled all this."

"Not from nothing," Granger said. "I had disconnected pieces. I didn't understand them, but it was a start. Also, I knew my friend."

"So?"

"This one couldn't have killed him, not close in like that."

"But getting from this idiot," Renaldo kicked Gambeau, who looked up for a moment, tried to shift further from Renaldo, and resumed his sulking, "to me was impressive."

"You shouldn't have complained to Cartabona."

"It never occurred to me that you would ever come back. I'm curious, American, where did you find the first piece?"

"It was given to me. Someone had tucked a note with names and an address in Havana into the patch box of my friend's rifle. I thought you knew that. Isn't that why you had Chavreaux steal it?"

Renaldo grinned. "Did I have him do that? But no, I didn't know where it was. I suppose Étienne hid it there."

Granger said nothing about Martine's actions. Not that it mattered now, but he felt protective. She'd risked—and lost—enough already. But a new thought occurred to him. "Did you have him killed, too?"

"Étienne de Lautin? Of course not! Why? No, he dropped dead all on his own. It presented a new problem. I realized belatedly that Diego may have given him certain things for safe keeping. I needed to search that house. I had it done once, before you returned, again before you took possession, and then a third time, but found nothing."

"So you thought Martine was keeping it close. That's why you were courting her?"

Renaldo shrugged.

"So what went wrong in Havana?" Granger asked. "It sounds like a perfect theft."

"Nothing is perfect, not even honesty. What happened? We were found out. I do not know how. But I was arrested first. Atilio moved the gold, as you suggested. You see, he did do more than just give us a place to stay, but that makes no difference now. There was no proof against either of us, only suspicions. You were correct about our benefactor. He could not tolerate the scandal. So we were separated. Atilio sent to Mexico, I to Ste. Genevieve. I grew accustomed to the idea that it was all lost."

"Then Diego showed up."

"And he told me he knew what we had done. That Atilio was dead. And the map he had left behind was no longer useful to me, that instead it was his proof of what we had done and he would use it if I said or did anything to threaten him. I hadn't even known about the list of names until then. If he had kept his peace, I would never have become convinced that I could find it and take it from him. I realized that he was just as much at risk as I was, since I could denounce him, as you suggested."

Renaldo stretched and craned his neck. He looked around the forest through which they passed.

"I became angry with him when he undercut me with the horese trade I had been acquiring from your man Dodge. I was going through this one." He nodded toward Gambeau. "But it turned out he was stealing from me as well. Treasure an honest man, señor. They are as rare as truth. But I lost a great deal when Diego cut me out of the arrangements with Dodge."

"The attack from the British gave you a chance."

Renaldo was silent for a time. Granger peered into the thickets.

"The money you paid me," Granger said. "Where did you get it?"

"Diego. He threatened me then paid me a sum. He thought to appeal both to my fear and my greed." Renaldo laughed. "A mistake. Because of that I came to believe the rest was here. Somewhere." He was silent for a time. "I am sincerely sorry for your friend. He should not have been there. It was unfortunate."

"Unfortunate for you."

"Most assuredly. Without his death, you would never have returned, I think."

"He wasn't the only reason."

"No? But without it, you would not have felt compelled to pry into matters that should never have been your concern."

They rode on for a time, not talking. The track narrowed.

The first shot struck Cruzat's horse. The second the corporal driving the wagon.

Renaldo stood and dropped his arms around the dying soldier, lunged away from Granger, and off the wagon, into the woods. Granger twisted around to try to bring his weapon to bear, but his wound stabbed painfully. By the time he could get into position to shoot, Renaldo had dragged the soldier into the brush.

The mules started forward and Granger dropped his rifle to grab the reins.

There was a third shot. Granger turned and saw one of the rear soldiers fall, and his horse, riderless and frightened, charged forward. At the last instant, the animal veered into the woods.

The shots came from his left. Granger retrieved his rifle and jumped from the wagon. He stumbled and struck one of the slender trees at the edge of the road. The wind left him in a burst and he slid to the ground. He gulped air and his shoulder lanced with pain. He saw his rifle lying on the ground. He tried to reach for it. Pain knocked him back. He made another lunge, fell forward, and grabbed the barrel.

Gambeau crouched in the bed of the wagon. The mules in their harness danced, but one of the surviving soldiers now had them by the mouthpieces, holding them in place.

"Get—" Granger started to yell, but it came out in a breathy rasp. He swallowed, cleared his throat, and filled his lungs till they hurt. "Get down!" he yelled.

In response, Gambeau raised up a little to see him, and the side of his head exploded, and his body fell forward.

The last rear-guard soldier was on foot and led his horse past Granger, past the wagon, toward the front. Granger pulled the rifle into his lap. The pan had lost the powder. He tugged his horn around and filled it, snapped it back, and cocked the hammer.

He pivoted around where he sat and crawled, one-handed, into the trees.

He was recovering from the shock to his body, breathing easier. He made his way east, keeping close to the road, until he came to where he thought Cruzat had fallen. The horse lay across the road, still breathing, but blood was bubbling from a wound in its chest on the right.

"Señor."

Off to the left, Granger saw movement. A few yards further he found Cruzat and his soldier, in a patch of snow. Cruzat's right leg was stretched straight out. He had a pistol in his left hand.

"My ankle," he said. "I do not think it is broken, but it will not take my weight."

"Renaldo jumped from the wagon. Your corporal is dead, plus one other soldier that I saw fall. Gambeau is dead, too."

"Gambeau?"

"Witnesses. He's killing witnesses."

"Who? Chavreaux?"

"That would be my guess. Those were very precise shots. He still has Ham's rifle."

Cruzat closed his eyes.

"Stay with him," Granger said to soldier. The man, eyes large with fear, nodded, but Granger had no idea if he understood him.

Another shot broke the stillness.

Granger crawled back to the edge of the road. The soldier holding the wagon mules hunched off to the right, opposite the side Renaldo had leapt into. Granger tested his weight on his right arm; the shoulder twinged, but it was not incapacitating. He would be in great pain tomorrow. If he made it to tomorrow. He wrapped his hand around the rifle and scurried across the road, into the opposite brush.

It was very different woodland from where he had grown up, but some lessons remained the same. Quiet. Move slowly. Watch the shadows. He moved several yards into the woods, remembering how to step silently in this snow-packed undergrowth, and then veered west.

After about thirty yards, he paused to study his surroundings, and listen. This was the hard part for most men. He had seen several young soldiers die because they did not trust that sitting still would not make them a target. They would fidget, then they'd move, and a second later fall over, wounded or dead. War was not like hunting. Game did not shoot back. Yet some of the same disciplines applied to both.

The woods were quiet after all the shots.

There. A delicate crackle, the crunch of snow and twigs. Granger looked. That way. He brought the rifle around, studied the detail, looking away to clear his vision of the confusion, looked again.

Someone was coming closer. Not directly, but angled toward the road. Granger saw shadows shift. Now that he knew where to look, he could listen more selectively. The slight brush of cloth on a branch, the soughing of cotton or buckskin or linen on itself as the wearer bent, turned, stepped. Granger waited, hearing the approach. He raised the rifle.

A shadow, a bright patch not quite the same color as the foliage around it, a movement, and a man stepped between two saplings carrying a musket. Granger did not recognize the shirt, but he couldn't see the face, not yet.

A few more steps.

Davidet. The other one who had been playing cards with Gambeau and Chavreaux, and also worked for Gambeau, peered resolutely toward the road.

In a fluid motion, Granger aimed, sighted, fired. Pain erupted in his shoulder, his ears rang, his vision hazed briefly.

Davidet spun around, a shocked look on his face, and dropped.

Granger scrambled forward and snatched up the musket, then took three noisy steps west before turning south again and moving silently. He assumed they were setting up a cross-fire on Cruzat. Three of them, two now. So one would likely be on the other side of the road and the last one several yards west still, close to the road.

After a few dozen paces, he stopped and reloaded the rifle. It took longer because he had to rely on one hand. Prepared once more, he tucked the musket under his left arm, and when he knew he was well west of the ambush, he made his way back toward the road.

He reached the edge without seeing or hearing any sign of his prey, and eased out from cover and looked east. The wagon still stood in the road. One of the saddled horses had wandered into the trees to the north.

He pulled back a few feet, squatted, and listened.

Steps came crashing behind him. He started to rise and turn, lurched to the right as Renaldo, hands free of the manacles, slashed downward with the sword he had taken from the corporal, missing Granger's foot by inches as it struck the ground. Granger let the musket fall and tried to bring the rifle around.

Renaldo swung again, catching the rifle mid-stock with a blow that jarred up through Granger's arms. He staggered, his grip loosened, and Renaldo plunged into him, jamming a hand, palm forward, at his face. Granger dropped the rifle as he ducked his head, then scrambled back and to the side to evade another sword blow that sent small branches flying. He tripped and fell backward.

When he looked up, Renaldo, breathing hard and grinning, had the musket aimed at his face.

A shot came from Granger's right. Renaldo staggered, blood spraying from the Spaniard's left shoulder. He recovered instantly and fired the musket into the woods just as Granger surged off the ground. Renaldo tried to swing the musket into him but Granger was too close, too fast. The first punch, a left, he drove up into Renaldo's ribs. The second, a right, he slammed across Renaldo's cheek.

Renaldo stumbled but did not quite fall. He managed to scoop up Granger's rifle. Granger reached for the sword abandoned between them as he heard the hammer draw back. He wrapped a hand around the sword's grip, continued into a roll, came around and jammed the blade up, deep into Renaldo's stomach.

Renaldo gasped, his face stretched in shock, ghastly pale. Granger pulled out the sword, stood, and snatched the rifle from the dying man's hands. Blood flowed down Renaldo's shirt and pants, dripped onto his boots. He took two steps back and sat down hard.

Granger leaned in close. "The gold was here all along," he said. "Diego brought it with him."

Renaldo looked puzzled for a few moments, then his eyes went wide as he fell backward and stared, unseeing, up at the sky.

A crunch brought Granger around, aiming. Neptune stepped toward him, a hand over his left hip. Blood colored his pant leg.

"Just a crease," he said. "But *damn* it hurts."

"Russell?"

"Still hunting Chavreaux."

"Cruzat."

They stepped into the road and ran up to the wagon. In the back, Gambeau lay face up, eyes open. At the front, the mules were still held by the lone soldier, who by now was terrified and trembling, but still holding position.

Granger and Neptune entered the woods where Cruzat lay. Both he and his man were still there, alive and waiting.

"Renaldo is dead," Granger said. "So is Davidet. He was the third man. We still don't know where Chavreaux is."

"This has been most disorderly," Cruzat said. He drew his leg up. "Sprained, I am sure. With assistance, I should be able to walk."

As Granger began to reach down to assist the lieutenant governor up, a movement to the far left caught his eye.

He turned.

Two shots sounded almost simultaneously, one clearly louder than the other.

A ball smashed into the tree just above Cruzat's head, showering him with small wood chips.

Granger, rifle pointed into the woods, searched for the tell-tale trace of smoke. There. Not twenty yards away.

How did he miss?

He hurried forward. It would take less than a minute for an experienced rifleman to reload. And then he came upon Chavreaux, stretched out face down in a confusion of snow and grass. The hole in his back was enormous. Ham's rifle lay a few feet from his outflung right hand. Granger knelt by it and looked around.

Someone stepped from cover.

Salvatore. He approached, his face expressionless, eyes fixed on the body between them. He held the musket Granger had seen in Cortez's house. He stared at Chavreaux's corpse for a time, and then reached down, took hold of his hunting shirt, and rolled the body over.

Salvatore straightened. His face contorted with hatred, and he spat on the dead man.

"He will live," Eliana said. They sat in her parlor. She held a glass of rye whisky, but she had tasted none of it. "In truth, I do not know if that is good or bad." She looked at Granger. "He seems so much less than he was. He speaks now. Not much, not like he once did, but some. In time, it may be more. I hope it will be enough."

Cortez, sitting beside her, squeezed her hand.

"I hope so," Granger said. "I am curious, if you don't mind. How did you manage a royal pardon for him?"

"My family has influence," Eliana said. "Even so, it took time. It was necessary. We could never go on with such a thing unresolved. Once Diego sent word of the *Declaración jurada*, it was easier." She looked up at him. "We might have succeeded with just one, but both…"

Granger swallowed. "Señora, I have something I must give back to you." He pulled the sheaf of letters from within his coat. "You asked me how I knew you. I took these the day we found my friend here. I had no idea what was in them, but I thought they might tell me something about the man who owned this land and why Ham might have died here."

Eliana stared at the pages. "My letters…"

Cortez stared at them. "I thought they had been stolen."

"No," Granger said. "Forgive me. They became a bond to this place, something that tied me here and gave me hope that I might learn the truth."

Eliana shuffled through them. A faint smile ghosted across her face. "You read all these?"

"I did."

Color flooded her cheeks briefly. "Then you know us better than…I am at a loss, señor. Thank you so much for their return."

"I appreciated the glimpse into what's possible between two people." He paused before adding, "Or more."

They looked at him and Granger instantly regretted the remark. But suddenly Cortez and Eliana laughed.

"If there is anything else we may do for you—" Cortez began.

"There is. Two things I'm still puzzled about." When Cortez raised his eyebrows, Granger continued. "The stallion killed in the stable. I don't understand why it would have been here. I assume it was Diego's prize horse." Cortez pursed his lips, remaining silent. Granger went on. "Which leads me to the other thing. Who is upstairs? Diego or Atilio?"

Cortez's eyes narrowed. "Tell me, señor. Those two fine rifles, your own and your friend's. Can you tell them apart?"

"Yes."

"Could anyone else?"

"No, probably not."

"Does it matter?"

Granger grunted. "I suppose not." He stood. "One more thing. My friend's body—we buried him in your plot. If I may, I'd like to recover it and send it home to his family."

"Of course," Cortez said. "I will assist you."

"That would be very kind of you."

Cortez fetched Salvatore to help and the two men worked at stiff ground into the afternoon until they dug down to Ham's shrouded corpse. Granger could do so little. The abuse he had taken left him feeling bruised and now he could barely raise his left arm. Cortez provided a canvas wrap and Salvatore lifted the body up to them.

Granger jumped down into the grave, surprising Cortez. He then took the shovel in his left hand and jabbed into the wall until the gold coins spilled out again. He looked up at Cortez. The expression on his face gave Granger his final answer and told him why he could expect no more.

Thirty-two

Russell came back after taking Granger's kit down to the ferry landing.

"Everything ready?" Granger asked.

"Everything," Russell said. "You *are* coming back?"

"Absolutely."

"Good. I'd hate for things to go back to the way they were before."

"How was that?"

"Dull." Russell turned toward the door.

"Russell, you need to know something—"

Russell stopped. "That Salvatore shot Taylor? I know."

"What are you going to do about it?"

Russell was silent for a time. Granger could see the muscle along his jaw working. Finally, he looked up at Granger.

"Nothing. As long as he stays away from me for a time. He was guarding Cortez's place. Probably thought we were Gambeau and his men. Can't fault him for that. But I don't want to see him. Not yet."

"Martine's staying in the house. She can help run the store. I would appreciate it if you made sure she—"

"She'll be fine. Tayon and me, we'll make sure she stays fine. And Neptune is staying on, he'll be there regularly. I'm just curious about one thing. Why'd you tell Cortez about the money?"

"It's theirs."

"Uh huh. He stole it fair and square, is that it?"

Granger laughed. "He gave us a goodly amount. There should be enough to see the store through a lean year or two. Just take care of things till I get back."

"This one—Cortez—he didn't know where it was, did he?"

"I don't think we need to know all the answers. Is that all right with you?"

"Absolutely, Major." He touched the peak of his hat and left.

Granger went out the rear door, into the shop. Martine was straightening blankets on a shelf. She did not smile at him.

"I'm going now," Granger said.

"Is this necessary?" she asked finally.

Granger looked at her, standing there with her arms folded, an impatient scowl on her face. He hugged her, but she gave nothing back. Just stood there, committed to her disapproval.

"Yes," he said finally.

"I don't understand. You have resolved the question of your friend."

"I have resolved his death. Yes."

"Then what? I said we must put it behind us before we can discover what there may be for us. You have done this."

He lifted Ham's rifle. "I must return this and his body to his family. Now I can restore it where it belongs and give my friend his proper burial."

"You could send it back with Russell, or someone else."

"This is something I have to tend to personally."

Her frown deepened. "How long will you be gone?"

"I should be back by August at the latest."

"Do you expect me to wait?"

He looked up at that. She met his gaze, eyebrows raised, challenging.

"No," he said. "But I would be very glad if you did."

She looked angry for a moment, and then her face softened. She nodded. "Not if you're gone another three years." She frowned suddenly. "I am coming with you."

"What? But—"

"Do you think I have nothing better to do than wait here wondering if you will return?"

"It's a long way."

"So? You could be killed and I might never know. You have shown an exceptional tendency to get shot at since I've known you."

"I *will* be back." He touched her face. "There's no war now to hold me."

"There will be. Sometimes I think men make them so they don't have to keep their promises."

"I kept all my promises to you."

"Yes. You did." She pulled him to her and kissed him, a long exploratory kiss that left him anxious and aroused when she stopped. "And I am keeping my promise to you. I will be with you. You said you want me. Leaving me behind does not inspire confidence. Do you want me or not?"

He touched her face. "I want…"

"What? What do you want?"

"To be a river for you."

Her expression changed. For a moment, he thought she would smile. But she took his hand, squeezed, and stepped back.

"And I wish to travel that river, Lieutenant."

Acknowledgements

Among the myriad folks who have been supportive and helpful along the way, I'd like to say thank you to:

Donna, Jim Fournier, Tom Ball, Vicki Daniels, Kris Kleindienst, Danielle King, Shane Mullen, Randy Schiller, Cliff Helm, Shualee Cook, Jim Mosely, Left Bank Books et al., Timons Esaias, Bernadette Harris, Lucy Holmes, Rich and Annette Hudson, Terry Ryder, Jen Udden, Nicola Griffith, Kelley Eskridge, Daryl Gregory, Ellen Datlow, Henry and Donna Tiedemann, Scott Phillips, John Lowrance, Nathan Lowrance, Tom Dillingham, Allen and Linda Steele, Carolyn Gilman, Lloyd and Carolyn Kropp, Keith Byler, Danica Geaslin Byler, Maia and Jim Funkhouser, Trevor Quachri, Sheila Williams, Gordon van Gelder, Janet Berlo, Chip Delany, Tim Powers, Scott Edelman.

Also those who are no longer with us who mattered along the same road: Harlan Ellison, Lucie Beaudet, David Hartwell, Gene Wolfe, Gardner Dozois, Kate Wilhelm, Damon Knight, Earline and Gene Knackstedt, and so many others who made it all special over the years.

About the Author

Mark W. Tiedemann was born in St. Louis in 1954. A lifelong reader, he early on became interested in science fiction, pirates, cowboys, and secret agents, in no particular order. After a few early attempts, he settled down to try to write in the early 1980s, shortly after meeting his partner, Donna, who encouraged him (because she liked the stories). This led to his attending the Clarion Writers Workshop in 1988 and shortly thereafter the first few published stories. Although the majority of his work is science fiction, he has always been interested in history, and finally decided to see what he could do along those lines. He continues to reside in St. Louis, having grown to appreciate its idiosyncrasies more and more as time goes on.